"*BIRTHSTONE* IS DAZZLING. Mollie Gregory dishes the dirt with wicked finesse ... *Birthstone* glitters from the first page to the last."—REX REED

"HERE'S A NOVEL THAT HAS IT ALL ... powerful men and women, opulence and decadence, and most of all, primitive passions in high places."
—MAUREEN DEAN, bestselling author of *Washington Wives* and *Capitol Secrets*

"A PERFECT DIAMOND—faceted with a dynamic story, fascinating characters, and sparkling settings."
—JOHANNA KINGSLEY, bestselling author of *Scents* and *Treasures*

Birthstone

They paid the ultimate price for love....

LINDY WYMAN OLIVER. She lost the sparkling privilege of her birthright and gambled her deepest passions to regain it.

FLETCHER AVERY. His burning ambition for fame would destroy lives and shatter hearts.

EDWARD WYMAN. The son Lindy never knew—until past secrets threatened to make them lifelong enemies.

Birthstone

All that glitters is not gold.

BIRTHSTONE

A searing page-turner that unmasks Hollywood's most gifted elite—the stars and star-makers who would do anything to come out on top.

BIRTHSTONE

From the lush extravagance of Beverly Hills pleasure-palaces to the exotic allure of Budapest and Singapore, they dared to seize their most glamorous ambitions—and risked losing everything in a tide of passion and revenge.

BIRTHSTONE

The dazzling story of one woman's triumph over her family's tragedies . . . a story that picks up where Mollie Gregory's *Triplets* left you breathless for more!

"Finely etched characters, intricate plotting, and raw human emotion illuminate this rich novel of a Hollywood family caught in a web of secrets . . ."
—Carolyn See,
author of GOLDEN DAYS

Jove Books by Mollie Gregory

BIRTHSTONE
TRIPLETS

Birthstone

Mollie Gregory

JOVE BOOKS, NEW YORK

BIRTHSTONE

A Jove Book / published by arrangement with
the author

PRINTING HISTORY
Jove edition / December 1991

ISBN: 0-515-10704-2

Jove Books are published by The Berkley Publishing Group,
200 Madison Avenue, New York, New York 10016.
The name "JOVE" and the "J" logo
are trademarks belonging to Jove Publications, Inc.

PRINTED IN THE UNITED STATES OF AMERICA

10 9 8 7 6 5 4 3 2 1

ACKNOWLEDGMENTS

Many people gave generously of their time and their expertise to help me with this story. I especially want to thank those who educated me about California mental health facilities and correctional facilities: Dr. Arthur F. LeBlanc, who led me through various scenarios that would suit the character of Belinda, and, also, Dr. Richard A. Miller and Dr. Robert Benedetto.

Also extremely helpful were Jonathan Rendell, Dr. Howard Krauss, and my brother, Andrew Griffin, who managed in quite different ways to give me information and insight.

In another vein, I am grateful to the unstinting and generous efforts of friends who tirelessly read this manuscript at various stages, and who made excellent suggestions—Katherine Rembold, Lorraine Despres, and Krista Michaels. I'd particularly like to express my gratitude to my editor, Leslie Gelbman, whose suggestions and courtesies along the way made the path an enjoyable adventure.

A reality check: The outside tile mural cited as background in chapter 18 is fictional, adapted from artist George Johanson's real tile mural called "Northwest Power," which actually hangs in the Bonneville Power Administration in Vancouver, Washington. In chapter 25, the Hollywood building cited is a design amalgam of three Hollywood buildings in that area.

FOR KRISTA

PROLOGUE

1990

The crowd below the building looked up with one face.

Traffic had been diverted around the intersection to a slim trickle north and south. The sidewalks and part of the streets were filling with people behind yellow ties. A fire truck stood down the block like a shiny red lump surrounded by men who alternately looked at the sky, then at the ground. Police were coming together in knots, looking at the crowd and at each other.

"Fucking jumpers," a police sergeant grumbled. "Can't make up their minds. Get us out here on the double an' look at 'em up there, going to have coffee and bagels next." He glanced crossly at his officers on the roof, and on the street, hurriedly shutting off traffic. "Jump, you poor son of a bitch."

"The nets, Jim?" a younger officer asked his sergeant nervously.

"Yeah, yeah, keep your pants on."

An air of multitudinous expectation was forming in the crowd, ascending the building, reaching up to where two figures stood on a top-floor balcony of the oldest high rise in Hollywood.

One figure rocked against the balcony railing, hands propped flat against the warm iron, elbows out. The other stood stiffly nearby, angled toward the first with a posture at once afraid and sympathetic. The noon sun was high and hot. Only when one of the figures moved was it possible to distinguish them from the statues affixed to the building. The crowd below was both near and far to them, for sound travels oddly at such heights, flooding up and spreading out like birds lofting, tacking in a draft, gliding.

The crowd stirred and the sergeant looked up sharply. One

figure, angled tensely toward the other, was beating a hand against the railing, demanding, threatening.

"Oh, Christ, get ready!" the sergeant said.

The younger officer, panicked, started off down the street toward a second fire truck that was just pulling into place.

But on the balcony, the figures stopped moving. They were staring at each other, their postures defiant. The wind blew at their clothes, lifting a jacket in the bright light.

The sergeant waved angrily toward the fire truck, shouting. But the answer was lost in the sudden intake of breath from the crowd, a sound of shock and suction. One figure had lunged, trying to pull the other figure toward the fragile railing. For an instant they rocked in an anerotic embrace which was, even so, swollen with expectations. Then one broke free. From the ground it was impossible to tell if the leap was willful—suicidal—or forced. The image was that one of them flew out, arms akimbo, feet apart, head up, an arabesque of death.

A groan rolled out of five hundred throats below, mounting into a scream to meet the figure as it plunged down, clothes pressing against bone and muscle, the body turning slightly, swimming in air, dropping with amazing speed.

It slapped onto the emptied avenue with an opening and closing sound, a flattening sound, the unforgettable sound of flesh hitting stone.

Police rushed to hold back the horrified and gratified crowd, who were now silent. Some turned away, sickened; others stared at the still body.

The woman lay on her side, knees drawn up, one arm flung over her head, the other broken beneath her, half her face pancaked against the pavement.

"Ah, fer crissakes, get a sheet."

A thick blunt stream of blood was oozing out somewhere beneath her body, seeping slowly, eating asphalt.

"She was pushed," a man with binoculars in the crowd whispered to the sergeant.

"Mister," the sergeant said, "will you please step back. No one pushed anyone."

On top of the building at Hollywood and Vine the remaining figure hugged the railing, head bowed, jacket and hair lifting in the wind.

CHAPTER 1

JUNE 1985

It was an unusual fog for summer. Indifferent to the packed, jammed-up city, actualized in disrepair, the fog churning through Los Angeles that dawn swirled along the freeways from downtown skyscrapers to Santa Monica beaches. It deadened the rolling noise of trucks, cement mixers, gunfire, cars, helicopters. It wound down the big boulevards like Olympic, Pico, Sunset, and Central where movie stars and gang leaders, lawyers and gardeners—the teeming mass of three million people—were either getting up or going to bed. Anglos were now the minority here, though few realized it. L.A. was being remade. Just after daybreak, the fog fanned across Beverly Hills, tumbling over luxurious houses, charging the moats of their wide lawns. It distorted and obscured the heavy beautiful trees in this neighborhood terrain which seemed untouched by the metastasizing urban disorder around it.

A boy of thirteen was leaning against a Seward Johnson sculpture—a whimsical sentinel posted on the grassy parking strip of the massive brick house. The boy was trying to fix a strap of his duffel bag which had just torn loose. He bent to the task, intent, the fingers of one hand working at the strap.

A single car slipped past, disappeared into the fog around the curve in the placid Beverly Hills street. A cloudy vapor eddied in its wake, masking shrubs and the way ahead. The boy stared into it, uneasy. He looked at his Swatch watch: 7:15. His ride was late. The bang and boom of The Police doing "King of Pain" beat in his headset. He gave up on the strap and, taking two hand-size rubber balls from his pocket, he began juggling with his right hand, throwing the first up, then the second, catching the first, and repeating.

A woman appeared through the fog, walking toward him, and that was strange because she wasn't wearing a running suit. She was approaching steadily with a quick, light step. He felt a shiver of anticipation. He dropped a ball, nailed it with one foot, picked it up and held it against the other in his hand.

She was old enough to be someone's mother, but not old enough to be his; she looked wiry, more delicate than most mothers he knew. His mom, Patsy Wyman, had a thick waist and a lot of tiny lines under the powder on her face. But this woman had a curvy, springy bod. He couldn't see her breasts but he could see a jouncing beneath her jacket. The mystery and the challenge of sex took hold of him; he was never free of its grip for long. He was glad his mom and his grandma, Diana, couldn't read thoughts. No one could. Well, maybe his dad could. Vail was psychic; his mom joked about it.

The boy glowered at the stranger separating herself from the fog. She was closer now and she looked vaguely familiar. He straightened up. Was she one of his parents' friends? Some instinct told him she was not and that she did not belong here. Yet, he felt he knew her. Her chocolate brown hair fell around her face to her shoulders. She wore a red bombardier's jacket and stone-washed jeans. She looked hip, especially the way she walked—determined yet sexy. She definitely wasn't a mom.

She stopped and looked up at the house, then down at him. "Is there one of you at every gate?" she asked, lightly.

He stared at her. Her eyes were deeply set, ice blue, ringed in dark blue. "You looking for an address?" he asked. His right hand gripped the balls, his left hung straight down by his side, just behind his jacket pocket.

"I think this is it."

"This is my house," he said, doubtful that it was the one she wanted. "Who are you?"

The woman hesitated. She didn't look like she wanted to be there. She glanced quickly across him. "My name's Oliver," she said to the house looming behind them. "What's yours?"

"Wyman."

The woman's delicate face was really pretty, not wimpy, he thought, but her expression was set as hard as marble, and she had a wise glint in her eye, like she didn't take any guff.

He tossed one ball up, made the catch, but stumbled against the sculpture. Gripping the balls in his right hand, he reached out, dropped both balls and lifted his left hand for balance.

He had no left hand: it ended in a stump at his wrist. The woman's eyes widened, a look he was used to. The balls bounced and rolled. He snagged one; she stopped the other, picked it up, handed it to him. "Here," she said. He took it and jammed it hard into his pocket, ripping the seam. Coins fell to the sidewalk. The woman knelt down; the boy knelt, too. Embarrassed, irritated, he concentrated on retrieving the coins. When he looked up, she was offering him two quarters. Her face was close to his. A current went through him, something hasty and familiar. He took the coins. His right pocket was ripped. It was awkward to get the coins from his right hand into his left pocket, the one without the rip, so he hooked a finger around the strap of his duffel. The woman, still squatting beside him, reached across and unzipped a side pocket. The boy dumped the coins inside. He placed his stump against the pocket and held it down while he zipped it shut with his right hand.

"It's a birth defect," the boy called Wyman said. "Some kids get them. Don't pay any attention to it."

"No," she replied softly, "I was just thinking about mistakes."

"My name's Eddie," he said with energy to prove he didn't care if he had fingers or not. "No-fingers Eddie. Gimme five!" A lot of adults didn't know what that meant but this woman put out her palm. He lobbed his fingerless hand down toward it, and laughed like a half-grown wolf—with knowing delight.

"Hey," she said, joining in. She had a laugh like sugar, grainy and sweet.

"Are you here to see my mother?" He stood up.

"Yes. Is she up yet?" She rose, too, quickly, lightly.

"Probably."

"I'm an early riser myself," she said. "I like mornings."

"They're okay. Lot of fog today."

"I like fog," she said. "It always burns off." She tilted her head. "What are you doing out here by yourself?"

"Waiting for my ride. Going to camp." He didn't tell her that he and his father had argued last night about this very subject: Edward had not wanted to go to camp at all, meet a bunch of new kids, put up with the testing and the taunts about his missing hand or the artificial one he had in his duffel bag. His father had insisted he take it and wear it.

"What kind of camp?" she asked.

"It's for artistic kids," he said, mockingly.

"Oh, are you artistic?"

"Nah, my folks just think I am."

A car barreled around the foggy bend at the top of the street and pulled to a stop in front of them. "Gotta go," Edward Wyman said, waving at the two other boys in the car with their father. He grabbed his duffel bag, pulled open the car door, and jumped inside.

Belinda Oliver watched the car bearing her son slide around the curve and disappear. She hadn't seen him for five years, and then only at a distance, outside his school. He'd been waiting for his ride with a crowd of other eight year olds. Then, too, he'd climbed into a car and had been driven away as she'd looked after him. Finally, she'd pulled her own car into the street, and had begun a five-year odyssey that hadn't ended until today.

Standing in the fog in front of the big house, Belinda Oliver was memorizing the features of her son's face from his thick unruly yellow hair, his brow with the short horizontal crease in it, his dark hazel eyes, his childish nose, and impertinent, definite chin. He had a round, comforting face. He resembled his father. From a corner of a dim room with heavy furniture and a green glass desk lamp, his father stepped into the light. One hand was seductively outstretched, a smile of comfort and longing on his broad fifty-year-old face. Archie was always in that dark study, like a prisoner or a ghost. It had been the first place they'd made love. It had been an opulent room that now, worn thin by memory, seemed banal.

She cut it off. She looked up at the house, imagining her family inside it. She hadn't seen them in at least seven years. It had been a mistake to come back. Perhaps she would not go inside. Coming back to them confused her. She felt drawn to them, and repelled at the same time. She didn't want to come clean or explain or relive the past. But the people inside that house had a hold on her. She had to face the old ghosts. She had to smother fear and shame.

Diana Wyman always rose at six o'clock in the morning. Fully dressed now, back straight, unwilling to give in to physical alterations, she was moving to a small walnut desk in the corner of her large, airy sitting room on the top floor of the house. She was eighty-five, but her imperious bearing and the reflection of her youthful beauty, like a recollection, made her look younger. As she moved, she pinned her wavy white hair up with a tortoiseshell clasp. That done, she picked up a china cup fringed with forget-me-nots and carried it to the desk.

She sat down carefully. Her long fingers picked up a fountain pen. She began writing a letter to California's Senator Cranston about President Reagan's wreath-laying visit to the Bitburg Cemetery in Germany where Waffen SS officers were buried. Diana remembered World War II as clearly as she remembered the war in Vietnam—clearer, in fact. With calm deliberation, she wrote the senator that this incident proved Mr. Reagan was hopeless as a national leader, "a most improbable president." She wrote a strong letter: all Diana's letters and opinions were strong. She was also well-informed: she read the *New York Times* and the *Christian Science Monitor* every day, along with a number of weekly magazines. She had worked on human rights committees and in liberal political campaigns since the thirties.

She glanced at a pile of other correspondence, topped with an invitation to a charity event promoted by a bright but silly woman who raised millions for crippled children. Diana was condescending about such efforts; they had their place but her interests ran to issues, not hospitals. This attitude did not prevent her from being invited to many events; she was the mother of famous and prominent children, a set of triplets. Her son, Vail, was a critic; her daughter Sara, a film director, had lived in Italy for years; Sky had been an American film star. Diana balanced the pen above the paper, a slight half smile on her mouth, thinking about the good years with Sky, enjoying the memory until, as always, it soured. Sky had died, wastefully, ignobly, ten years before. Diana's hand fluttered over her eyes; she shifted an envelope and a card; she turned her face toward the window. But she did not see the poinsettia tree outside: she saw the face of her favorite child and heard her voice.

Downstairs, Maria Estarte, the Wymans' housekeeper and cook, was refusing to let the Oliver woman in to see Diana.

"Tell her Lindy is here," the woman said.

"Wait here," Maria said, coolly. She was a trim, intelligent woman from Guatemala and she was not about to let someone she'd never seen before roam about the house. The hall telephone rang, a line Maria answered for the family. She crossed the expanse of brick red tiles and picked up the telephone. "Wyman residence," she said. She saw movement out of the corner of her eye. The woman was starting up the stairs. "Come back here! You can't do that!"

"Oh, yes, I can." The thrill of rebellion shot across her face. She didn't even pause on her way up the staircase.

Diana's concentration on her letter to Senator Cranston had been invaded by the dream: she'd had it again last night. She's in a huge, once fine but now forbidding house, the back of it open to the fresh air, like a set, like a bombed-out building. Upstairs, she hears her triplets—Sara, Vail, Sky. Diana starts up the steps that curl around to the second floor of the ruined house. They are rickety, unstable. She grabs at the railing, looks up: open sky through the roof, engulfing black clouds beyond. She must reach her children! The railing shudders, a horrible rusty yawn warns her the stairs are pulling away from the wall. She tries to save herself, looks up in panic. Sky is peering down at her. "This is the house that Diana built!" Sky yells.

Behind her, in shadows, that horrible Patrick grins at Sky. Diana clings to the railing, rides the sickening yaw of the staircase. Suddenly, Sara is beside her, cooing: "We'll all be exposed." Somewhere above with Sky, Vail is laughing.

A sound in the room shook Diana out of the dream. She turned: her granddaughter was standing in the doorway. Was this possible? "Heavens! Belinda!"

Belinda smiled tentatively.

"How long have you been standing there?"

"A minute." It was not until she entered the room that Belinda realized how much she herself had changed. Though the room was new to her, everything in it had been part of her grandmother's life, and they were objects Belinda remembered well. But she herself was different.

"Where have you been all this time?" Diana's voice trembled.

"Well, for the last year, New Mexico, other places."

Diana's dark hooded eyes shone, an accusation. "They release you, what we were all praying for, and you disappear! So cruel."

"I wrote you."

"And now you just turn up." Diana pressed her lips together. A tear slipped down her cheek. "I'm so angry that you wouldn't come home. Almost five years . . ."

Belinda stepped briskly across the room, leaned close and kissed the air next to her grandmother's cheek. The familiar scent of powder and rose water met her.

"I couldn't come back, Grandma. After the scandal I caused you, I thought I should stay away."

"We *all* suffered, Belinda." Her granddaughter spoke in a flippant tone Diana didn't recognize.

"Yes, there was plenty to go around," Belinda said: a statement.

Diana tapped at her cheek with a handkerchief, still gazing at Belinda. Her face was thinner, which made her striking eyes seem larger. It was like looking at another version of Sky. "You resemble Sky now that you're older, not so much like Sara."

"I never looked like Sara," Belinda said.

Fresh tears came into Diana's eyes. "Why are you here now?"

Belinda looked at the ceiling for aid. "It's time."

"You're my only grandchild," she murmured. "But I don't even know you anymore." There seemed to be no rest in Belinda; everything about her was quick—her movements, her step, her speech, yet she kept her distance.

"Maybe we can get reacquainted, Grandma." Belinda put her shoulder bag down on a chair and glanced at the room. It was a comfortable sitting room of soft blues and greens, her grandmother's favorite colors. A door to the left stood ajar, Diana's bedroom. "This is very nice, Grandma." Diana nodded, cataloging her granddaughter.

"I saw him outside," Belinda said, looking at a little Sevres dish.

"You couldn't have. He's not here," Diana replied. Her elegant, musical voice, the voice of a younger woman, was under control now.

"Well, I did. He was outside the house."

Diana looked down at her bony fingers and her manicure. "You have no rights here," she said quietly. "I mean with Edward, dear."

"Yes, that's so. I concede."

Diana glanced up at her with the air of someone at once victimized and belligerent. Belinda ignored her and picked up a brass Chinese box.

"Eddie . . . he looks grand," Belinda said.

Diana rose and shut the door. "How would you know? You have no comparison."

"I like him; he seems sort of jovial, jaunty. I'm glad. He said he was going to camp."

"I'd rather talk about you, dear," Diana said. "What have you been doing all this time?"

"Working on nonunion films under an assumed name."

"Honestly," Diana said, distressed, "an assumed name? What are you going to do now?"

"I don't know yet." She put down the brass box. "Aren't you glad to see me, Granny?"

"Of course I am. I'm surprised, that's all." She sat down in a cane chair. "You mustn't disturb anything here."

"What do you mean?"

"You know."

Belinda recognized a painting of ripe stolid fruit in a bowl. It had been a fixture in her grandmother's rooms for years. She'd always thought the thick fruit ugly. "All right. I won't disturb anything. I don't want to." Belinda crossed the room, knelt beside her grandmother, and embraced her. "I had to come back."

"Darling, Belinda . . ." she whispered, completely taken aback by the display.

"You wouldn't say any of these things if Sky were alive. You'd just say 'I'm glad you're back.' "

"Shush." Diana's curved, high-backed cane chair enfolded her on each side like a woven hood. "Sit down over there, dear," she said, pointing at a dark green chair.

Belinda sat back on her heels, her face blank. "Sorry," she said, rising. She sat in the other chair.

"When they released you they didn't even tell us, you know.

The first we heard was your note from Canada."

"Families are the last to know."

"And then you just stayed away—months could go by without hearing from you."

"Yes, well, I had a lot to . . . work out. It took a long time for me to get used to being free, having choices, making decisions." She was trying hard to keep emotion out of her voice.

"You were always very intelligent."

"I still am." She looked at the familiar pattern of the old carpet in the new room. "I was in that hospital and that—that place they call a school for over five years," Belinda said lightly, tossing her hair back from her face. "I spent my *college* years in there, from seventeen to twenty-four." A girl of sixteen was screaming and throwing food in the dining hall, her arms like windmills, her face red and twisted. Spittle and food flew out of her mouth. "My own Vietnam war," Belinda murmured.

"What?" Diana asked.

"Nothing."

"You come here—why didn't you let us know? We could have prepared." Diana thought briefly of her son, Vail, and his wife, Patsy, and shuddered.

Belinda was on her feet again, touring the room. "I felt that if I made an—appointment—I might not go through with it. It's hard to be here."

"This is your home."

"I'm the skeleton in the closet. I'm the girl gone bad." She stopped and gazed at Diana. Her pale blue eyes looked wintry, hard.

"Don't be impertinent." Diana tilted her slim head. "Of course, we tried and tried to get those people at that institution to see sense, tried to get them to release you. You were never crazy. No one in my family is crazy. But once you're in their grip, all those officials, once you're in their machinery, they won't let go. It's those authorities, we tried to get you into a private institution, but the state," she spat, "the state runs everything. We had no choice, and you were sent to that awful public place, that juvenile institution. People just don't have any rights anymore." Diana was dabbing at her eyes with her hankie again.

"No." Belinda couldn't help smiling. Then she clocked the effects of age on her grandmother; it kept her mind off her boiling feelings. Diana's energies had once come in quick bursts, hurriedly shut down by an indomitable self-possession. "A dynamo disguised as a lady," Sky had once giggled to Belinda.

The door opened and Vail Wyman stepped into the room. He was wearing an Armani suit, a pocket handkerchief, highly buffed shoes, and he was tying his tie. "Oh, sorry," he said in his animated voice that slid up and down over the syllables.

"Uncle Vail," Belinda said.

"Lindy!" His worst nightmare. He forced a smile. "What are you doing here?" He advanced across the room. Up close he could see her much better, the pale, deeply set eyes, the mass of dark hair. "Where have you been?" Vail had just done his tie, now he jerked it loose.

"I've seen you a lot on television, Vail," Belinda said. "You're *the* Los Angeles media critic now, aren't you?"

"Did you just get here?" He looked at his mother, then back at his niece. "God, this is so surprising!" He slumped in a chair. "You—we—sometimes we didn't know if you were dead or alive—"

"I wrote—"

"Skimpy notes. No return address."

"I'm sorry, Vail. I didn't want to be found." Her intensity startled him.

"Vail, you left your wallet." It was Patsy, coming through the door carrying a briefcase in one hand, the other holding out a wallet. Her triangular face was turned down, her cropped brown hair fell around her cheeks, her eyes were fixed on one shoe. She turned her foot. "Damn shoe." Patsy's voice was soft and high, a voice people liked hearing. "Vail, we're late." She looked up. Her eyes widened. "Lindy!" She's back, Patsy thought. Is she here for Eddie?

Vail was out of his seat, going to his wife, putting an arm around her waist. Diana leaned back in her hooded chair.

"Where have you been?" Patsy cried, trying to keep her voice under control.

"She's been traveling, working," Diana said.

"You should have told us you were coming," Patsy whispered, staring at Belinda.

"I know, I know. I didn't think it would cause such a—"

"My god," cried Patsy, "where have you been?"

"She's been in Canada and New Mexico," Diana said to her daughter-in-law in her usual faintly condescending tone.

Vail made a critical gesture at his mother, but Patsy said, "You've had a chance to take this all in, Diana, but I haven't. I'm just bowled over."

"It's a long story, Patsy," Belinda said. It had always been hard to shave the truth with Patsy. Belinda anted up. "I had to stay away. I had to get to know myself all over again. I couldn't do that here."

"Five years is a long time," Patsy said. She stared at Belinda, an open examination, a challenge. Belinda's voice had changed—the melody was gone. The wiry body, the eyes, the straight nose and expressive mouth had gelled: she may have come from Sara's womb but she looked like Sky's daughter. She also seemed younger than her thirty-one years, as if she'd been preserved in a sunless incubator which hadn't wrinkled or aged her. "You'll stay here with us for a while?"

"Sure," Belinda said, "thanks."

"I have to be in court—I'm not often in court but today's the day and—and Vail has to drive me—the other car's—oh, never mind."

"You run along," Diana said.

Patsy bristled. "We won't just rush off. We'll have a cup of coffee."

"That's okay," Belinda said. "I'll still be here tonight."

Diana rose. "Belinda and I will get reacquainted."

There were alarming undercurrents in the room that everyone ignored.

"I'm stupefied," Vail said.

"I'll drive," Patsy said.

"No, you won't. You're too upset."

"I'm not upset, Vail. I am much calmer than you are. Don't slam the door." He got into the driver's seat and slammed the door. Annoyed, Patsy climbed into the seat beside him.

Vail backed out of the garage too fast, turned in the middle of the street, and took off. The fog was almost gone.

"Do you think she's okay?" he asked. "You know what I mean. God, so many years—I began to think she wouldn't come back. Where's she been?"

"Getting herself together, I expect."

"For five years?"

"Getting over being in a girls' prison and a state hospital takes time."

"She's got to be an emotional convict," he said. "Of all the women in this family, Lindy's the one I've never understood—even before the tragedy."

"She'll probably tell us where she's been tonight. And slow down," she said. His driving was atrocious, notorious. The Beverly Hills police, she maintained, could always see him coming and either swerved out of the way or pulled him over out of habit. "Vail, for god's sake!" she yelled as they narrowly missed sideswiping a bicycler.

"She could have called us," he shouted, lifting both hands from the wheel of the car. "And when she was—inside—she wouldn't let us see her! You remember that day—?"

"Yes, Vail—"

"They turned us away! We'd gone all that way."

"She didn't want to see us. I think we reminded her of Eddie, reminded her of everything."

"Doesn't she think we suffered?"

"Keep your eyes on the road." Patsy put her hand on his thigh without thinking, an automatic gesture. "She looks good, don't you think?"

"Please don't be upbeat and civilized." He was rushing down Robertson toward the freeway, twenty miles over the speed limit. "After what she did, how do we know—I mean, we have to be careful. She'll be right in the house. Can she be trusted around Eddie? God, she's back, I can't believe it!"

Patsy looked at the cars getting out of Vail's way as he roared up the ramp and slapped onto the freeway heading toward downtown Los Angeles. She picked up the car phone and punched in her office number. "Betty, I'm going straight to court on the Halliburton defamation case . . . for the continuance. . . ." Vail cocked an eye at her, listening. "I'll be back by eleven," Patsy said. She replaced the phone in its box. "I don't think Belinda expected us to be shocked. I think she expected something else."

"What?"

"Platitudes. Distance. Hostility."

L'Affair Belinda had hung over the family like a shroud. At age seventeen she had shot and killed a man. The family's disgrace had become the unspoken family secret. Most of the publicity of her crime and imprisonment had been suppressed, for the Wymans were from a powerful California family, born of oil and railroads, and more recently from films and television.

Of everyone in the family, Patsy had known the most about the Belinda Wyman case by the time of its hearing in the early seventies. At the time, Patsy had been a young attorney with the great firm of Banning, Bode, Carter, and Nye. Representing Belinda, Banning had engineered the manslaughter plea bargain that had sent her for two years into the California Youth Authority system. Patsy, now an entertainment attorney, had made it her business to learn just what had awaited Belinda in the Ventura School for Girls—Ventura School for Girl Thugs, Patsy had discovered. More than any other member of the family, Patsy understood Belinda's situation there, and later, at the Patton State Hospital. That knowledge made Patsy feel intensely divided about Belinda. But no matter how much sympathy she had for her niece, her sudden reappearance changed everything.

"I wish we could have had our own children, Vail."

"Edward's our son. Nothing will ever change that. We raised him. We're his adoptive parents. Lindy didn't care a damn about Eddie."

"Vail, she was forced to give him up."

"She wouldn't even let Eddie come to see her there."

"Would you want Eddie to see you in a state mental institution?"

"All right, all right!" He hit the wheel, exasperated. "But *she* told you to tell him his mother died, and that doesn't sound like a lot of maternal warmth to me."

"The big lie," Patsy mumbled. "I hate it. We shouldn't have gone along with Diana. We should have known better after what happened between Sky and Lindy—"

"That was different."

"How? Lindy didn't know she was Sara's child until—until that night. Sara and Sky should have told her right at the first." It was an old argument between them but Patsy rose to the reengagement.

"Sara was ashamed," Vail said, "and Sky wanted to be her mother so much, and don't forget Mom—"

"Ah, yes, Diana. God give me strength," Patsy said with feeling. "She still thinks she's moving this family around like marionettes."

"Oh, she does not." Vail's mouth curled into a ripe and winning smile. "You just have to be aware of her little predilections."

"You always stick up for her," Patsy said, angered. "You're fifty-five, you're one of the most sophisticated critics in this country, certainly one of the best known, and you're acting like a little kid."

"You weren't a triplet," he aimed at her, smiling crookedly.

"The unbreakable goddamned triplet bond," Patsy intoned.

"You didn't grow up with Diana."

"Thank god." But she heard the laughter in his voice.

"Why, she did everything for us. We owe her—"

"Stop it, Vail. Don't tease. I know you're as shocked as I am by Lindy's reappearance."

Patsy always saw right through him. He cut across three lanes of solid morning traffic. "Anyway, we're not triplets anymore."

"When's Sara getting in?" Patsy asked.

"A couple of weeks. I'll call and warn her."

"When she gets here, we'll tell Edward everything," Patsy said.

"No! We don't even know if Lindy's back for good. We don't know if she can be trusted." Vail ranted on. "*Can* she be trusted? People are released from those wards all the time and they stay out a few years and they still fall apart. Was she crazy?" he demanded of the rearview mirror. "Is she okay now?"

"Lindy doesn't look to me like someone who's going to fall apart." Patsy thought of the tense but composed young woman she'd seen in Diana's sitting room.

"Are you a shrink now?"

"She's Edward's mother."

"She isn't! *You* are. Does she want to take Eddie away with her? Why is she back? There's got to be a reason."

"Sure there's a reason," Patsy said.

"Yeah, to take Eddie."

"Oh, no," she replied softly, "it can't be that."

"God, you're calm. Don't you care about Eddie?"

"Of course I do." She felt tears burning in her eyes. "How can you say that?"

He reached across and grabbed her shoulder with one hand. "I'm sorry, honey. I'm upset. You're the best mother that ever was." He took Patsy for granted—everyone did. She was always cool and logical. But she'd struggled to become a lawyer when women hadn't been lawyers, and she'd struggled against his family to be herself. She loved Eddie fiercely and she'd always tried to keep the problems in the family away from him. "I'm sorry."

"He's as much a part of my body and soul as if he'd come from my body," Patsy said.

"I'll fight her to the last breath. Jesus, Patsy," her husband howled in his pain, "what's she going to do?"

"What are any of us going to do?" Patsy murmured, watching Vail hit the exit at fifty miles an hour.

CHAPTER 2

The Wymans were used to power and responsibility: Ned Wyman, Vail's father, had come from a distinguished California financial family. Over objections, he'd married Diana Whittaker, a woman who'd said she was without family, but who in fact had been the illegitimate granddaughter of an oil and railroad tycoon, a California family even more powerful than Ned's. When Diana had expected twins but had given birth to triplets, Sky being the surprise third child, she'd raised them to succeed at all costs. Sky had been lucky and pliant. Her accidental early fame had changed the lives of every family member. Sara and Vail had struggled against the attention and the comparisons by failing noisily and publicly, personally and professionally, until they were well into their thirties. But through it all—the competition, the glare, and the pressure—the triplets never betrayed the absolute trust each had for the other.

After Vail dropped Patsy downtown, he rushed back on the Hollywood freeway, snapped in and out of traffic-clogged lanes, and headed west toward his office.

Vail was short, five feet, six inches. Physically, he resembled Sara more than Sky—reddish hair, hazel eyes, a sharp, straight nose. Also like Sara, he had an explosive, outgoing, and unpredictable manner. Women had always found him attractive, for he gave them the impression that he understood and cared about their thoughts. As early as high school, he'd found he could successfully seduce women just by listening. That this was true never ceased to astound him.

Vail had wanted a son in the fervent way of some men who grow up surrounded by women. Eddie had been only a few days old when he and Patsy had brought the child home.

Overnight, Vail had changed from a self-indulgent happy husband to a devoted and attentive father. He diapered Eddie, fed him, sang to him, bought him toys and books long before he could even sit up, supervised advances in prostheses, buying him the best as he slowly grew into each size. For the next decade, Vail rearranged his schedule around Eddie's schools, father-son dinners, soccer practice, and rock concerts. Eddie was the center of his world and gave that core a special resonance.

Thinking about Eddie made Vail happy. He started singing "Lucy in the Sky With Diamonds," as he drove off the Highland exit, which dumped him eventually on Sunset. He turned west, reminding himself to call Sara. When she heard about Lindy's reappearance, she'd have a range of reactions—each bigger than the last. He was fond of Sara, and had become closer to her since Sky's death. But he'd been bound to Sky in an indefinable psychic way that still thrilled and appalled him. Since childhood, he'd had what the family had called "Vail's dreams." They weren't dreams but waking visions that came to him in brief splitting headaches. The first had come when he and his sisters as little children had been on an "educational tour" of Europe with Diana in the middle thirties. They were about five. Vail had refused to go to lunch in a small German town because it was "bad." He'd been dragged there, screaming. Sara and Diana had ridiculed his dread, but Sky had not. That was the day Nazi storm troopers attacked a baker as a small distressed crowd that included Diana and the triplets stood on the street and watched. Sky had taken Vail's hand. Years later, he'd seen Sky's death on the edge of the reservoir long before it happened. But he'd denied the warning.

Since then, he denied nothing. On a day he'd been making a new meat sauce in the kitchen, he'd suddenly known Patsy was in trouble. He'd raced out to the yard as she'd come tumbling off a ladder, breaking her shoulder. Later, her shoulder in a cast, Patsy had joked about his warning. Her whole universe was real and could be parsed. To Vail, sleeping dreams were distorted unreal images of another world running a parallel track beside the waking world. Waking "dreams" were real, but it did no good to go around talking about them.

* * *

Vail's office was a bank of large rooms on Sunset Boulevard where the trees thickened and the boulevard cut away from West Hollywood to approach Beverly Hills. He peered through the windshield as he approached the left turn into the parking lot beneath his building. He'd hit both sides of the entrance and had crumpled both fenders, not once but twice. He waited for a space in the oncoming double lanes of traffic, then crept toward the garage—a dark mouth opening in the building. Horns began honking at him: he gave the lead car the finger. The front of his hood rose up over the indented driveway and dipped down for the descent. Vail squinted at the opening and tried to judge the distance between his fender and the edge. But he couldn't see to the sides, and the dark entrance also seemed to distort his field of vision. He couldn't tell if his fender was a foot or half an inch from the wall. He accelerated and skimmed through the opening.

"Cutting it pretty close there, Mr. Wyman," the attendant said.

Vail got out. "Like life," he replied airily. Nothing in his voice gave away his panicky fear. "Maybe I'll get a driver!" he said, stepping into the elevator. The doors slid shut. Or, a new head with new eyes.

That afternoon, Diana Wyman and her old friend, Leonora Lytton, were taking their monthly luncheon at the Bel Air Hotel. They both wore superb hats.

Leonora was all angles, a regal hawk, while Diana was sleek like a beautiful fish; Leonora's beautiful voice and speech had theatrical cast, while Diana's was effortlessly perfect but a shade artificial—the high-class American speech of an earlier century, taut, understated. Sometimes Leonora slipped into the vernacular for effect. Diana never did.

The Bel Air was tucked in a wooded hillside of sycamore elms, tree ferns, palms, and bougainvillaea far up Stone Canyon in West Los Angeles. A private meeting place for decades, the modest, ordinary frame buildings with their red tile roofs and faint Spanish air, had once been stables. The two elderly women were seated in the dim, cool dining room near a window that looked out on a banana palm. Beyond it, two spoiled swans glided complacently on a pond.

The past was a durable bond between Diana and Leonora. Both had been part of "Old Hollywood," a halcyon, perhaps mainly imaginary era when Hollywood professionals had felt like a family. Leonora spoke of it as "the time before everything cheapened." She had a more intimate connection to old Hollywood—as a well-known New York stage actress she'd come to Los Angeles in the 1930s. Diana had not arrived till the fifties when Sky appeared in her first picture.

"You wouldn't have believed it, Diana," Leonora was saying with banked energy about a mutual friend. "So many lifts. And she must be seventy, maybe more, who knows? She has a dead face, my dear, still as stone." She tapped her breastbone. "And in here, too, a pebble. If she were cast tomorrow, she'd have nothing to give. Sad, really, such fear."

"You're not usually so unkind, Zip," Diana said, distracted. She straightened the silverware.

"I'm reporting! It has nothing to do with kindness."

"I'll say."

"You wait, Diana. When you see the poor thing, you'll know."

Their daughters, both actresses, formed a second bond between them. They had met on Sky Wyman's set in the fifties when Sky was at the top of her form, and Leonora's daughter, Pauline, had been struggling for roles. They became close friends in the sixties when their daughters' situations had been reversed. Sky had been trying to make a comeback. Pauline Lytton, by then a television comedienne, had agreed to play the role of Sky's sister in a film which the producer insisted Sky could no longer carry by herself. It had been a bad period and Diana and Leonora had spent a lot of time commiserating with each other: Leonora had always been baffled by and irritated at Pauline, who, she'd said, had betrayed the family escutcheon by working in television. But Diana's myopic pride in Sky had remained undimmed by trivialities like alcohol or drug abuse or plummeting celebrity status.

"How many pictures did you produce, Zip?" Diana suddenly asked her.

"Oh, you know, not many."

"But why did you start producing?"

"We were broke, my dear. I took a page out of Katharine Hepburn's book and optioned the plays I wanted to make. Once you control the rights—"

"I never produced anything," Diana interrupted. "Except the children." She patted her forehead with her lacy pink handkerchief.

Leonora narrowed her eyes. Diana's fixed, slight smile froze. She couldn't shake the undertow from her dream about her triplets or the sudden, disorienting arrival of her granddaughter.

"Belinda's come back. It's troubling. We're all thinking about the effect this might have on Edward."

"What effect?"

"Little Edward is Belinda's child," Diana said.

"He *is*? I always thought he was Vail's."

"When Belinda had her troubles, I thought it would be best for Edward if he had a more stable atmosphere."

Leonora laughed merrily. "Diana, what a peach you are— so understated." She was trying to remember what Belinda's "troubles" had been; Diana wouldn't tell her straight out, she knew.

"Oh, dear." Diana sighed. "We try to do what's right and then—things happen." She reached for another wheat cracker and broke it in two. "Don't pay any attention to me, Zip, dear. I'm a little depressed today."

Leonora was now thoroughly aroused. She started talking about Booth, her own granddaughter, hoping to stir more of Belinda's story out of Diana, but Diana sat listlessly in her chair, one hand bent at the wrist, her David Webb bracelet caught at her thumb knuckle, the thin blue veins snaking under her skin.

"You know, Zip, I think it would be a good idea if Edward went to boarding school," Diana said finally. "Perhaps someplace in Europe . . . such fine schools. My triplets were practically raised in Europe—of course that was before the war, you know—but I always thought it gave them breeding, something to aim for, something above American standards, which can be so low and commercial. I know it did wonders for Sky's taste in roles."

Leonora frowned, the hard realist. Diana was always moving her family furniture around on the set. She'd been her daughter's constant companion, a manager-mother, but Leonora knew from

Pauline how much Sky had resented it.

"Nothing can replace a fine education," Leonora said neutrally.

"I'm not sure that Vail and Patsy can handle this situation with Belinda."

"What situation?" Leonora asked. "Stop making these veiled comments if you want me to follow."

"Edward doesn't know he's Belinda's child."

"Good lord, why not?"

"She didn't want him to, what with the institution and her dreadful circumstances. . . . It seemed cruel, considering his hand and all." The image of Edward's handless wrist came into Diana's mind. "A penance," she muttered, closing one bony fist.

"Edward knows he's adopted, doesn't he?"

"Of course." Diana's deep hooded eyes glanced away from her friend toward a lush banana palm. "Belinda told me this morning she doesn't want to disturb anything, but I'm not sure that she'll be able to resist."

"What's she like?" Leonora asked.

"Belinda? Difficult to say. Oh, quite pretty in a delicate sort of way. Not a real beauty, like Sky, and rather hard now. There's something—I don't know—counterfeit about her. She was always impulsive, rash, but now she's locked down. She thinks she's in control but she's not."

"What do you mean?"

"Well, Zip—how would you be if you'd spent years in a mental institution, and then, after release, you don't go back to your family, but run off doing heaven knows what, hiding from yourself?"

"Maybe she feels more confident now."

"I wonder if she's used to making decisions, if you follow. I wonder about her stability."

"Sounds like she's been pretty independent."

A diffident waiter delivered their salads and disappeared. "Is she going to be living with you?"

"We don't know yet." Diana looked at her friend with an ingenue's openness—pure fakery.

Leonora was struggling to recall what incident had put Belinda in an institution. It had been years ago, but it had shocked the Wyman family down to its Continental Army beginnings—an ancestry of which Diana was very proud. It had been in all the papers . . . San Francisco! Belinda had been at college there when everything had come apart.

"She looks quite well, considering," Diana said. "But you and I know what it's like to be a mother, and if Edward's around, Belinda may want to have him back. She may not be able to stop herself."

"Perhaps she won't stay," Leonora said brusquely.

"I think it would be better if Eddie went to that wonderful school in Geneva." She lined up her butter knife on the plate. "I won't let her take my family apart again," Diana said in a passionate and trembling voice that was ice cold at its center.

"My dear," Leonora said, taken aback, "I don't see what you can do." Diana did not say anything. She picked up her fork and speared a piece of tomato delicately. "In the long run," Leonora said, "I find that it really doesn't matter what we do."

"Oh, yes, it does." Diana's hooded eyes regarded her friend. "I will not sit by like a stone."

The kitchen in the Wyman house was known as Vail's kitchen. He had designed it. A central work island and range floated in the middle of the long, well-lit room of bright tiles and stainless steel appliances. Copper pots hung above the island. A window herb garden at one end was augmented by the larger herb garden outside the kitchen door in the backyard. Vail had installed sinks for food preparation and another sink area for cleanup. The atmosphere was of a working area where the preparation of good food brought joy.

"Mr. Vail," Maria Estarte, the cook, was saying in her slightly accented English, "do not rearrange this dinner, please."

"No, no," he said, with relish, setting out the other ingredients for the salad. "Would I do that to you?"

"You would and you have." Her strong arched nose and oval face was pure Mayan Indian. Maria was, in fact, a university professor. Her husband was a doctor, studying to be admitted to practice in the States. They had won asylum.

Vail plunged into his cooking, relieved that the day before yesterday he'd taped his next two weekly reviews and could concentrate on the fresh garlic and olive oil for his famous Caesar salad. He beat the dressing snappily with a whisk, put the bowl aside, went into the dining room, and set the glossy round table. He was arranging the flowers in the center of the table when Patsy and Belinda came in.

He peered at Belinda, squinting. "You've changed a lot," he said. She looks like Vic, he thought, and like Sky. Jeez, a lot of Sky in those eyes.

"How?"

"Less impulsive?" he tried, not expecting to be asked.

"I've been with all kinds of different people, Vail." She turned to Patsy. "Do you still hate your name?" Belinda asked her.

"Yes, but I've given up trying to get anyone to listen to me. At least they call me Pat in the office."

"*You've* changed, Patsy." She seemed to be the stabilizing force in the family now. "You're the family's *consigliere*."

Patsy laughed. "Not bad for the daughter of a Reno blackjack dealer and former beat chick," Patsy said.

"Flower child," Vail corrected, smiling. He was proud of his wife, who'd changed from a reticent, unsophisticated girl into the warm cogent woman she was today. She had a sweet, tough nature. It had been Patsy's sexiness that had first attracted him, but it had been his friend from the Korean War, Bondy Goldstein, who'd seen into her heart long before Vail. "She doesn't express herself elegantly," Bondy had said, "but she's sharp and she's honest." If not for Bondy, Vail might never have married Patsy.

Patsy was staring at the table. "Who else is coming?" She pointed at the fifth setting.

"What?" He counted settings: "You, me, Lindy, mother . . . Oh. Sky." His faced blanked.

"Sky?" Belinda said.

Vail was removing the setting.

"He counts her in sometimes without thinking," Patsy said. "Sometimes Sara, too."

"We were triplets a long time," Vail muttered. Occasionally he could feel Sky in the room taking up space. He was sure she was there.

"What was it like?" Belinda asked. "Being a triplet."

"Always plenty of competition and company," he said.

"Sounds like being in camp all the time," Belinda said. It didn't have much reality for her.

Vail put the extra silverware back in a drawer. "I'll tell you the best thing."

"You could read each other's thoughts," Belinda said, raising an eyebrow.

He looked at her sharply. "No. The best thing was having the same experiences at the same time. We all learned to read and write at the same time, or horseback ride or dance. My sisters didn't lag behind because they were younger or make me feel small because they were older. Now *that* was *great*."

Diana came into the dining room wearing her slight smile as naturally as her dinner dress with a Belgian lace collar and her usual complement of jewelry—bracelets, earrings, and a diamond brooch.

"They were such beautiful children. I couldn't help but overhear," she said, glancing swiftly, critically, at the table. She straightened one of the roses in the vase. "Let's go into the sitting room. It makes me tired to stand." She took Belinda's arm. "Everyone commented on my triplets when we lived in Europe. I wanted them to have the very best tutors. Edward should have the best, too. Why, Vail was absolutely marvelous at French and German, a natural ear for languages." They breached the living room and Diana, straight as a yardstick, sat down in a Sheridan chair.

The room was huge, twenty-eight feet high at the ceiling's sloping peak. At one end, nearly ceiling high, a tall arched window looked out on the city. The walls were white, laced with dark beams and wainscotting. Along two walls, about halfway up, a mezzanine loft extended back, expanding the sense of open space. It was lined from floor to ceiling with books and contained cozy groups of sofas and chairs. Below, on the lower level, the room was elegantly and traditionally furnished. In one corner, a grand piano; on the opposite wall, a double pair of French doors opened onto the patio.

"Do you remember, Vail dear, the time Sky lost her dolly in, where were we—Switzerland? Such a dickens, and so stubborn! And the other one—"

"Sara, Mother."

"Yes, she thought I was going to leave Sky behind. Can you imagine?"

Vail said to Belinda: "What I remember is Paris where Sara and Sky and I found an attic room, a sort of cubbyhole 'way up in the Ritz. Mother couldn't find us for hours." He chuckled.

Diana adjusted a bracelet. Vail gazed at the neighbors' huge poinsettia tree. Patsy sipped ice water. Everyone was relieved that Edward was away. Belinda studied them covertly: Patsy's kindly, gritty realism; Vail's spirited, emotional intelligence; her grandmother's gravity. She'd taken their respect and affection for granted, and she'd lost it. She wanted it back, without pity.

"Well, you'll want all the news, Lindy," Vail said, filling the gap. "Sara's been filming in Europe." But suddenly he wasn't sure that Lindy wanted to hear about Sara. "She was over budget," he said, looking away. This family's a mire, he thought.

Maria came in and announced that dinner was served.

They were well into the culinary joint effort between Vail and Maria when Diana said to Belinda, "But you used to draw so well. I remember you doing hundreds of those cute caricatures of everyone! Didn't you keep it up?"

Vail groaned inwardly. His mother was talking to Belinda as if she'd just returned from college.

"I did some drawing," Belinda replied, thinking of Maisie, one of the prisoners in the school, as they'd called the California Youth Authority prison, who'd torn up all her drawings. It had been a serious power move. Belinda had responded by putting a tablespoon of cayenne pepper in Maisie's stew when she'd been on kitchen duty. From then on, it had been war. Belinda had not realized that war in the school could be deadly.

"The best therapy for me," she said to her grandmother, "were the theatricals at the hospital." They'd called Patton State Hospital the "loony bin," "the nuthouse," and, "the Home," because many would never leave it. "I had a way with some of the patients as actors. I enjoyed that," she added, shyly.

"That's perfectly natural since your mother, Sara, is a film director, and Sky was an actress," Diana said.

"Sara is not my mother," Belinda said. Her voice was hard, her manner abruptly defiant. "I don't even know her. Sky was my mother. Sky was the one who made cookies with me and arranged my schooling. Sara wasn't around to do that."

After a silence, Patsy said, "So, you've been working on some location shoots."

"Nothing big. There was a television series that was shot in Seattle for two years. I worked as a secretary to the location manager. I was a secretary to a documentary producer in Hawaii. I worked as a waitress before that—"

"A waitress." Diana moaned. "Oh, why didn't you come home?"

Belinda stopped eating. "I couldn't face you," she said.

"Your *family*?" Diana cried.

"I was hanging between two sets of realities, and neither were very appealing—you all and the loony bin. I wanted to see if I could make it on my own. There was— I wanted to punish myself, too, as if the state hadn't done a good enough job."

Patsy heard Lindy's cynicism, the root of her niece's toughness. Belinda had been a protected young girl of seventeen, at the top of her private school class when she'd entered Berkeley as a freshman. A few months later, she'd been in jail. Now she doesn't trust anyone, Patsy thought.

"You could go back to school," Vail said.

"I graduated from college by correspondence courses."

"Why, that's great," he said. "Congratulations." Belinda said nothing. "I was thinking of school more as a social venue— meet new people, maybe find someone special—"

"I don't believe in love, Vail," she said.

Silence settled over the table.

"I have made a few plans. I took a new name—Belinda Oliver."

"What?" Vail said.

"Rash," said Diana.

"Oliver *is* Victor's name," Belinda said.

"You have to face your life with your own name," Diana replied.

"No, I don't."

"So you've taken your father's name," Patsy said. "I don't think I've seen any of Vic's thrillers recently. I wonder how he's doing."

"He's fine," Belinda supplied. "I called him a while ago."

"You *spoke* to him?" Vail asked.

"Yes. We've met off and on. He used to come and see me in the hospital when he was in the States."

"You let *him* see you and not us?" Vail said, surprised that he was hurt by this.

"I wanted to get to know him."

"But I'm your uncle," he shouted. "You're part of our family! I'll take care of you."

"Vail, calm down," Patsy said.

"I don't need to be taken care of."

"Vic's her father," Patsy went on. "It's perfectly natural—"

"I'm not saying it's *un*natural," Vail said.

"I have changed my name, Vail," Belinda said evenly, "because I can't have a life as Lindy Wyman anymore. There was too much press." She pushed back a hank of her dark brown hair with a dismissive gesture that implied a concern for appearances she would have denied.

Vail felt rushed into a discussion he wanted to have later. "I didn't want to bring this up now, but what are you doing for money?"

"Vic's helped when necessary," Belinda said, dabbing her small mouth with the heavy napkin. "I'll get a job." With this announcement, her eyes looked even bigger and more deeply set: stubborn. "Something in films, I don't know what exactly."

Diana, sitting across from Belinda, was wondering if her sympathy for her granddaughter had idealized her over the years. The woman Belinda had become seemed stranger and more complicated than Diana remembered. She felt Belinda was part martyr, part victim, a woman who rebelled against tenderness, and was, most of all, self-destructive. It hardened her resolve to remove Edward.

"I think you are right to find a job," Diana said, gazing at the slightly overblown roses. "A métier—everyone needs pride."

Diana was the only woman Patsy knew who demanded pity and respect at the same time. She saw fresh evidence of this now: Diana had just embraced Belinda's announcement, and had made it her own decree. At the same time, Diana's voice had held a note of pathos as she'd said the word "pride."

"Lindy," Patsy said, "how do your plans include Edward?"

Vail stopped eating.

"It's too late to change what was—and is," Belinda said. "I don't want Eddie to know I'm his mother. For his sake. Let's just leave things as they are."

"That's wise," Vail said.

"We're just postponing the inevitable," Patsy said.

"I'll get a job," Belinda went on. "I'll have my own place. Maybe Eddie and I can be friends someday. But I won't live as Lindy Wyman again." She broke a bread stick in half. Everyone was looking grim. "Cheer up, there's family precedent here—it was Sara's choice to give me up—"

"That was a different time," Vail interrupted. "You don't know anything about Sara's choices; you can't imagine the pressures Sara was under."

"I don't care what they were, Vail. It *wasn't* my choice to give up Eddie, I was forced to. But the result for Eddie is the same."

"I don't agree," Patsy said. "I might tell Eddie myself."

"Patsy!" Diana and Vail said together.

"You all can put your heads in the sand, but I'm not going to join you," Patsy said. "And as for you, Belinda, if you want to keep secrets, why did you come back?"

"I told you, I had to put down the burden. I couldn't go on with my life unless I did."

"I don't believe you." She looked at Belinda shrewdly.

Belinda stilled. "I don't care if you do or not, but it's true." But more was demanded of her, and she knew it. "I can't be Eddie's mother. You both have done a great job with him. He looks like a terrific kid. But I lost my youth. I spent my college years in a reform school and a mental hospital. You just don't know what living in those places is like. It's a weird, split world where everything's decided for you—*and* it's life threatening. When I finally got out, I wasn't fit to—I could hardly order a cup of coffee. I ran away and I did a lot of stupid jobs and some okay jobs, and now I want to move my life forward. I want to feel good about living my life, but I couldn't do that until I came here. I won't disturb anything for Eddie."

Vail sipped his wine. He felt sorry for all of them.

"But, Lindy," Patsy pressed, "Eddie believes his mother died. I didn't like saying it then—"

"Don't blame yourself," said Belinda.

"Well, I'm not!" Patsy snapped.

"I told you to say it."

Belinda looked as if she'd performed well on a test. But Patsy was chilled. Incarceration and her escape into dead-end jobs had not cowed Belinda; it had changed her deeply. Patsy wasn't sure she was going to admire the result.

After Belinda went upstairs, Diana, Vail, and Patsy remained in the living room, not looking at each other.

"She can't handle a real job," Vail said, breaking the silence.

"Looks like she's been doing just that," Patsy said. "She needs a challenge."

"She's tired of running," Diana said.

"Running takes different forms," Patsy replied. "She's still running if she won't come clean about Eddie."

"Don't start!" Vail said.

"You're not the only one this is hard on," Patsy said sharply.

"Yes, Vail, think of Patsy," Diana said in a tone of voice that always irritated Patsy. "There's so much bias against mental illness. The social stigma. And it's always the family who's to blame." Diana refastened her brooch. "I never thought Lindy was mentally ill."

"*Mother*," Vail said, "you think what she did was normal?"

"Of course not, dear," Diana snapped. "But there's no madness in our family."

"What would you call what she did, Mother? An act of sanity?"

"Vail," Diana said, "we don't know what went on in that room between Archie and Belinda. We only have her word for it." She took off an earring and studied it.

"The subject here is Eddie," Vail said, but he knew he was surrendering to his mother, and he hated his abdication. Hated it. He turned to Patsy. "Do you believe all that stuff about her not wanting Eddie?"

"No, not completely."

"I don't either. I'll never believe it. Maybe we can get her married to someone; she can have another child."

"She doesn't want another child," Diana said, rising. "She wants something very much, but not another child."

*   *   *

In the darkness, the armoire was a solid mahogany lump against the wall facing the bed. Its bulk dwarfed the other lumps—a small table, an upholstered chair, a Bombay chest. The door to the room was invisible in the dark.

Belinda lay in the guest room bed infatuated again with the sensation of self-will. She'd felt the rush every night since she'd been released. She could go to the door and open it— it wasn't locked. Was it? No. Maybe it had been locked while she was in the bathroom. She leaped from the bed, banged her shin against an ornamented chest. The pain did not deflect her. She reached out for the doorknob and twisted it. It opened.

Back in bed, lying on her side, feeling sleepy and good, she stared at the armoire hunched in the dark against the wall. Gradually, she was aware that one of the massive armoire doors was opening. Slowly, Belinda raised herself up on her elbow.

The door was open. Inside, in the gloom, Sky was leaning against the back wall, her arms folded across her chest, her white face surrounded by her black hair bleeding into the shadows.

"Jesus Christ, I'm hallucinating," Belinda said out loud. She would close her eyes and Sky would be gone.

But that did not happen. Sky turned her face up, lifting it toward the window's faint light, going for the key light, a gesture that Belinda had seen hundreds of times. "God, I really am crazy." She felt sweat in her hair and a chill down her back. She was suddenly more terrified for her reason than of the apparition before her. But the image of Sky drew her with a loving pain: Sky was her mother, not Sara.

Sky stepped out. She was wearing white linen slacks and a sheer cotton blouse with full sleeves that Belinda remembered well. Transfixed and frightened, Belinda watched as Sky came toward her, stretched out the palm of one hand, tucked it beneath Belinda's chin. Her hand was soft and small.

"You'll be all right, Lindy. I know you'll be all right. I love you, my sweet."

Her pale, cool fingers slipped slowly across Belinda's cheek.

"Oh, Mama," Belinda whispered, immensely soothed, immensely lonely. "I've missed you so." Tears rolled from her eyes. A blunt, lengthening pain drew through her.

Sky was moving toward the door to the hall, receding. "Don't go." Sky nodded, agreeing, and disappeared in the darkness.

Belinda was sitting on the edge of the bed, leaning forward, her hands behind her. She had no idea how long she'd been sitting there. The armoire door was closed.

"Sky's make-believe daughter, that's what you were," a doctor had once said scathingly to her. "She wasn't your real mother and your friends weren't really your friends, they just wanted to be close to your mother."

When Belinda had been eight, Sky had made her birthday cake: white icing with misshapen red roses, one of them tilting vigorously toward the center. Finally, the maker had given up perfection and had drawn a big red icing smile in the center with two lopsided rosebud eyes. There were dancing lessons, art lessons, tennis lessons. When she hadn't been shooting a picture, Sky herself had driven Lindy to them. When she hadn't been shooting, Sky read her stories at night, cuddled against her in the wide soft chaise.

Belinda sat on the bed, crowded by her past. She compared her youth with Sky to the dry, violent desert of the school and the nuthouse. She smelled the tart disinfectants and ripe bodies; she heard the echoing cement and linoleum halls, the sudden screams, the furtive buzz of people stacked in every room like bees in a honeycomb, never silent, always shifting, turning, moaning. The monotone of the dayroom television set had not been another drug but her connection to the changing world outside. Inside, there was no safety anywhere, night or day, no safe place to sleep. One night, in the school, she'd awakened when a hand had slammed over her mouth: her bed was surrounded by inmates, whispering, menacing, laughing. Other hands held her down. Belinda had fought, twisting, arching. The woman she'd come to know later as Maisie appeared at the foot of the bed and had told her softly how things worked in her dorm. Then they'd beaten her and fondled her and had stolen everything she'd brought in from outside—money, soap, perfume, cigarettes. She'd lived every day as if another person sat beside her constantly, listening to her breathe and think. After a month in the school, Belinda's childhood memories belonged to someone else.

She leaped out of the bed and turned on the lights in the spare room. I will not give in to this, I will not, she told herself. She went to each piece of fine furniture, felt it, proved it. She wouldn't allow any of them—Maisie or Ruby or the guards or the nuthouse freaks—back into her life.

She was left with the present. She felt the hot ancient rage at Sara and the jagged triumph when she'd conquered her fear of the menacing inmates and guards. In the school, everyone distrusted authority and every inmate felt worthless. Belinda wanted respect and the need propelled her. For, looming over everything, bigger than before her imprisonment, was the uncertainty she'd had since childhood: how could she live up to Sky? High and ill on Haldol, she'd seen Sky's old films on the loony bin's dayroom television set. The distance between herself and the woman who'd raised her so tenderly seemed too great to be closed. And it wasn't only Sky; everyone in the family was someone to be reckoned with. Even Sara had pulled herself out of decline and envy to a point where Vail had called her "a complete professional." What could she, Belinda, do in the face of such triumphs?

And what about Eddie? It was painful seeing him, painful and wonderful. She'd come back here to face herself, to face her people, but most of all to see him. Had she really meant what she'd said to Patsy? Yes. She could withstand the guilt, the need to confess, the need to be who she really was with him. Eddie was lost to her, and that was right. He was Patsy's; he was Vail's. He was Archie's.

But who was she? She felt like a shell. She had to fill herself or find out what was inside that had never come out.

CHAPTER 3

"Come in quick! I'm surrounded by women!" Vail waved Schurl, his oldest friend and the producer of his television show, into the house.

"All those sisters, wives, mothers," Schurl said, laughing. He stepped inside. "You only have one of each."

"It always seems like a crowd."

Schurl was about fifty, a big man with heavy, kind features. He still wore his shoulder-length, sandy hair in a ponytail. "Sara here?" Schurl asked, hopefully.

"No, not yet."

"She okay? It musta been hard for her, losing Reed."

"Yeah, tough," Vail said. "They were married about fifteen years. The party's really for Sara—she just wrapped her film in Milan, first one she's shot since Reed died."

They walked into the living room where the sunshine through the high arched window threw a crosshatch pattern on the carpet. A wind in the night had blown the smog away exposing the city below. The double set of French doors were open to the patio and the vibrant flower garden.

Vail said, "You can buck Sara up. She's always liked you."

Schurl smiled warily, too pleased to believe it. "Oh, well, I always thought the world of her, Vail. What did Reed die of?"

"Heart attack." Vail snapped his fingers. "Like that."

Schurl contemplated the impermanence of life, which reminded him of their television show. "Anyone else here yet?"

"No. You're the first. What do you want to drink?"

"Just a beer. Vail, I came early because I want to talk to you about the show."

Vail was opening the beer. "What's up?"

"The network says they want to talk about a slight change of format with us."

Vail handed him the beer. "That means they've made up their mind."

"I think it's something we can accommodate." Schurl sipped his beer. "They feel the show needs a younger perspective." They had actually said to Schurl that Vail was old and traditional.

" 'A younger perspective'? What the hell does that mean?" Vail was alert now and uneasy.

"We'll find out next week. I want us to sit down with Jack and talk it through. They mentioned Neil doing a two-minute segment on teen movies each week."

"Neil?" Vail said, astounded. Neil Sheffield was his right arm, the only assistant who'd lasted five years.

"He's had local experience before he joined us—"

"They want to put Neil in front of the camera?" Vail asked, incredulous.

"I'm sure everyone's open, but I don't think it'd do the show any harm."

"It cheapens the show, waters it down! Jesus, Schurl—" Vail was about to launch into an intense tirade against network and commercial interference when Belinda walked into the room. "Belinda," Vail said, distracted, "this is Schurl, an old friend and the producer of my TV show. This is Belinda Oliver."

"Schurl?" Years ago she'd heard about Schurl, but he'd been on the east coast and had not come west to do Vail's show until after her trial. "That's your first name?" she asked, offering her hand.

"Yes. And last. I'm down to one name. It's easier than the original Polish: Szczeyliwicz."

"And your first name?"

"Wojciech."

"Great. Schurl."

"Have we met before?" he asked her.

"No," she said truthfully.

Schurl was puzzled. The Oliver woman looked a lot like Sky. It's the eyes, he told himself.

"Where'd you two meet?" she asked.

"At the Café Puccini in San Francisco," Schurl said to her.

"It was Ferlinghetti's," Vail corrected.

Schurl smiled tolerantly. He was an easygoing man. "Anyway, North Beach, late fifties. Vail was out of the army—the so-called Korean conflict was over—and I'd dropped out of college—studying anthropology."

Belinda listened encouragingly. She dimly remembered conversation about Schurl now. "You were part of the beat generation," she said.

"Dharma bums on the move," Schurl replied laconically, but he'd made the connection. This was Lindy, Sara's daughter, the girl gone bad.

"Schurl was an antiwar mobilizer in the sixties," Vail was saying, "a real steady force in my life, one of the few guys who always kept his principles."

"Now you're a TV producer," Belinda said. "Big jump from demonstrations."

"Vail and I make a good team," was all Schurl said.

The front door opened, then slammed shut. "That has to be Sara," Vail said. He glanced at Belinda.

"Schurl," she said, taking his arm, "let's you and me go outside."

Vail's sister was in black, a contrast to a mane of shoulder-length, curly, bronze-colored hair that flew out from her head dramatically. Her hazel eyes, high cheekbones, full mouth were laced together by a bold, beckoning expression. She was fifty-five, like Vail, but she looked younger. Elegant and sleek, Sara could always find the center of a dance floor, the center of a hot conversation, or the center of someone's joy or discontent. She was standing by the door, staring into a mirror when Vail stepped into the foyer.

"Hi, honey," Vail said.

"Oh, Vail," she whispered, "I'm so nervous about Lindy."

"Let's go in here." He motioned toward the study.

"Where is she?"

"Outside, with Schurl." He shut the door.

"That's good. He's so comforting." She took off her cape and tossed it on a chair. She passed a hand over her head; white streaks rushed up from her temples into her bronze-red hair. "How's she look?"

"Good. Harder. Sara, you have nothing to reproach yourself for. If it hadn't been for you, she wouldn't have gotten out of the hospital as soon as she did."

"Has she asked about me at all?"

"A little," he said. Sara was a brash, competent woman, unafraid of controversy, but now she looked timid and anguished. "Sara, I'm sorry, I know you're having a hard time without Reed—"

"I'm not in turmoil, Vail." She struck a pose.

"You look like it." He went up to her. "Please, no I'm-the-eldest-triplet crap now. You put in your time playing protector to Sky, to me—" He took her arm. "Settle down and let me help you."

"I need to know—if she's forgiven me."

"Sara, what difference does that make now?"

"It makes a difference to me! I don't want to go to my grave without her forgiveness."

"What's between you and Lindy can't be resolved tonight."

"I can try," she said in a lofty tone.

"I'm concerned about what Lindy's going to do when Edward comes back tonight. She's been saying that she just wants to know Eddie as a friend, that it's too late for her to be his mother, and that she doesn't want to upset everything."

"What's Patsy say?" she asked.

"She's—ambivalent."

"I don't believe you. Anyway, we should have everything out in the open."

Her brother looked irritated and unhappy. "Can't you come over to my side on this, Sara?"

She frowned, deepening the vertical line in her forehead. "No, Vail. Eddie's got to be told. Lindy may change her mind later and then—"

"Let's just take this one step at a time, shall we? I don't want a major drama tonight!"

"Okay," Sara said airily. "I don't want to upset you. As a matter of fact, I want to take Lindy back to Italy with me. There are fine art schools, a complete change of scene—"

"Sara. It's too late for you to mother her."

"I just want to make the offer."

"Don't risk it, Sara."

"I've always risked everything."

A knock came at the door: it was Maria, her black hair glistening under the hall light. "Good to see you back, Ms. Wyman."

"Thank you, Maria."

"A messenger just left this letter for you."

Sara shut the door, turned the manila envelope over, then opened it. A sealed letter fell out. Sara's face compressed, and she groaned. "Not another . . ." Her hands shook as she opened the letter, glanced at it.

"Another what?"

"After Lindy was released, I began getting these nutty, awful anonymous letters!" She slapped the letter against the back of a chair.

"Give it to me." Vail took out his thick glasses and started reading. " 'Sara Wyman,' " Vail read. " 'I haven't forgotten about Lindy. I will personally make sure she pays for what she did. I have told you before some of the ways she will die.' " Vail looked up. "How many of these have you had?"

"A few off and on."

"You should have told me."

"The letters stopped. I haven't had one in a couple of years."

Vail frowned, then read on. " 'She's corrupt. She corrupted lives. I know you and your family bought her out of a seat on death row—where she belonged. As her mother, you are the most to blame. I will not rest, I will never rest until she is dead, horribly dead.' Jesus . . ." Vail breathed, shook his head. "What have you done about—these?"

"I called a lawyer," Sara said, "and I hired a private investigation firm that handles crazy threats, but even they didn't find anything. Then the letters stopped."

Vail was turning over the envelope but there was no address. "We'll call the messenger service—"

"The letters come in the mail to them with typed instructions and cash. Twice they were left for me in my office in Rome and no one could even remember how they got there."

"Ah, it's got to be a crank, Sara."

"It's not a crank. There's someone out there, clever and full of hate and pain, waiting for her. And it frightens me."

Belinda was on her way to the kitchen when the front door opened. Eddie was in his fashionably torn jeans, and carrying his duffel bag. Except for a sunburn, he looked exactly as he had two weeks ago when they'd met in front of the house in the fog.

"Gee, you still here? I forget your name."

"Belinda Oliver. Yours is Edward. How was camp?"

"It sucks." He saw two waiters hovering over the dining room table. "What's going on?"

"Your father and mother are giving a party for Sara."

"The bride of Frankenstein's back already?" he asked lightly. Eddie brought his hand to his temple then combed it up toward the top of his head. He made a wild face. "Remember Elsa Lancaster's hair in the movie? The white in it's supposed to look like electrical charges? Sara's the electrically charged aunt." He dropped his arm. "Where do you come from?"

"San Francisco," she said, seeing again his faint resemblance to Archie.

"San Francisco's the max, isn't it?"

"Oh, yeah," she agreed and he laughed.

"Are you staying with us?" he asked. Eddie liked her: she was easy to talk to and wasn't one of the movie or TV heavies who ruffled his hair and pretended to listen to him when all they really wanted was a good review from Vail.

"Just for a while."

"Where's Mom?"

"Patsy's in there with someone called Schurl."

He picked up his duffel. "Oh, Schurl—he's real." And he was off.

Sara entered the garden head high, a prime-time woman, a wide, if somewhat fixed smile on her foxy face. But nothing could ease the anxiety, guilt, love, and longing she felt for the daughter who was not even a friend.

"Sara," Schurl said, "you are breathtaking." He took her hand in both of his. Sara did not see the fondness in his eyes. She was looking at Belinda who stood alone across the garden.

"Excuse me, Schurl, there's someone I have to see," Sara said, taking back her hand. She started across the lawn, thinking of all the words she wanted to say to her daughter, but instead seeing Lindy at two years of age, both arms raised above her head, wanting to be picked up.

"Belinda, I'm so glad to see you," Sara said, leaning in to kiss her cheek. "You look wonderful."

Belinda drew slightly away. "I'm no kid anymore," she replied, laughing. Her voice was like Sky's, but harder.

Oh, but you are, Sara thought, to me. She said: "I was so concerned about you but I understood why you couldn't come back as if nothing had happened." Sara put an arm around Belinda's waist; Belinda moved outside its circle.

"I drove into the hills the other day," Belinda said, "and looked at Sky's old house."

God, Sara thought, even from the grave Sky sends a shadow. "Did you go in?"

"No. I sat outside awhile, thinking about Sky, about growing up there, school plays, everything."

Sara knew that Lindy's veneration of Sky, whether real or pretended, was a way to chalk out the distance she felt from Sara. "I'm glad you're back," Sara said, cutting through. "Can we spend some time together tomorrow? I need to talk to you."

Her daughter hesitated. "I don't think tomorrow's good."

"It's important."

Across the patio with Vail and Schurl, Keith Llewellyn was witnessing what he considered an odd, awkward conversation between Sara and a younger woman. He knew Sara, as any serious writer would know a producing director, and Keith was a serious writer. It was Sara's attitude of a supplicant toward the younger woman that struck him. Sara's body was tilted forward as if she wanted to make amends, as if she owed the younger woman.

"Who's that with Sara?" Keith asked Vail, indicating Belinda.

"Friend. Belinda Oliver."

Keith gazed at Belinda, trying to see beneath the cagey, formal surface, a surface that was, he thought, false yet without guile, and strangely appealing. He sensed she was struggling to maintain some kind of public equilibrium. Keith could relate to struggle.

"Introduce me," Keith said to Vail.

"Haven't you already got enough women, Keith?" Vail said. Keith was talented, ambitious, and kind; women flocked to him.

"Quantity cannot compete with quality," Keith said.

It was almost as hard for Belinda to remeet Sara as it had been for her to see Eddie again. Sara talked on, trying to be engaging, inviting Lindy to Italy with her, describing art classes in Rome, relating episodes from her filming in Milan. But underneath her colorful stories Belinda knew Sara was pleading with her. Finally, her mother stopped talking in mid sentence, too proud and too sad to go on.

Belinda bent her head toward the woman she hadn't forgiven, and whispered: "I'm not going to make this easier for you, Sara. Why don't you take a clue from Grandma, strike a pose and don't look back?"

"What do you mean?"

"Grandma's pose is that she tolerates me but doesn't want me here. Patsy's is pity for the convicted felon trying to fit back into normal life." She arched one brow. "Or pity for the mother manqué."

"Oh, Lindy," Sara said, tears springing into her eyes.

"I like Vail's best: guarded antagonism. Don't sweat it," Belinda said, "I've had rougher times." She turned away and walked across the garden for breathing space. Her face burned in the cool evening. She sat down on a stone bench. Two weeks of being monitored by Vail and Patsy and Diana had drained her. The weight of the past outmatched her. She thought she'd conquered her anger at Sara, but just seeing her brought everything back. And underneath that coil of emotions, she was really angry at herself because she was doing to Eddie what Sara had done to her: Belinda had been raised as Sky's daughter, not Sara's. The night she'd learned who her mother really was had exploded in her face and had changed her life. Someday it might explode for Eddie, too.

"I can't let this go." It was Sara, putting a hand on Belinda's arm. "Belinda, I must talk with you." She moved her daughter away from the newly arriving guests until they stood by the jacaranda tree. "I wrote you about the letters, Lindy, when they first started." Belinda sighed. "Then they stopped but now, today, they've started again. I wasn't in this house ten minutes—"

"Sara, I'm not interested in the nuts out there."

"You listen. What kind of a mother would I be if I didn't warn you about this, tell you what I think?"

"It's too late for you to mother me, Sara."

Sara stopped moving. "All right, I made a lot of mistakes, but I'm not wrong about this. This letter is a threat. It's serious. I'm going to get another investigator on it, I'm calling the police—"

"Oh, great, my best friends, the cops."

"Lindy, this person is clever. Isn't there anyone you can think of who'd do this?"

Belinda appeared to think about this. "No, no one. It's probably someone who hangs around courtrooms."

"But they're writing *me*, as your mother."

"The whole country learned how you handed me off to Sky. It's not a secret now, was *then*, certainly hasn't been since the hearing, anyone could know you're my mother. I don't want to be mean about it but when you think about it, it's really a hoot, your testimony, and I'm sure it grabbed the public's imagination."

Sara felt deflated, frustrated.

"What would make you happy?" Belinda asked her, lightly. "Is this letter why you wanted me in Rome? What makes you think the writer's an American? Might be some Italian pizza boy who wants to upset you."

"Lindy!"

Belinda relented. "What do you want me to do?"

"Be careful, keep your head down, be warned," Sara said.

"I won't live in fear anymore, Sara. I've already done that, every night. No more. If the letter writer wants me, they can find me. I'm not keeping my head down." She started to walk away, then turned back. "I think it's a crank and you're getting overexcited."

"You sound just like Vail," Sara said, shaking her head.

Belinda moved toward a small table set up with wines, mineral water and sandwiches. As she poured a glass of water, and selected a sandwich, she waited for Sara to approach her again. But she did not and when Belinda turned around again, she saw that her mother had returned to the main group across the yard.

Belinda sat down on a stone bench under the jacaranda tree, her body turned away from the party. She wasn't as cavalier about the letters as she'd pretended, but neither was she going to let them dictate to her. They were from a crank, Sky had received many odd and repulsive letters, too, the cranks of the world all had pens. She leaned against the stone backing of the bench. She distrusted Sara's focus on the letters.

"My name's Keith Llewellyn."

Belinda turned quickly. She saw a tall, barrel-chested man in his mid thirties. He had dark thick hair, animated green eyes under dark brows, and a bushy mustache. "Mind if I sit down?" He sat. "Parties"—he sighed—"can get on the nerves. And you are?"

"Belinda Oliver."

"Shake," he said. She had a glass of mineral water in one hand, a sandwich in the other. He took the sandwich and ate the rest of it. "Now." They shook hands. Keith had the no-style style: torn jeans, T-shirt, baggy jacket that hadn't seen a pressing in months, mussed-up hair.

"What do you do?" she asked.

"Screenplays. I do screenplays."

"You rich? Got a Jag? A pool? Mortgages?"

"I drive a major heap. I rent an apartment. Status makes me tired."

"All you care about is the work, right?"

He grinned. "Something like that." After a silence, he asked, "You know a lot of people here?"

"No."

He nodded at a tall man with hunched shoulders whose weight was going into his face and his stomach. "That's Teddy Monroe, screenwriter," he said. "Used to be a playwright. Wrote the first play Sara Wyman was ever in. Damn good. Now he's eccentric, cantankerous. But I like people who are different. Some people call him a hack but I don't think so. And over there, a producer—he used to work out of his car, literally, and now, after everyone turned him down, he's got a hit TV show, the one about City Hall." Keith's face didn't move much as he spoke; his manner was sturdy, somewhat solitary but definitely friendly. "See that woman? She's one of the best second-unit directors around, and the woman next to her is a bang-up camera operator."

"That's what I'd like to do someday: direct."

"Yeah? Well, start with second-unit, then you have footage to show." He examined her lightly then gazed back at the party. "Half of Vail's staff's here, too. That's his assistant, Neil Sheffield," he said, pointing to a good-looking man in his twenties with blow-dried red hair.

Keith was surprised at himself. He usually didn't talk much at parties. "How do you know the Wymans?"

"Long story. I'm just visiting."

"Yeah, Vail told me."

"What did Vail tell you?" She tensed again.

"That you were visiting." A group across the patio distracted Keith, laughing suddenly and loudly, leaning away from each other. "I saw you talking to Sara when I came in," he shouted over their laughter.

"You know Sara?"

"Everyone knows her. She's a classic." He downed half a glass of red wine in a gulp.

Belinda felt her guard going down. She was suddenly aware that she wanted a friend very much.

"I don't get away enough," Keith went on. "It's important to get out of this town, keep fresh, keep learning. Vail could use more of that but he's nailed in here. Now, Sara—she's a woman of the world."

"You like her?"

"I admire her." He smiled. "Mucho grando director, gets on the set, takes it over—in a nice way, y'know, no hot games, no hair balls. But she's not here often—does her thing in Europe. I don't blame her. She's a woman of beliefs; that's how she strikes me. What do you believe in?"

Belinda didn't know what she believed in. "Sweeps week," she said, lightly. "And you?"

"I believe in doing it my way." He ran a finger under his mustache and his face stilled.

"How indulgent."

"Only if you have nothing to say or to give," he said. "There are lots of people who want you to do it their way—be bribed, be less, go along, live here, live there, get a computer, laugh at their jokes, be available, rewrite the ending. See?"

Belinda found herself thinking of Nathan who had certainly done it his way but under very different conditions. His family had sent him cans of designer talcum powder and the scent of it came back to her.

"What?" Keith asked her.

"Just thinking of someone, guy named Nathan. Met him on a huge sloping fresh-cut lawn early one morning. Like an engraving, that morning. He did it his way, too." Nathan had been slow, and lithium, combined with other drugs, made him slower. His family had stuffed him away in the nuthouse; he would never get out. "The first thing he said to me was 'Am I here?' I said that as far as I was concerned he was. He said, 'Good. I wasn't sure.' "

"Often wondered that myself," Keith said. "Who was he?"

"Just a crazy actor."

"And where did all this happen?"

"On a shoot in North Dakota," she lied.

"Why'd you think of him?"

One good thing about the school: it had taught her how to size people up quickly. "He was decent. Like you." She smiled and flipped her hand.

The party was getting bigger and moving toward them. Sara, Vail, and Diana were suddenly near; Belinda thought they were smiling at Keith. Or were they smiling at her? Keith was rising to speak with Teddy Monroe, who was cackling and pointing—at her? Belinda looked away, saw not Patsy's garden but the sloping lawn of the nuthouse. Nathan had managed to hang himself, bent on doing it his way.

"It was your idea," Vail was saying to Sara. "You were the one who wanted to take the horseback ride, not me!"

"Vail," Sara replied, "don't you remember anything right? It was Sky who got us all on that horse!"

Belinda was shoved back in time: Sara and Vail never remembered anything in their childhood the same way. Keith began talking with Sara about the American film business versus the art. He gazed at her respectfully as she criticized the American dream, American international interference. "There are only two filmmakers in the States who turn out consistently original material: Warren Beatty and Woody Allen," Sara said. "A big country like this, and only two?" Vail joined in, arguing boisterously with her; the kind of banter that substituted for hugs.

Someone said, "But why don't you work here, Sara?"

"Hollywood is dangerous to women's health."

Keith was back, towering over Belinda. "Food," he said. "They're actually serving food." His restless green-gray eyes looked at something behind her.

"Would you like to get out of here?" she asked him.

"Now?" he asked, startled.

"Yes."

"Where?"

"Just down the block, get some air."

"Maybe later," he said.

Close by, his eyes fixed on Sara, Schurl was bending down to whisper to a woman Belinda didn't know, maybe the camera operator. A long look slid out of the woman's eyes toward Belinda—or was it toward Vail? The crowd became a wall of rolling eyes and moving mouths, voices rising and receding. Belinda wondered: were people whispering about her? God, this *is* mad, she thought, a paranoid Haldol high, she'd called it before. Haldol, the drug of choice at the state hospital, hadn't agreed with her. The psych-techs, the nurse-keepers, had given it to her anyway.

Why was she feeling this way now? The roar of the party swelled. Then she knew. This was Patsy's and Vail's world now, not hers. She was an alien in her own town. She'd grown up here; she knew every shortcut from the Palisades to Silver Lake. But she had no idea where her old friends were now. The only people who were real to her were the girls in the school or the nuthouse where time had stopped.

She took hold of Keith's arm. "Let's get the fuck out of here," she said.

They were walking around the block. "This feels better," Belinda said.

"Better than what?"

"Oh, I don't know," she said, heartily. "Better than a knife in your ribs."

"Yeah," he said, eyeing her. "It feels better than that."

"Is Vail a good critic?" Belinda asked.

"There's no such thing as a 'good critic.' He's powerful. He can save a show that's been buried by its distributor or he can kill a show."

"Do people hate him?" she asked.

"Sure, lots. I don't, but then he liked the two pictures I wrote. If I put my heart into a piece of work and he smeared my guts all over the TV screen one night, I'd hate him. And he's perfectly capable of doing that." The street was dimly lit and hilly and still. "Were you born in L.A.?"

"Yeah, one of the few," she said.

"Me too. I just got back from Wales. Wanted to see where my grandfather came from."

She stopped walking. "Aha! Your face is kind of rugged like I imagine Wales," she said. It was, she remembered, a land of slate houses and slate roofs and slate tombstones and ravens. "Your grandfather alive?"

"No, he died in the mines. My dad got out playing soccer. He played all over the world. Anyway, back in Wales, I met a cousin who still works there. Mines are a lot more mechanized than what my dad told me about, but those aren't robots digging out the coal down there—men still do it. Lot of pride in the mines," he said quietly, looking at a tree as big and dark as a thundercloud. "Been thinking about that. My dad was successful, but he never talked about pride. Maybe he didn't have any. Maybe he lost it."

"Where's your dad now?"

"Dead—alcoholism. Liver went belly-up. Let's head back," he said.

"Not yet. You go if you want."

But he didn't. "What's your line?" he asked.

"I don't have one," she replied with a tilt of her head and a great smile. "I'm still thinking it through."

They fell silent again, passing the huge lighted homes and their proud trees. Belinda was strange, he felt, very strange. "You look a little familiar," he said. "Were you an actress?"

"Nah, I hate acting, all that interior mumbo jumbo."

"You're full of it. I bet you really love actors." She was irritating, like his sister.

They rounded the last corner, heading back to the house. Faint party sounds drifted from it on the balmy air.

"Thanks for the walk," she said. "I don't like crowds."

He thought of hooking an arm over her shoulder, but she seemed too skittish and remote.

Belinda felt she'd been at the party forever. The few late-stayers, including Schurl and Keith, were sitting on the patio, drinking coffee and wine. They were debating the new Soviet star, Gorbachev, a dialogue that collided with an analysis of last year's film, *The Killing Fields*, a post-Vietnam effort about Cambodia which Vail had called "a brilliant propaganda film."

Belinda was sitting near the double French doors when she heard Diana's lowered voice from the living room.

"Patsy, dear, she's . . . unstable." Belinda heard Patsy murmur something impatient but cajoling. "No," Diana answered, "I'm afraid of what she might do to Edward."

". . . can't discuss this now," Patsy said.

"I've spoken with Dr. Davis . . ."

Belinda jumped up, disturbing the languid conversational waters around her. She knocked over a cane side table on her way through the double doors into the living room.

"What the hell?" Vail demanded.

"Damn you," Belinda hissed to Diana. "Is this the way it's going to be?"

Diana's hand flew to her mouth. She looked alarmed and embarrassed.

Outside, on the patio, Vail was on his feet; Sara, Keith, and Schurl were rising, too. Belinda saw the shocked expressions tacked on people's faces. "I won't live this way!" she said, not caring what any of them thought.

"Of course not," Patsy said, reaching out for her.

"Don't touch me."

"Stop this," Patsy said, "and come into the kitchen." She began walking through the dining room.

Belinda followed her. "I'd like to be treated like—oh, forget it," she mumbled to Patsy's back. "I've been fine without any of you for a long time." But she was ashamed of her outburst.

On the patio, Vail watched them moving out of earshot. Irrational, he was thinking, defiant, uncontrollable. She'll end up on the ash heap. He saw Patsy push through the kitchen door, Belinda go with her, and the door swing shut. Had his mother retreated upstairs? he wondered. Vail sat down as Schurl was saying, "Did you hear about Markham's shoot in Brazil? Second unit went out in a helicopter to look around, got lost, had to land on a hill, some Indians appear and Markham says, 'Hi, we've got tickets for the Hollywood Bowl here.' . . ."

Inside the kitchen, Patsy said: "I'm sorry you had to overhear that."

"I'm sorry I—lost my head out there," Belinda said. "I was wrong to come here."

"Maybe. I'm not sorry you did, though."

"Don't maneuver me. I've had enough of that for a lifetime."
Belinda was pacing Vail's huge shiny kitchen, past fleets of
appliances and a mile of tile counters. "I was right the first time
around before I came back here—I can't put it behind me until
I break with *all* of my past." She stopped in front of a stainless
steel refrigerator. "And that means all of you. Everyone seems
to have a plan for my life. Vail wants to get me out of here,
maybe marry me off!" She hooted. "Sara wants me in Italy
with her, going to art school—ludicrous." She thought of the
letters. "I don't even know Sara, and I don't want to."

Diana pushed open the kitchen door. "What a wretched,
dreadful scene. I don't want you to be unhappy. You're my
only grandchild!"

"I'm sorry, but I'm out of here. I'll get my own place as
Belinda Oliver."

"You're running away," Diana said. "Don't be a coward—
you were never that."

"Grandma," Belinda said with a laugh, "I know you want
me to be happy—somewhere else. And I'm going to give in
to that."

"If you leave, do it because you want your own life. I know
there's nothing here for you but pain and memories."

"Lindy, do what's best for you," Patsy said.

Belinda said, distracted, "The people out there—they all
know about me, don't they?"

"No," Patsy said. "No one knows." Like Diana, she was
divided about Belinda; Patsy wanted to help her, but she now
felt that Belinda would only survive if she left the house.
And it was suddenly important to Patsy that Belinda survive.
"You're right, Lindy," she said. "If you stay, you'll never
grow up."

"I was stupid to think that I could go back. You can't know
what it's like—this readjustment."

"That's true, none of us can," Patsy said. "I'll help you
find a job. You can say that you're my cousin. But don't just
run away again and don't make up too many deceptions. Lies
always come out. Sara would agree about that."

"Who is *she* to give advice?"

Patsy clasped her hands together. "You lead your life; let
Sara lead hers. Lindy, one of my clients is a director. His

assistant just quit. He's not an easy man to work for, but if you can stand him, you'll learn a lot."

"Thanks, Patsy," Belinda said with more grace than she felt.

After Belinda left, Patsy leaned her elbows against the cool tile counter.

Diana suddenly sat down. "You handled that just right, Patsy."

Patsy whirled, angry. "I didn't handle her at all! She's just running! And don't think we've done any favors for the family—we haven't."

"She'll be happier somewhere else, without the memories."

"Memories? She'll never get rid of those." Patsy sank into a chair at the table. Had she known since Lindy came back that she couldn't stay? There was no question that her absence was better for everyone today, but how about tomorrow? Patsy felt something lock in place. It wasn't a good feeling.

Keith was driving home. The old Mustang's friendly rattles and clicks and squeaks kept him company. The draft from a tear in the convertible top cut across his face. He was a little drunk. After Belinda's surprising blowup, when things had calmed down, he'd gone into the house to get his jacket. He heard hushed, fervent voices from Vail's big kitchen. He wanted to get closer, listen in, but he was afraid Vail would discover him, so he'd gone back outside. Who was this Belinda Oliver, he wondered, a woman who must be in her late twenties but was somehow unformed? She was tough, yet full of struggle and terror. She fascinated him.

He drove down a street lined with ludicrous, stringy hundred-foot palm trees, their tiny mop tops dancing in the breeze. He visualized the worn leather belt at Belinda's waist, tucked in under her blouse, her slim thighs and bony ankles. He shouldn't have taken her back to the party. What might they have talked about? What might they have done? He could see his hand on her waist, feeling the bone and skin. He could see her earlobe under a sheath of dark hair. But it was the tumult in her that drew him, the iron in her that kept whatever was inside in check. She was present in the way that something wild was present—wary, alert. She was locked up behind her face with both fire and ice in her eyes. He didn't know if she were going to burst into flames or freeze. She probably didn't know either.

The walls of the room were papered in a Victorian-inspired design of twisting grapevines, pointed leaves, and tumescent bunches of pale grapes.

The caller sat deep in thought at an antique fruitwood table, contemplating action apprehensively, then reached tentatively for the telephone, pulled back, snatched the receiver off the hook with sudden decision, and dialed. The number was ringing. The caller was nervous, excited, counting the rings: one, two, three, four. Click.

A woman's voice with a Latin American accent answered. "Wyman residence."

"Sara Wyman, please," the caller said tensely, leaning forward.

"Ms. Wyman is engaged at present. May I take a message?"

The caller's body stiffened. "Tell her to get on this telephone!"

"What? Who is this?"

"Tell her that there's nowhere Lindy can hide."

"What?"

"Tell her to keep her eyes on Lindy because I'm going to make her pay for what she did."

"Who are you? What is this?"

The caller hung up, spun around, arms bent as if in physical pain. A moment later, a paperweight was pitched through the window.

The sound of shattered glass stopped all motion in the room. The caller drew a shaking hand across the table and sat down, breathing hard. Very slowly, a widening grimace stretched across the caller's mouth. The first sounds of a laugh started with a sigh and were followed by a bubble of sounds breaking out in a howl. The caller's eyes fixed not on the broken window, but on visions of Lindy Wyman.

CHAPTER 4

Fletcher Avery, film director, was leaning back in his chair, his hands clasped behind his head, his dark eyes fixed on the ceiling as a nervous young woman read lines with his assistant director. Fletcher was casting *Force Field*, a post-Vietnam adventure film.

At thirty-five, Fletcher was an aging enfant terrible in American pictures. He was trying to find his own version of what everyone billboarded as "a man's prime." He had all the hallmarks of it: vigor, ego, moods, drive, talent—a seductive combination. But pride and doubt battled inside him. He'd had big successes in his twenties—pictures that had shaken the industry and whose characters, like E.T. or the Muppets, had become part of popular culture. From those heights, Fletcher's thirties had seen his first failures; his last two films had bombed with reviewers and with audiences. Failure baffled him. It was outside his experience. It happened to other people. He couldn't find what he called the "rip cord" to the eighties, therefore, in *Force Field* he was going back to what he knew: war, pathos, blood, betrayal.

He cocked his head to one side, listening to the actress toss lines, listening for the note, the tremor, the brass that would seal her into his vision, into the role.

Fletcher's face was handsome in a mashed, lopsided way: he looked like he'd been in a car accident, but he'd only grown up in a tough neighborhood. The prominent planes of his cheeks drew attention to his nose. It was strong and bent left—a fighter's nose. His eyes sat under the ledge of his forehead, dark, intense. His mouth was a wide double band, soft, blunt—emotional but not sensitive.

He tilted forward, ruffled his long curly dark hair with his stubby competent hand, put his other hand on the desk top. "Thank you, Tracy. I saw you in *White Water*—that sorta low-key—"

"Smart-innocent-girl-in-a-raincoat part."

"Yeah. Great. Well, thanks, Trace, gotta think here."

She squinted at him. "I can give it more—"

"No, not your fault. I'm looking for someone more . . ." He wanted to say more talented than you are, bitch, but he said, "More sassy."

"Oh, let me try—"

"Thanks. It's the chemistry." It was his executioner's voice. He stood up. He had a medium build, but his air of command made him seem tall. The actress called Tracy put down the script, gathered up her large bag, slipped her bare feet back into her sandal heels, tugged at her floppy canvas hat, picked up her jacket from the old sofa. "Well, 'bye," she said, "and thanks, Fletchie." He watched her tight little buns on parade as she retreated.

Fletcher Avery's office was a block away from Paramount Studios in a new honeycomb high rise of square cubicles inhabited by producers and directors and writers. Fletcher paced to the windows, glowered at the sunshine. "Isn't there one actress in this town with half a frontal lobe?" he demanded, turning to face his assistant director, Burton "Buttons" Botsford. "Maxie is such a juicy little role—easy, fun." Buttons Botsford stared back. "Where's Sam? I thought we were meeting to discuss the role."

"He sent word," Buttons replied. "He won't meet with you unless you guarantee him the lead."

"What? Five years ago that cocksucker couldn't get arrested!"

"Yeah, well, now he's the actor of the century."

"I'm the director of the century!" Fletcher stormed. "That does it! I wouldn't cast him if he danced in here on his fingertips."

Buttons knew Fletch meant it. "Too bad. The role's perfect for him."

"And where's Opal?" Fletcher demanded of the bighorn sheep's head protruding from one wall. Opal Douglas was his casting director.

"At the dentist. Root canal."

Fletcher winced. Dentists scared the shit out of him. "She deserves it after what we've seen this morning! Why does she keep sending Tracy in for these kind of roles?"

"That's Opal," Buttons said, "tenacious." The action of his life with Fletcher right now teetered between frenzied casting sessions, swarms of phone calls, and driving out to locations that might double for Malaysia.

Buttons was a short, compact man of twenty-six with cheerful good looks, plenty of stamina, and big ambitions. He said: "Fletch, about location. For the stuff around the fishing boats, there's always the cove at Catalina."

"Catalina sucks," Fletcher muttered, looking at a stack of pictures. The telephone rang. "Is this one out there?" Fletcher asked, showing Buttons one of the pictures. "She sorta looks like Maxie."

Buttons opened the door. In the outer chamber, a rollicking, nervous mass of beautiful women gossiped about their last jobs, their favorite films, and their agents.

"Yeah," Buttons said, closing the door, "she's there."

The phone kept on ringing. "Holy shit, that fuckin' Marianne," Fletcher boomed, affronted. "How could she quit on me now!"

Buttons knew Marianne, the secretary-assistant-slave, had had good reasons. "Fletch," he said, "you go through secretaries like a machete through palm fronds."

Fletcher yelped with laughter and snatched up the telephone. "This is the ninth rung of hell," he growled, immediately handing the telephone to Buttons.

"Yeah? Hey, Damon, how's it going?" Buttons said.

The door opened. "Patsy!" Fletcher cried, leaping to his feet. "Hang up," he ordered Buttons.

"I'll call you right back." Buttons hung up.

"Cull that bunch out there," he said, tossing his head at the outer office. "Just bring in the top three." Buttons saluted and left for the triage session with the beautiful women. "Patsy! How's my lawyer?" Fletcher shouted with real pleasure.

"Smart," she said. He was one of the few in her professional life who she allowed to call her Patsy.

"How come I'm so lucky? God, you look great!" She was

wearing a sharp Banana Republic outfit. The buttons on her shirt were tight across her breasts; her safari skirt was wide and full, her boots the right mix of rough chic. "Where's your bush hat?" He laughed. "Hey, sit here." Fletcher swept a pile of *Variety* magazines off a chair.

"I was down the street at Paramount," she said. "I only have a minute." She put down her briefcase.

"Ah, Patsy, stay awhile. You're the one constant in my life." She was his lawyer, his surrogate mother, and his shrink.

Patsy laughed out loud. "Don't con me," she said. "You avoid constancy like the plague. You love commotion and hardship. Your personal life is in an uproar—and you're addicted to working on location, the more hazardous and exotic the better."

"Yeah, yeah," he said, happy she'd found him out.

Patsy McAulis Wyman, a senior partner in the Steiner, Niden, and Harris law firm, was part of her clients' careers. She made things happen for them: negotiated contracts, initiated and packaged projects, handled profit participation plans, supervised career moves. When her clients were or felt they were in trouble, they called her. It was a reciprocal relationship because, to a large degree, her status in the firm depended on the success of her major clients, like Fletcher.

"Jerry called me," she said.

Fletcher threw himself into his chair. "Jerry! All these years—love the man, call him my Sundance Kid—but he's refusing to up the budget so I can shoot in Singapore! I mean, we're practically on top of Singapore, for Chrissakes. There's a four-lane freeway as big as the Santa Monica from Singapore to Melaka. Can't he read a map?"

"Jerry's been your producer for eight years, Fletch, he knows."

"But you've been my attorney since I started out, Pat. You and I're like this." He held up two fingers, pressed together.

"Fletch, listen—don't blow this. You're working for hire through the studio—"

"The studio's boy," he mumbled.

"You've got an inflexible budget. It's unforgiving and that's the deal. You agreed, Fletch."

"Aw, Patsy, I know . . ."

"The studio won't interfere with your vision of the script

and they'll keep their hands off your production—except for major casting. But no budget changes. How's Martin like the script?"

"Loves it. 'Course it was created for him."

"We don't want any major casting changes. How's Pepper doing on the divorce?"

"Rancorous. Susan's being a shit," he said of his wife. "God knows what it's doing to Hope, she's only three. It's a tragedy. I can't get to see her—" Fletcher choked up. "I got problems on all fronts."

"You always do." She and Fletcher had been together longer than any relationship in his life.

"And listen to this! Dave—dynamite script two drafts ago, now he's got back problems, can't sit in a chair an' rewrite a scene on a fuckin' computer. And Roland—"

"Who?"

"Roland, my production manager—corrupt SOB. I fired him. Got Yvonne with all her Pac rim ties: she knows people out of Singapore and Bangkok for the Malay sequences. Hey! Did Vail get the inflatable totem pole—wasn't that a gas? He's such a good guy. I really appreciated what he said about *Alms*," Fletch crooned. Patsy smiled: even Fletcher wasn't immune to Vail's power. *Alms for Oblivion*, Fletcher's last film, a love story spun around an early Alaskan exploration, had been poorly received by most critics and most audiences. But Vail had liked it. "How's Eddie? Still goin' out there for soccer?"

"Yes, Fletch."

"I'm gonna get that kid a great map of Malaysia for his map room."

Patsy changed tempo. "I've got to get rolling. Have you found an assistant yet?"

"God no. Marianne—I went to the wall for her. Everything's fucked up— Did you see that snake pit out there?" He flung an arm at the door. "Got some damn temp who can't work a can opener—"

"Well, Fletch, I have someone for you—Belinda Oliver."

"No, no more women! I want a guy."

"Don't be a fool, Fletcher. Women are the only people competent enough to keep this town running." He chuckled; he liked being contradicted by people he respected even more than he liked subservience from those he despised.

"She's no kid," Patsy went on. "She has some experience but I don't think it's a lot—"

"Which means I can mold her." He laughed.

"You're difficult, but you're talented," Patsy said merrily, heading toward the door. "I figure that if Belinda can handle working with you, she can work anywhere."

Fletcher was on his feet. "Send her over today before I execute the asshole out there."

"She can't come today. She'll call you."

"Patsy, I love ya." He opened the door and kissed her cheek. "But I'm looking for a guy."

"No, you aren't. You're looking for Belinda Oliver." She marched out.

Fletcher shut the door, sat down at his desk with a huge sigh. He felt the rot inside him: could he crack out of the failure box he felt closing around him? Was he one of those guys he'd always felt sorry for—a rocket at twenty, all burnt out at forty?

"Buttons! Next victim!" He laughed to ward off his dread, leaned back in his chair, laced his fingers behind his head, ready to be surprised.

The train rolled and rattled sluggishly through a Colorado mining town, then picked up speed for a straight stretch before the long climb into the Rockies.

Victor Oliver, a tall, supple fifty-eight, was standing in his compartment, nude except for a pair of briefs, swaying with the train, watching the woman on the bed peel off her bra. And he was trying to remember her name. He'd met her in the dining car. She was on the far side of her forties, he judged, a headstrong woman used to pleasure. Rubens could have painted her. Barbara!

Vic looked his age but he was still a hunk, as lean as he'd been at thirty and proud of it. His only exercise was walking around the cities of the world or around his little farm in Ireland. Hard living was mapped in the deep wrinkles dug in under his eyes and down his cheeks. His angular, assertive profile, his dark blue eyes, had not softened. He was tough and graceful; he'd seen much he wanted to forget, and he'd forgotten a lot.

He shifted his eyes to Barbara's breasts and her rosy nipples. Her white satin flesh moved up as she stretched her arms toward him. But he remained apart, excited by what he saw in her eyes. Barbara's captivating, wanting face was saying *now*. He'd seen the shades of that look many times—each woman had her own variation. Barbara's mask had dropped and the essential brass-frank woman shone through: the look that excited him most when it emerged. It was as unmistakable as a scent.

He embraced her fully, pressing his mouth against her breast. She combed her thick, pointed fingers across his graying temples, raised his head, then clamped her mouth to his with open appetite. His groin was curling inward, massing familiar sensations that reached back to the base of his spine as he gently put a knee between her legs and opened her up for the feast, sure they would both dine well.

Vic Oliver was a poor boy who had made good. Born in 1927, the son of Russian emigrants named Oumansky, his father had abandoned Victor's mother in San Francisco. When success came to Vic, he'd changed his name to Oliver, cutting the last tie with his father. Vic grew up in the San Francisco Tenderloin district, and later on the "avenues," once that repository of unacceptable "Frisco" people who wore "paper collars." Old enough to do a stint in the army right after the war ended, he went to night school on the GI Bill, majoring, at his mother's insistence, in engineering. Vic had no talent for it. He liked drawing and he wanted to be an architect; his mother felt he was reaching too high. He and his mother, alone in the world, stuck together—and he stuck to engineering until he took a summer job stage-managing a little theater group. That's where he'd met Sara Wyman. She was a rich girl who'd stood in the shadow of her sister, Sky. Vic recognized pain when he saw it, and Sara had had a heart full of it.

Barbara was dressing, hanging onto the bathroom doorknob, one shapely leg poised on the end of the bed to receive her stocking. Her breasts tumbled, gelatinous ivory against the lacy rims of her bra.

"You are divine," he said, from the bed.

Fully dressed, she blew him a kiss from the doorway. "Get some rest," she purred. "We don't get into L.A. till six tomorrow night."

Vic sank back into the bed, turned out the lamp, pulled up the shade, and gave himself to the motion of the train careening through the thick darkness. He wanted a cigarette: why did cigarettes have to be bad for you? Why was everything good bad for you? He closed his eyes but the summer he'd met Sara clung to him like the humid sweet and sour scent Barbara had left in the room.

That summer of 1955, the little summer stock theater had been buzzing. Sky Wyman, beautiful, introverted bit player in the group, a definite loner, had been screen-tested and cast in a film in Hollywood. Everyone had been surprised that Sara, the extrovert triplet and a lead player in the group, had been passed over. Sky had not liked acting; Sara had loved it.

"A sideshow, Vic," Sara had said on her return from a press conference in Hollywood shortly after her sister had been cast. "They lined us up—the triplets. Vail and I are packaged publicity for Sky." Vic remembered a moment just before Sara had begun to cry: she'd raked her curly, bronze hair and it had snapped back to its original wiry position as if she'd never touched it. She'd stormed around Vic's room at the Post Street Residence Hotel, feeding on envy. Why had she been in his rooms? He couldn't remember. They weren't lovers; they weren't even special friends. The triplets—especially Sara and Sky—had been under their mother's thumb—escorted, sequestered, chaperoned—no one had been able to get close to them. He'd watched Sara's performance in his rooms, astonished, admiring, a subaltern. For as long as he could remember, Vic felt socially inferior. Sara, with her passions, her flair for the dramatic, her showy good looks, had seemed far above him, like a treetop or outer space. In that distance had come a fatal attraction.

Longing and fascination gelled; Sara became special to him. Her parents, the condescending toads, had mocked him. Vic grimaced in the dark on the train, remembering his first ghastly dinner at their home. But he'd become Sara's first lover anyway. They'd shared the kind of love that flourished in energy and defiance. They'd eloped. Ah, Sara, Vic groaned. It had been with Sara that he'd had his first true physical intimacy with a woman, and it rode with him even now, buried deep in a special place, undisturbed by all that had come after he'd left her—the horror years. He'd been lost during those years, clinging to the edges of life. He'd paid richly for leaving her. He still felt guilty, for the craven way he'd left her, not once thinking that she might be pregnant. Belinda was the incarnation of his cowardice with Sara.

Except for his late but solid success as a writer, the most important person in his life was his daughter, Belinda. He hadn't met her until she was sixteen, and he could still feel the shock, the exuberant joy, and helpless bewilderment of discovering that he had a child. But it hadn't been his fault alone that he'd had no part of her childhood: he shared the blame with Diana Wyman. Victor Oliver loved women, but he hated Diana; and he was ashamed of his youth that had made him gullible and vulnerable to Diana's manipulations.

He yanked down the shade, turned on the little lamp, and pulled out his notebook. He could have been more candid with Belinda before she'd got into all the trouble; he could have—hell, what did he know about fathering, what could he have done differently? When she'd come to him, pregnant with Eddie, as it turned out, he'd told her to talk to Sky or Sara. He hadn't known anything about pregnant teenagers. He'd gone off to Deauville! Guilt.

The train was slowing for some kind of crossing. Vic pulled up the sheet to his naked chest and smoothed it out as he moved to happier thoughts. He congratulated himself for gaining Belinda's confidence over the years of her ordeal, for sticking by her, for knowing how things worked enough to help her. He hadn't been allowed to be a father until she was practically grown, but he was trying now to be a perfect father. He thought that meant being strong and supportive and looking good to his daughter, not showing weakness or failure or anything that she might not respect.

He looked at a page of notes for his new novel in his notebook; he didn't know what any of them meant. Must have been drunk when he'd written them. He tossed the book aside and turned out the light.

Vic Oliver had a poised, manly way of moving, and even on the swaying train, his walk was sexy as he headed into the dining car for the first breakfast sitting. He felt his spirits sag when he spotted Barbara waving to him from a table for four. Oh, well, he thought, sitting down and smiling warmly, recreasing the creases in his face, what was an embrace with Rubens without a little payback? He shook out his napkin and started talking about Ireland.

"I didn't know you lived in Ireland," she said. "You must give me the address."

"Oh, I don't live there," he lied. "Just rent from friends occasionally."

"Where *do* you live?"

A couple from Australia sat down beside them and immediately engaged Barbara in conversation about the Grand Tetons. Barbara knew a lot about America and was glad to share it. But she kept one eye on Victor, who was staring out the smudged window at the rugged, beautiful country.

"This is Victor Oliver," Barbara said, a pronouncement. "He's on a United States book tour set up by his publisher." The Australians perked up, a gratifying response. Barbara said, "Tell them about the tour."

"I only have two cities left, Los Angeles and San Francisco," Vic replied. He smiled his autograph smile but there was no heat in it. His book wasn't selling well—like his last one—and the tour was being cut back.

"Oh, I read one of your books!" exclaimed the Australian woman. "It was a very bloody thriller—practically everyone died."

"How do you like the tours?" her husband asked him.

"Frankly," Victor said, "I hate them." The man looked astonished. "Not the people I meet—readers are great. It's the travel." The man nodded sympathetically; travel was the pits. Victor was lying again: he hated everything about tours.

The fate of his book distressed him. Maybe he was drying up; he certainly had the money problems to prove it. His editor was hinting that his books weren't "eighties" thrillers, that he needed a new take on his subject. But Gorbachev's new *glasnost* had thrown him a curve. Though the Russians and the Eastern Bloc were still the archetypal NATO enemies, the literary sands under Vic Oliver had shifted. He had to shape a different kind of story. Did he have the energy to adapt? He felt spent. Once, writing had been fun for him; now it was hell. Could he write fearlessly, like a youth, again? He felt old and dated when he faced the blank page.

Victor gazed at Barbara and sent her a clue. She smiled languidly and reeled him in. Barbara would give him relief today—the sweetest ride in the universe. But Vic was an introspective man. With Barbara, and all the women like her, he was only dodging his fears about the rest of his life and ducking his anxiety about seeing Belinda for the first time in two years. He wanted to find a way to suggest that she bring Eddie, too. Maybe they could begin to be a little family. Eddie was, after all, his only grandchild, as far as he knew.

Eddie was approaching his house from the back, hoping to get into his room before anyone saw him. It was not to be. He skirted the garage just as Patsy pulled into the driveway. She waved. He waved back, keeping his face averted. "Wait!" she called out.

"Can't!"

"Edward Andrew!" He stopped. "What happened?" she said, coming up to him.

He turned around. His shirt was torn; he wasn't wearing his artificial hand. He had a black eye swelling shut, a long scratch on his forehead, another on his arm, dirt caked his legs, and he was limping.

"Nothing."

Patsy put her arm around his shoulders.

"I'm okay," he insisted.

"I'm not." She walked into the house with him.

In the downstairs bathroom, she examined his cuts. "Your face is clean," she said.

"Coach helped me out."

She dabbed disinfectant around the scratches and into his eyebrow. He didn't flinch. "Who was it this time?"

"Tommy."

"Again? What's his problem?"

Eddie shrugged. It had been really bad today because though it was no secret, somehow Tommy had found out that Eddie was adopted. They had fought not only over Eddie being "a cripple"—Tommy's favorite taunt—but about his parents.

Patsy bent down and examined his ankle. "Mom! I'm okay!" She straightened up. "Take the picture."

"Oh, Eddie, your collection's big enough. Wash your legs off."

"No, I want the picture uncensored."

She took the Polaroid camera out of the table drawer in the hallway. Eddie lined himself up against the wall and leered into the camera. She snapped it, handed him the shot, put the camera back in the drawer. "Great," he said, watching the gray shapes metamorphose into color, definition.

Eddie's room on the second floor was wallpapered in maps: maps of the world, maps of the solar system, a map of the ocean floor, maps of separate countries, historical maps. His favorite was a copy of a fifteenth century map of what people then had thought North America looked like. A tall double bookcase crammed with paperbacks and a huge poster of Pelé, world-renowned soccer star, were the only breaks in the maps. One corner of the room was media: television, VCR, tapes, cassette deck, speakers. Jeans and sweats lay on the chairs, across his bed, under his desk. Soccer memorabilia and gear were scattered throughout. Patsy followed Eddie inside his sanctum, glanced around, said nothing. It was his space by family rule, and inside it he could do anything except sleep on the same sheets for more than a week.

Eddie went into the small adjoining bathroom, removed his hightops, put a foot in the tub and washed his leg. Patsy followed him in there, too, put the lid down on the toilet, and sat. "Mom, privacy, privacy."

"What was it about?"

He slapped his wet foot down on the rug. "My hand! My hand! What do you think it was about?" Patsy looked at the floor. "They don't want a cripple playing soccer."

"Who cares about them?" Patsy demanded, lighting up, angry. "*You* want to play, don't you?"

"Yes—"

"Coach David wants you to play. A lot of the kids want you to play because why?"

"Because I'm good," he mumbled.

"That's right. When *you* don't want to play anymore, *then* you won't play."

Eddie dried his foot with a towel. His arm, ending at the wrist, was caked with dirt. He put it under the tap and washed it off.

Once, Eddie had believed that as he grew older he would grow a hand. He clearly remembered the day in school when he knew that, no matter how old he was, he would never grow a hand.

Gym class had been the worst, excused from push-ups, excused from swimming, excused from basketball. Being excused made him feel deformed. He had covered this by alternating between truculence and his sunny, outgoing charm. He quickly acquired the reputation for being erratic. Eddie didn't want special treatment; he wanted to be treated like everyone else. Some teachers looked at him with pity, and he loathed that. Others had trouble looking at him at all and wouldn't call on him in class. He finally told his parents when they questioned his widely varied grades. The three of them had worked out what Vail invariably called "the strategy." Eddie began to see each teacher's prejudice as a challenge to be surmounted or converted. By the time he was in the fifth grade, he'd begun to be accepted. But more than anything else, Eddie wanted to be *like* everyone else. When he hit junior high, he knew that would never be.

Sports had been the scenes of his worst defeats until Coach David arrived. He'd started a soccer team. Vail had insisted that Eddie go out for it. Eddie had had enough of sports; he was making a name for himself as a brain in American history. Vail had challenged him, had bought a soccer ball, and had started kicking it around in the backyard. It was a game of tactics and ball control. It was the one game in which no one but the goalie could touch the ball with a hand. Perfect. Eddie went out for the team and won a place. At eleven, he wanted to play inside left forward like Pelé, and score at least one goal per game.

"Please let me look at that eye, Eddie," Patsy said.

He was combing his hair in the mirror. "It's okay, Mom."

Patsy went back into his room. She and Vail had long ago decided that they would not treat Eddie any differently because he had only one hand. He would not be babied; their standards for his behavior would not be lowered; they would buy him the best artificial hand, see that he knew how to use it, but they wouldn't insist he wear it unless he wanted to. Most of all, they would *be* there for him. But of all the years of fights and hurts, this one was the worst, thanks to Tommy, a fourteen-year-old bully on the soccer team. Tommy couldn't be ignored, because he won goals and he was a good student.

Eddie came out of the bathroom, took the Polaroid from his pocket, and pinned it up to join others of him at various ages on a bulletin board on the back of his door.

"A real rogues' gallery," Patsy said, eyeing the pictures of her bruised, scratched, pummeled, muddied, triumphant son.

"Yeah," he said, satisfied. "All the other kids look worse."

"Oh, honey," Patsy said softly. She put her arms around him and hugged him. "I wish you had an easier time." Tears came into her eyes.

Eddie broke away from her. "Don't cry, Mom. God, you never cry! It was just a scuffle." His mom was always calm and steady, the exact opposite of his dad. But now real tears were drizzling down her cheeks. "Mom, cut it out. Everything's cool."

"I'm sorry," she said. "I know it's all right. You just have a lot to deal with and I wish I could make it better." She rubbed her eye with the back of her hand. Eddie handed her a T-shirt. "Thanks."

Patsy sighed as Eddie pulled open a drawer, looking for a clean shirt. Everything seemed to be converging on them at once; Belinda's reappearance, Eddie's fights with Tommy, and his passage to the time when he would be asking more about his real mother and father. And then he would know she had lied to him. She hadn't lied about anything except Belinda.

"Mom, the fake hand's broken," Eddie said.

"That's okay, we'll have it fixed."

"No, Mom. I don't want to wear it anymore."

The front door downstairs slammed. "Anyone home?" It was Vail.

"Up here, honey," Patsy called out.

Vail was wearing his favorite Armani jacket and his Gucci loafers. "I've been thinking Italy all day, so we're going to have Italian food tonight," he said, coming into the room, full of his plans. "Stopped in the market, got some fresh basil, found some great tomatoes—" He took a good look at Eddie. "Wow, what a shiner, Son. What's the other guy look like?"

"Existential, Dad—a wipeout," Eddie said. "I'm all cleaned up now." He waved at Patsy.

"Let's see," Vail said, peering at his eye which was now firmly swollen shut. Edward held his head up for his dad's inspection. "Did the school nurse look at it?"

"Ah, Dad, it's nothing."

Vail said, "We gotta think of a strategy to get that Tommy. It was him, wasn't it?" Eddie nodded. "Yeah, we need a strategy—something to take him down a few pegs, what do you say?"

"Yeah, Dad, great."

"You can't keep beating the poor guy to a pulp every month." Eddie laughed. Patsy smiled, wiping away a tear, putting her arm around Vail. "You change your clothes, then c'mon downstairs, Son, and we'll strategize while I cook."

Patsy giggled as she and Vail went down the stairs. It was "family night," no Maria, no guests. Vail cooked with aggressive joy, and during dinner they each hashed through their separate weeks.

Eddie turned on his tape deck and flopped on his bed as The Byrds' biggest and oldest hit filled the room. But Tommy's screeches sailed over the music: "Your real mom gave you up because she didn't want a fuckin' crip!" It had been like hearing his most secret fear shouted out in public.

Eddie had known for as long as he could remember that he'd been adopted, but he hadn't wanted to ask Patsy and Vail about his real parents because he didn't want to seem disloyal. Patsy and Vail were as cool as parental units could be as far as he was concerned: aggravating, loving, and supportive. He'd gone through a period of resenting them, about feeling they'd been forced to take him, but that was over. He had won the battle about his room, about riding a bike, about playing loud music. But he wanted to know more about his real parents. He knew both of them were dead, but he didn't know when they'd died or how or what kind of people they'd been except that his real mom had been Aunt Sara's daughter. That made him part of the family, and for that, he was glad. Sometimes, when he was mad at Vail especially, he hated his real mom for giving him up. Because Eddie knew that she hadn't died when he'd been born. He could remember standing between two adults in a white room. One of them was holding his right hand, the other held his left wrist. He was looking into a woman's face who must have been squatting down to talk to him. Had she been his mom? *Had* she given him up because of his hand? Had she, as he'd once overheard his parents argue, done something wrong? Had that eventually caused her death?

Edward turned over on his bed, threw an arm across his forehead, and stared at the ceiling where he'd tacked a map of the universe. Had his mother been so bad that he'd been born without a hand as her punishment? Edward writhed. He knew this couldn't be true. Vail and Patsy had told him scientifically how hands or feet sometimes weren't formed. There was a scientific reason. But the dread that he'd been marked because of wickedness in his mother and father still crept up on him in moments like these when he felt low.

Downstairs in the kitchen Vail tossed some crushed garlic into the hot olive oil in a frying pan. It sizzled and the aroma filled the kitchen. He was thinking about Sara and the letters, about Maria's report of the telephone call, about her inability to tell if it had been a man or a woman. "A deep, breathy voice," she'd said. "Strong." It had pushed Sara into immediate action, and before she'd left for Europe, she'd rehired the investigating firm, which had, so far, come up with exactly nothing. Sara was right to insist on doing something but Vail had no confidence in any lasting result.

Patsy was sitting in the breakfast nook, reading that morning's newspaper.

"Guess who's coming to town, Vail?"

"Who?"

"Victor. He's signing books. He'll be on television. There's a big ad in here for his new one."

"I don't want that man in this house."

Patsy dropped her newspaper. "Did I say anything about inviting him to stay with us?"

Vail was cutting up fresh basil. "I hate it when Vic comes to town," he said, vehemently. "I don't want him anywhere near Eddie—especially now that Lindy's back."

CHAPTER 5

E ast of Vine, west of Vermont, south of Sunset, and north of Wilshire described the heart of the area known as "East Hollywood." Once a white working-class neighborhood, it was now as ethnically diverse as any community in America and the prototype for the new Los Angeles. Immigrants were shaping Los Angeles in the eighties, just as other immigrants had once shaped Manhattan at the turn of the century.

Berendo Street was a jumble of gas stations, restaurants, family-run corner stores, forties bungalows, and new, light-framed apartment buildings in pastel colors. A corner unit of one of the new apartment buildings was to be Belinda's home for the next five years.

When Vail heard the address, he was appalled. "She'll be shot! My god, no one lives in Hollywood anymore! Even the pigeons are on crack!" Patsy said the choice "held challenge," but she insisted they let Belinda "do it her way." When Diana jotted down the address, she frowned. "Close to the studios," she murmured. "Pleasant little bungalows, as I recall." Diana hadn't been in Hollywood for decades.

For Belinda, the East Hollywood terrain held several attractions. She'd never meet anyone on the street who might once have known her. She could get lost there, and found. It was a universe of racial and national variations that she'd come to know in the state institutions. She didn't have to fit into anything: everyone was different—neighbors could only greet each other with a smile because no one spoke the same language. Compared to this animated, struggling, sometimes dangerous neighborhood, Beverly Hills was sterile. Since her release from the hospital, Belinda had been high on freedom and excitement. Risk gave her a jag. Tranquility bored her. East Hollywood was perfect.

On the afternoon that Patsy called her about Fletcher Avery, Belinda was sitting at her desk in the front window of her fourth floor apartment, writing a letter to Eddie. She knew she wouldn't mail it, but it connected her to him and to the rapport she'd felt between them. She told herself that Eddie probably had not felt it, but she wrote him anyway—about the neighborhood, about the Korean grandmother carrying an infant fastened to her back with a scarf, heading down the street with a string bag to shop at the corner; about the retired Chinese home owners at the end of the block who tended their minuscule, perfect lawns every morning. She drew Eddie a sketch of the Salvadoran father next door coming home from work and swinging his child up in both arms. She wrote about the restive, arguing Armenian men who owned a solid block of homes and who sat on their front porches playing backgammon. About the Guatemalans, Thais, and Filipinos, each group encased behind their cultural walls. Some of them smiled at Belinda, most did not.

Her doorbell rang. Startled, Belinda looked through the peephole and saw a middle-aged Filipino woman and a young boy standing outside. She opened the door.

"I'm Dr. Suico," the woman said. "I live in your building. I have the office next door—acupuncture?"

"Oh, yes," Belinda said. "I've seen your sign out front."

"I'm trying to get a new neighborhood watch organization started."

"Come in."

"We won't stay long. This is my grandson, Joseph. He's five." His face was shiny, his eyes black like his hair, which had been wet-combed back from his forehead.

Dr. Suico was short and light boned with a round face, dark brown eyes, and graying black hair. She sat down in a chair and opened up her briefcase. "Everyone on this block sees their children growing up with the other children," Dr. Suico said. "Most of the children speak English, so, the trust begins. But it is slow."

It developed that drugs and crime were bringing neighbors together. "Reverend Kim, he's a Methodist," Dr. Suico said, "is trying to dispel the Salvadoran garment workers' distrust of their Korean employers."

"I don't understand," Belinda said.

"The Koreans are generally disliked because they own many new buildings and they have the money to build more. It is said the Koreans are taking over," Dr. Suico said softly. "It came to a head when a Korean girl fell in love with a Salvadoran boy on the next block."

Dr. Suico's grandson was restless. "I'll draw you a picture," Belinda said, taking out a sheet of paper and a pen. She sketched a few deft lines on the page—a caricature of the child's large dark eyes and round face. Dr. Suico talked on about the neighborhood watch. Belinda drew the little boy, accentuating his timid smile, remembering the day of her sixteenth birthday—the day she'd first met Victor. She'd been sitting in Diana's living room drawing Archie. He'd been sitting opposite her, one leg crossed over the other, his head back comfortably against the high wing chair, smiling at her dreamily. She could see her pen skimming across the page, caricaturing Archie's personal, physical style in a few strokes—a powerful mixture of compassion and sarcasm. She'd exaggerated his wide sensual mouth that turned up at the corners, a charming but mocking smile. She'd liked Archie; he had become part of the family, the architect and guardian of Sky's recovery from the accident that had sliced her face and arms into ribbons.

Victor had appeared on that day of the drawing. Later, she'd met Archie on the landing of the stairs. He'd asked her how she'd felt meeting her father for the first time. "Cool," she'd replied as Archie's eyes had settled on her in an entirely new way.

"Oh, but that is very good!" Dr. Suico said of the drawing of her grandson. "May I keep it?"

"Sure."

"And will you come to our first meeting?"

"Yes, sure."

After they left, Belinda went back to her desk in the window. Archie had saved Sky. But, as she looked out the window of her apartment, Belinda knew now that after the accident Archie had become Sky's supplier. As Belinda turned sixteen, Sky hadn't been present in her life. Belinda had thought she'd been there, but the woman she'd called mother had been living in a narcotic dream.

Belinda had graduated high school a year early and had

been accepted to UC Berkeley at the age of seventeen. UC was across the bay from San Francisco. Archie's practice had been in that city, but he'd flown down to Los Angeles twice a week to counsel Sky. It had been during Belinda's first year of college that she and Archie had driven out to Sausalito, though she couldn't now think why they had done that; it had had something to do with Sky, something he had to pick up for Sky. They'd been driving back across the Golden Gate Bridge when he'd started telling her about his failed marriage and about his daughter, then fifteen, who'd been living with him since the death of his wife a few years before. He'd switched to his own childhood, about growing up in "the mausoleum," his mother's old family manse on Nob Hill. "I was blond like every California boy ought to be but I was big and clumsy as a teenager. Underneath, I'm just a lonely guy who knows that half his life is over." She'd been flattered that such a respected man had allowed her to see him as he was. The air between them in the car had felt loaded, charged.

He'd pulled up in front of the "mausoleum." Archie had to pick up some paperwork before he flew back to Los Angeles. He'd invited her in while he sorted the files. "You can meet my daughter," he'd said.

The family room was soft and comfortable with a tiled fireplace and built-in bookcases. His daughter wasn't home. Belinda had followed Archie to his study, a dark room with heavy furniture and a green glass lamp. He was coming around the desk, his hand outstretched. He'd touched her hair, letting his fingers slide down its length to her breast. His eyes appealed to her but his manner was confident. He pulled her to him, pressed her body close. "I know how to make you feel so good," he said, his voice low and comforting. Belinda stood on tiptoes to put her arms around his neck. His beard was soft as a fur against her throat. Her back tingled at his touch, and her heart beat hard. Embracing him was illicit and reckless, a reach far outside her experience, all the protections she'd had since childhood. The risk and the promise were intoxicating. Archie kissed her, burying his lips in hers, thrusting his tongue inside. She leaned back in his arms and let him fondle her breasts through her blouse. She took off all her clothes and twirled, nude, on the rug. He knelt before her, both big hands on her waist, and kissed her between her legs with his thick, wide mouth. Her legs shook, she was on fire, he put one finger in her navel and she felt the fire down to the soles of her feet. He cupped her buttocks with both hands and pressed her hips to his face, his merry tongue licking and his lips sucking. Finally, she couldn't stand it any longer and he'd covered her with his big body, slowly poking her, prying her apart, separating her from everything she'd ever known.

"This is our secret," he'd said later, lying next to her, nuzzling her.

Whenever he'd been in San Francisco, they'd made love in the manse. Her new appetite matched his. It was as if a pump had been opened inside her; she never tired of the new feelings that drenched her. Nothing between them had been censored—anything was permissible. She'd needed his touch, but most of all she needed the compliment of being adored by a man of experience and stature. It made her feel grown-up and valued. People fought to be his patients, listened to his advice. It was forbidden, but Archie had wanted only her. He said she was attracted to a man of his age because she'd never had a father. He would teach her about men, he said. It would be their secret.

One night, Belinda had come out of the study, where most of their "lessons" occurred, to find a girl about fifteen in the cavernous hallway. She was starting up a flight of gently spiraling stairs, a curious but beautiful architectural fancy curling up to a wide landing. Archie had admonished his daughter gently for getting in so late. He introduced Belinda as a patient. The girl had said nothing, not even hello. She hovered on the stair like a bird caught in mid flight, her pale, angry face and blond hair outlined against the dark paneling of the stairwell.

Belinda looked down at the letter to Eddie on her desk. Through Eddie, Archie would always be with her. It was the connection that defied death. She began writing again, but she felt divided about it. Even if she never sent the letters, she knew that with Eddie she was repeating her own history and she felt guilty. But she needed to keep in touch with him.

She folded the letter, put it in an envelope, dated it, and sealed it. Then she tucked it into a desk drawer with the others.

* * *

The next morning was hot and sunny when Belinda swung out of her apartment to keep the appointment with Fletcher Avery. She wasn't worried about the interview: she'd lie. She couldn't tell anyone she'd been in a mental ward or that she'd been bumming around the country to blot it out. She'd lied before about what she'd done. But this felt different because she was meeting a man Patsy knew; Patsy was a collaborator. Belinda weighed the real and the fictitious past. She passed the nursery school, run mainly by East Indians, where the tiny toddlers from a dozen different countries lined up in front of a flagpole, pledging allegiance. Farther down the block she passed the Thai market and the Armenian bakery. What drove them all in this desperate, borderline struggle between safety and danger? The American Dream, the chance for a new life. It was the same for Belinda.

The woman Fletcher saw in the doorway of his office wasn't what he wanted—she wasn't a beauty and she wasn't a man.

"How old are you?" he asked.

"Almost thirty," she hedged.

"Don't look it." Her features were delicate, her narrow face was surrounded by thick dark brown hair, her eyes the color of blue ice.

She could feel his disappointment like a draft. This man was doing Patsy a favor. Belinda felt like walking out on him, but she'd been on the run too long.

"How do you know Patsy?"

"Distant cousin," she said, sitting down.

"Don't look anything like her."

"No," she said. "I always wanted to; she has a great face, so pert and smart."

Savvy Fletcher sat back, listening to his instincts. They always told him the truth and he relied on them totally. Don't hire her, his gut said. But this Belinda Oliver was an odd-ball—tough surface but scared, too, somewhere deep. Oddballs appealed to him.

His hands were still knotted behind his head as he fired questions at her about the kind of jobs she'd done and why she wanted this job, but he didn't listen much to her mainly fictitious answers; he seemed to be hearing something else. Sometimes he answered his own question or just left it in the rubble, piling another on top of it right away.

"The idea here is that you make my life easier," he said, freeing his hands. "In twelve weeks, I'm going to be in Malaysia, shooting *Force Field*."

"I can make your life easier."

He looked up. She did not look away.

"I can do that," she repeated.

Her icy blue eyes gazed at him. Suddenly, she smiled. It transformed her face. She wasn't giving anything away, but the gift was there and he knew it. The room felt warm.

"It's kinda a shit job," he said in a new voice. "Why do you want it?"

"I need it," she replied. "Besides, I'll be good at it."

The sharp, exhilarating sense that he'd collided with her shook him. He jumped up, started talking about the demands of pre-production, about the script changes, about the customs agent in Malaysia, about his production manager.

As he marched around the room, tapping the windowpane, hitting a chair, punching the air, she knew she had something in common with Fletcher Avery. Anger drove him; daily life was a war. "This film's about the kind of conflict you take in with the air. It's everywhere!" he shouted. "There's betrayal, death in this picture. Civilized—what is that? We don't know what 'civilized' is anymore. No one's 'nice.' Ha," he exploded, "it's the mirror of Hollywood." He spun around. "But there are moments of real decency, characters who *try*." He burned the word into the air. "They try to do right, to understand." He raised both arms upward for punctuation. Fletcher Avery was a believer. His movies were famous for their unromantic violence, for characters at polar ends trapped in a hard, stupid, jealous world run by greed where the faint light of someone's honor flashed brightly in a vast nighttime sea. "Movies shape our world, you know. Ever think of that?" He brought his arms down. "Anyway, we're a month into pre-production."

Belinda knew all about pre-production. She pretended not to know that much. She watched his stubby hands moving in the air. When he moved to the window and snapped the blinds she observed the way his back grew out of his waist and broadened into his shoulders. In the school and in the loony bin, sex had been payment for protection, institutional baksheesh that ranked with drugs and cigarettes. "Going down" took on a whole new meaning inside: descent, bribery, submission. It had nothing to do with sex. None of it did. It was all power. But even those acts of anger and vulnerability had not erased the powerful hunger she had to be touched, held, mounted, claimed.

Years of isolation, restrictions, and humiliation crowded against her as she sat motionless, watching Fletcher flop down on the sofa, jump up, pat the bighorn sheep on the nose, straighten a stack of papers on a shelf. Opposing desires moved against her in waves: to be licentious, to be free, to indulge in her appetites; to do nothing at all, to be safe, to hide.

Fletcher was standing beside her, waving the script. She must remake her life; she must avoid attachments, do nothing to endanger her freedom. But she felt awakened, connected, as he leaned down, knocking his knuckles against a page of the script. She felt the yearning inside open like a trench. She sat back in her chair to steady herself.

Abruptly, Fletcher tossed the script on the desk. "It's against my better judgment," he said, walking away. "But the job's yours if you want it." He turned and surveyed her.

"Why against your better judgment?"

He laughed. "I don't know." He sobered up. "Because I can't figure you out." He shook a finger at her. "But I will."

She rose. "I'll tell you tomorrow."

"I thought you needed a job!" he said, an accusation.

"I want to talk it over with someone first. You got a problem with that?"

"No later than tomorrow!" he barked.

The Windsor was an old Los Angeles restaurant on Seventh Street near the Ambassador Hotel. Once an aristocratic neighborhood—home of the original Brown Derby and the Coconut Grove—it was now half a mile from the Ramparts—the highest crime area in L.A.—and half a block from a precinct known colloquially as "Koreatown." A mile east, the burgeoning downtown district, with its forty-story, gleaming high rises was reshaping the area for robust corporate enterprises unconnected with show business. In this part of Wilshire

Boulevard, producers didn't rent offices, newsstands didn't sell *Variety*, professionals didn't wear tight jeans and ostrich boots. The lawyers, real estate magnates, and accountants wore three-piece suits and read *The Wall Street Journal*.

The Windsor remained unchanged and unbending, a dowager out of a different era. Ruby banquettes lined the curved corners around the brass and marble bar, overhung with crystal lamps. Thick worn red carpets deadened sound.

"Victor, you never stint," Belinda said as they settled into a booth.

"My motto. Life is too short to stint. You look beautiful," Vic said. "I could take you to any restaurant—Le Fouquet in Paris, Fogher in Rome—anywhere! Wanna go?"

Belinda had always felt flattered by Victor. He had a way of throwing attention on her like a sable. He was on her side. She couldn't explain his influence, but he affected her profoundly, and she accepted that. She savored telling him about her interview with Fletcher Avery.

"Not sure I like that neighborhood you're living in," he said as their waiter glided away from them with their drink order.

"Don't you start," she said. "I've already heard it all from Vail. It's a wonderful neighborhood—except for one street and that's blocks away."

"Drugs?"

"What else? But the threat's uniting the neighborhood. And the building I'm in is very well run."

"But why don't you live in a better place?" he said, gruffly.

She stared at him. They had never had a conversation like this before. "No one ever asks where I come from, or who I know, or who I am."

"Okay, lamb. Okay." He sighed. When it came to Belinda and her tragedies, he felt helpless even as he was called upon to perform.

They fell into the pattern they'd established when he'd visited her in the school and later in the nuthouse: he listened carefully to what she said and he sometimes offered her advice; she softened her voice and felt herself becoming childlike. Tonight, they started out by reminiscing.

"Don't you remember?" he said, laughing. "It was your sixteenth birthday. You wouldn't take my gift." At the time, it had killed him; all the Wymans were standing around, watching him meet her. "You turned the package over and said, 'Is this supposed to make up for all the time you've been away?' You were a very cool number even then."

"But you did fit the romantic picture I'd made up about you," she replied.

"Oh, yeah?" he said, pretending to doubt her. "What was that?"

"You know, that you were tall and handsome and you had a sense of humor."

"I'm a diamond in the rough, lamb, that's me. Remember what you did next? You gave back the gift! 'You haven't earned the right to give me things.' So self-possessed."

Victor was dimly aware that he wanted to be the figure in her life that no other man could compete with. He saw her as someone who deferred to his experience, someone made independent who needed help, someone he needed to repay, whose fate he was partly to blame for.

"Vic, what did you do before you wrote books?"

"I was a wreck of a man," he said, smiling only with his mouth. "I never did anything worthwhile."

"No, tell me. I want to know."

He gauged her with his hard, dark blue eyes. "No, you don't," he said finally. "See all these wrinkles?" He laughed and squinted at her. "Life."

"Didn't you ever fall in love again—after Sara?"

"Not really. Yes and no."

"What did you do before you started writing?"

"Knocked around, held odd jobs. I didn't know what I wanted to do." Except stay out of jail, he thought; I learned how to do that, finally. "My life was pretty dull." But he knew he was going to have to throw her something. "I worked as a waiter once on a steamboat line up and down the Mississippi. Damn near killed me. We'd work breakfast, lunch, and dinner, get off at about eleven at night, party all night, then get up at six. I was too old for that." Not old, he thought, drunk and stoned on hash. He'd been fired, thrown off in St. Louis where he'd slept on the fuckin' streets for a month.

"Victor," she said, "I never really thanked you for everything you did for me when I was at the school and later, too, at the nuthouse." He waved one arm brusquely, dismissal.

"No, I want you to know how important it was." He had regularly flooded her with the maximum amount of money and cigarettes which she'd used to bribe favors from inmates, nurses, and guards. "You really made a difference, like you knew what I needed in there. Did you?"

He was trapped. "What a clever girl you are," he said. "I was in jail once, vagrancy." He hated admitting it. "I was young, bumming around the States, and I spent five days in jail, and I saw that bribery was a way to alleviate some of the, er, problems that can arise." Victor had been jailed for vagrancy, but he'd also been jailed for a minor theft in Nevada, a year in the can that had cured him.

"I'm glad you told me," she said, "because I don't really know much about you."

Her enthusiasm for candor was lost on Victor who felt that she wouldn't respect him if he told her the full truth about his life after Sara: he'd lived on the edge and had clawed his way back from it. He noticed a woman rising from a table across the room, her breasts heaving beneath her blouse, her hips moving in circles.

"I was offered a job today," Belinda said. "With Fletcher Avery. He's a director."

"Well, I know he is." The woman was slipping into a coat, camouflaging her attributes.

"The job's sort of secretarial but—"

"Lindy, you don't want to do something like that—be a secretary."

"But it's a good job."

"Lindy, aim high."

"It is high, for me," she said, disappointed.

"Look, I want you to come to Ireland, stay with me, maybe go to art school there, how's that sound?"

"Jeez, aren't you glad I've got a job offer?"

"Sure I am—"

"And you're away from Ireland most of the time. What would I do?"

"Well, study, relax." It hadn't occurred to him that he *would* be away a lot.

"I want the job. People respect Avery. He doesn't do the fly-by-night productions I was working on. I think I can make something out of it."

"But, Lindy, burying yourself in that kind of a job, I don't see the point. Those little jobs are demanding—long hours. You can't run away from reality in an eighty-hour work week."

"What do you mean?"

"Well, how about the Wymans? How about Eddie? Have you dealt with all that? You have to come to terms with them."

"You just invited me to Ireland. That sounds more like running away from reality than working for Avery."

But Vic was wrapped up in his own visions. "I was hoping we could arrange it so that, after everything was settled between you and Vail and Patsy, that you and Edward could spend some time with me. I only have one grandchild and he doesn't even know me."

"Vic, that's not going to happen. I'm not a mother—I never was. A mother's more than giving birth. Eddie's happy with Patsy and Vail. It wouldn't be right to take him away."

"No need to make a decision this minute."

She knew she'd made him angry. "Vic, if you want to be a grandfather, you talk to Vail and Patsy about that."

"That's a kind of cold thing to say," Vic muttered. Belinda had been strong at sixteen; now she was tough. "You don't have to be harsh to be strong."

"Here we are!" The waiter docked at their table and put their drinks down with a flourish. Victor was relieved by the interruption. He didn't know how to get back to solid ground with her. "I want what's best for you, you know that, don't you?" he said briskly.

Belinda nodded, but she suddenly wasn't sure. She'd always felt comfortable with Vic because he wasn't part of the Wyman past. But she realized there were people in the nuthouse she knew better than Victor. There was something shadowy about him. She knew Archie better than she knew Victor.

"Let's talk about this job offer," Victor was saying. "You haven't had a lot of experience."

"I've had jobs in films before."

"There's all kinds of work out there."

"I like Avery. He's exciting. His new picture's going to be shot in Malaysia, and I want to go."

"Did he say that?"

"No."

"Even if he did, I'd take it with a grain of salt. Just keep some perspective."

"I have perspective," she said.

They worked hard to keep the dinner rolling along in the shallows of surface affection, but for the first time their conversation was strained. When she looked at her watch on the way to the ladies room, she was amazed that only ninety minutes had passed.

As he drove her back to her apartment, she felt Vic had failed her in some crucial way she didn't want to examine. "I'm going to take that job," she said. Fletcher Avery was different—bold, open. Fletcher Avery was a means of escape.

"Look at that, Lindy," Victor said. "A sofa, right out here on the parking strip. How can you live in this neighborhood?"

"I'm not on this street, Vic. I'm one block over. We have home owners over there."

When he stopped the car in front of her building he looked around. "Well, you're right," he said. "Your block is better." He turned to her. "I'm sorry our dinner didn't turn out the way it might have." He didn't know what she needed from him. "I want to help."

"I know."

"Lindy, please let me get you a little condo in a nice neighborhood."

"No. I want to do it myself."

He inhaled sharply. He had said exactly the same thing once to a woman who'd reached out to help him. "You'll find that ultimately we never do anything by ourselves."

His daughter got out of the car almost gaily. He knew she was relieved.

Belinda let herself into the building and started up the stairs. Maybe she'd disappointed him, but she felt disillusioned, too. She counted on his approval, she'd relied on his shrewd, resourceful assistance. But tonight, something had altered between them, a shift in temperature like the first sign of a fever.

CHAPTER 6

DECEMBER 1985

I t was one long howl:
*WHO'S THE . . . WHERE'S THE . . . CHANGE THE . . .
DOES HE . . . WILL HE . . . WON'T HE . . . HOW ABOUT
THE . . . BOND SHIPPING AGENT LISTS YVONNE'S
SCHEDULE CASTING BUDGET INSURANCE AIRFARE
MELAKA INSECT REPELLENT BOOM MIKES SCRIPT
CHANGES SICK PILLS WORK WITH JERRY . . . HOW
MANY VEHICLES MEALS TICKETS FAMILIES EXTRAS
SCENES JUNGLES ROADS RIVERS SETUPS PROPS
LABELS CHILDREN BIRDS LOTIONS FAVORS LENSES
FILM ROLLS . . . THEY FORGOT THE CHANGES.*

The day Belinda took Fletcher Avery's job had been almost
six months ago. Fletcher had messengered a script over to her.
The note clipped to the cover said, "Read this now." At that
moment, she entered what Buttons called "the whirl." Since
then, the good of the picture displaced every other considera-
tion: sleep, food, comfort, health, family obligations.

The film story, *Force Field*, was a variation on Vietnam
war tales: twin brothers, Don and David, played by the same
actor, Martin McCarthy, are separated when Don enthusiastically enlists in the 101st Airborne. David, fervently antiwar,
burns his draft card, hides out in Santa Cruz as a lifeguard.
The story turns into a hunt when, toward the end of the
war, Don is reported missing; David comes out of hiding
and goes to find him, eventually locating him in Malaysia
where Don has now become a freaky, shrewd mercenary. It's
David's job to turn him around psychologically and bring him
home. *Force Field* was a big ambitious picture, cutting back
and forth between the U.S. domestic scene in the middle seventies and the wind-down, defeated action in Southeast Asia.

The next day she'd reported for work. The outer office was pandemonium. A huge bulletin board, divided into sections, outlined the months of pre-production, production, and post. Beneath this, a large coffee table kept discarded scripts, *Variety, Hollywood Reporter*, film magazines off the floor. The main secretary's desk was being used as a dumping ground and coffee tray. A nubile young woman in jeans and a silk shirt sat at a smaller receptionist station. People rushed in and out from other rooms, waving clipboards, fabrics, scripts, cards. *Force Field* was unlike any of the small productions Belinda had served on. *Force Field* was a juggernaut.

Fletcher was standing in the center of the outer office; he wore a jacket emblazoned with red letters: *WRITING IS COMBAT*. People huddled around him as he talked to a tall bald man with wire frame glasses on his nose and a pipe plugged into his mouth.

"What's that?" Fletcher demanded of Belinda, pointing at a five-foot roll of heavy paper under her arm.

"My lunch."

Fletcher snorted. "Oh-oh. Tough girl. What'd I tell ya, Jerry?"

"That's right," Belinda said. She unfurled a map of southeast Asia.

"I already have one of those," Fletcher said.

"Now I have one, too." She peeled open a drawer of the secretarial desk, fished in it for pins and tacked her map to the wall.

"We're not shooting all over southeast Asia," he said.

"I know. See? Here's Malaysia."

"I'll be damned," he said, peering dramatically at the map. "Troops!" he called out. "This is Belinda Oliver, the new aide de camp. Be nice to her today. She doesn't know how much trouble she's in." Fletcher sent her a quick, compelling smile. "That's Jerry," he went on, pointing at the lanky man in glasses with the pipe. "He calls himself my producer." Jerry bowed gravely. "That's Burton Botsford—Buttons to everyone, my assistant director. And those three muses over there are a few of our assistants, part of the permanent staff for casting and pre-production—Margie, Jeanie, and Ellen." They were pretty, perky women in their early twenties. "Answer the telephone," Fletcher finished, walking back into his office. "Then come in here and I'll tell you what we think we're doing."

Later that first day in his office, Fletcher said to Belinda: "I see everyone. I talk to everyone." He hiked his feet on his desk. He was wearing calf-high elkhide cowboy boots. "But some people are more important than others, like Jerry and Buttons. Opal Douglas is my casting director—ferocious memory for names, credits, faces. Opal," he rhapsodized, "has the Eye." He looked at Belinda. "You know what the Eye is?" She knew, but she shook her head. "She can spot talent. She's great at visualizing the role and filling it with that perfect matchup. I trust her. And she'll argue with me, too. She'll go to the wall. I like that. The other important person to you at this stage is Yvonne Duret, our production manager. She was Omar Bradley in another life. She lives in Hong Kong, but she'll be working out of Singapore soon. Yvonne organizes everything—where people sleep, eat, travel, how the freight goes, who's driving what, how many people for how many days at how much per person—that sort of thing. Now!" He snapped his feet from the desk and stood up. "In addition to answering the phones with the other muses, there's night work—sample reel screenings till we get everyone cast."

"The actors' reels."

"Right. I want you there with your notebook."

"I can't explain what's going to happen," Buttons, Fletcher's assistant director, was saying to Belinda. Crazy pretty ice blue eyes, with dark blue rings, he thought, it was impossible not to look into them. "You've only been here a few months. I don't want to shock you. But maybe nothing shocks you."

It was nine o'clock at night in Fletcher's office. *Force Field* had changed it's schedule five times and it was four months late. Buttons almost never stopped to talk. He conducted business on the run, his hands gripping scripts and charts, his short thick legs carrying him everywhere at double-time speed.

"Try me," Belinda said. "It's chaos now."

"*This* is not chaos. Trust me." Buttons cheerfully snapped his perennial bow tie and propped one hip on the corner of her desk. "On Fletch's set there's always a sense of danger." He leaned close, hunching his round shoulders, shifting his weight. "Fletch is after a thrill—an artistic thrill. After *Alms* wrapped—"

"*Alms*?"

"*Alms for Oblivion*. Fletcher's last film. After it wrapped, one actor told me, and believe me, he was having an orgasm, he said he felt completely used up—ravished." Buttons's closely set eyes were hard like agates. "I'll never forget the look on that actor's face. That guy loved intellectual and emotional punishment, *moral* punishment." He tweaked his bow tie again.

"Get out of here," she said, skeptically.

"Fletcher raises punishment and atonement to new planes."

"I like Fletcher."

"We all do. He's gifted. But you'll see, if you're around. Fletch uses people up fast."

"He won't use me up."

Buttons eyed her and laughed.

Belinda said, "How long have you known Fletcher?"

Buttons stopped by a wall mirror to survey his bow tie and jacket. "About four years." He looked at her sharply in the mirror. "You'll love it in the jungle with Fletch." He spun around. "We're gonna do the jungle whirl."

"I've been in whirls before," she said.

"Not like this one." He waved at her and left, whistling.

The Malay Peninsula was a bulging tail of land, resembling a snake that had swallowed a mongoose. It protruded south from another long tail, Thailand. Both were sandwiched between the South China Sea and the Indian Ocean. A narrow strip of sea, the Strait of Malacca, divided Malaysia from Sumatra. Singapore sat at the tip of the Malay Peninsula; north of it was the town of Melaka where much of the shooting was planned. Farther north, Cambodia and Vietnam swelled into the South China Sea. To the east of the Malay Peninsula lay Borneo. Borneo. Belinda listened to the sound of the word in her head. Doom, hardship, impenetrable jungles, *Three Came Home*. She'd seen the movie on TV half a dozen times in the hospital—Claudette Colbert, of all people, imprisoned by the Japanese during the war in . . . Borneo. Belinda put her head in her hands and closed her eyes.

"You can't sleep here." It was Jerry Markowitz, the producer of the picture. He was staring at her map. Jerry was always calm, a quality necessary to strike a long working partnership with Fletcher Avery. He took out his pipe lighter, stepped forward and held the flame to one curling corner of the map.

"God, what are you doing?" The flame gnawed into paper.

"Birth by fire," he said softly. He smiled under his mustache, pressed the heel of his palm against the paper, snuffing out the flame.

Wary, she reorganized her thoughts about Jerry. "What happens on productions as big as this one?" she asked him.

He started to load his pipe. "We move a lot faster than General Patton did. We'll set up a production office in whatever city's the base camp, and right now the main one's Singapore."

"I thought Singapore was out."

He grimaced, holding the pipe in his teeth. "Fletcher usually gets his way. It *is* closer than Bangkok. Anyway, you and I and the production manager and Fletch and half a hundred other people will be in that production office—" He turned his gangly body and raised a long arm. "—till the coffee turns into seawater or until the bond company takes over the production and throws us all out, whichever comes first." She knew he was joking but she also knew about bond companies which guaranteed—insured—the finish of any picture. A bond company had shut down one of Sky's last pictures.

"Fletcher says I'm not going. I'm supposed to hold the fort here."

"Ridiculous. The fort's moving to Asia."

WHERE'S THE FREIGHT RENTAL PROP LISTS . . . HE WANTS THE BRUTS HELICOPTERS REPLACEMENTS ZOOMS TRANSMITTERS BULLHORNS MINIBUSES MARTIN'S WINNEBAGO CASTING CALLS EXTRAS BODY HOSE AK47S NUDE SCENE MEKONG DELTA. MEKONG DELTA? WE'RE NOT SHOOTING IN VIETNAM. WE ARE NOW.

The first person Belinda saw the next morning was Opal Douglas, casting director. "Is he in? What a silly question. Fletch!" She trotted into Fletcher's office, looked around, came out. "Where?"

"I don't know."

Opal put her hands on her hips. "Keep track of him! Watch him!" At forty, Opal was short and stocky but she had an appealing, sulky prettiness, and artfully tinted strawberry-blond hair. She bobbed and bounced when she walked on her short legs in high spike heels. Her contact lenses had transformed her hazel eyes from pebbles into emeralds. She looked like a cat.

Opal was powerful. Through her and her network of people, particularly in Europe, Fletcher could snare every name with an acting credit, plus a thousand wannabees.

"Are you going to Singapore, too?" Belinda asked. "I'm doing the Singapore list. Is there a lot of casting there, too?"

"Yes. The Asian hordes." She was consulting a leather-bound notebook. "I've set Fletch up with someone there through Yvonne."

"I talk on the phone almost every day with her," Belinda said. "She sounds great."

"She's the best, that's all. I'll be down the hall." Opal bounced out on her high heels.

The "casting room" was just another office where Buttons, Jerry, Fletcher, Opal, and assorted muses screened auditioning actors for the main supporting and the smaller but lively speaking roles. This was the room in which arguments broke out: "I want Bob!" "The studio will never go for him!" "Fuck them." "They have casting control, Fletch. Be a good boy." "Fuck you."

Fletcher controlled eight important supporting American and Asian roles in which he was determined to cast unknowns—a gamble. On casting days, the corridor outside the room hosted actors waiting to read. Belinda passed them hourly. They leaned against walls, gripping the "sides," the script scenes, mumbling, gesturing self-consciously, pacing, grimacing. Waves of hope and desperation rolled off these actors. They were worried about their ages, their bodies, their faces, their inflections, they were anxious about whether they were wanted or needed—personally, professionally, metaphysically. These were the actors whose impassioned voices often shot up from the Room, laughing or wailing or shouting obscenities.

Belinda was dodging from one phone call to another that morning when the director of photography, an Italian-American named Bruno Brusari, stepped into the office.

"Bruno," he said with a warm smile that divided his white goatee from his white mustache, "the DP."

"Belinda," she said. "Head muse."

"Welcome to Armageddon," he said. Bruno was a legend. He'd worked on one of Sky's last films, but Belinda had never met him. He looked solid, stubborn, proud.

"The look isn't right for Ted," Fletcher was shouting as he pounded into the room in the center of a phalanx of people.

"The look is Ted all over!" Opal argued.

"No, show me some more. Gotta be out there somewhere. Bruno!" Hearty handshake, back pumping.

"Fletcher!" Belinda waved a telephone message at him.

He ignored her. "Enter," he said to Bruno. "I been thinkin' about that cemetery scene—crane shot . . ." They sat down in his office with Buttons but didn't close the door. Fletcher's voice rose, ecstatically describing scenes not in concepts or emotions but in gear: industrial cranes, interiors with Panaflex, light, zoom lenses, prime lenses, filters, labs, film buys, dailies, and video.

"I want to use the Australian lab," Bruno said. Bruno dictated the gear he needed and people he'd take with him.

"Nah, let's stick with Los Angeles, with CFI."

"My reasons are these," Bruno pressed on, his voice low. "The dailies are starker, higher contrast over the States' labs, Fletch." In actual fact, the DP's former girlfriend was now living in Sydney and he was contemplating his R & R from the production. "I'm taking all the gear from L.A. to make sure that it works. Don't want any funny breakdowns." After an hour, Bruno left.

"Now, what?" Fletcher demanded of Belinda.

"The insurance broker called," she said. "Something about not liking the script."

Fletcher grimaced. "Shit. The scenes are too risky for him, right? Damn bond companies—wouldn't know a creative setup from the trunk of their cars. Nah, I'm kidding, this one's great. Script's going to change anyway. Get him for me." He started to walk toward three strangers who'd just come into the office, but he turned back to Belinda. "How are you holding up?" he asked gently.

"I love bedlam."

"More screenings tonight."

"I love sample reels."

"Are you always so accommodating?"

"No," she said.
"That's a relief."

The room was small, intimate, grimy. On the screen, one actor was bending over another actor, threatening him with a psychotic sweetness.

"His agent wants a minimum of two days' work for the role," Opal was saying to Fletcher at the screening that night.

"I like his quality," Fletcher muttered.

"No," Jerry said. "No more money."

"Jerry!" Opal exclaimed. "That's nothing."

"Goddamnit, Jer, don't you ever look at anything except the bottom line?" Fletcher demanded.

"We're gambling on these unknowns," Jerry said.

"If you turn him down tonight, I'm going to put him back in the lineup tomorrow," Opal said. "He's perfect. And he's going to be big. You're an idiot if you don't see it." Fletcher glared at Opal with respect. Under certain circumstances with certain people he enjoyed being bullied. It was a currency of communication.

· Belinda looked at Fletcher's profile in the half light—the jutting crooked nose, the truculent jaw, the gentle hollows in his cheeks. He looked nothing like Archie or like anyone she knew, but she felt psychically close to him. She understood his war. In the last few months, two sensations had come in gusts: she wanted to make love with Fletcher; she wanted to *be* Fletcher. The rotating seasons at the school and the nuthouse had taught her that nothing was as bad as her anticipation of it, and nothing, she knew, would ever be worse than the nuthouse. Risks that might turn others off, turned her on. Just thinking about having sex with Fletcher was scary—and thrilling. She didn't feel nearly as scared contemplating ambition, no matter how far out of reach it seemed. Being someone, being respected drove her as much as her secret appetite for Fletcher.

She came back to talk about billing and minimums and Winnebagos and matching actors to roles.

"What happened to Curt?"

"He'll work for less because he wants to work with Fletch," Jerry said happily. "He likes the script."

"How about his schedule?"

"It'll work around ours."

"I want to see Lee, too."

"I told you, he won't take a part that's smaller than the one he had in *Waltz*. And he won't take less money."

"Christ. He'd have been perfect. Let's look at him anyway."

"You don't have a prayer," Opal said. "Besides, he's uncontrollable."

"I can control him," Fletcher said. "He'll do it for me."

An actress on the screen was losing her mind, screaming and throwing things. "So forced," said Fletcher. "Next."

Another actress was up on the screen. She was young but her features were heavy, simple. Belinda thought of Quake and Princess in the nuthouse. Everyone had nicknames, and Quake had come by hers because of the dread she caused. She was a cunning woman with such stupendous anger in her dark eyes that to feel her gaze was to feel the shadow of death. She had heavy, crude features, and heavy hair. Princess, a muscular but tiny woman, said she'd been committed because of a sin and that the mental health system was just a way to control the artists. In the dayroom one morning Quake had suddenly struck Princess in the mouth, knocking out two teeth. Then, she'd twisted her arm back and snapped it. For a large woman, Quake was very quick. Everyone had gone berserk, and two of them—a woman called Jo, another called Singer—had piled on top of Princess like jackals. The others stood aside and quivered. Belinda noted who was dangerous and who wasn't; later she'd learn who snitched and who could be bribed.

Belinda smiled in the dim light of the screening room. She would not have survived the loony bin without the salubrious teachings of the school.

"Goddamnit, take it off," Fletcher was groaning.

Another sample reel popped on. The actress this time was in a bathing suit on a raft. "Look at her skin, look at the way her legs move," Fletcher crooned. "Jeez. She's having a love affair with the water. Is she going to drown?" he whispered, excited. It was the erotic innuendo mixed with the threat of violence in his voice that alerted Belinda. "Great, great," Fletcher breathed as the actress disappeared in the water. "Get her."

"I knew you'd love it," Opal said.

At ten o'clock, Fletcher called a halt. "I can't see anymore. I don't know what I'm watching." Jerry, Opal, and Buttons rose, started to straggle out. "Stay, Belinda. Two memos. Here. Just sit down and write. Do 'em up tomorrow first thing." Everyone left. Only Buttons gave them a second look. Belinda picked up her pen. She was so tired it felt like a foreign object she'd never used before.

Fletcher seemed to be collecting his thoughts about the production, but he said: "Where were you born?"

"What? San Francisco."

"Ah. Gorgeous dame of a town."

"The memo?" she asked.

"Tell me about your life."

She sighed. "Ordinary. Married, divorced, looking for work. Here I am."

"Are your parents alive?"

"My dad."

"Oliver . . . Oliver . . ."

She gave up. Eventually, he'd make the connection. "He writes thrillers."

"Victor Oliver?" She nodded. "Well, well." He considered her. "You're good at this job. You pick up on things, like that call from the bond agent. You knew that was important. How come?" He reached out and drew a finger down her cheek, a director's gesture.

She tapped her temple with the pen. "Good sense."

"I want you with me in Singapore, Belinda. Such an old-fashioned name." He leaned across the arm of the seat between them. "You are a great girl."

"I'm a woman, you sexist freak."

"Yeah." He evaluated her, his face inches from hers. "Stick with me on this one, Belinda. I'm going to need a lot of support. I'm going to run you ragged, use you up. Can you take it?"

"I've had worse."

Again he ran his finger down her cheek, outlining the bones down to her sharp chin. "You are a mystery." His wide lips smiled dreamily. "But all that has to wait until we've transferred this lunacy to Malaysia!"

The telephone on the console behind them rang politely. But Fletcher did not move his eyes from Belinda's face. "That's

Yvonne Duret," he murmured. "She's going to tell me about all the things she needs and doesn't have."

In Singapore, it was early afternoon of the next day. Yvonne sat at a little desk heaped with papers and five stacked clipboards. Her shiny black hair was cut short and straight like a helmet, her eyes were dark blue, her skin ivory. She was wearing a telephone headset to keep her hands free. On the terraces below her, a garden of splashy flowers was in bloom. "I need answers, Fletch. You're finally shooting in eight weeks. I need to see the pictures in your head—that's the only way I can make any decisions." She smiled, patiently, sweetly, even, and focused her eyes on a Chinese silk tree as Fletcher's voice came hurtling through the telephone. She'd worked for him and for Jerry before; she knew their tricks. "True, Fletch, but it's a fourteen-week shoot! How can I make all this work if I don't know which actors and what gear, which vehicles to take where—I need answers, padre. You keep changing the script!"

"Listen, my little whirlwind," Fletcher bawled at her, "I'm not here to make your life easier."

"I'm going through a lot of people out here to get you the best, you know that." Yvonne focused on a bed of disorderly orange flowers far below. "Okay, as soon as I get the *revised* script, I can talk with the shipping agent. . . . Of *course* he's good. . . . Vietnam? Who said anything about shooting there? Why are you telling me now? Why not wait till we're halfway through the shoot? . . . I see. Okay. I'm signing off now, have to check your local casting. Ten four. Ten four, you dog." She heard Fletcher laughing as she hung up.

Yvonne took off her headset, jumped up from the desk, and started stuffing papers into a satchel. She was riding the point. But soon the others would pour into Melaka and Singapore: people who built things, people who found things, from candlesticks to dynamite, people who found real places, magicians who made things appear to be different than what they were. As production manager, Yvonne's job was to assemble the crowd at some date in some place for some kind of shooting, get them contracts, transport, rooms, meals, medical care, and baby-sitters. She was ninety pounds of sparkle—until she felt a director or a producer made a choice she disagreed with—then she fought hard. Sometimes she won; sometimes she lost. Either way, Yvonne was fiercely independent. She couldn't imagine another kind of life than the one she'd built for herself.

The night before she was to leave for Singapore, Belinda sat at her desk in the Berendo Street apartment, writing a letter to Eddie. "You are too young to know how much it means to me to be back in my own city, to be working again with first-rate people, to be accepted." She paused. They would not be so accepting if they knew who she really was. "I know you are well and happy with Patsy and Vail. Knowing that has brought me a lot of comfort in a cold place for many years. I want to spare you what I went through. I know I can't spare you all of it, but maybe, just by writing once in a while, by letting you know me a little, I can forestall that awful moment when, despite what any of us do, you'll realize who I am."

The pretense of the letter hit her. How was she going to save him from anything? She wasn't even mailing these letters. She was in some private communication with herself. She balled up the letter and threw it into the wastebasket.

Her doorbell rang. She looked at the clock. Seven-thirty at night.

"Dr. Suico," she said, opening the door. A Japanese woman and a child stood politely behind the doctor.

"I am sorry to interrupt," Dr. Suico said, "but Mrs. Katasawa and her daughter would like to ask a favor. They have seen your drawing of my grandson, Joseph, and Mrs. Katasawa wishes to purchase a similar picture of her daughter. It is for the child's father, on his birthday tomorrow."

Belinda didn't groan, but she felt like it as she ushered the little group inside, placed the girl on a chair, and took out a drawing pad and a pen. The daughter Katasawa was the fourth child Dr. Suico had brought to her door. In the neighborhood, Belinda had become known as the woman who drew the children.

CHAPTER 7

JUNE 1986

Fletcher loved waking up in a room and not knowing where he was. He'd slipped out of his slot of time and space. He floated, an entity without memory. He simply was.

Pale dawn light filtered through the slatted blinds of a tall window, striping a white cushion on a rattan sofa. His jeans were flung across it. The spatial disorientation ended. He was in the Shangri-la Hotel in Singapore. They'd arrived last night. It was six in the morning.

Each day on location, it was Fletcher's habit to take time that was his alone and walk. He pulled on his jeans and a shirt and hit the streets of Singapore.

It was a tropical island city-state with skyscrapers. The harbor lay somewhere ahead of him. The day was already hot and the humidity high. The streets had been brushed off by a thousand brooms, and every wrapper had been picked up.

The city of two and a half million—Malays, Chinese, and Indians—was already waking up. Fletcher walked as if he'd lived there a year, swinging along in different areas of town, down to Arab Street, a hodgepodge of bazaars, shops, and mosques. Languages trailed him: Tamil from southern India, Malay from the peninsula, Mandarin from China, English from Stamford Raffles and the early colonialists. Muslim Malays had once lived in villages called kampongs, long since gone; Arab Street was the only Muslim neighborhood left. He turned and set a fast pace to Change Alley, a narrow street of oriental bazaars, then on to Chinatown, where the old Chinese streets were called "shophouses." They radiated out from People's Park where ferns and creepers draped the giant trees. Along Seragoon Road, in Little India, he stopped in a songbird café for a coffee. Hanging from beams were dozens of handmade wooden cages, from which the birds trilled and traded songs.

Fletcher stirred his coffee. He was glad to be an ambassador of the world. Not bad for a little boy from West Virginia. Film crossed all barriers; film companies went everywhere. He loved his crews, amazingly adaptable professionals, working in lands they'd never seen with people they'd never met, entrusted with millions of dollars to paint, build, cast, decorate, scrounge, serve, light, shoot. They slept in trucks or in hotels; they ate strange foods; they worked eighteen hours a day, sick or well.

The songbirds piped into his thoughts. Fletcher listened, nodding, watching idleness die. The production was months late getting started, but what the hell, it all took time, that was the business, a network of strangleholds, delays, changes, betrayals, joys.

He set his jaw. He was ready to start the combat.

Keith Llewellyn's dog was named Bob, a simple solid name for a golden retriever who, according to Keith, was smarter than most directors. Every morning, around six o'clock, Keith and Bob trotted down the deserted Santa Monica streets to the track at the high school six blocks away where they ran for two miles and watched the sky grow light, if it was winter, or watched it turn a ripe blue, if it was summer. Sometimes the track bored Bob and he'd zigzag off in a wide circle, intercepting Keith at the bend, loping ahead, doubling his distance. Sometimes Bob just lay down in the center of the oval green and watched, panting. Keith had found Bob five years before in a cardboard box on Hollywood Boulevard, a puppy, lean and cranky and frightened. Food and love, Keith mused, running, food and love is all.

On this cool June morning, as Keith trotted along on the track with Bob beside him, he was mentally going over what he would write that day. He visualized his workroom, the second bedroom of his apartment. It was painted white. He saw the long black table, the single chair, the bookcase, the computer and printer, the bulletin board where he put pictures and clippings, insults and congratulations. His favorite was from a Hollywood wit, "Klong: a sudden rush of crud to the heart." Keith had felt klong a few times, that mix of fear and shame. His next favorite bon mot was a headline which he'd

clipped: "HAD ENOUGH?" That was it. It always made him
smile; he didn't know why.

Keith felt the air deep in his lungs. He thought of the
woman he was currently spending a lot of time with, about
the gloriousness of her glorious red hair and her singing laugh
and her fine mind. But he knew she wanted him to change his
life, which he wasn't going to do. He liked his simplicity—his
apartment that looked out on the trim unpretentious courtyard
with its silly fountain, his lack of car payments, pizza on
Monday nights at the local pub, his unadorned, uncomplicated
independence. His life did not lack direction; he was on the
path of his choice as surely as he ran on the track every
morning. But his unspoken, often not even admitted anxiety
was that he would not find a match, or would not recognize
her when he met her, that he'd settle for someone and live
his life knowing the compromise. He'd been married for six
years and divorced for two. It had taught him how wrong he
could be about a match.

Bob was zigzagging in front of him.

Keith was on his last lap when he felt the idea take root and
flower, a process that always astonished him. One minute it
wasn't there; the next it was fully grown. He saw it clearly,
whole, like a great tree against a blazing horizon; he sensed
it like an emotion or a color. Unconsciously, he slowed his
run, tasting the beginning, the middle, and the end of the
idea. The central character was a tough twenty year old, a
little eighties girl-thug with a heart, a bandit in the making, a
rascal in deep trouble, squeezed by the indifferent and opposing forces of crime and law, the issue of which is unequal
justice. He stopped running, bent over, breathed, savoring his
new companion. He even knew what he'd call it: *Indictment.*
Bob ran around him, barking.

When Fletcher returned to the Singapore hotel that morning,
Yvonne was waiting for him in the production office, a small
second-floor meeting room. He bellowed greetings at her and
wrapped his arms around her, feeling the tight press of her
ribs and back. The room was already filling up with newsmen,
radio interviewers, talent agents, actors, technicians. The telephone was already ringing.

Belinda came bouncing into the room, clipping her hair back from her face with a barrette.

"Belinda! This is Yvonne," Fletcher called out.

"Yeah, know you from the phone," Belinda said. They shook hands. Yvonne was surprised at the firmness of Belinda's grip.

Fletcher said, "Where is everyone?"

"Above the line, like your star, Martin, and then Jerry, Buttons, and Belinda are right here in the high-priced Shangri-la with you. Department heads are at the Goodwood Park Hotel, the former German Club. Other team players are scattered around the area at smaller, cheaper hotels."

"Where's Raffles?" Belinda asked.

Yvonne laughed. "You don't want to stay there. Shabby, with indigestible food. Full of noisy package tours stomping about."

"See?" Fletcher said, happily. "Nothing's sacred."

He went off to the other nerve center, his hotel suite, to meet talent agents and take telephone calls. Yvonne turned to a table heaped with papers. She was making budgets in local currencies for each country they'd be shooting in.

"Buttons Botsford, as I live and breathe," Yvonne said, sarcastically, as he came flying into the room. "How lucky can I get?"

Buttons shook hands with her. "Yvonne Duret encore. I knew you'd be here at first light," he said without enthusiasm and danced away.

Belinda noted the strain between Buttons and Yvonne, but said nothing. All morning, Yvonne worked the phones, committing to members of the crew, confirming the art director with Fletcher, and the editor who'd travel with the shoot, cutting "along the line of march." In the afternoon, the continuity supervisor called in. A woman of fifty, she'd worked every Avery film. Jerry arrived and appropriated a separate adjoining room. Belinda swung between Jerry, Yvonne, and Fletcher. She hung on the telephone with Yvonne and the shipping agent confirming lists of equipment into and out of Singapore, into and out of Melaka, into and out of wherever. The production accountant telephoned: he wouldn't be on board for five days to do the final budgeting.

"We'll need four cars," Yvonne announced. "Minibuses for gaffers, reporters, props, wardrobe, sound. A camera van, a jeep, a special effects van, construction trucks, an electrical truck, a pickup, a catering bus."

"That's a lot," said Belinda.

"No, it's not. Fletch is really holding it down this shoot. Or Jerry is." She winked at Jerry across the room, leaning against a desk top, his long legs extended, his shoulders hunched. His pipe percolated smoke.

But later, Yvonne hung over Belinda's desk, her voice tight: "No! The *local* location managers are arranging that transport, and those extras, and those permits."

"I'm not a mind reader!" Belinda shot back. "Get out of my face."

"No one's perfect!" Yvonne shouted with glee. Belinda wasn't as confident as she seemed. "See this guy? He's the Malaysian location manager for the highlands shoot—budget for five days of shooting up there. Hells bells, we need two more assistants for Kuala Lumpur."

"I added two and someone took them out." It was like living in a cone of sound and energy and emotion. "Are we shooting the end in Vietnam or what?"

"Unclear," Yvonne replied, rattling papers, checking another clipboard. "But put in a location manager and an assistant there just in case. *And* secretaries for each manager to type up the call sheets, carnets, revisions—*bilingual* secretaries."

"Didn't mean to shout," Belinda said. "Just shout back."

That night, after a dinner of eggs in spicy sauce and vegetables in coconut milk, Belinda and Yvonne walked back to the hotel through a narrow street of bustling shops. Yvonne stopped. "These are easy to mail," she said, holding up a small soapstone chop about the size of a finger. "Kids like them—you get your name in Chinese carved in the end. You use it with sealing wax."

Belinda bought one. They walked on.

"You were married, right?" Yvonne asked.

"Yeah. Divorced." Belinda frowned. She didn't like lying to Yvonne.

"Who're you sending the chop to?"

"Son of some friends." They rounded a corner into another

small street of brightly lit shops. "You and Buttons don't get along," Belinda said.

"No, we don't," Yvonne said cheerfully.

"Why not?"

"Buttons wants to be the only crew member who's really close to Fletch. But Fletcher listens to me—and on the last shoot, Buttons got jealous. I don't mean he's gay—he just wants all of Fletcher's attention. We just never hit it off."

That night, Belinda wrote Eddie. "This is a chop. You use it with sealing wax to seal letters. It leaves a 'signature'—a design—when you press it into heated wax. I'm on a location shoot with Fletcher Avery and a cast and crew of what feels like thousands. Everyone's going in different directions but we'll all end up in the same spot—shooting the film. Amazing, really." She wrote him about Singapore and the plans for the rest of the trip. Conflict and guilt about the letter dogged every word, but she couldn't stop. She needed to write him. She needed to acknowledge her connection. And as she wrote about the cast jealousies and the problems of mounting the huge production, she felt it was better to write than not to make any connection with him at all. If Eddie got to know her a little through letters, maybe he wouldn't judge her too harshly later on.

"You wouldn't know from what I've written so far that these are grown-up people," she wrote, "but in many ways they're real tolerant of each other, of mistakes or tempers, and they try to do better the next time around. Film companies, as Fletcher is fond of saying, are America's ambassadors around the world, so we all try to be as good as we can be—which only means that we are human. Sometimes we don't reach the mark we set for ourselves. But we try. Sincerely yours, Belinda Oliver."

Except for casting, all other efforts were bent toward the imminent recon trip to the old town of Melaka on the Malay mainland. From there, they'd turn inland to the highlands north of it, and then on to Kuala Lumpur, the capital of the Peninsular Malaysia. Their mission: final decisions on harbors, roads, cemeteries, churches, a shed, a rice field— the building blocks of the film, scene by scene, place by place. After seven days on the road, they'd come back to the main production office at the hotel in Singapore. Then, when everyone was hired and cast, when everyone from the States had arrived, when the vans and trucks and cars had been rented and tested, when the equipment arrived, the little army would set out for the first locations—probably in Melaka.

But that would change. Everything changed.

The ribbon of road wound through parallel walls of solid jungle. The coast forests were mangroves and swamps, but the lowland forests began a few miles to the east, and there, the huge trees stood ninety feet tall, their branches sprouting sixty feet above the ground, a triple canopy rain forest.

"It's the oldest rain forest in the world," Yvonne said, everyone's tour guide. "Makes Africa's or South America's look young . . . what's left of it."

"Yeah," Fletcher said, making sounds of a Black and Decker motorized saw, "timber!"

Yvonne, Fletcher, Jerry, and Belinda were traveling in an air-conditioned van. The art director, Buttons, Bruno, and various assistants rode behind them in another vehicle.

Emerald green rice paddies glittered under the sun. Huge brown bullocks stood as motionless in the paddies as the wooden houses built on stilts. Luxuriant papaya trees framed the houses and batiks hung on clotheslines. On their left, the sea was a deep blue, skirted by brick red sand and old, bent-over coconut trees.

The monsoon winds met at Melaka near where the Indian Ocean linked up with the South China Sea. Once this great Asian port had controlled the ancient spice trade. Now, weather-worn Melaka was an old, fabulous junk pile.

Fletcher, Yvonne, Bruno, and Belinda stood at the end of Jalan Gelanggan, the main street, staring down through an arched warehouse window at a narrow alley below, the decrepit but functioning dock.

"This is the shot when David first sees his brother," Fletcher announced. "We'll pick him right out of the crowd."

Bruno rubbed his white goatee, squinting.

The big antique junks with their high bows and raised

poop decks bobbed beside the wood pilings, looking just like fifteenth century Chinese junks that had stopped there loaded with silks and porcelain and camphor. But now, the neglected, aging vessels carried only charcoal. A line of laborers ploughed back and forth from decks to dock, their backs bent under the sacks of the fuel.

"Don't you wish we were doing a Malaysian *Taipei*?" Yvonne asked, seeing the romance in Fletcher's eyes.

"Yeah, in a way." He turned to Belinda and pointed toward the mouth of the river that fed into the Strait of Malacca beyond. "Can't you see a two-masted trader, her sails full blown, pushed right into the harbor here by the northeast monsoon? They take off the cloves and nutmeg, and load on stuff from India like carpets. The winds change and the southwest monsoon drives them home! Goddamn, wish I'd grown up here."

The noise on what Fletcher called the main drag was horrendous: horns, hammers, bullock carts pounding over rough pavement, scores of rattling sewing machines, shouting vendors. The heat was oppressive. Fletcher and his little entourage made their way by car and by a three-wheeled bicycle, a tri-shaw, past Chinese shophouses, past the oldest Chinese temple in Malaysia, built in the fifteenth century even before the Portuguese settled in to trade and dominate. And after the Portuguese came the Dutch, leaving their neat, square, orange brick buildings and their beds of tulips; past the Porta del Santiago, a gate without a wall, past forts and churches, ruined and working, up to the Bukit China cemetery for the graveyard scene on a hill in back of the town. Weeds covered the old Chinese tombs, some of them dating back to the Ming Dynasty.

At noon, everything stopped. Siesta. The square emptied, the traffic halted. The only action anywhere was at the food stalls facing the sea where the cooks whipped up Malay, Chinese, and Indian dishes.

"Hiya," Fletch said jovially to the Malay cook at a stand, "we're from Hollywood. Give us satay."

"Satay?" The cook looked at Tujah, the group's translator, their local production guide. He was a small light-boned brown man with a cast in one eye, and he spoke Malay, English,

Mandarin Chinese, and Tamil. His laugh was a high wheeze.

"Tell him the hottest satay in the world for me," Fletcher said.

Tujah evaluated Fletcher kindly, as he might a sick child or a fool, then he turned and ordered. The Malay hot dog snack, little skewers stacked with chicken or beef, had been marinated for how long no Westerner knew in peanuts, spices, coconut milk, and chili peppers. Fletcher waited, making small talk with Yvonne, eyeing Belinda. She wasn't wearing a bra under her cotton shirt, and her slacks were of a sheer East Asian weave. Her hips were pear-shaped, her breasts pointed, her ankles bare.

The satay arrived. Tujah and the stall's owner/cook stared politely as Fletcher hoisted a skewer and slipped two chunks of beef into his mouth. Belinda and Yvonne waited. Everyone waited. "Goddamn," Fletcher cried, swallowing, "That's the best satay in the east! I say so! Got to be!"

Gently, Tujah pushed the little plate of raw cucumbers toward him. Fletcher took one, crunched it down, followed up with another meat and fire lump from the skewer. "More," Fletcher said, his voice softer. He ate another cucumber slice. A thin watery red line appeared at the bottom of his large dark eyes. Tujah offered him an onion but Fletcher declined. "Try one," Fletcher said to Belinda.

"Don't do it," Yvonne warned her.

Belinda looked at Fletcher and knew she had to do it. She took a skewer and gently bit off a piece of meat. Folded into her mouth, she began to chew, and then she felt the searing flame eat her tongue. Her eyes popped open, her face flushed. She would never feel her mouth again.

"Water!" Yvonne said. But Belinda refused. "God, you're as crazy as he is."

"Yeah," Fletcher said, grinning. "She's all right." Tujah and the cook nodded, smiling. "Make 'em tough in Hollywood."

"Beer?" Tujah asked him. Fletcher nodded, starting on his second skewer, handing another to Belinda. Buttons raised his eyebrows; Bruno folded his arms.

"Fletch! Belinda!" Yvonne ordered. "Stop that! No Westerner can take that stuff at its hottest."

"I can," he said, his voice now very soft and breathy. "So can she."

"Don't you have anything to say?" Yvonne demanded of Buttons.

He pressed a hand to his chest. "No, not me."

The cook was fairly dancing about his shack, taking other skewers off the fire and slathering the deadly sauce on the meat. Belinda felt the beads of sweat opening on her forehead. She was on fire from her lips to her stomach.

"We've got to go on," Yvonne said, disgusted. "We'll miss the light on the square for the market scene."

As they walked, Yvonne said in a low voice to Belinda, "He gets that way. Thinks he's outside normal reactions, normal rules. Won't give in. Doesn't mean you have to do it, too."

"It was a test," Belinda said. "I had to do it." Her seared mouth was worth the reluctant admiration she'd caught in Fletcher's eye. There was danger about Fletcher. It appealed to her; it was familiar.

Two days later, the Jerry-Fletcher recon group were six thousand feet above the hot and steamy sea level flats in the Cameron Highlands. Cameron, a nineteenth century British surveyor, had been the first to explore and map the area. After independence, the Malaysian Tourist Development maintained the highland golf courses and hotels the British had left behind.

The narrow road, fringed with bright splashes of orange impatiens, cut into the green skin of the hills. The forest at this level was chestnut and oak; the dense jungle growth was so implacably deep that visitors were warned not to stroll off the road. Malay houses, decorated with carvings, crouched on the plateaus of the steep green mountains surrounded by terraced tea plantations and strawberry farms. Far above, the limestone mountains rose one behind the other, each a different shade of blue gray, blending distantly into the sky. The air was crisp and cool.

"Why have we stopped?" Belinda asked from the rear seat.

"A python," Yvonne said. It lay across the road like a thick rope, twenty feet long.

"Hell, run over it," Fletcher directed.

"No. Very bad luck," the Tamil driver said.

"Sometimes, they just lie there, not moving at all for hours," Jerry put in. "I remember a shoot in Thailand—"

"Goddamnit," Fletcher said, "we can't hold up the line just for a python to get it together."

"This is nature," Yvonne said to him. "Even you cannot change it." She got out of the car. Belinda piled out after her. Soon everyone was out except for the driver.

They were stopped in a pocket of high mountain jungle that stretched as far as they could see on either side of the road. Belinda stared into the green tumescent mass of leaves and vines and trees. Red trumpet flowers dangled from the edge of the canopy.

Jerry came up to her. "Awesome, ain't it?" he said about the jungle.

Belinda nodded. The journey was changing her. "I feel as if everything I've done doesn't really matter," she finally said. "In fact, we don't really matter."

"There are two kinds of people," he muttered. "Wiser ones who understand the indifference of nature, and less wise ones who think they matter."

A yell that sounded like "Scram!" made Jerry and Belinda turn to look at Fletcher. He was standing on the other side of the van, willing the python to move out of his way.

Belinda laughed. "And then there are others who think they control nature," she said.

"Fletcher," Yvonne called out, "take a break."

Suddenly, the sun disappeared, the weather turned eerie and misty. Clouds were rolling over the mountains. It began to rain. Everyone piled back in the vans and slammed the doors.

"Look!" Belinda shouted.

The python was undulating across the road and disappearing, headfirst, into the jungle.

"So long, serpent," Fletcher said. "Have a good life."

Ye Olde Smokehouse was a colonial relic of Tudor design surrounded by lush landscaping. Its rooms overlooked the fifteenth fairway of the golf course. Jerry, an avid golfer, was ecstatic.

"Fuckin' British protectorate!" Fletcher bawled as they went inside. The public rooms were from a different age, composed of mahogany beams set against white plaster walls. In the lobby and the bar, portraits of British officers and displays of antique pistols lined glass panels; couches surrounded the fireplace, issues of *Country Life* magazine nestled in baskets, end tables supported bowls of huge gaudy roses. It looked like Ye Olde Smokehouse had invented the "splash of soda, old boy."

Yvonne took Jerry aside. "There's only one telephone downstairs in the bar. I picked this place for its R & R."

"Bless you," he said.

She consulted her clipboard and called out to Fletcher, "There's a spot near here where you can film the last chase. It's promoted as a jungle walk but actually you have to crawl on your hands and knees up and down the bloody ravines."

"We can't do the chase in a ravine, Yvonne."

"Would I do that to you? There's a flat stretch."

"How's the transport around here?" Buttons asked. "Seems real isolated."

"The beaches at Pinang Island are five hours away by car, Kuala Lumpur is a bit closer. Nearest airport is in Ipoh, tourist spot. Rental cars, all that."

Fletcher checked his watch aggressively. It was still misty and gray outside. Cream tea with scones was being served in an enclosed garden. "Just one phone?" he asked Yvonne.

Fletcher's line of march stopped in the highlands. It was the off-season; they had the candle-lit dining room to themselves except for an elderly British couple, the Hayers, who were quickly sucked into the group's hilarity.

Stories swirled around the table as the steak and kidney pie, the beef Wellington, and the other British-style meat slabs arrived with their boiled potatoes, watery vegetables, and quantities of red wine.

Belinda, Jerry, and the Brits were seated across the table from Fletcher, Buttons, Bruno, and Yvonne. Jerry, cutting efficiently into his Wellington, began telling a chain of sadistic or *gemütlich* production tales. Fletcher's legendary charm blossomed as he added asides to Jerry's stories. "That guy supplied the dope on his own set," Fletcher said, "and did you know, Jer, that he trains show poodles, too?" His eyes softened. Tenderly, he lifted the crust of his kidney pie and slipped his fork inside. He turned the fork, plumbing the pie slowly, glancing upward at Belinda with a naughty, vulnerable look. "And that writer," Fletcher went on, still gently rooting around under his pie crust, "what's-his-name—"

"Malcolm," Bruno supplied.

"Yeah, his ma was an invalid and that's how he relates to people. They locked him off the set." Fletcher grinned slowly at Belinda, turning his fork under the pie crust, searching blindly, poking. Everyone else was talking loudly about hairdressers who tyrannized their stars, of saintly directors, of acts of thievery and generosity, but Belinda couldn't take her eyes off Fletcher's half cloaked fork stirring around in the kidney pie. A smart, sexy smile stretched his blunt lips.

Belinda, dropping her eyes only when necessary, dipped a rounded small knife in a mound of butter and brushed it across a piece of soft brown bread. Fletcher was watching her. She bit into the bread, leaving a scollop-shaped, precise pattern of her teeth imbedded in its buttery blanket. She put the bread with its bite mark down on a plate, a trophy, glanced at Fletcher, licked her upper lip, licked the inside of her cheek.

Fletcher's fork shot out of his pie crust like a diver breaking the sea's surface. On the end of the fork was a nubbin of kidney, round, fat, reddish-brown, organic. He put it in his mouth and chewed lazily. Belinda inserted a celery stick, licked it, then bit into it noisily. Fletcher narrowed his eyes, sank his fork into the middle of his pie, sending broken crust chips sinking into juices. Belinda started in on a slab of steak, carving a long streak through its red, rare flesh, skewering a piece, lifting it, dripping, into her mouth. Fletcher, one hand reaching out for bread, the other still busy with his fork in the pie, was talking to Bruno, but she knew he was watching her chew, and she chewed slower and slower.

Yvonne took another swallow of wine and said to Buttons, "Fletch's a benevolent demon."

"No! He's a heretic," Buttons yelled, loving his leader.

"Sure, that's me," Fletcher said, putting greasy spalulate fingerprints on his wineglass. "And maybe Mr. Hayer, our gent from Great Britain," he said, slyly. "Look at the face, the way he sits. He doesn't give a damn what people think." Mr. Hayer lifted his Celtic jaw and smiled frostily. "Maybe Belinda, too, our lady of the secrets who keeps her own counsel."

"I'm just shallow, Fletch," Belinda said, sending out a complete smile, raising her glass, drinking deeply, leaving a red wet line on her lip.

"Sure," he barked. "Shallow like Catherine the Great." He laughed and speared a cauliflower and sucked the buttery surface before it disappeared in his mouth. He rolled it like a marble in there, then bit down slowly, like a vise closing. He waited for Belinda's return. She forked up a tiny new potato, dipped it in horseradish and the red juice of her steak, took a bite and let her lip trail across it as she nibbled. Fletcher was tugging on a piece of bread, gripped in his teeth, separating crust from heart. He speared another kidney lobe, held it out to examine it. "Now let's take Buttons next," he said, his dark eyes rolling toward his assistant. "Loyal and afraid, competent and anxious . . ."

Yvonne, feeling the wine, watched Fletcher prove once again his remarkably accurate perceptions of everyone around him. People were his food and drink, but even in the dining duel with Belinda—and Yvonne had only seen the last part of that—even when Fletcher seemed deeply involved with any of them, his understanding was objective, remote, uninvolved.

"Aw, I haven't got any business sense," Fletcher was saying to Buttons. "Yvonne does that, Jerry, god bless him, does that." He saluted Jerry with his smudged wineglass, then turned to the awed British couple. "All I know is culture, the creative expression, what's inside that actor, how to get it out. I'll never be rich, but my life belongs to me. I just can't do what other people want, huh, Jerry?"

"I've lived to regret it," Jerry said, pushing his plate away, biting his pipe.

"I'm not here to please anyone but myself and my actors." Fletcher basked in the group's approval of his authority. With a giant sigh, he rose. "Everyone had enough food?"

They adjourned to the bar for coffee, brandy, cigarettes, more stories. Fletcher claimed erotic overtones in everything. "Look at the veins!" he bellowed, pointing at a glossy rubber plant. "Look at the light rubbing against the corner of that wood, caressing the hollows."

God, Yvonne thought, here we go. Soon he would say something scary and uncouth.

"How *about* that python?" he demanded of the group.

"Big mother," Buttons commented.

"Actually, it was young," Yvonne put in. "If it had been full grown its tail and its head would've been inside the jungle on either side of the road."

"Yeah, the big snake," Fletcher murmured. He lifted his eyes and stared into the beamed ceiling. "I can see that tubing curled around Belinda's waist with its head chucking her under the chin." He made a pointed snake's head with his hand and shoved it gently at her throat. He turned his hand downward toward her belly. Then he took his hand away and humped it across the low table. "Wrapping her in its coils, gliding down her body. . . . I got it! The porno movie of all time—the lady and the snake." He lowered his voice. "The snake's twisted around her, she's lying like this, stretched out, he's got his head inside her, he's squeezing her to death, slowly ploughing her, in ecstasy and death. . . ."

"Fletcher, for God's sake," Jerry said.

"It's a love story," Fletcher said.

"The hell it is. Just a simple male fantasy."

"That's true." Fletcher's tone was amazed, as if Jerry had just discovered something rare and unique. "That's why pornography survives so well. Men think eroticism is a painted, scantily dressed woman but that's moral dishonesty. And when women collaborate with it, they're exploiting themselves. It's a corruption of themselves." Under the ledge of his forehead, his dark eyes shifted to Belinda. "Whaddya think of that?"

"I think it's bullshit."

Fletcher led the laughter.

Everyone finally tottered upstairs. At her door opposite Belinda's, Yvonne said to her: "Got the picture?"

"Yes," Belinda replied.

"Lock your door," Yvonne said, laughing.

Belinda's room was decorated in major chintz with antique furniture. She sat down in a flowery chair opposite the armoire. She turned away from it toward the window, remembering her dream of Sky in Vail's house. It didn't take another armoire to bring it back. She pushed open the window for a slice of the night to blow away the disturbing dream. The odor of roses and decay rose up from the garden.

Archie was bending over her, leaning on one arm, the other hand trailing through her hair. His lips were damp and full.

She turned away from the window, feeling for Fletcher the same rush of addicted, fascinated attraction that she'd once felt for Archie. A savage drink to the lees. The carnal feelings had been inside her all these years, preserved hard like amber. She had no practice with intimacy. The school had taught her sexual commerce, not giving. But Fletcher was compelling because his instant and complete intimacy required no effort, no soul-searching. With Fletcher, it was all or nothing.

Belinda shut the window. But Fletcher still intruded. He was danger, hovering over her, grinning at her with his wide flat lips and his deep-set eyes. The leaf, the embracing serpent—Fletcher was daring her. Do you dare to feel? Do you dare to feel again? How much will you gamble?

"What's up?" Fletcher asked. He was leaning against the edge of the open door of his room, his hair rumpled, his eyes tired. He was wearing a pair of jeans, no shirt; his feet were bare.

"You and me," Belinda said.

He eyed her, then stepped back from the door. "By all means."

When the door closed, she put her arms around his waist and leaned her cheek against the curly hair on his chest.

"Oh, well, well," he said.

His skin was warm and damp. Could he feel her heart beating? His hand cupped the back of her head. She pressed against him, slipping her arms under his, curling her hands behind his back, pressing her breasts into his hard chest. She didn't feel the tight curling signal from his groin. He brushed his lips against her cheek, a dismissal. He was in a different mood now. He stood passively, kissing her face once more, and then once more again. She broke away, took his hand, led him to the rumpled bed in the next room, and lay down.

He stood beside the bed, gazing down at her speculatively. "You're a good actress," he said. "Did you have every move planned?"

She bolted from the bed. "You shit," she said. "You're a fake."

He caught her arm as she went through the open doorway. "Stay," he said.

"The hell I will."

He laughed. "I want you to stay. I was lying here thinking of you."

"Crap."

"I don't care." And he didn't. He tried to draw her back into his arms, but she escaped into the next room. He got to the door before she did.

She backed away. "Let me out."

"Not now." He leaned against the door casually as he might lean against someone's mantel in a crowded room. Very slowly, his arm lifted between them. He reached for her hair with the same wary concern he'd extend to a feral animal. His hand landed lightly on the side of her head, gently combed down her hair to her jaw. "You've been mine," he whispered, "since we met. And you knew it then."

"Ridiculous—"

He seized her arms with both hands and kissed her hard, without distance, without confusion. It was a relief. But as the kiss grew and she imagined that his lips were swelling against hers, she felt as if she'd rather be anywhere except inside these strange arms.

He hooked an arm around her neck and started to guide her back into the bedroom. "No," she said.

His fingers moved to her shirt, avoiding her breasts, nimbly popping buttons. "You don't give an inch, do you?" he said. He opened her shirt. "Ah," he sighed, gratified. He ran a finger across both rounded mounds trapped in the bra. "Ah." His fingers dropped to the fastening between the pale fleshy mounds and popped it open. The stiff lace fell away. She put her fingertips between his skin and the waistband of his jeans, then moved them down to the distended lump below and pressed hard. His fingers danced across her naked breasts. He bent and licked them wetly while one hand lifted her skirt, bunching the material up to her thigh, his fingers walking to the edge of her panties beneath. He spread one hand against her, palm down, holding her, undulating, pressing in and out against the tight material. She leaned back against his arm as his hand slid inside her panties, fingers closed. He held her softly. One finger detached and found an inner secret lip. She took her hand away from the warm angle between his legs and undid the top buttons of her skirt. It fell partway, and she lifted her foot slightly to step out of one side of it. Fletcher's hand, still pressed against her inside her panties, moved against the wet glossy skin.

Belinda sank to the floor, half in, half out of her skirt. Fletcher removed his hand, slipped it out of the loop of skirt, which fell away. Gently, he pulled off her shirt, too, and looked at her as she lay on the carpet. Then he knelt beside her and slowly rolled down her panties, peeling them down to her ankles, kissing the terrain of skin and bone in their wake. He lifted her hair at the back of her head and pulled her head up and peeled off her bra. He knotted it around her ankles, closing them, stripped off his jeans and slowly moved over her, holding himself above her on both arms, kissing her face. When he stretched on top of her, flat, he pressed against her, hard and eager but in no hurry, nuzzling inside her little by little, sending out waves of heat under her skin. She gripped him to her. They rocked together until suddenly, he reached down, released her legs, and plumbed her. She yelled. He smiled, a conformation that freed his face in a completely new way.

"Lie still a moment, my love," he said.

"I can't." Her body was someone else's, swollen, vibrating, unfamiliar.

He slipped an arm under her waist to bring her closer. "Then fly away home."

Hours later, they lay in the four-poster bed. One of Fletcher's arms curled around her shoulder, his other hand held a cigarette.

"Yvonne told me you grew up in West Virginia, in a small town," Belinda said.

"No, no biographic notes after the great lay." He chuckled. But after a few moments, he said, "My dad was a hay and corn farmer in a land that only grew coal." He blew out a cloud of smoke. "He was a man without dreams. He died when I was eleven. My ma kept her dreams, I never knew how. I think she married for love—and lived to regret it."

Belinda burrowed closer to him. The fingers of her hand were knotted in his hair. "Brothers and sisters?"

"Three of them died before they were out of the orange crates we called cradles, all 'cept Rose—a real looker. Her first husband was a truck driver, the next one was a contractor, and the last one's in real estate. She lives in California. She was the one who brought me out there, actually."

"So, what happened when your dad died?"

"Mom took Rose and me back to Maryland but our dear grandparents wouldn't let her in." He shook his head in the dark. "Real beauts they were. Pretentious poverty is what they lived in, didn't have a pot to piss in, but my mom had married 'beneath her,' so she'd have to take her punishment."

"They chucked her out," Belinda said.

"You got it. That's the folks. Sweethearts. So mom worked as a department store clerk, a waitress, a nursery school teacher. We moved around a lot, but ma was never involved with other men—I didn't have that to contend with. Then, in 1968 I turned eighteen just in time to be drafted to Vietnam. At least I missed the Tet Offensive. I did a year's tour—a lifetime." He put out his cigarette. "I've heard guys say it wasn't anything much, but they're hiding. They'll hide all their lives. When I got back alive, I wasn't afraid of anything." He propped up on an elbow. "You're not afraid either, but you're scared to death." He broke off, laughing, and lit another cigarette.

"So are you," she said. "I know it when I see it."

He puffed on his cigarette. "So tell," he said in the absent way some men question women.

"Tell?" Princess was hissing at her, her neck hooked forward, her pointy chin out, "Do what they want and they'll let you out." She tapped Fletcher's arm. "You want me to tell you about how I went to college for a year and got married?"

"You're a liar," he said, amused.

"I wasn't in Vietnam, I was in Berkeley staging antiwar demonstrations in 1972."

"And then you got married. Did you have children?"

"No."

"Just married, divorced, and that's that?" Belinda nodded. He laughed hugely. "I don't believe you. God, what a piece of work you are. You fuckin' seduced me. I like that." He pressed one hand inside her thigh. "Do you always do what you want?"

"When it suits me."

"I made you do it, you know," he whispered, kissing her breast. He drew away to look at her. "That satay really burned, didn't it?"

She put her hand between his legs and watched him close his eyes. His lips parted. "I thought my head was going to blow right off my neck," she said, softly.

"Me, too," he breathed. "Thought I'd die."

Eddie was sitting on the edge of the patio in a pair of ripped jeans and a long-sleeved shirt, holding a letter from Belinda. Patsy sat behind him at the table, making notes on a legal tablet.

" 'There's a time in every production when you feel that it's completely out of control, when people are screaming, when nothing works, and everyone swears they've never experienced anything like *this!* before. It's a stampede, and we're going over the edge . . . !' Sounds wild, huh, Mom?"

Patsy nodded. These letters from Lindy to Eddie bothered her.

Diana came out on the patio. She, too, had a letter from Belinda. She sat down under the umbrella at the table with Patsy. "Such a dear letter," Diana said. " 'Traveling along the roads, which are pretty good here, one sees lush greenery everywhere, dotted with the bright red clothes of the women in the fields. Everyone is very kind and helpful. I could live here forever.' Isn't that sweet of her to write?" Diana finished.

Eddie stuffed his letter in his pocket.

"Yes, Diana," Patsy said, seeing that Eddie, too, had noted the different tone of the two letters.

"How is your schooling, Edward?" Diana asked him.

"Great, Grandma. I beat that kid Tommy to a pulp."

Diana sniffed. "I'm not sure that's anything to be proud about. I'm surprised your mother condones such fierceness."

"She didn't," Eddie said.

"Just how did you manage to 'beat him to a pulp,' Edward?" Patsy asked.

"I dared him to a one-armed fight in the gym with a referee and everything. Coach tied one of our hands behind our backs. It was a fair fight and we had to shake hands after it."

Patsy smiled at Diana.

"Edward, where's your new hand, dear?"

"I don't like wearing it." He looked down at the stone flagging.

"Well, you ought to, dear. I thought it looked fine. I'm sure your mother agrees."

Edward looked at Patsy. "I don't agree, Diana," Patsy said

briskly. "I think it's Edward's decision."

"Finally, if it's my decision," he said, "then I'm not wearing it." He looked at both his relatives truculently, expecting one of them to go on the attack.

The cordless telephone near her on the table rang. Patsy picked it up. "It's Fletcher Avery from Malaysia," she said. "Yes, Fletch, how are you?" Eddie signaled his mother he was leaving and she waved him off. Diana also rose and walked slowly into the house.

"Great! The shoot's aces," Fletcher said.

"Where are you, exactly?" Patsy asked.

"In the Smokehouse."

As he described it to her, he stretched out his legs and gazed at a huge arrangement of pink and white roses that flowered on a table beside the telephone. "I want you to talk to Jerry. He's being a shit. I've got to have more money. It's outrageous, me having to ask for money." But he didn't have his back into the conversation; he was thinking of Belinda. His gaze wandered to the space above the fireplace where a painting of some man in a tight military uniform stared into the middle distance. Patsy was saying something he missed. "Just talk to him, Patsy. You can turn him around." He heard her say something about the script. "I'm rewriting it."

"You be careful. That script is what got you Martin. He loves that script just the way it is. Don't—"

"I'm improving it! Listen, Patsy, only have a min. About Belinda."

"What about her?"

"Her secrets fascinate me. I got an instinct about these things. Where'd she come from?"

"Geographically? From San Francisco. Fletcher, what difference does it make?"

"None. Just curious."

"Vail's fond of her," she said meaningfully. "So am I."

"She's all round great. I'm a little in love with her."

"Don't you fool around with Belinda," he heard Patsy say, striking a warning note in her voice. "Is Belinda there? Can I talk to her?"

"She's off on a jungle trail," he replied. "Anyway, I didn't call to talk about Belinda."

"Right," Patsy said. "When do you get back to Singapore?"

"In a few days."

When they hung up, Fletcher went out to the rose-filled garden patio and looked across the golf links to a corner of a mountain obscured by a misty fog. He thought of the dark jungle trail he'd explored that morning with Buttons and Belinda, of his feeling of being watched by the teeming life from behind the jungle wall. He saw himself making love to Belinda on the green mosaic floor as pythons slithered around them, over them, pressing them, as butterflies as big as birds fluttered and watched.

The truth is, Fletcher said to himself, Belinda's under your skin. He hadn't felt like that in years. It felt very good.

CHAPTER 8

Victor couldn't remember which city he was in and it scared the shit out of him. A woman was sleeping next to him but he didn't know who she was. He felt dry and light-headed and ill; he knew he was still drunk. It was three in the morning.

He arose slowly. He felt like an insect; he imagined his eyes extended, swollen, and crisp, on stalks from his head; his body felt as if it would snap like a twig; he had no lungs, just openings. He moved to the window feeling vulnerable and ugly and alien. The view wasn't high enough to give him a clue to his surroundings. He gripped the windowsill and turned. The woman stirred. He went over to her, peered at her in the dim light. Not a clue.

He examined the room. A hotel and not a very good one. As quickly as he could, he moved on his reedy insect legs to his clothes flung into a deep chair and felt around for his wallet. Finding it, he climbed carefully into his slacks and pushed his arms into his shirt. His head wasn't throbbing because he felt he didn't have any blood, just air sacs and slits in his armor. His movements were jerky. His neck shook. He sat down to put on his socks.

When he woke up, he was on the floor. It was dawn. The window was streaked with rain. The woman was no longer in the bed. He got up on his hands and knees. Now his head felt like he was wearing a pair of barbells for a hat. He struggled over to his jacket, put it on. His wallet was gone. He sat down on the floor, resting his back against the foot of the bed and watched a sickly sunlight advance across the rug. "Salvage," he said to himself. "I've got to salvage what's left." But he couldn't get up to begin the rescue operation.

So he sat at the foot of the bed, all head and abdomen, encased in his exoskeleton. He tried to think back, but he could only conjure up the dinner with Lindy in Los Angeles and he knew that had been months ago. His thoughts drifted away, his and not his, and he found himself wondering how soon Lindy's heart would be broken again by another man's appetite. Acutely, out of context and proportion, he lamented not seeing her first Christmas play, not escorting her to her first father-daughter dinner, not being around to shake hands with her date to her first dance. His mind eddied and jumped, independent of any efforts or direction from him, as he tried to find the months between the time he'd seen Lindy in Los Angeles and now. He saw her retreating into her apartment, waving good night. "You'll find that we never do anything by ourselves," he'd said to her that night. Who'd helped him get out of the morass of his life after he'd left Sara? he asked himself. The image of the London woman came back to him, chunky, plain, hot. Generous. She'd been a writer and had teased him into writing something for a magazine. He'd loved her hugely. Tears formed in his compound insect eyes. I never loved Sara, he thought, grimly. I just admired her and took her mother's money. He saw his life as complete wreckage as he sat by the foot of the bed in the advancing light.

"Get up," he ordered himself. "If you can't write at least get up off your knees."

He tottered on his insect legs to the window. There was a huge building across the street which he'd never seen before. He looked down about three stories. People were going to work. They looked like people everywhere in rain hats and umbrellas. London? he wondered. If only it weren't so painful to blink, he could focus his eyes.

His trembling hands rummaged in his jacket pocket for his notebook. His last entry was dated a Monday, in Belfast. Was this Belfast? There was nothing for it. He would have to go downstairs and ask someone where he was. A wave of nausea swept over him. He leaned against the table until it subsided. But most of the nausea was shame and that did not pass.

He was at a crossing and he faced it squarely. He clung to the edge of the table near the window, fully acknowledging his failure of heart. He wasn't going to surrender to booze and women again, goddamnit, never again. He was going to get back to the remaining business of his life—writing. It was, simply, the only card he had left. He wouldn't tolerate the look in Lindy's eyes, and in his own, if he failed.

On his way to the shower, he saw the telephone on the nightstand. He picked up the receiver and dialed "O."

"Bonjour!" a merry voice said.

Victor Oliver was in Paris.

Belinda and Yvonne were driving an extra jeep back to Singapore from Melaka. The road along the shore was broad, the afternoon hot and calm. On their right, visible over the rises and around the curves, the brilliant Strait of Malacca gleamed and rolled.

But it could have been Lake Erie. Belinda was inhaling the narcotic fire; she was seared and hungry for more. The satay, the passion, the production had fused. For the week of the recon, the indistinguishable days had been frantic passages to the nights with Fletcher. This morning, she'd come out of the hotel in Melaka to find him standing alone on the street waiting for their caravan of cars.

"How are you?" he'd asked.

"My condition is called euphoria," she'd said, stopping in front of him. "I grin a lot. I get smiles back."

He'd wrapped his arms around her and rocked her. "I am taken out of myself."

"Fletcher Avery? Taken out of himself? Never."

"Even me, hardball."

"So I got into the work as a location underling," Yvonne was saying gaily, driving around a bend, tossing her helmet of black hair. "Then this nut called Fletcher came along, shooting his first film in Hong Kong, and he made me a location manager. His second movie was partly shot in the Philippines, and I worked that one, too. He was different back then."

"How?" Belinda asked through a web of sensations that had nothing to do with Yvonne. Fletcher was kissing her thighs, her ears, her mouth, her feet.

"More confidence in himself, easier on everyone, less spoiled. His reputation spoiled him. Got big too soon. He just wasn't as hard to work with then."

"I don't find him hard to work with."

"You wait till crunch time." They drove in silence for several miles.

"How'd you get over here?" Belinda asked. "You're American, aren't you?"

"Yes. My mother was an American but my father was French and when I was a child, he was managing a rubber plantation in Indochina—Vietnam. He'd been raised there, and for a while it was pretty peaceful." Yvonne turned to look at Belinda. "I was ten and I loved it. I used to have a white crested hornbill as a pet—almost a pet, she didn't live in a cage or anything. She had real dark eyes. Hornbills are big birds and she'd come flying out of the sky when I'd whistle. . . . Whoosh, whoosh, I can still hear her wings. . . ." The jeep rattled over a dip in the road as they passed a long line of still palm trees. "Then the guerrilla warfare started and the French were driven out. So I did most of my schooling in the States."

"But you didn't stay in Los Angeles," Belinda said. Fletcher's lips and tongue licked her fingers and her palms. Fletcher, on top of her, reared up, blocking out the light from the window, an expression of joyous pain locked into every line and muscle in his face.

"I could have," Yvonne said, passing a bullock cart rattling along the side of the road. "But I really missed great old war-torn Southeast Asia. So I got a job with Run Run Shaw—the movie king in Hong Kong." She laughed. "What a time we had!" She looked up. "I guess you got it all out of me. Tell me where you got your film experience."

"Just odd jobs in Hollywood."

Yvonne ran a hand through her thick black hair. "Whatever you choose to tell me will stay sealed. I never talk."

Belinda wanted to confide but she didn't know how. "I had some trouble with my family, and I left and I never went back. Traveled around a lot, took any old job around a shoot. Like that."

They were passing a small town built on stilts. Yvonne turned east for the final leg into Singapore. "Martin's getting in tomorrow," Yvonne said. "Going to be hot times. He doesn't like the revised-revised script."

"More rewrites? God, we're running out of time."

"What are you going to do about Fletcher?" Yvonne asked suddenly.

"I don't know that I have to do anything," she snapped.

"Hey, you're pretty quick on the trigger."

"Sorry." She looked at Yvonne's short, tight profile. "I feel like I'm flying and being attacked—all at once. I never felt quite this way before. You remember the first day in Melaka, eating the satay? That's where it started. If I can get used to the heat of satay, I can get used to Fletcher."

"Don't kid yourself."

"I can handle it."

"If you were the Duchess of Windsor, Imelda Marcos, and Madame Defarge all rolled into one"—Yvonne laughed—"you couldn't handle Fletcher. No one 'handles' Fletch. He's a man who works best under strange, harassing conditions. An affair adds to the drama."

"He does have a dark side," Belinda said to the rice paddies. She didn't care. She lived for his touch, for the cascading sensations that she hadn't felt in years.

"Everything that goes wrong, all the hardships, turn him on," Yvonne said, cheerfully. "Turmoil's inspiring. Big emotions, like passion or betrayal, according to Fletcher, can't get out any other way. Very seductive."

The combustible connection between Belinda and Fletcher had preoccupied everyone on the recon trip. Yvonne had seen huge love affairs swamp productions on location before; they were like hurricanes, dramatic and disastrous. Belinda and Fletcher, yawing off course in a squall, had caught them all by surprise.

"This isn't your ordinary, garden-variety love affair, is it?" Yvonne said.

"No," Belinda said.

"It might have repercussions—besides the craving you two can't hide," Yvonne said. "Everyone's talking about it."

"They are?"

"How could quiet, low-profile, unemotional, tough little Belinda be doing this?"

"Is that what they're saying?" Belinda looked at the green fields sweeping up to the hills in the distance. "I'm surprised I can still love, frankly, that I'm willing to feel something so big." He *is* like fire, she thought. I'm addicted. "God, I can't believe this thing with him," she said out loud.

"You know, I liked him right away, but I was afraid of him."

"*You*? Tough nut Belinda afraid? I don't believe it."

"I just realized that I'm kinda afraid of men, period." She had never voiced that before, and inwardly, she shrank from Yvonne's reaction.

But Yvonne only said, "Why's that?"

"I don't know," she hedged. "Being brought up with women, maybe. I didn't even meet my father until I was sixteen. I like him but I don't know him."

Yvonne nodded. "You don't know Fletcher either. He's drinking too much. My mom was an alcoholic. I know. At least he's not doing coke—is he?"

"Coke? Jesus, no, not that I've seen—"

"Fletcher tries everything five times. Mind if I give you advice? Don't get too involved with him, Belinda. If you do, don't take what he dishes out. Stand up to him or get out."

"Why do you keep working with him if you don't like him?"

"I do like him, but I see him clearly. He was the crown prince until his last two films went in the bag. I couldn't abandon him on this one."

"Does he have a lot of affairs on locations?" Belinda asked.

"Actually, not many. One or two I can think of. The work's too demanding, and the pace is catching up with him. He's not twenty anymore."

"I never thought I'd feel this close to anyone again," Belinda said.

WE NEED LOCAL MANAGERS TRANSPORT EXTRAS PERMITS CATERING CARNETS ASSISTANTS TRANSLATORS TRI-SHAWS . . . SINGAPORE . . . ASSISTANTS . . . IS HE SHOOTING IN VIETNAM . . . NEED LOCATION MANAGER ASSISTANT SECRETARIES SCRIPT CHANGES CALL SHEETS REVISIONS TRILINGUAL . . . MORE SATAY.

Singapore. One week before shooting.

The production office in the hotel was a clamorous hellhole of piled-up papers and jostling, shouting people striding around with clipboards. Belinda now had an assistant, a

Chinese woman who, among other chores, photocopied the script changes daily. Every department head was in a different town or couldn't be found. Everything was revised ten times over. The days were laced together with coffee, tea, cigarettes, dry sandwiches, jangling phones, questions: Extras in where? Ipoh? Is that a country? Hotels? Martin's Winnebago? Caterers?

Martin and Fletcher came out of an adjoining room. "Marty," Fletcher was saying, "it will all work. Believe in it." Martin did not look like a believer. He was not tall or muscular but he had an intense presence, accented by a wave of dark curly hair and brilliant blue eyes like cornflowers. Marty glanced at the pandemonium in the office. His usual sunny smile had faded. His face was set in a power scowl. He left without a word.

A cacophony of budgeting, bargaining, pleading, compromising raged through the office. Last minute casting added to the confusion. The rotund Asian casting director, Mr. Chen, stylishly turned out in a silk suit and a diamond pinkie ring, commanded stacks of sample reels. Crowds of exotic or desperate actors from all of Asia, it seemed, poured into the office, vying to play the minor roles: men in suits or turbans, women in saris or jeans and halters. One man, dressed as an ancient Thai monarch and leading a baby elephant, stood outside the hotel holding a huge sign in Malay, Thai, and English: *Hire me and love God.*

The equipment was taking over, and the support vehicles, customized vans that held the equipment—cameras, lights, sound, the generator. "Fletcher," Yvonne said, "I estimate it will take ten work days just moving the stuff to the locations I've scheduled and back again."

"Got to be less. Bruno," Fletcher called out, "I don't give a shit what your Aussie lab says, they've got to pay the cost of sending dailies back to us: Make them do it."

Bruno only nodded; he was talking to Jerry. "I don't want to argue this every time, Jerry. You don't want the stuff breaking down in the jungle and us with no replacements. Do you?" He left muttering about the backup camera, prime lenses, and the Nike crane.

Belinda and her assistant were making equipment lists for the shipping agent. "Lighting truck—cables, lamps, butterflies, flags, turtles, stands . . . Here's the revised list for the sound truck: mikes, cordless radio mikes for actors, two transmitters, walkie-talkies, bullhorns, a thirty-five millimeter projector with screen to show rushes on location, the video setup." Her assistant checked them off. "And the radio setup," Belinda finished, "so we can talk to the production office." In Melaka, Yvonne had rented a production office, a cramped little room next door to a restaurant.

Belinda stared at Fletcher's back. He was sitting on her desk, gesticulating at Mr. Chen.

"But what do you want, Mr. Fletcher?" Mr. Chen wailed.

"Someone talented!"

The hall outside was full of Malaysians and Chinese, Jerry was on a telephone cajoling the studio in Los Angeles, and Yvonne was struggling with the production accountant, a bald man in a commando shirt, horn-rimmed glasses and a crew cut. "Which crew members go everywhere?" Yvonne showed him the list. "Which are picked up locally?" he asked. "And, how about Malay extras? How many?" She tapped the sheet. He scrutinized the figure suspiciously.

Belinda sank into her chair. "Is *this* a *picture*?" she muttered, and started laughing. It was an ordeal, a mass of twisted, spitting problems that had to be solved a week ago. Fletcher's spectacular madness, and the way everyone fell into step with it, accepting it, was as deranged as her time in the loony bin. The difference was that no one here had been coerced to work on the picture. Just because all the haggard, yelling people around her had chosen to be here, did that make them less crazy than Ghost or Princess or Quake in the nuthouse dayroom? Did it make any difference? No. *Force Field* was a runaway train, and she still couldn't get off.

Buttons was watching Belinda. It was not hard to imagine her in bed with Fletcher; it was only hard to imagine her staying there. He looked at the line of her jaw where it joined her neck—aristocratic, sweet, chilly. He watched her hips swing and her breasts jiggle as she swept around the room. He looked at Yvonne, frowning down at her figures. Yvonne was everyone's friend, except his. He had always felt tense around her. She always challenged what he said or how he said it.

He went over to Belinda. "Ever wonder why we lost the war in Vietnam if we can't even put this mother together?"

He cackled a laugh and hopped away.

The towering and complex organization of the big film made everyone's nerves jump.

"Jesus H. Christ, how long is this going to take? Can't you do a simple budget?" Fletcher screamed at Yvonne. His astounding and unexpected rage detonated in the crowded room, transfixing everyone except Mr. Chen, who kept smiling.

"You're lazy, Yvonne!" Fletcher accused her in the terrible silence. "You know what they say about directing—that it's all compromise, a patchwork of doing what you can, letting the rest go. Not for me! Not for me! Don't you know that by now? I get what I see in my head on the screen. Either you do that job or you're out!"

Yvonne stood in front of him and didn't move an inch. "Don't you ever talk to me that way again, Fletcher Avery, or I will walk." Her voice, usually in a middle to high range, had dipped into a lower register. Her cheeks were bright pink.

Under the shelf of his hair and forehead, Fletcher's dark eyes condemned her.

"What's it going to be, Fletch?" Yvonne demanded.

Fletcher laughed. "Ah, c'mon, Yvonne, you know me. I'm emotional." He wrapped an arm around her. A stirring went through the packed room like a breeze. "You're the best. I apologize." He hugged her.

A trail of light skittered through the picture window and dropped onto the floor beside the bed. Belinda coiled her body around Fletcher's and caressed his long curly hair. "Would you have fired Yvonne?" she asked.

"No. Oh, I don't know," he said in an exhausted voice. "Sometimes it's just too fucking much."

"I'm going to sleep in my own room tonight," she said.

"No, you aren't." He pulled her tightly against him. "I want you here. You make me feel good." He rubbed his wide mouth against hers and licked the inside of her cheek.

The telephone rang. Fletcher groaned. "Who died?" he muttered, reaching for the receiver. "Yeah, Avery. What? Gary?" he said. "Are you in Los Angeles? What's the—?" Gary was Martin's agent. Belinda sat up and turned on the light. "Is this some kind of fucking joke?" Fletcher roared in a voice of outrage and panic. "That son of a bitch!" He was climbing out of bed, dragging the telephone with him. "He can't do that!" The phone slid off the bed table and dropped onto the carpeted floor. Fletcher pulled it along as he strode right, then left, shouting. "That part was written for him! The whole fucking picture was created for him!"

Fletcher didn't hang up. He dropped the receiver and stood, naked, in the middle of the room. The agent's voice sputtered into the carpet. "Martin's left Singapore," Fletcher said in a dead voice. "Quitting the picture."

"Why?"

"The script no longer reflects what he first saw in it." His face, lit on one side by reflected lamps outside, was contorted into a pale, still mask.

"You'll get someone else," Belinda whispered.

"Sure! In a *week*?" He pulled a sheet off the bed and wrapped it around him like a shroud. "Martin *is* David and Don—every nuance of those men comes from him. I can't find another actor—I can't create a whole new character!" Ever since she'd joined "the whirl," Fletcher had been obsessed with the story and the characters, speaking of them like friends or enemies he'd known a long time.

After a protracted silence, he said, "Get Jerry and Buttons up here."

When they arrived, disheveled and anxious, Belinda went down to Yvonne's room and tapped at the door.

"Martin's quit," Belinda announced when Yvonne answered the door. She had a bathrobe on over a pair of slacks.

"There goes the budget." Yvonne opened the door wide. A goosenecked lamp on a table behind her spotlighted neat stacks of papers.

"You want to go upstairs? Buttons and Jerry are up there."

"The last thing I want is a midnight conference with Buttons. I'll wait till I'm called. They'll have to call L.A." She motioned for Belinda to come inside. "Fletch'll probably pull it out of the fire."

"Without Martin?"

"Sure. Don't be grim. The trick now is to get around the studio's casting. They might insist on someone who's dead wrong for the role—tilt the picture." She brightened even more. "But, hey, Fletch might get someone better than Marty!"

Belinda stared at the woman who was becoming a friend. "You're good for us," she said. "You're good for me. You always see the positive."

"It takes work, believe me. You ought to try it, scrape some of that hard edge off you."

"I can't get over this thing with Marty. Fletcher did it to himself—he kept changing the script."

Yvonne shut the door. "Yeah, we're our own worst enemies."

"It's another celluloid rocket with no passengers," Vail sighed. He, his former assistant, Neil Sheffield, and his new assistant, Sandra, were sitting in a plush Los Angeles screening room watching a highly promoted, twenty-first century cop flick.

Vail didn't feel well and he didn't want to review this movie with its thousands of special effects made at the cost of a zillion dollars which could have rebuilt Mexico City. He felt Neil's trim, gym-worked body stir in the seat next to him. Neil would like this film because he liked the director. Vail was fond of Neil though privately he called him "the chipmunk" because he looked inoffensive and trustworthy— "like a local news anchor." Vail called all local news anchors "chipmunks."

"Lordy, lordy," Vail said in the darkened theater, "it's mighty hard to believe in the importance of movies today, but mighty easy to see the disregard most filmmakers have for that importance." Neil made an agreeing sound. "Not going to find any ethical standards here."

Over the years, it had been Vail's habit to mutter or shout his immediate reactions to Neil, who'd taken them down in shorthand. But over Vail's objections, expressed only to Schurl and the network, Neil was going to be elevated to an airtime reviewer of "Teen Flicks," a two-minute segment on Vail's show. Vail still called all the creative shots, but he knew the show would change.

Vail's new assistant, Sandra, was smart and willing to please but she had not yet earned a nickname. Sandra was now taking down notes. From transcriptions of this raw material, Vail composed the narrative for his reviews.

"Where'd he get that disk thing?" Vail asked Neil.

"The silver dollar? Off the body of the hookerette."

"When, for God's sake?"

"Few minutes back, in the scene where the heavy metal marshal pries open the hookerette's mouth. The dollar's lying on her tongue."

Neil glanced at Vail. The film was well made but Vail was missing details of the action again. Maybe his boss wasn't paying attention because the picture was great commercial trash. Even so, Vail would watch it through closing credits; he never cheated. Neil made a note about the coin detail in the hookerette's mouth. He would add it to others he was collecting of what Vail missed.

Vail shivered in the warm room. More often now he couldn't see key action as clearly as he had a year ago. There was something really wrong with his vision, but he couldn't quite define how. Darkened screening rooms or theaters had turned into black holes. Driving at night was the worst: the streets turned into dark dangerous tunnels.

Out of nowhere, Sandra's arm came into Vail's line of vision. "Jesus," Vail said, "don't jump around like that!"

"I was just stretching," she said.

"Well, quit it," Vail said. He'd forgotten that she was even there. He faced front and watched the body of the hookerette being loaded into a van. Even though Sandra was sitting right next to him, he couldn't see her unless he faced her. That scared him.

Vail's office suite was a jumble of handsome, faintly literary rooms. *The Color of Money* and *Platoon* were being heavily promoted for their releases that year, and the outer office was crowded with movie junk that flowed from studio publicity and promotion departments as solid waste flowed out of New York: stand-up displays, one-sheets, magazines, releases, helmets from *Platoon*, a pool cue from *Money*.

Bookcases and film memorabilia were the major decor items in Vail's office, augmented with invitingly scattered antique chairs and sofas. The rooms said that the on-air critic at the top of the pole read books, appreciated geography and history, enjoyed a longer view than the last five years of hit films and an aesthetic more developed than California Modern.

Vail was a tough and uncompromising critic of movies and television. Some people said he was tough because he was cynical and disappointed in what was produced, but Schurl knew better: it was because Vail loved and respected film. Schurl called him the Alfred Katz of media—a critic of the visual who would comment on television, cable, film, and even music videos. Vail was not stuffy. He was animated and precise. His ratings were high; he delivered his criticism with energy and delight. "If the makers of this film could just take their hands out of the till long enough to let a single, justified, moving moment of truth live between the characters, the audience would have the yardstick it needs to see just how phony *Rocket Express* is."

Movie reviewing was sometimes an adjunct of the studios' publicity department. In his younger years, Vail had seen the danger of becoming a studio mouthpiece, not because he was so big at the time, but because television was so powerful. He maintained people watched him because he wasn't there "to put people into the theaters, but to make them consider what they are seeing."

Vail was sitting in his office at his Duncan Phyfe desk when Schurl came in. "It's settled. Neil starts the teen flick wrap-ups next month. He gets a researcher and a secretary."

"You know how I feel about that."

"Look at the upside. It'll expand the show's base."

"I am not in a long-running soap, Schurl. I'm a critic."

Schurl didn't want this conversation again today. He was off to Italy for a month's vacation where he hoped to see Sara Wyman. He had, in fact, chosen both time and place in order to "run into" her.

"Vail, guess we're a go!" Neil said, coming into the room. "Oh, hi, Schurl."

"Congratulations," Schurl said.

Vail pushed out of his chair, went around his desk, and offered Neil his hand too. "I don't want to catch you saying, 'gee whiz,' or 'rad' on my show."

"Thanks, Vail. I'll sure try to do myself and you and the show proud," Neil said, unctuously. "Oh, and Sandra said not to forget your appointment with your doctor at five o'clock."

"How could I forget? I hate doctors."

Dr. Steiner was lean, tall and quiet. His hands were cool and smelled of soap. He sat on a stool in front of Vail, who sprawled in a leather and metal examining chair. The room bristled with optical machinery.

"Mr. Wyman, you have a disease called retinitis pigmentosa," Steiner said.

"Sounds like a fancy name for pinkeye. What the hell is it?"

Steiner shifted slightly, assessing Vail Wyman's ability to absorb bad news. "You spoke of having difficulty seeing in the dimly lit theaters, and you say you've virtually given up driving at night."

"Night blindness," Vail said, "not enough vitamin A or something." He knew that what was coming wouldn't be good.

Dr. Steiner pressed on, his voice composed. "The first symptoms of retinitis pigmentosa are often associated with problems with darkness—but it's not night blindness, it's a narrowing of the field of vision." Dr. Steiner looked at the chart open on his knees. He spoke slowly. "You have lost most of your peripheral vision."

"Well, if that's as bad as it gets," Vail said, "I can live without peripheral views of life."

"Unfortunately, it will progress. Your vision will slowly narrow to a central island. And then it will close off."

Vail pressed his shoulders into the chair. The news terrified him. "Say again?"

"Retinitis pigmentosa narrows the field of vision, gradually."

"What do we do?"

"There's nothing we know of that stops the process."

"God, there must be something."

Steiner's smart, sad eyes apologized for the limitations of medical science.

"I'm going blind? I can't believe that."

"Yes." This was typical of people absorbing bad news: they denied it, wrestled with it, but later, most of them dealt with it.

"But I'm a film critic. Everything I do depends on my eyes. This can't be happening." Dr. Steiner met Vail's gaze steadily. "Does this process take years or months—I mean, how long do I have?"

"Each case is slightly different. You might have three to five years, possibly more."

Vail stared at the floor. "I can't take it in." Suddenly, he looked at his watch. "I have to go."

"I want you to make another appointment," Steiner said. He had long ago scrubbed his language of expressions like, "I will want to see you again," or "Be seeing you."

Vail shook hands with Steiner, took the appointment card from the receptionist, rode down in the elevator, crossed the lobby, went through the double glass doors and stood on the sidewalk on Beverly Drive. He had no memory of how he got out there. He took his left hand out of his pocket, raised it and slowly brought it around until he could see it. It was at about a forty-five degree angle from his body, halfway from his side to his face. He turned, facing east; he could not see the traffic six feet away at his side. He turned back. A red sports car was honking irritably at a gray Mercedes in a line of traffic backed up at the light. The early spring heat wave that was baking Los Angeles, hitting record levels, rode shimmering air currents off the cars. He could see the cars directly in front of him, but people around him, passing him on the sidewalk rose up suddenly like ships from a deep fog. He shut his eyes. Blind, he would not be able to find his way to the curb. He stood rock still. Where was pride, what was effort, motion, dreams, desire if he spent his last years in the dark? He thought of Patsy, of a certain tone of voice he'd heard from her occasionally, a mixture of pity and impatience. He thought of being no good to anyone blind, of losing her, of being alone in his darkness.

"Go home," he said to himself. "Go home."

Diana Wyman was sitting at her desk watching a blue jay hop from one foot to another in a tree at the end of the garden. She had just received a note from Belinda which described the filming in a village outside Melaka. Her granddaughter's tone of compressed excitement reminded her of Sky and her first shoot: "Mother, it's like flying in the air. I was frightened but I was meant to fly." Diana pressed her lips together, limiting pleasure and regret. Sky was always with her, but when she'd read the letter, Belinda became Sky, and Sky lived again. Diana had felt a fleeting rush of joy. But it was over now. The blue jay leaped into the air and soared through the heat.

"Mom."

"Darling Vail," she said, "I didn't expect you home this early. Is Patsy with you?"

He shook his head and sank into a flowery upholstered chair.

"What's the matter, dear?" Diana said.

"Nothing. Tired."

"I just got a letter from Belinda. She's really enjoying her work. Isn't that wonderful?"

Vail nodded. He felt dizzy with grief and fear. He felt that he was at an end where he could and would say anything and it wouldn't matter. He was in his fifties and he felt like a boy, longing for comfort. "Poor Lindy," he muttered.

"She's all right. This is a very good letter."

"I didn't mean that. I never got to know Lindy, she was always so wrapped up in you and Sky and her great grades—"

"She was a particularly brilliant student."

"A waste." Had he ever felt affection for Lindy? he wondered. Now they were joined through Eddie, a clandestine link.

"Nothing in life is ever a waste, Vail," Diana said.

Vail felt tears in his eyes. He removed his glasses and looked away toward the window, a bright hollow of light at the end of the room. "Schurl's going to see Sara in Italy while he's there," he said. "Great about Sara coming back to live for a while, don't you think?"

"If that's what she wants," Diana replied. "I disapprove of her taking Sky's house."

"Oh, Mom, let it go. Kitty wants to live in Hawaii and she didn't want to sell it. I'm glad Sara's coming home." Diana sniffed to show her disapproval of Kitty, Sky's longtime companion who had inherited the house in the Hollywood Hills when Sky died.

"It's a beautiful house and Sara will like it," Vail tried.

"It's a silly little house," Diana corrected him, "and I don't think it's a good idea for Sara to live in it. Like taking Sky's place, almost."

"You never understood Sara, Mom."

"Well! I certainly understand my own daughter, Vail."

"No, you don't. And I think that's very sad." He expected her to keep arguing but she turned away.

He thought of the year he and his sisters had been twenty-four—the blazing magazine covers, the overwhelming reviews of Sky's first film. Her fame had plunged the family into a vortex from which it had never escaped. "Sara had to live with comparisons all her life," he mumbled, hating his halfhearted way of disputing his mother.

"You were compared to her, too."

"Mother, I was a boy—it was different for me. I got the good fallout." He'd been welcomed everywhere. Women had slept with him just because he was Sky's brother. "It was hardest for Sara. It ruined years of her life."

Diana rose and pushed her shoulders back. "I have some tea over here," she said. "It will be like old times, dear. Remember when you and I used to have tea while the girls played in their room?"

He nodded and felt like sobbing. He raked his fingers roughly through his graying russet hair. "Fine." He looked around the room quickly, checking his peripheral vision. Diana handed him a cup of tea and a spoon. "God, sometimes I miss Sky so much," he said emotionally.

She reached out and stroked his hair. "I know, dear. You above all."

"The three of us were always together. We shared everything. And despite the rough times between Sara and Sky, despite all the separations later, you know, we always cared about each other; we never betrayed each other." His eyes filled with tears and he looked down at the cup shaking in his hand. "I'm proud of that," he murmured, believing, as he always had, that one reason they'd stuck together was to protect themselves against Diana's protracted interference in their lives. But in his deep unhappiness and his fear this afternoon, he felt he could even forgive his mother that. "A triplet relationship minus a triplet. The road's good but the vehicle's missing a wheel." He wanted to confess his terror of certain blindness. The hugeness of it pressed on him. Eddie would grow into a man but Vail would not see the changes, he would always look what? Eighteen, twenty? How old would Eddie be when Vail lost his sight?

He took a deep breath. "Where's Eddie?"

"Rehearsal for *Streetcar*," she said, returning to the small table and pouring another cup of tea. "He's so proud to be cast as Stanley Kowalski. Though I think the school could have picked a less salacious play—"

Vail cleared his throat. "I love Eddie."

"Edward, dear. He likes Edward."

"I couldn't love him more. I always wanted a son. God, I hope I've been a good father to him."

"Why, Vail, darling, you've been a handsome father to Edward. Why ever would you think not?"

"I was thinking of Lindy . . ."

"But you and Patsy are his legal adoptive parents." She stirred her tea. "I received some wonderful mail from that boarding school in France for boys his age, boys in the arts."

"Mom, I don't want to send Eddie to boarding school."

"It would broaden him, dear. Aren't you glad you traveled and learned languages?"

"It's not the same. He'd be all alone. We were the triplets; we always had each other." His mother was still standing, looking down at her cup. He imagined what it would be like to see only her handsome face and nothing else in the room. She would look like a cutout.

"I think you're making a dreadful mistake, Vail. The longer Edward's here, the more temptation is—well, put in dear Belinda's path."

Vail gulped his tea. "I don't want to fight about this. I'm not sending Eddie away."

"If you'd just take a minute—"

"Mother! Drop it."

"But, Vail—"

"Just once, stay out of it!" He shot to his feet, gripping his china cup. "Nothing will make me part with Eddie—not you and your damned fears, not Lindy and whatever she's up to. Never, never will I give him up! Do you understand?"

"I only meant that you haven't thought through what a long court battle might—"

He flung the empty cup at her. It missed and broke against the wall.

"Vail!" Diana cried out, one hand shooting to her face as though the cup had struck her.

"I can't remember one thing in this family for forty years that you've not interfered with—Sara's career, Sara's marriage, Sara's child, *my* marriage, *my* career, Sky's lovers, and now Eddie." His voice was hoarse. "You drove Sky away from you, hounding her. She wasn't a star as you like to believe at the end—she was a drunk trying to dry out and make good again. She was wretched. I look around at my life and I count my blessings that it isn't worse—because of you. I don't have a lot of courage but I showed a little when I married Patsy over your continuous objections—"

"I won't listen to this!" Diana shouted in a surprisingly strong voice.

"You interfered with Belinda's life before she was even born. How do you think she felt, sitting in that courtroom listening to her father—whom she barely knew—confess why he'd left Sara? Because you *bribed* him to leave—a straight business deal!"

"That man wasn't good enough for Sara; he was holding her back. She was putting him through college, working as a filing clerk—it turned my stomach—"

"It wasn't your right!"

"It was my right," Diana said, coldly. "Just—get out of my room. Get out now." She sat down stiffly, her back to him.

Vail cleared his throat. His face felt frozen. He could taste his bitterness but when he opened his mouth to speak, he said, "I'm sorry."

"It's too late for that. Leave me. Now."

He was furious at himself for not saying all that had been choking him for years. His legs felt like iron.

He was at the door when she said, "And when she takes him away from you, don't come to me."

"It takes balls to make a really bad film," Fletcher mumbled in a soft, defeated voice. In front of him, the actor who had replaced Martin was coming down a narrow forest path as if he were coming out of a shopping center.

"Okay, cut. Print," he said louder. "He just doesn't get it; he never will."

Martin's replacement grinned, lifted his shoulders to ask if the shot was okay, then getting a nod from Fletcher, he walked away from the giant vine-wrapped tree to the clearing beyond where his Winnebago shimmered in the damp heat. They were on the edge of the jungle, no more than twenty yards from a cart path leading back to the main road. "Let's wrap it for today. Back to town."

Bruno looked up. "We got another hour of light left." He'd

never known Fletcher to quit early, especially when they were ten days behind schedule.

"I've had it."

Instantly, everyone started moving equipment, talking into walkie-talkies, lighting cigarettes, yelling for gear, wrapping up.

They'd been shooting for four weeks. Everyone was tired, and many were demoralized. Fletcher couldn't help that; they'd all been on rough shoots before and this was certainly one of them.

"We just haven't recovered from Martin's defection," Belinda telephoned later to Yvonne, who was in Saigon preparing for the last week of shooting. The studio had virtually forced Fletcher to take Ben Carmody, a rising young star with one box office hit about nuclear subs to his credit. Carmody was charismatic but he was more at home looking good in a navy jet than in acting a demanding double role on a tough shoot. "Buttons calls Carmody 'the cartoon,' " Belinda said.

Yvonne yelped. "Buttons would."

"We all miss you," Belinda said. Yvonne had been away from the shoot for a week, and with her had gone the last bright spirit.

"How's Bruno's leg?"

"Not good. Day before yesterday that rattan bamboo bridge collapsed. All the gear went into the river. Bruno hung on to the broken end of it, just swinging there over the water— except for his leg. That was in the water. That scratch is a festering sore now. Doctor gave him some salve and is keeping him in a chair, but Bruno won't quit. I know he's in agony."

"Gee, sounds like the happy group I used to know. Give my love to Fletch and Jerry. Tell 'em everything's set at this end. Saigon welcomes them."

Belinda lowered her voice. "They're having some kind of running feud about Carmody. Buttons is mediating. He's really a great guy."

"Buttons's a sweetheart," Yvonne replied, sarcastic.

"Don't sell him short," Belinda said. "And this fight between Fletch and Jerry is serious."

"Nah," Yvonne said. "They'll make up after the shoot's over."

"They're not working well together. Everyone's suffering. Yesterday they spoke to each other only through Buttons."

"Aha! Buttons finally has some power."

"C'mon," Belinda said. "Why don't you and he make up?"

Yvonne chuckled. "You just want everyone to be in love like you are."

By the time the production moved to Saigon, Jerry and Fletcher were enemies. It came to a head after a day's shoot in killing heat twenty kilometers outside the city.

"This is the last time you do this to me!" Jerry was yelling. His face was beet red; sweat poured down his lean cheeks.

"Tell him," Fletcher shouted at Buttons, "that if he'd gone on the fucking recon here, he'd have a right to shout. But he didn't and he doesn't!"

"You've just thrown away a million dollars with this move! This place looks just like Melaka!"

"Tell him it looks *nothing* like Melaka except to a tasteless, dull bastard like him!"

"Tell him yourself!" Buttons screamed at Fletcher, losing it. "God, I'm sick of this shit!"

"You runty, good-for-nothing son of a bitch, you do as I say!" Fletcher roared back at Buttons.

"Fletcher!" Belinda exclaimed, shocked. She knew he loved Buttons.

Fletcher turned on her. "Stay out of this, bitch!"

"Don't speak to me like that!" she yelled.

Soon everyone was shouting at each other. "You're fired!" Fletcher roared at Buttons. "I never want to see your fucking face again! You're through!"

"You're a pig, Fletch," Belinda said.

"What a flash," he replied.

Buttons was striding away from the vehicles, away from the circle of equipment, down an overgrown path that led toward a scrubby forest a hundred yards away. Everything they'd worked on all day was in the opposite direction.

Fletcher spun around. "Stay out of my way, Jerry. I hate your guts."

Belinda looked after Buttons. He was trotting now, his shoulders hunched. "Buttons!" she cried. "Wait up!" She started to run when the sound detonated the heavy liquid air.

Buttons was lifted ten feet off the ground, his arms and legs flying out in a shower of earth and leaves. He rose, twisting, as the terrible sound reverberated, throwing her back, then he thudded into the ground. "Buttons!" she screamed, running headlong toward him.

"Belinda!" It was Fletcher. "Don't move!" The anguish and the fear in his voice stopped her, and she turned. Fletcher was charging toward her. Behind him, Jerry was physically holding back two grips and the sound man. Ahead, Buttons was screaming.

"Mines!" Fletcher yelled. "Don't move!"

Buttons's screams were like geysers, shooting out of him, arching in the air, falling, rising, continuous. He was twisting on the ground about twenty yards ahead of her. She drew a sight line between them, and walked.

"Be-lin-da!" Fletcher called, agonized. "Don't!"

"Stay away from me!" she shouted over Buttons's shrieks. But Fletcher was coming on. She ran, keeping the direct line she thought Buttons had walked in view. Now Jerry was yelling at her, "Stop moving!"

Fletcher caught at her arm. "Hold it."

"No," she said, twisting away from him.

He looked fierce, controlling his panic. "Stay behind me." He started walking the last yards to Buttons.

"Oh god," Belinda moaned, looking down at Buttons, feeling the tears rush into her eyes. Buttons's legs were blown off, and blood was seeping out beneath his belly.

"Gimme your belt," Fletcher said to her, taking off his own. "Okay, man, we got you. Doc's coming. Hang on." He was wrapping his own belt around one stump and pulling it tight. Belinda handed him hers.

Buttons looked at Fletcher with love. "Knew you'd come," he murmured.

"Yeah, man, always with you. Love you."

Buttons rolled his eyes toward Belinda. "Belinda, girl, whadda girl you are . . ."

Fletcher was tightening Belinda's belt around Buttons's left stump. His hands were shaking as he tried to unbutton Buttons's shirt. He ripped it open. "Shrapnel," he said, looking at the small wound oozing blood in Buttons's groin. "Medic!" Fletcher yelled without looking around. "Medic!" His voice was high and raw. Belinda took off her blouse. Fletcher stuffed it at the wound. "Press on that," he said. "Hold it tight." He leaned around her and felt for the beat of Buttons's jugular. "He's fainted."

Half an hour later, the set doctor and Fletcher had carried Buttons out of the field while Jerry radioed for a helicopter. In two hours, Buttons was on the operating table.

It was after midnight. In the hotel, Belinda was waiting for Fletcher. The room was sterile and cold and beige. People called asking for progress reports, and she had none. Yvonne was down at the hospital with Fletcher.

Belinda wet a washcloth with cold water and pressed it over her face. But behind her eyes, she saw Fletcher raging at Buttons that afternoon, callous, remote, intensely involved in some inner wave of power over others. She took the cloth away from her face and threw it in the washbowl. Fletcher's reckless disloyalty to Buttons ate away at her own small measure of trust. She raised her arms, dropped them, dried her face, went into the other room.

She was standing at the window, looking out on the bright street below. She felt dizzy and moved around the room, opened a drawer in the nightstand. Inside, sheets of folded stationery were neatly banked against each other. She took one out, sat down at the table.

Dear Eddie, A ghastly day of excess and accident. People go out of control and regret it the rest of their lives. It isn't that they mean to do it; they allow it and have bad luck. The mine is there, the gun is loaded. Fletcher will never recover; something in him died today. I've been there, I know.

She saw Archie staring at her from the floor, his hand on his bloody throat . . . She heard Princess calling for her from the latrine, a high wail . . . "Lindy, save me from sin, save me, save me. . . ." Belinda had not moved to aid her. *Sometimes, all you can do is hang on, laughing, for the next one,* she wrote.

Would Buttons live? She looked down at the letter. Soon *Force Field* would be finished. But the film was a ship breaking up in a rough sea. Everything would change. Everything had

already changed. Everyone would pack up and go back to the
States. Would she go back to her apartment? Would she turn
back into Fletcher's secretary? No, she knew she wouldn't.
What picture would Fletcher do next? How long would they be
in Los Angeles? She didn't have to go with Fletcher wherever
he went. But she wanted to. *Even in love . . .* she wrote. Shit,
she thought. I don't know what love is. Eddie, you're better
off without me. But she wanted to see Eddie. She wanted
Fletcher to be with her. She wanted to go home. She tore up
the letter.

The door to the room opened.

"He'll make it," Fletcher said. "Without his legs." He
slammed the door and sat down heavily. "Yvonne's staying
at the hospital in case Buttons wakes up tonight. He'll be
flown back home in a couple of days. It's a miracle he's
alive, a bloody miracle."

"I know." She heard again the need and the panic in Fletcher's voice as he'd shouted at her over Buttons's screams. She
sat down on his lap and curled against him. "You love Buttons.
You feel deeply. You love me."

"No, I don't. I use people up. I injure them. I can't help
myself."

"And I love you."

He sighed. "Don't." He pressed his face into the crown of
her head, into her hair. He wrapped both arms around her. His
chest heaved. Belinda ran her hand over his unshaven cheek
and brushed his tears away.

CHAPTER 9

It was as though a great battle had been hard fought, and lost. With a send-off attended by the entire company, Buttons was put on a plane for Los Angeles. After that, the last days of the shoot were monotonous, somber; the production submerged into itself. And then it was over. People dispersed. The ship broke up.

Fletcher refused to edit the picture in Los Angeles. He and Belinda decamped to Sydney, Australia. He stopped talking about producing his own picture and, while editing, began to rework a project set in New Zealand that he and Jerry had been developing together for the last three years.

But Belinda knew that neither the beauty of the Great Barrier Reef nor the adventure of the Outback drew him there: Fletcher needed distance from a recuperating Buttons, from his own guilt.

Then, in February of 1987, with the edit of *Force Field* still unfinished, Jerry broke up the partnership. It was this event that brought Fletcher and Belinda back to Los Angeles.

Fletcher hated hospitals. People went there to die. That hospitals were also places where people were made well again did not move him from this conviction.

"I can only take five minutes of this," he said to Belinda as they stood outside Buttons's door.

"We simply cannot be in L.A. and *not* see him," Belinda said crossly. "He's not suing you; he's been an ace."

"If I land in a hospital," he groused, "just order the casket because I'll be dead before it arrives."

"Get yourself together," Belinda said. She pushed open the door.

"Buttons!" Fletcher called out boisterously, striding into the room with a big grin on his face. "How're ya doin'?"

"Fletch, good to see you. Belinda!" Buttons was sitting on his bed under a coverlet. His legs ended at his knees.

Belinda went over to him and gave him a quick hug and a kiss. "You look wonderful," she said. He looked pale and five years older.

"I am wonderful," Buttons replied. "Sit down there and tell me the news."

Fletcher clapped Buttons on the shoulder and sat down in a chair. "Film's going to be okay," he said. "We're editing in Australia. I can't stand this town." He leaned forward, clasping his hands tightly in front of him, staring intently into Buttons's wan face. "Listen, pal, let's bottom line this. I want you to be okay, I want you to have everything you need and deserve and I've told the studio that. I'll go right to the wall for you."

Startled, Buttons glanced at Belinda. She nodded. "Fletch, I don't blame you or anyone. It was an accident. My lawyer would kill me for saying this, but I know you, and I know you mean it. We want—"

"A generous settlement and I'm right behind you, buddy," Fletcher interrupted. "That field was supposed to be swept for mines before we got there."

"I don't want Yvonne to be creamed because of it, Fletch."

"Well, it was one of her people," Fletch said.

"But Yvonne wasn't to blame, Fletch!" Belinda said.

Buttons reached up, grabbed a bar above his bed, and hoisted his body to a higher sitting position. "Fletcher, this is between you and me, right?" Fletcher nodded vigorously. "I will not spend my life blaming and punishing and suing people. I've had a lot of time to think about it. Now you work your end and I'll work my end and maybe we can get the insurance guys and the studio to do the right thing."

"Ha! Those cocksuckers'll penny ante us down till we're old," Fletcher said.

"Think positive," Buttons said. "Belinda, why are you both back here?"

Fletcher slapped the air. Belinda said, "A problem with Jerry over the New Zealand project. We came to get it straightened out with Patsy." Her glance settled on a stack of scripts. "What're those, Buttons?"

"Friends sent them, agents sent them," he declared. "I look

at that stack, and I do my exercises, and I know that someday I can direct from a wheelchair. And that's what keeps me going."

"Atta boy," Fletcher said, uncomfortable. "Way to go."

After they left, Buttons let his shortened body slide down in the bed. He could feel the tears working at the back of his eyes. He snatched a book from the shelf beside him and opened it violently. He looked at the print, couldn't take it in. He slammed the book shut. With a cry, he threw it across the room.

Outside the hospital, the sky was low and gray, the air warm. In the car, Fletcher leaned his head against the steering wheel. "Poor son of a bitch," he mumbled. "Sitting there with no legs and acting like he's gonna be a fuckin' director. Breaks my heart."

Belinda said, "He's inspiring. He can teach all of us."

Fletcher's head snapped up. He started the car. "Then you're as big a fool as he is. He isn't going anywhere." He gunned the car, careened around the parking lot, threw a ten dollar bill and the parking stub at the attendant, and sped away.

"Fletcher, slow down and calm down. We won't be working on anything if we're both dead."

He slowed down. "Yeah. You're a peach." He put his big square hand in her hair and tugged gently.

In another part of Los Angeles, Sara Wyman shut a wrought-iron gate and started up a set of narrow, granite steps. Above her, Sky's small turreted house looked unchanged from the day in 1975 when Sara had last seen her sister. Diana had declared it was "morbid" of Sara to be living in Sky's old house, but Sara felt she was at last making her peace with Sky by repainting the interior, bringing in a carpenter, replacing cracked tiles, letting in the sun. By living there.

The peace was broken by the anonymous letter that now arrived via her agent in London.

You're her mother! You're responsible for making her! She's an agent of evil and I will set it right. She will not escape me. She's robbed and she's saved and she can't have it both ways. No one can. I won't let her. All of the guilty are discovered and I will bring her to final justice. She isn't worth anything. I am the avenger and she won't escape. She ruins everything she touches, don't you know that? Watch her. You'll see . . .

The tone of it was scary, but it had made Sara strangely sad, too. Beneath the bravura threats, the cry of rage and pain, there was also a cry for help. And parts of the letter didn't make sense, like "she's robbed and she's saved and she can't have it both ways." What the hell did that mean? And, would she ever know who wrote these letters? She doubted it. The police, the investigators had not produced any answers.

Sara looked up at the house to take her mind off the letter. It was tucked into the Hollywood Hills, far up Beechwood Drive, on a forested hill of scrub oak and eucalyptus. At night, great horned owls hooted and coyotes slinked through the trees. At dawn, she could see deer trotting down the road. About three hundred yards north lay the reservoir. Residents dubbed it "Lake Hollywood."

Edward was sitting on the grass in front of the house.

"What a surprise," Sara said.

"Yeah, well, I thought it was time I came over. Guess you've been here a while. And I was curious, I admit to curiosity." Eddie was in high fashion Nikes that resembled shoes best suited for space, a ragged pair of jeans cut off above the knees, a T-shirt, a jacket, and a gold stud in his right ear.

"Curious about the house?" Sara asked, unlocking the door.

"And Sky—and you, too," he said, as they stepped inside. He looked up at a circular window on the landing of the staircase above him. "Wow, great window. So this was Sky's house. When was it built?"

"Nineteen twenties. Sky bought it in 1959. Diana was really put out."

"Why?"

"Oh, because Sky was known all over the world but she chose a home that isolated her."

"Not prestigious enough," Eddie said. "So, this isn't where you all grew up?"

"No. Only—your mother. Vail and Sky and I grew up in San Francisco."

Sara waited for a question about Belinda but Eddie only

said, "Oh, yeah, I forgot," and he made an impatient gesture.

"I hope you'll come and visit often." She gave him a big hug, then led him deeper into the house. The rooms were airy and bright, and smelled slightly of new paint. "We can sit out here," she said, stepping onto a flagged terrace that overlooked the "lake." She sat down in a chaise. "You've grown a lot."

He straightened immediately and smiled. "Almost fifteen now."

He was taller than Vail, more like Vic's height, Sara thought, pleased for Vic. Slender like him too, with the start of a handsome face that might be angular in his twenties. Patsy had told her Eddie was a popular boy in high school. But he was also impetuous and had a chip on his shoulder; he took offense easily and was involved constantly in minor scrapes. "But drug free, Sara!" Patsy had declared.

Eddie looked around, cementing images. "We finally got Dad to hire a driver. I dunno why he suddenly agreed. He did a one-eighty."

"About time." She was trying to figure out what was different about Eddie. He'd always been an easygoing, generous child. Now he seemed distracted—even nervous. "And Diana—she okay?"

"Oh, yeah, Grandma's rad. 'Cept she's really mad at Vail about something." He drew himself up stiffly and peered at Sara down his nose, "doing" Diana. Sara laughed out loud. It wasn't hard to get reactions out of Sara, but they were gratifying because they were instantaneous and big. He knew Sara was his grandmother, the mother of his real mother who'd died, but Sara had always seemed like a dramatic aunt, flying in from Europe for Christmas or for a screening of one of her films. "I saw that film, *Winter Wheat*, that you made with Sky," he said suddenly. "Playing at the Vista down in Hollywood. Dynamite."

"Thanks, Edward. And I hear you played Stanley Kowalski at school."

He grinned. Sara fascinated him, the flamboyant, brassy-haired triplet who swore and smoked and drank red wine for lunch, who'd lived in Portofino and Rome and directed small, noncommercial movies. "Why did you move back from Europe?" he asked.

"Too many memories."

He liked that in Sara—she answered directly. "You mean your husband who died?"

"Yes. I spent a year trying to control my grief about Reed, but it was really controlling me. It was time to come back. I lived over there since 1965, Edward."

"Vail said you were in some—films back then. Acting."

She nodded. "He probably said 'racy.' They weren't very good. Sky was so famous, I didn't know what to do with myself. People got close to me because I was Sky's sister, not for any quality in me. Or, so I thought. What's up with you? Something I can help with?"

"Nah, I'm okay. Hey! You know that Belinda Oliver? She's been writing me from Malaysia and Hong Kong and Australia—she actually works with Fletcher Avery."

"What's she write?" Sara had never received a letter from Belinda.

"Sort of travelogue letters, and stuff about the production shoot, scoping out the problems, real immediate stuff. Mom's giving this party and Fletcher Avery's going to be there," he said, respectfully.

"Avery's been a client of your mom's for a long time."

"I guess, but Mom doesn't talk about it."

Sara was thinking of Lindy's letters to Eddie; a terrible thought was taking root in her. "Do you have one of Belinda's letters on you?" she asked.

"No. Why?"

"No reason. You like Fletcher's work?"

"The best. You remember *Alms for Oblivion*?" She nodded. "When that came out I guess Vail and me were the only ones who liked that movie. There's this real corn dog at school, writes the newspaper. He did an analysis of *Alms*, and I did a rebuttal. I mean, no one liked that movie and now look—it's a real classic."

"Yup," she said, "some movies build slow." Sara noticed how well he concealed his missing hand; he did everything with his right, keeping the other arm by his side, or clasping his left wrist with his right hand in front of him.

"It's too bad about the accident on his new picture, the guy who was blown up." He made an explosion gesture with his hand.

"Shoots can be dangerous, but that accident was an old land

mine from the war." She tapped his arm. "You're not wearing your artificial hand."

"No. I don't want to. When I have it on, I feel like I'm missing a hand. But when I'm not wearing it, I feel natural— I don't feel like I'm missing anything."

"I never thought of it that way," she said.

"The whole thing makes me cross with my body. I don't want to wear anything, Aunt Sara." He looked at Lake Hollywood.

"Then don't."

When he spoke again his tone had changed completely. "I wish I had two hands."

She put her arm around his shoulders. "I know you do, but it's what's in your head and your heart that counts, not whether you have two hands or two feet."

"Mom and Dad say I don't have to wear it, but I think they really want me to. Dad's been talking about the implants now where the wires or whatever are put into your shoulder and the hand moves when you want it to. But it doesn't look like a real hand."

"Then tell them you don't want to wear anything and tell them why. They'll see it your way." She hugged him again. "I'm so glad you came to see me. Want a sandwich or a soda?"

They went into the kitchen, where she built two big juicy sandwiches of prosciutto and cheese and tomatoes. Then they went back outside to the terrace and talked movies for an hour. She found his opinions knowledgeable, young, and quirky.

"Y'know, I get this dream sometimes," he said, balling up his napkin. "Had it again last night and I think you're in it. Is that weird or what?"

Sara lowered her eyelids. "Edward, I *have* known you since you were born."

"Yeah, well, in this dream—you want to hear it?"

"Sure."

"The room's absolutely bare, painted white. There's a cot or a twin bed in it—no headboard or anything. And, you know how big things look when you're little? I'm hanging onto the leg of this bed and I can just see over the top of the coverlet. I'm looking into a woman's face who's squatting down to talk with me. But I can never remember when I wake up what she looks like." He lowered his voice. "Sometimes I tell myself that the woman without a face is my mom. Suddenly, something happens to her. She jumps up, and I don't know where she goes, but I can hear her crying, and a minute later, the door flies open and men in creased trousers come in, sorta milling about, and when I look up, someone like you with your color hair kneels down in front of me at my eye level, and she shakes my hand. Then suddenly, someone picks me up—I just fly up off the ground—and you sorta rise up with me, but you aren't holding me—someone behind me is but I can't see who—and then we're going through all these green hallways and I hear these steps echoing like marching, and way down the hall I hear some woman screaming—wailing, really. And I wake up."

Sara looked up into a spidery eucalyptus tree. Vail had been one of the men in the suits. From a toddler's point of view, Eddie was describing the visit she and Vail had made with Eddie to the prison school in Ventura to see Belinda. Patsy and Vail had taken him out to see her nearly every month. But this time, Belinda had started to cry, and then she'd screamed, "I don't want to see him again! Take him out!" Just as abruptly, she'd had a change of heart and had wept to have him back. But by then, one of the staff had intervened. Belinda's appeals had been heard all over the building.

"I'm curious," Edward said. "I mean, about my mother and what happened."

Sara was desperately torn. "I think you should talk to Patsy and Vail about that," Sara said.

"What kind of a person was she? I mean, I wanted to ask you—" He looked down at his hand curled around his other wrist. "It's been bothering me." He was gearing himself up and she could feel his effort. "Would she have given me up because of this?" he said suddenly, lifting his stump.

"Oh, no, Eddie! Your mother once said that she loved you more because of your hand."

"She did?" he asked, doubtfully.

"Yes. God's truth." Sara was nothing if not convincing with the truth on her side.

"So what kind of a person was she?"

"Very smart. A brain." If he asks me how she died, Sara thought, I'll tell him everything.

"*Was* she?" he said, pleased. "And beautiful, like Sky? And you?" he added, hastily.

"Yes, but more like Sky than me. There are some pictures of her somewhere."

"Yeah, I saw some of her as a child, and one in high school, but Mom said she didn't like her picture taken."

"That's true. She looked like her father, too. You remember Vic?"

"Sort of. Not real clear. Had a real rugged face."

"I saw Vic a couple of months ago, just before I left Europe. He's taken a place in Westwood, and he's working on a new book. I know he'd like to see you."

"Yeah, maybe."

"He's your real grandfather, you know." Sara had met Victor at a coffee shop in London's Waterloo railway station as she was leaving for the States. As usual, he'd been handsomely turned out in all the superficial ways, but the need in his voice had moved her. "Vail won't let me see him, Sara. Can't you help me? Isn't there anything I can do?" She was sure he was in Los Angeles for Eddie as much as for his work.

"How'd you feel about getting to know him?" Sara asked Edward. "I could have both of you over for dinner."

"Okay by me, but Dad and Mom are antsy about it, and Grandma doesn't like him. She calls his novels, 'cheap.' "

Sara laughed. "Grandma only reads Jane Austen or the opinion columns in the *New York Times*, Eddie. But if you want to get to know him, I'll help," she said, realizing as she spoke that her words weren't just for Vic but for herself, too.

"I dunno, Sara. Might upset Mom and Dad." His sunny face had closed. He rose. "Have to go," he said.

After he left, Sara lay back on the chaise on the terrace and closed her eyes. It's beginning, she thought. Soon there'd come a time when Eddie would ask all the questions, and he wouldn't let go until he had all the answers.

Down the hillside a neighbor's big dumb shepherd dog was barking, his signal to the region that he had seen a squirrel. Sara opened her eyes. Thank god Edward didn't look like Archie. The first time Sara had seen Archie, he'd been standing in this very house on Vail's wedding day—a tall, broad man with thick blond hair and a bushy blond mustache. She'd stepped close to shake his hand. His mustache had arched over his full and sensuous mouth, framing it. She'd felt a current buried in him, a seductive instability held tightly in check. But his mouth belonged to a man who bolted into pleasures. Archie had been a psychiatrist; he'd been a man who'd loved music. Everyone in the family had admired him except Vail and herself.

The shepherd stopped barking. Sara was certain that Archie had been Lindy's first love; first loves were always so risky. She leaned back in the chaise, thinking about her first love, Victor, the man who'd had no chance to be a father, who now wanted to be allowed to be a grandfather.

She put her hand in her pocket for a cigarette and felt the anonymous letter. She didn't want to touch it. She took her hand away. Even though it was full of hate for Belinda, using Sara only as an intermediary, a monstrous suspicion was forming: what if Belinda was the writer? Sara pressed one hand to her head. Could her daughter be on a self-destructive course so well screened that she, Belinda, was not fully aware of it? Could her daughter be, in fact, crazy?

Patsy Wyman's office decor balanced nicely between femininity and business: the furniture and walls were a dignified gray, but that color was tempered by the sprightly American folk art that she collected, bright cushions and a ruby-red Bukhara rug.

Her twenty-second-floor office was in Century City, a westside section of Los Angeles, that had once been the back lot of Twentieth Century Fox. Patsy was staring out the window, imagining the ghosts of Darryl Zanuck and William Fox striding along the shopping malls below the towering high rises.

She didn't want to look at Fletcher. He was sprawled on the sofa behind her. "That goddamned Jerry! Who needs him?"

Patsy left Fox and Zanuck to their devices and finally turned around. Fletcher's combative face looked young and tired. "I know you feel betrayed," she said.

"I spent years working on that New Zealand film project with Jerry," he said in a soft, outraged voice. "How could he give it to Ray to direct?"

"The Buttons incident," Patsy said. Until the notoriety of the accident subsided, until the final depositions and payments were settled, it would loom over Fletcher's professional and emotional life. And what affected Fletcher, affected her.

"It'll work out with Buttons," Fletcher said. "We see eye to eye."

Patsy sighed. "Eventually it will work out, I agree. You're generous by nature, Fletch, and everyone has been rather civilized, for a change. But right now, it's a thing in the road."

Fletcher picked up a book, stared at it, hefted it. "I feel guilty. I shoulda protected Buttons." He slapped the book down and pushed to his feet. "Listen, Patsy, I'll produce my own stuff. You set it up. I'll be hot again."

"Fletch, sit down and listen. There are repercussions from Buttons's accident. They are financial, professional, and emotional. They'll affect your career for a while. Let's not go off half-cocked."

"Producing my own stuff is going off half-cocked?"

"Not in the larger sense, but right now it is. Just finish the edit and follow up with another solid picture for the studio with a good producer."

"Every director in this town is producing his own stuff. They're all ministudios. They got platoons of people attached to them."

"Not every director in this town owns his own stuff, and none of them have just come off a shoot five mil over budget, six months late where the AD got blown up."

Fletcher flung himself down on the sofa. "My life used to be simple. I picked a film, I directed it, it was a hit."

Patsy suppressed an irritated remark. Fletcher seemed younger than Eddie.

"I don't want to horse shit around with producers any more!"

Patsy advanced, her hands on her hips. "It won't do you any good if you try to mount a film and you can't even make a deal. You want that all over the street? C'mon now, let me handle this, set you up with a great producer."

Fletcher was shaking his head.

"For god's sake, at least think about it."

He headed for the door. "No. It's time for me to get out from under."

Upstairs, in her rooms, Diana was pinning up her hair but it made her arms tired. The afflictions of age irritated her; she lost patience, and her mouth felt tighter. Tight mouths were unattractive. She shook her head, relaxed her mouth, and made another assault on her hair.

There was a soft knock at the door. "Mother," Vail said. Slowly, Diana walked to the door and opened it. Her son was dressed in slacks, sports shirt, and a baseball cap. "Mother, please come down to the party."

"I'd rather not, Vail," she said, coolly. She held the door partly open, but did not invite him inside.

"Belinda will be expecting you," he tried as a last resort.

"If she wants to see me, she'll come up here."

"Mother, this—problem—between us. Can't we let it go?"

"I just don't feel up to a party, Vail."

"What do you want me to do, beg you to come down?"

"Certainly not."

"I've apologized; I don't know what else to do."

Her son's hurtful remarks still burned her. "I don't know why you were so hateful to me over Eddie and his schooling. I was only trying to be of some use."

"It wasn't over Eddie, Mother, it was over a lot of things."

"I don't think I'll ever forget it," she finally said, but his abjectness touched her. "I shall try to move past it."

"Good, Mother. That's all I ask."

The doorbell was ringing. Vail started down the stairs, muttering about mothers.

Belinda and Fletcher stood in the hallway. When Vail heard that they were a couple, he'd been elated. He was willing to pay for their wedding if it would divert Belinda from Eddie.

Vail hugged his niece briefly. "This guy must agree with you," he said. She seemed less combative. "Howya doin', Fletch?" They shook hands fiercely.

Eddie was standing in the archway between the hall and the living room, his arms folded across his chest, his blond hair combed out in a tangled, loosely curled, shoulder-length rock-star style.

"Edward!" Belinda said, delighted. "Fletcher, this is a big fan of yours."

Fletcher put a lot of shoulder into his handshake with Edward. "What's happening?"

"I thought *Alms* was a great film," Edward said.

"Thanks, pardner," Fletcher said, clapping him on the back.

Sara came out of the living room, her shoulders back, a smile lifting her eyes, her red-brass hair done up on top of her head.

"Sara Wyman," Fletcher said. "A pleasure to meet you. I saw *Solazzo* when I was in college. Was that the first film you directed?"

"Yes," Sara said, pleased, shaking his hand.

"It caused quite a stir. I don't think anyone knew what the damned thing was about." Fletcher laughed hugely.

"You're really getting tall, Edward," Belinda was saying. His face was thinning out. In only a few years, he'd be a man.

"Thanks for your letters," he said. "You draw really well."

"This the kid you hauled that thing all the way from Malaysia for?"

"Yes. It's outside, Eddie," Belinda said.

Sitting on the backseat of Fletcher's open, top-down convertible was a huge, elaborate bird kite, four feet wide and as many long. Covered by tiny designs cut out of translucent paper—red, brown, and black—it had a sharp nose like a plane and a wide tail like a bird. Silvery tassels hung from the tips of its outstretched wings.

"That's beautiful, Belinda," Sara said.

"What's this?" Edward asked, pointing at the long protruding wood pieces at the neck.

"Makes it hum when it flies," Belinda said. "Sounds weird. But good." Conversation seemed easier with Edward now, but Belinda was conscious of her mother's eyes on them. "Think you can get it off the ground? It's a real skill."

"Sure!"

"I took lessons, just in case you run into trouble," Belinda said. "Kite flying's a great sport in Malaysia. Competition is fierce."

"Who wins? I mean, what are the rules?" Edward said, examining the triangular tail.

"Whoever flies highest. Like life."

"Sensational," Edward said.

Fletcher wanted to show Edward how to fly it right away.

"Belinda's going to show me," Edward replied.

Fletcher gave way, laughing heartily. "But girls always get their lines twisted up. It's a man's sport."

Belinda scowled.

"I'll wait for Belinda," Eddie said. Holding it with his good hand under its belly, and using his stump as a support, he hefted it out of the convertible. Fletcher saw his missing hand for the first time.

"Yeah, guess I'll never be a film editor," Edward shot back defensively, irritated at the pity on his idol's face.

Fletcher laughed at Eddie's aggressive defense. He thumped him on the shoulder. "You can do better than that, kid. Be a director!"

Eddie laughed, won over again.

Patsy was in the back garden. Fletcher greeted her hugely, taking center stage, his high male energy by turns adorable and wicked. "Patsy," he said, "let's you and me make up and take off for the Bahamas." He hugged her around her waist and kissed her cheek. "Kid," he shouted to Edward, "your mom has saved my ass regularly." He swung Patsy into a savage tango; he was band, soloist, audience, and dance director all at once. The thing about Fletch was that he was crazy, but acceptably so, Belinda thought. He made her less suspicious of her own sanity. He made her feel normal. Bizarre behavior was in.

Fletcher wore down and deposited Patsy near Belinda at the picnic table. "Pat, you gotta forgive me, but I have to leave early, okay?"

"We'll all need a rest by then," she said, pouring glasses of wine from a pitcher. She handed one to Fletcher, watched him drink half of it at a gulp. He wandered off toward Eddie and the kite.

"Are you talking about marriage?" Patsy asked Belinda.

"Oh, I don't know."

"Of course, it's not too late—"

"For another child?" Belinda interrupted, laughing. "Is that what you want?"

"I want you to be happy," Patsy said. "When you get to know me, you'll see that's true."

"Sorry, Patsy. I'm suspicious by nature."

Patsy offered her a glass of wine. "When I first heard about you and Fletcher, I was happy for you but I was anxious, too— Fletcher's track record is strewn with discarded bodies." Patsy wondered how Belinda would react to a dramatic rejection.

"Be careful. He can be selfish and callous."

"Patsy." Belinda laughed. "I've had plenty of practice."

Patsy was taken aback. "Lindy, I've known you for many years. We're part of the same family. Why wouldn't I care about you?"

"Eddie."

"I won't compete over Eddie, Lindy." Her warm blue green eyes looked cold. She lowered her voice, and though no one was near them, she pulled Belinda to the side of the table. "You're not in an institution anymore; you don't have to cover your back or pick powerful people to protect you or curry favors. I made it my business to know what happened to you in those institutions. Do you think none of us cared? Do you think we just went along with our lives and never gave you a thought? Your mother told me that when you were sent away her life just ended. How do you think you got transferred from the state hospital into that private hospital? Sara and Victor bribed the hospital administrator to allow it, that's how."

Belinda looked astonished and skeptical.

"Sara's never going to tell you and I can't imagine that Victor would offer it. But Vic knew what to do for you in there, didn't he? The cigarettes and everything? He was the one who bribed one of the psych-techs to look out for you a little."

Belinda flashed on the psych-tech who'd had a slightly friendlier attitude. "I didn't know. I felt so cut off from everything."

"You don't have to be at war with the world out here. It *is* a war, of course, in its way, and you're tougher than most," Patsy said. "But you might think of how helpless we felt on the outside, wanting to make it better, utterly unable to do anything much. . . . So just don't give me any lip about Eddie and competition. If you've changed your mind and want to suddenly raise him, I'll make that mighty hard for you."

"No, Patsy, I haven't changed my mind."

"I thought you might have, all those letters," Patsy said to the bank of wineglasses.

"I just had to stay in touch. I guess I thought that if he got to know me a little, well, if he ever learned who I was, he wouldn't hate me so much."

"You mean the way you hate Sara?"

"I don't hate her. But I don't care about her either." She looked at Sara, standing across the yard, smoking a cigarette. The smoke trailed up and around the wide brim of her sun hat. "But I'm grateful if she got me out of that nuthouse."

Fletcher was watching Belinda talking with Patsy, her peppy little body moving with her words, then stilling, to listen. Suddenly, she was starting toward him. He imagined her legs under her slacks, the downy hair on her arms, her indented ankle, the slight curve of her nose, her mysterious eyes, so hot, so cool. He felt his jeans tighten at the crotch. He imagined himself burying his head in her open belly, gnawing on her delicious guts. He reduced her to the size of a doll, bagged her, carried her off. He laughed. He wasn't tired of her. Nothing ever seemed to shock her. She could say things to him that would take the top of his head off but only when he was naughty. Belinda never seemed scared; she never pulled punches. He wrapped a big arm around her waist and squeezed hard. "Let's get out of here," he whispered. But she shook her head.

Later, Diana appeared as Belinda and Eddie were straightening the lines of the kite.

"How beautiful," she said. "Whatever made you think of something so wonderful, Belinda?"

"I don't know what came over me," Belinda muttered, smiling at Eddie. Patsy and Vail made a fuss over Diana's arrival and introduced her to Fletcher, who kissed Diana's hand. "I am always thrilled to meet matriarchs," he said, staring into her eyes.

"Indeed?" Diana replied. "And why is that?"

"Such quiet power," he said, letting go of her hand.

"Looks prehistoric," Keith Llewellyn called out, seeing the kite. He was coming into the garden with a striking blond woman.

"Oh, there's that nice writer," Diana said.

"Pterodactyl," Keith said, coming up to them. His hair was ruffled, one knee of his jeans was torn. The blond was also in jeans. Her gestures were expansive and she seemed to know everyone.

"Eddie," Vail said, "you remember Keith Llewellyn."

"Hiya," Eddie said, glancing up from the bird kite. "Pterodactyl, huh?"

Keith nodded solemnly. "Direct descendant. Where'd you get it?"

"From Belinda."

Keith looked around. "Hello." He shook her hand. "Fletcher, how's it going?"

Fletcher said, "I'm still cutting the Malaysia shoot." He slapped Keith on the shoulder and eyed his beautiful companion.

"Sorry to hear about that accident with the cameraman," Keith said.

"Assistant director."

"Right. A real tragedy." Llewellyn didn't toss off the word; he said it with empathy and understanding.

"You wanna fly the kite, Keith?" Edward asked him.

"Hey, how about me?" Fletcher demanded happily. "I helped get the bloody thing over here."

"Belinda's first," Edward amended quickly.

Vail was standing before the smoking barbecue. A stack of raw hot dogs and hamburger patties sat on a tray beside him.

"Grill 'em," a voice said from one side. Vail swiveled around to face Keith Llewellyn. "They won't cook unless you put them on the fire, pal."

"Patsy does all the grilling around here. Smoke gets in my eyes and I can't see a thing. Have a beer. I'm glad you came. You and your gorgeous friend. Is she an actress?" He turned his head to see Keith's rugged face and some of his normal irritation fell away. Keith was so decent, the kind of guy you'd want on your right going into battle.

"Singer and dancer," Keith said of his blond date. "I hear Fletch is going out on his own," Keith said. "I'm having my agent send over a script of mine."

"Ah, Keith, Avery deals in broad strokes. Your stuff's more subtle. He'd miss the point."

"He might not."

"I wish you luck." Vail screwed his face up, intensely ambivalent about Fletcher. But it would solve everything if

Belinda would marry him and settle down and have another child. "God, he's a difficult man."

Keith laughed, a warm tumbling sound in his chest. "Yeah, that's Avery all over. How's Belinda?"

"Belinda should settle down."

"I don't think you do that with Fletcher," Keith said.

Edward was being persistent. "Let's fly it now."

"Oh, not here," Belinda said. "There's not enough room."

"C'mon, let's try," Eddie urged her.

Shit, Belinda thought, I hope I can do this. Nervously, she took up the towline. "Gotta be careful here," she said to Eddie. "Trees over there." She judged the wind was blowing away from the huge jacaranda tree and decided to risk it, giving the kite a boost from one end of the big yard to the other, gradually playing out the towline to give it enough lift.

Suddenly it was up, slipping into the sky, framing the sun, flying and floating. "What wonderful freedom," Belinda said, watching it.

Sara had been watching Belinda, waiting for a moment to speak to her daughter about Eddie.

"What's the matter with you?" Diana asked Sara. "Quit fidgeting." Diana was sitting in a chair under an umbrella, her feet propped on a stool, a visor cap on top of her white hair.

"We're all making a terrible mistake with this charade," Sara said to her.

"I'm sure I don't know what you mean, Sara Bay."

Her mother's dark round sunglasses gave her face the look of a skull. "Mother, those glasses don't suit you."

"Don't you think so? Edward gave them to me." Diana's hands fluttered up to the lenses, then back to her lap.

"Take the line," Belinda called out to Eddie. "It tugs hard, so hold on." She turned to Fletcher, who was itching to fly it. "I shouldn't have given in. Too tricky getting it back down without damaging it, hitting everything."

"Yeah," he grunted, reaching out as Edward struggled with the towline.

"I can do it," Edward cried.

Everyone looked at the kite in the sky except Sara, who was looking at Belinda. An expression of amazement and deep pleasure settled on her daughter's face as she followed the kite and Eddie across the yard. Then, she stopped, frowning, making a gesture of impatience that seemed to be answering an inner dialogue. Everyone was shouting at Eddie, at the kite. Belinda took hold of a laurel branch and started stripping its leaves. Occasionally, she looked speculatively at Fletcher, and then she turned all the way around and stared at Sara. In that instant, Sara thought of the letters, coming from someone mercurial and disturbed. Could they really be a cry of help and confusion from Belinda?

A gust of wind caught the kite and was carrying it off. "Run! Run!" someone shouted. Eddie was struggling with it, Keith was reaching out to help. The yard emptied, leaving only Sara and Diana.

"Those thoughts," Diana said, staring at the kite above the trees, "are unworthy of you, Sara Bay."

Jolted, Sara said, "What thoughts?"

"What you were saying before about Belinda. Let Eddie be Vail's son. Just leave things as they are and everything will work out."

"I'm not going to do that, Mother," Sara said.

After a frantic struggle, one near crack-up, and many calls of alarm and advice, Belinda managed to get the kite down safely by running around the house to the street and reeling it in down the block.

Late in the afternoon, Fletcher left. "Where's he going?" Eddie asked Belinda.

"He's got a date with his daughter. She's four."

"Thanks for the kite. Really cool," he said.

"You're welcome. How's school going?"

"Fine. It's high school now, you know. I'm on the soccer team."

"Yes, I heard. Got a girlfriend yet?" It had been a glib remark and she was instantly sorry she'd said it because Eddie's sunny face went blank. She'd trespassed.

"A million," he said. "I'm beating them off."

"Listen, if I'm in town long enough," Belinda said, in a different tone, "maybe you and I can take the kite out to the park. Give it a real test."

"Okay by me," he replied. "But I'm meeting some friends for soccer practice now, and I thought I'd give it a test flight on the field." A few minutes later he and the kite were gone.

Diana went upstairs as Keith and his blond friend came up to Belinda. "Good seeing you again, Belinda," he said, taking her hand and holding it.

"Yes?" she asked.

"No, nothing," he summarized, letting her hand go. "Just thinking about my new script." The blonde threaded her arm through his and waved bye-bye at the crowd.

"Let's talk," Sara said, startling Belinda. She followed Sara across the yard to the patio, thinking about what Patsy had told her. She wanted to say something to Sara about it. But Vail and Patsy tagged after them.

Sara swept the wide black sun hat from her head and took off her dark glasses. "I'm hoping you'll be in town for a while, Belinda."

"No. Fletcher wants to get back to Australia."

Sara considered Vail, then said to Belinda, "What are you thinking of doing about Eddie?"

"Sara!" Vail barked.

Patsy sat up alertly.

"Edward came to see me a few days ago," Sara said. "He's beginning to ask questions. I didn't say anything—except about Victor."

"Victor?" Vail said. "Whatever for?"

"Victor's his grandfather," Sara replied impatiently, "and he wants to get to know Eddie and I don't see why not."

"Well, I do," Vail said.

Sara ignored Vail. "Wouldn't that be all right with you, Lindy?" she asked.

"Sure. Victor always mentions Eddie when I see him."

"Wait a minute," Vail said. He felt revolution and defeat coming on. "There's no telling what Vic would say. He's not in the family."

Belinda rose. "Then you deal with Victor. Sara, I can't—I don't want anyone to tell Eddie who I am." Her voice shook. Sara reached out to her but she moved away.

"None of this will ever come out," Vail said with energy. Vail wanted to believe what Lindy said about not wanting Eddie back, but he didn't trust her. "Patsy, you tell her."

But Patsy hesitated, caught between her head and her heart.

She hoped for Eddie's innocence, but, unlike Vail, she knew that one day it would all come out. The problem was getting Vail to surrender to the inevitable.

Sara sprang forcefully into the silence. "Lindy, think about what you're doing. You're only hurting yourself and Eddie."

"That's not true!" Vail said.

"It *is*. It's a repeat of old family history and, believe me, I know its consequences better than anyone except you, Lindy."

"You don't know what I feel," Belinda said quietly to Sara. "Please don't press this now."

"We're running out of time."

"I don't want to be lectured about consequences that started with you, Sara. It's because I care about Eddie that I've given him up as a son. He and I have separate lives. And I want a chance at my own life—finally. I love Fletcher and he loves me." She gazed at Sara. "If things had been different, Eddie and I would have been together. But they weren't different. I don't want to pull him away from everyone he knows—I want him to go as long as he can, not knowing. Maybe he'll never know—"

"This is a terrible mistake," Sara said.

"I don't want Eddie to find out that his mother's a former inmate of a juvenile prison and a mental ward," Belinda said. "I want to protect him from that."

"My god," Sara moaned, "we all want Eddie protected. Do you think I want him—or you—hurt? You've already been hurt. But, Lindy, you think you're protecting Edward but you're not. He'll find out—not from me, not from anyone here, but from someone someday. And then the demons will all come out and you, like me, will have no one to blame but yourself."

"Sara! Damn you," Vail shouted. "You're wrong!"

"I'm not wrong! I *know*! You're dead set against this because you're terrified of losing Eddie."

"Keep out of this. Leave it alone," Vail said.

"God, that's what Mother said to me about Lindy when I was alone and struggling in New York. And that's why we're in this mess today!" Sara snatched up her hat. "You're leaving yourself open to terrible grief," she said to Belinda. "Someone will use it against you unless you get up the guts now to tell Eddie you're his mother *and* that you're responsible for his father's death!"

"Responsible?" Belinda scoffed. "I wasn't just 'responsible.'
Are you honestly ordering me to tell Eddie that I killed his
father?"

"You'll have to tell him sometime," Sara said, "because it'll
all come out, with or without you."

For an instant, Belinda seemed trapped. She was poised for
flight but did not move. She looked at each of them quickly,
alertly. Then she moved.

Sara watched her angry daughter stride into the house. Could
Belinda tell right from wrong? Could she have fooled them all?
Was she, had she always been, insane?

Belinda Oliver shut the front door of Vail's house behind
her. She'd wanted to find the words to thank Sara for getting
her out of the loony bin, and now she was trying hard not to
hate her mother.

The street was quiet, like a scene under glass. Belinda
looked across the lawn to the maple tree and beyond it to
the sculpture guarding the gate, but she did not see them. She
felt a cold and familiar panic. Years ago, she'd run around a
small locked room, mouth open, cold air drying her tongue,
terror pressing at her. The flat cement under her feet was a
quaking bog. She was going to drown.

She was back in the room, sitting on the edge of the cot.
Dr. Davis's face was peering down at her, light shining off
his glasses. He took them off and wiped one lens with a
white handkerchief. "If you don't shape up," he was saying,
"I will put you in a ward for the violently insane." He smiled,
concentrating on cleaning his glasses. Terror pressed against
her again. Could he do what he said?

"Everyone in my ward is already insane," Belinda had said,
"and the nurses are violent."

Davis's look was chilling, and she knew she'd forgotten the
first rule of survival inside: play ball with the system and
always give the answers the staff want to hear.

"You killed a man," he went on quietly. "You killed that
girl in the Youth Authority school, and you will kill again."
His voice was hard, but his eyes were misting over. Or was
she imagining that? Had she mentioned Eddie? Was it before
that time with Dr. Davis or after it that the panic had raced her
around that stark small room? She had to get out of that room.

She'd smiled at Davis and lowered her head. "Yes, Doctor," she'd said. She'd learned the second rule at school before she'd been sent to the nuthouse: hold the panic inside.

How long had she been in that room, she wondered—a day? A month? A month of Haldol was like a day or a year: time rolled out on new chemical wheels, blunting days, crushing weeks.

She was on the street in front of Vail's house. Fletcher had taken a cab and left the convertible. She got into it and drove away. She knew she would not be back for a long time.

CHAPTER 10

SUMMER 1988

A month after Fletcher and Belinda returned to Sydney to finish *Force Field*, Victor called.

"I'm only here a few days," Victor said, "writing some articles. Let me take you and Fletcher to dinner."

"Fletcher's in Melbourne. You'll have to settle for me. I'm lonely as hell."

He directed her to a café overlooking the bay. The late afternoon sun dappled the water and threw beams of light on the checkered tablecloths. Wine and oysters arrived. Belinda said, "Very romantic, Victor."

Victor laughed and shrugged, realizing that he didn't know any other kind of setting for a long chat.

"What about the articles?" she asked.

"A magazine's asked me to write them—traveling in 'thriller' cities sort of thing." He'd forced the magazine editor into the series by hounding him. Since his experience in the Paris hotel room, Victor had stuck to business. His fear, finally, had outstripped his yearning for escape.

The sunlight streaked his craggy but still handsome face. "You seem different, Vic," she said.

"Yes, I had an experience that changed me."

"What?"

But Victor shook his head and smiled.

"Near death?"

"Sort of." He quickly changed the subject. "When are you marrying Fletcher?"

"We're too busy to get married."

"Well," he tried, "it's good to have someone, be close to someone, isn't it?"

"Yes, Vic, it's good. But it's an affair. I don't know how long it will last."

Affairs were events Victor knew well. "Best take it for as long as it's good," he said, "and not be afraid to let go when the time comes."

"Um," she said.

"What do you do on the productions?"

"Handy maid. It's called production assistant. What I've always done."

"Is that a professional capacity, something people aspire to?"

"Hardly. No one wants to do it for the rest of their lives. Fletcher has a problem about women working in pictures."

"How?"

"Control. Fletch has a problem with control."

Victor said, "Maybe he'll get better. What do you want to do?" He saw her smooth brow indent in a single frown line. Her pale eyes looked dark. The late afternoon sun brushed one side of her face.

"Direct. I want to direct."

It stunned him. "Like *Sara*?"

"God, I didn't think of that." The realization made her feel that she didn't know herself. She began to chatter: "Working with Fletcher every day, watching him . . . I've never been this close to a good director before and—" She laughed her sugary, grainy laugh. "Did you know that in the loony bin we used to put on theatricals? I directed a few of them. That's not a qualifying résumé"—she laughed—"but I was good at it. Vic, I'm not going to fit into a 'normal' life-style."

"Don't say that."

"The creative side suits me. I'm not so different there. Fletcher is crazier than some of the people in the nuthouse, but he's 'creative,' so he's accepted. Do you see what I mean? He's got a license to be different."

"Yes." Her words disturbed him. "I guess I don't want to comment, Lindy. I haven't met him. But directing for you—"

"Not Fletcher's kind of films, not big Hollywood pictures. I could do low-budget films. People wouldn't be risking that much."

"Why don't you keep your options open for a while, see how you feel later? The little I know about it, directing's an uphill road for women."

"I like telling stories. Someone said it was a way to make sense out of the real world, out of the anarchy." She wanted to tell stories about the kind of women she'd known in school—extreme women, women who came out of slime, whose lives were disposable like paper cups, women who survived against all odds. She thought of Maisie. The woman still scared her, but Maisie refused to go under. Maisie did the unexpected, one of the few white girls inside who'd used power.

"Vic, Patsy told me that you and Sara bought me out of the nuthouse. You must have bribed Davis."

"Well, we made an offer," Vic said, turning his wineglass by its stem. "Sara engineered it."

"No, Victor, she wouldn't know how. You would."

"We both felt, well, that you were innocent of the second manslaughter charge that had put you in there."

"I didn't have anything to do with that girl's death in the school. It was a setup."

"I know. Why were you framed?"

She stared into her father's dark eyes. "I wouldn't sleep with one of the girls."

Victor looked down at his wineglass. "So a girl died and you took the fall."

"Yes. No one liked her. She was a sneak, so anyone could have done it."

"How'd she die?"

"A fall in the shower." She narrowed her eyes, concentrating. "I didn't see it coming. I didn't have enough protection. Even Maisie didn't help."

"Maisie?"

"Tough girl who sort of ran things her way."

"You were only two months away from your release from the school when it all blew up," he said, reliving it. "We tried everything, we tried to keep you from another hearing but the goddamned system—" He looked up, his lined face drawn and angry. "We couldn't keep them from sending you off to the state hospital. It was your record—they just looked at the sheet and figured you'd killed her in a rage of—of—insanity."

Belinda laughed, a brittle sound. "Yeah, I wasn't fit to live with the gang girls anymore. Is that rich or what?" Victor was shaking his head. "I swear to you I didn't kill her," she said to the dark and light planes of his face. "Do you believe me?"

"Of course I do. Hey! Life's too short for this. I don't want to relive the past."

"Me neither." She shifted away from the sunlight. "Vic, about Eddie. I can't do anything." The lines in his face froze like cracks in a pavement. "I can't help you with Eddie." She leaned forward and clamped one hand on the edge of the table. "You want a relationship with Eddie? You do it through Sara. Leave me out of it."

"How can you talk that way about your own child?"

"Victor, he hasn't been my child since he was two days old." She felt tears form in her eyes and brushed them away angrily. "I cannot handle this. I'm not a go-between."

Victor looked away. "I was hoping you'd be going back to Los Angeles soon. I was even thinking of moving there myself. To be nearer to you and Eddie." A smile twitched his thin lips. "But Eddie's as far out of reach as if I'd been back in Ireland."

"I can't help that."

"No. I know." But his face was set.

"I can't. Don't rub it in."

"I'm not."

"You are. Look at yourself, sitting there grim and injured. I owe you plenty for helping me—"

"No, don't think that."

"I do think that. But I can't repay you with Eddie."

"You don't have to repay me," he said, amazed. "If anyone has debts here it's me. I left Sara . . ."

"Why did you do that?"

Victor inhaled. "I was young and stupid and greedy, and I had no confidence in myself. Diana convinced me I was bad for Sara and she gave me a lot of money to make my departure easier. It was shameful. It's always made me feel less."

Belinda looked at the glowing sea and knew that she and her father had struck the heart. "You wouldn't have told me that a year ago," she said. "You're very important to me. Do you blame me for Eddie?"

"I'm the last one to blame you for anything, Lindy. I—I want to be strong for you. I want you to count on me. If there's anything you need that I can give you, just tell me."

"No. I wish . . ."

"What? What?"

"I wish I could live one day without Archie on my back."

He nodded gravely. "Regret's bad."

"I'm not sorry about Archie," she said intensely. "I'm not glad, but I'm not sorry. I just wish I could get rid of the memory." Victor smiled bleakly and nodded again. "Do you always behave so well? Doesn't anything shock you?"

"Oh, yes, I can be shocked." He felt he was talking to her for the first time. "I'm shocked at our ability to recuperate, to press on despite everything. I'm shocked at the way people can love again after they've had their guts torn out for love." He smiled wearily. "I understand about Eddie, and I won't press you any further on it."

For several minutes they sat in silence, staring at the people on the shore beside the wharf, at the constantly moving sparkling sea. The tart smell of salt and sand did not restore them.

"I'm working on a new novel," he said. A smile twitched his thin lips. "Doing these articles," he said with a phony brightness, "has stimulated some ember of my old enthusiasm for writing."

"I didn't know you'd lost it."

He sliced the air with one hand. "Not lost it, just misplaced it for a while. No, that's bullshit," he said roughly. "I haven't been able to write for a couple of years. I've been running, drinking a lot, smoking again . . ." He left out the women. "Old habits stick like the devil."

Belinda was riveted. This closed, competent, sometimes foolish man was actually unlocking himself in front of her.

"What happened?"

He stirred. How could he tell his daughter about ending up in the hotel room on his knees?

"The particulars don't matter. It was a stupid way for a man of my age to behave—"

"What way?"

"I was dead drunk in a hotel room with a woman I didn't recognize who stole every cent I had on me."

Belinda's full smile opened slowly. "Oh, is that all?" she said, poking her tongue in her cheek and laughing. "Did you get your money back?"

"Are you kidding? You never get your money back, honey!"

Victor started to laugh and couldn't stop. "I didn't even know what city I was in," he sputtered.

The waitress came over to them, ready to be amused, too. Victor waved her away. People around them smiled tentatively, then broadly. Victor lowered his voice, but he was still laughing, "I was so goddamned embarrassed I thought I'd have to go down to the desk and ask some fool what town I was in—except I was so hung over I couldn't stand up."

Belinda's sides ached, from relief, from pain, from reconciliation.

Later, they walked on the wharf.

"Where's your book set?" she asked.

"Budapest. It's about the collapse of the Soviet empire."

"The fall of the Wall?"

"Yup."

"Science fiction."

"Fiction never hurt anyone," he said. He was sanguine about it. "I know the story will work. It feels right. You do anything a long enough time, you know when it's working. Got a lot of joy in it, this book—" Some of the wrinkles in his face shifted. "Mixed with the usual recipe of chaos and betrayal." He took her hand. "I want you to read the manuscript when I'm done, will you? It's really all I have to give."

"Hardly all, Victor," she said, touched.

Gently, he dropped her hand. His expression changed; somehow, her father had slipped away from her again.

"Sure, I'll read it," she said. "Maybe I'll get Fletch to make a movie from it."

Victor looked directly at her. "That would be a wonderful idea."

"Well, I can't promise," she said. "What's the title?"

"*The Crossing*."

She glanced at his creased face as the shadows deepened on the water. "Vic, what do you want most of all in your life?"

Victor looked stunned. He made a wide motion with one arm, dismissal and embrace. "I suppose I want to be taken seriously."

"As a writer?"

"It'll never happen. I'm a good hack and I know it. It's a good life."

"I thought you were going to say Eddie."

"I don't climb glass mountains. Besides, you're more than enough family for me."

Dear Eddie, [Belinda wrote.]

We've been in Sydney for almost eighteen months. You know what happens when film is exposed in a camera at a fast speed? When it's projected later, you get the opposite—slow motion. Weird, huh? That's the way the last year and a half here with Fletch seems when I look back on it: going at top speed, ending up slow-mo reality. Fletcher finally finished editing *Force Field*, and it's being released this summer "in a theater near you," as they say. We've been living in a great apartment in an old Sydney neighborhood—kind of nineteenth century place, located on a hilly, narrow street marked by ornate iron railings. We've been really happy here but Fletcher hasn't been able to mount his own production yet.

Belinda propped her clipboard at an angle and looked up.

Still as a stone, Fletcher was sitting across the room in a window seat of their flat, staring down at an antique street lamp. None of the neighborhood's beguiling architectural niceties drew his interest. Fletcher was afraid. He'd lost control of his life.

The reason was money. *Alms* had ended up in the red, and *Force Field* had come in way over budget. The first film he'd tried to put together had collapsed in development. The next one didn't even get that far. People were afraid that Fletcher would overspend in production. The third film he'd tried, *Guardians,* had gone all the way into serious pre-production. But *Guardians* had been delayed and was collapsing. During his frantic resuscitation efforts, Fletcher had flown back and forth from Sydney to Los Angeles. It was now clear that even *Guardians* couldn't be saved. He sat at the antique window overlooking a city he didn't know, afraid that he didn't have what it took anymore, that people didn't trust him, that any film he mounted, *if* he could even do that, would bust or be minor—both bad. He was afraid that he wouldn't fulfill his early promise. All of Patsy's warnings had come true.

Eddie, [Belinda was writing,]
don't produce a picture because you spend all your time
talking and not doing. I'm a doer; waiting kills me. At
least we're in Sydney, so I managed to get Fletcher off
the telephone and onto a ferry with me a couple of times.
Sydney Harbor is one of the biggest in the world—a glorious sight. Deep, azure blue water, like a precious stone.
I don't know how long we'll be here, or what's going to
happen. I'd really like to see you but Fletcher and I get
along better when we're away from Los Angeles. This
is a strange time, like limbo. But living with Fletcher is
like a series of cartwheels. Something will change fast.

Belinda watched Fletcher at the other end of the room,
sitting inert and muffled, like an animal waiting to die. Under
his aggressive bluster, she knew he was fragile. Even at the
top of his form, Fletcher felt empty and afraid. But when she'd
questioned him, he'd say fear was the wind in his sail, fear
gave him the edge.

Fletcher broke into her thoughts. "We're going back to Los
Angeles to check in. And this time, I want you to come
with me."

"No way." She hadn't seen the Wymans since that afternoon
on Vail's patio, and she wanted to keep it that way.

"Belinda! It looks bad if you don't come too."

"I can't help that, Fletch, I'm not going. You don't need me
there, you only need sounding boards."

"Bitch," he growled. She's my enemy, he thought; she's too
close to me, she knows me too well. "*Guardians* is dead. We
have to go back."

"I'm not going back," she said, "but you'll find something
else. You're too good a director to stand around and not
shoot film."

She's my best friend, he now thought, the one person I
can trust.

Belinda reread a page of her letter. The distance from the
Wymans was soothing to her. She'd kept the ground from
shifting under her and the cement slab from slipping into the
bog. The nuthouse and Archie seemed further away. She heard
about Patsy from Fletcher, but he never mentioned Vail, on

whose favorable review of *Force Field* Fletcher counted so heavily.

Eddie, now sixteen, answered her letters with news of his own, mainly about soccer and music—he was into postpunk augmented with sixties' groups, like the Beatles and Dylan. The kite she'd given him had crashed in a park. Occasionally, he mentioned a girl named Zoe. Belinda had also kept in touch with Yvonne, who was now working in Hong Kong. Buttons, she'd last heard, had organized a disabled persons hot line in Los Angeles. He was not directing.

As for Victor, the manuscript of *The Crossing* had become the center of her conversations with him, the core of their relationship, and the substitute for everything they still couldn't say. She'd dunned him and cajoled him to complete it, tracking him down in his "thriller" cities—Prague, Berlin, Stockholm—as he spun the articles that appeared in *GQ*, breathing life into his dwindling career. "Finish it!" she'd yell over the telephone at him. And Vic would laugh and say, yes, he would. By then she knew he was afraid to finish it, that unfinished it was successful.

Now it was June 1988. Victor had sent her *The Crossing* manuscript.

Belinda put down her letter and stared at Fletcher until he turned away from the window. "What?"

"You haven't read *Crossing* yet," she said.

"A hundred pounds of paper?" he said. "No way."

"It's good, damn you," Belinda insisted. "And it's timely. Gorbachev's changing all the rules. It's a modern thriller."

Fletcher was sulking. Fletcher was in pain. He did not have a production.

"You won't even introduce me to Victor."

"I'm certainly not going to do that if you won't read his book."

"You," he said, advancing on her, changing the subject, "*you* have a whole secret life you don't even tell me about."

"What *are* you talking about? You're with me every minute."

He pulled to a stop in front of her. "That's not what I'm talking about." Whenever Fletcher felt down, he attacked.

"You're canny and shrewd, Fletch, but not about me. Go expose other people's secrets. You like that, don't you?"

"It's my creative right."

"It's not your creative right." But Belinda knew that one day she would share everything with him. "Just read *Crossing*," she said. "Read it, and hire Keith Llewellyn as the screenwriter."

Fletcher snorted. "Keith *who*?"

"You know who," she said. "He's getting a lot of classy press around that film he wrote." The central figure in his new film was a woman spy, and the Australians loved spies. "He'd do a good job on the script for *Crossing*."

"Never. That guy just wants to poach on my territory."

"He doesn't want to direct."

"That's not what I mean," he said, darkly. "He wants you."

"He doesn't want me."

"You're very dense sometimes." Fletcher reached out for her with the sudden huge affection of which he was capable, pulled her to her feet, and held her tightly. "You want me to make a film out of Vic's crummy book?" he murmured against her ear.

"Yes, Fletcher." She hung on to him with all her strength. These were the best moments with Fletcher, the moments that always waited for them outside the net of daily struggle.

"Victor Oliver hasn't had a book that went anywhere since something called *Berlin Betrayal*. People think *Crossing* is farfetched and a downer."

"You sneak! You *have* read it. You've talked about it."

Fletcher chuckled.

"What do you care what people think? What do you think?"

"Well," he said, lightly, imitating Ronald Reagan who was leaving office, "I like it."

"Then do it. Call Patsy."

"Studios won't let me produce it. Won't let me produce anything."

"Studios, as you very well know, aren't the only outfits with money."

"I don't want to discuss it," he said.

"You're afraid."

He whipped away from her. "I'm not afraid of anything."

"Victor thought Geoffrey Venner might be interested in you doing a film of *Crossing*."

"What are you—my producer?"

"Venner is a big media guy."

"I know who he is. Your father, the thriller writer, travels in Venner's crowd? No way."

"He met him at the Galway Plate," she said. "That's the biggest race in Ireland."

"I know what it is."

"Venner's a big racing fan and so is Victor. Venner's looking for original programming for his network."

"I operate first rung. Cable is not first rung."

"Fletcher, get your head out of the sand. Television is major."

"All those TV outfits do is cheap, underbudgeted programming," he said, disdainfully. "They don't make *pictures*."

"A lot of great film directors are starting to make films for television."

Fletcher wasn't listening. "This Venner, he's like Ted Turner—he'll end up buying *Casablanca* and colorizing it." He started up the stairs. "I'm going to Los Angeles and you can come or stay, as you like."

Belinda sat down in the window seat. It was beginning to rain. When their affair began, the glow of its fire had cast her secrets into the shadows. The alchemy of passion and need had made them a couple practically overnight. She felt his power and his flaws, his heat and his cruelty. She felt bound to him even though she knew he wasn't good for her. She dreaded telling him about Archie—he wouldn't condemn what she did because he thought he lived outside the rules, too, but he would care that she hadn't told him. He could dog her, ridicule her, question her. He'd want to know every single detail. But, despite everything, Fletcher had become the foundation of her new life in the same way that Archie had once been the pillar of her old life.

Fletcher had become possessive. Archie had been jealous, too, but unlike Archie, Fletcher had a sixth sense about her. His words about Llewellyn were a case in point. She had, in fact, bumped into Keith at the Sydney Opera House a month ago, but she had not told Fletcher.

"Aren't you Belinda Oliver?" he'd asked, separating himself from a lovely woman who looked brainy and clever. "I'm Keith Llewellyn."

He was tall and barrel-chested. "The writer who drives a heap."

"Yeah. Last time I saw you was at the kite-flying party."

"Oh, yes. That seems like a different life," she said.

The intermission crowd around them had been noisy. Keith seemed utterly unchanged by the miniflurry of international press attention which his film about spies had attracted.

"Did you really sell your spy script for a million dollars?" she'd asked him.

"Yeah, it's sick, huh? But I look at it this way now—they spend thirty mil on the picture, it earns a hundred mil at the box office. Why shouldn't the writer get a mil?" He rubbed his hands together. "Next, creative control."

"So what does anyone do with all that money?"

"I don't know about anyone, but I'm setting up a nonprofit foundation to save the dolphins."

"That's really good, Keith."

"Why don't you have dinner with me?"

"I can't, thanks." She'd taken out her compact, glanced at her reflection, then snapped it shut.

"Don't do that," Keith had said. "Or do it fully."

"What?"

"The way you look at your face. Too quick, as if you don't want to see it."

"Are you nuts?"

The noise of the crowd mushroomed around them. He'd leaned in and kissed her quickly on the cheek. "Love yourself," he'd said. "All things come from loving yourself."

She'd put her hands on the soft material of his coat and nudged him back. He'd waved, and backed away. He took the arm of the clever, pretty woman and together they'd disappeared in the crowd.

In the cozy sitting room, Belinda looked at the graceful, rainy street outside and thought not about Keith but about Fletcher. She heard him pulling out drawers upstairs. The heat of wanting him engulfed her. She threw down her clipboard and scuttled up the stairs.

Clothes were tossed about the chintz room, heaved in the direction of an open suitcase. He was wearing a T-shirt and a towel.

"Dressed for love," she said, removing her jeans. She flung herself at him. They fell upon the bed, knocking over the suitcase, kicking aside clothes, frenzied, willing, mad, a welter of hair and skin and sweat, of oscillating arms and legs, pulsing breasts and groins, of bodies fused and going right to the bottom and rising again.

Belinda and Fletcher lay on the wrecked bed listening to the rain on the roof.

"Fletch, when you do another picture, I want a crack at second-unit director."

"You don't have enough experience."

"I can take the second unit out and shoot insert footage."

Fletcher sighed, thinking of the ways he could work around her, of how he could give her the title but not the responsibility. They'd had this conversation before and he was tired of it. "I'll think about it."

"Do you promise?" she said, doubting the ease of her victory.

"I promise."

"And, I want you to meet Victor," she said quietly.

Fletcher's response was to fling a heavy, muscular arm over his head. "About time. But I'm not doing a crummy TV movie." He propped up on an elbow. "Belinda, I've got to go back to Los Angeles with my hat in my hand. I don't want to go alone."

"I'll go with you, Fletch." But Belinda was not going back on her knees. She had a plan and she was going to put it into action.

CHAPTER 11

"Can't you control Fletcher?" Sidney Niden demanded of Patsy. He was one of the firm founders. His knowledge of mining foreign entertainment markets was prodigious. Niden had been Patsy's big supporter in the firm. But during the last year, he was, obviously, having second thoughts. "Your career is slipping because your biggest client, Fletcher Avery, is on the skids. He hasn't earned a dime, he's tootled off to Australia, refusing good deals, he delayed his edit, he missed his original Christmas release schedule—all because of some stupid, self-involved desire to produce! If you can't control him, toss him."

"I'm not throwing him over," Patsy said. "I didn't want him to produce, but he's coming back a chastened man and I think we'll pull it out of the fire."

"You've put all your eggs in one basket, Pat McAulis," Niden said. "I wouldn't put *one* egg in Fletcher's basket."

"Tell me what you think of *Force Field*," she said. "There's a lot of heat out there for it."

"I don't make predictions. I wait to see what it does at the box office," Niden said. "And it better make money. Can't you get him and Jerry back together?"

"I tried. It's not going to happen."

"Why haven't you put him together with David?" Niden said, mentioning a trusted producer who was a client of the firm.

"I thought of that. Fletcher wouldn't budge."

"Don't let him do anything until we know how *Force* does," Niden said.

"Hey, Sid, I'm not a rank amateur. We're *all* waiting for that. But Fletcher's threatening to take the Raydam offer."

Niden clapped his palm against his high forehead at the mention of Raydam, a small rich firm that had made a bunch of exploitation films. He groaned. "Well, they have the money and they'll let him have his way as producer."

"The deal is," Patsy said, "that he'd take less as a director in order to produce—"

"Don't compromise what he'll get as a director with Raydam. My God, Pat, what a risk."

She smiled at Niden. "But if he made the Raydam film and it was a hit, then I'd be right! And he'd own the film."

"If he's gambling, you're gambling!"

"Tell me something I don't know."

"You don't realize perhaps," Niden said quietly, "how much this might cost you in status with the firm."

"My situation can cut both ways," she said, lightly. "If Fletch and my other people are successful, I could start my own firm."

"Is that a threat?"

"Of course not. You know I'm happy here; you know I'm a team player. But I don't like to be reminded of things I already know, like how much Fletcher's failure could cost me, as you say, in status. I've been sitting on that one for a year. More!"

"I don't want to see you trash out," Niden said, not unkindly.

Patsy left Niden's office mumbling to herself. No one knew Fletcher's situation better than she did, or the risks attached to it. In the last year, Fletcher had not won a single hand he'd been dealt. The only card he had left was *Force Field*, and if it sank without a trace, Fletcher might sink with it. And everyone would say it had been her fault because she hadn't controlled him.

Belinda was an hour early for her lunch with Patsy. She was sitting on a square upholstered chair as big as a bush in a West Hollywood restaurant known as Trumps. Furniture, floor, walls, ceilings were a chalky, comforting off-white.

"Aren't you Belinda Oliver?" Tall, big-chested Keith Llewellyn was standing beside her huge chair, laughing. "Why do we meet at lunch and not lunch?"

"You again," she said. He wore an old pair of jeans with a good white open-necked shirt and a linen jacket.

He sat down. "Places like this give me the jitters. I like down-home spots, you know, fries and steak sauce. I'm meeting a friend for lunch but if she's late, I hate sitting at a table all alone, don't you?" His dark brown hair was ruffled, his eyes looked sharp and mischievous under his bushy dark brows.

"Yes," she said. "Everyone's clocking you to see if you've been stood up."

"Now there's the difference between us," he said with glee. "I figure everyone's waiting to see who you're gonna eat lunch with." He had forgotten the strange combinations in her, like the heat in her arctic eyes. "You still with Fletcher?"

"Yes. Has life changed you since you became a million-dollar writer?"

"Do I look changed?"

"You look exactly the same," she said. "It's a relief."

"And why can't we have lunch?"

"Because I already have a lunch date, and you do, too."

"I meant some other day," he said.

"Okay." Keith was handsome, eligible, and wholesome; she could imagine having a long, comfortable lunch with him. She saw him surrounded by intelligent, competent women. Why aren't I attracted to him? she wondered. Not disreputable enough, she thought.

"Why'd you want to see me?" he asked briskly.

"To talk a little business. Adapting a script from a novel called *The Crossing*."

"I haven't read it."

"It's still in manuscript," she said.

He rested an arm on the back of his giant chair and faced her. "A Fletcher Avery production?" She nodded. "What's your role?"

"Strictly informal. The author is my father, Victor Oliver."

"He is? I like his stuff. But it's been a while since he had anything out, right?"

"Yes, and this wouldn't be any million-dollar script, either." She felt she could say the exact truth to him, and it was a relief.

Keith waved at a beautiful woman who'd just come in the

door—his lunch date. He rose, and put a hand on Belinda's shoulder. "I'll think about it. Send over the manuscript."

Patsy had entered the dining area from the parking lot and had just been seated when Belinda entered from the lounge a few minutes later. Patsy didn't recognize Belinda. Her dark brown hair was dressed in a convulsion of curls around her pale face; she was glancing around the room with a confidence that made Patsy inhale sharply: it reminded her of the way Sky had entered a room. But Belinda had none of Sky's showmanship. Her head didn't sit on her shoulders at that cocky insouciant angle, and when she saw Patsy in the corner, she did not salute her as Sky would have done, she merely nodded and started forward.

Patsy rose and kissed Belinda's cheek. "You look wonderful," Patsy said. "Fletcher must agree with you."

Belinda sat down. "All good things come to people who fight hard."

Patsy's wardrobe had taken a conservative turn. She was wearing a toast-brown Yves Saint Laurent suit, and a bright blue blouse. Her hair was fashion-business hair, sharp and short.

"How's everyone?" Belinda asked.

"Diana's still chilly," Patsy replied. "Makes the house uncomfortable. I told you about her big argument with Vail— Eddie going to boarding school. Grudges in eighty-eight-year-old women are not attractive. I've always had problems with her. She used to baby Eddie about his hand, telling him he didn't have to learn to do things because he wasn't able to— we really had go-rounds about that one. But I won." She smiled, re-grooving the bowed lines bracketing her mouth.

The waiter handed them menus. Patsy opened hers and narrowed her eyes at the California cuisine. "Vail loves this kind of food, but it bores me," she said. She put down her menu. "How's life with Fletcher?"

"The most important thing in his life is how well *Force* does."

"We're all waiting for that," Patsy said. "What do you think of it?"

"The violence will put some people off," Belinda said, "and turn others on. It never felt right to me without Martin in the lead, but Fletcher thinks it's his best work yet."

"Yes, but what do you think?"

"I think it will make a lot of money."

The waiter arrived and took their order.

"Patsy," Belinda said, taking a deep breath, "I wanted to talk to you about Fletcher's next film." Belinda spread some pâté on a slice of bread. "You know he's been trying to produce because of Jerry." She tasted her bread and pâté; all food was bland after satay. Would all men and all work be bland after Fletcher?

"Sure, he wants to best Jerry for backing out of the New Zealand project. That's not the only reason, of course. What's up, Belinda?"

"Vic's written a new novel called *The Crossing*. I kinda shamed him into finishing it, and he sent me the manuscript. I think it's really hot and timely. Vic's got a friend called Venner—"

"As in Venner Broadcasting?"

"Yes. Venner's interested in it for his cable programming operation if he can get a first-rate director."

"Yes, I received a letter from Venner, asking for a meeting," Patsy said, quickly reviewing the plus side and the minus side.

"Fletcher doesn't want to do it; he thinks cable TV is crap."

"It's not anymore," Patsy said, and Belinda brightened.

"I think that *The Crossing* is a really good piece for Fletcher to do. It's set in Hungary and he loves location work; it's violent but it's got a weird, strong love story. I just have this feeling about it."

"So what do you want me to do?" Patsy asked.

The waiter floated up to them and handsomely deposited two salads.

"Convince Fletcher to do it. It won't happen unless you're behind it."

"As you know, I'm meeting Fletcher this afternoon—"

"Please don't mention this lunch."

"I won't," Patsy said to a grove of asparagus spears in her salad. "But I'll have to think about his doing a film for Venner Broadcasting."

"I spoke to Keith Llewellyn," Belinda said, "and he's interested in doing the script."

Patsy stopped eating. "Now you hold on. You let me strategize this or it'll go out of control faster than you can get back to your hotel."

"Ah," Belinda said, grinning, "so doing something with Venner Broadcasting *is* a good idea."

"Maybe. They're gearing up for an assault on the public's airwaves, making what they call first-rate films, spending money. Remains to be seen. What do you want out of this?"

"I want to help Victor," she said immediately, "because of what he did for me inside."

"And Fletcher?"

"He has to work on something or he'll really go crazy. And I want an assistant directing credit. Eventually, I want to direct."

Patsy eyed her. "You could have chosen something easier."

"Why start now?" Belinda said, sticking a look of mock wonder on her face. "I always choose the hard way." Patsy said nothing. "I have a feeling about this project, but Fletch has to be convinced to do it."

"No one can convince Fletcher to do anything he doesn't want to do. But he might do it for you."

"Yes, he might." She frowned. "Do you think he would— I mean, if I put it just that way?"

"We'll know after I talk with him, won't we?"

"Vail," Fletcher said, chuckling, "don't lie to me. I know you've seen *Force Field*."

"Not yet," Vail said, dodging it. The last thing Vail wanted was to argue with Fletcher. Fletcher Avery might marry Belinda, god willing, and that meant she might have another child.

Patsy pushed open the door of her office just as Fletcher was winding Vail into a corner. "Guys, please."

Vail ducked around Fletcher. "Honey, where have you been? I thought we were having lunch."

"Vail, that's tomorrow," she said, irritated. He was always doing this now, mixing up dates.

Fletcher said, "C'mon, Vail, I know you've seen it—I looked at the screening logs. You know that crane shot, over the Melaka street at dawn? Now don't tell me you don't get a terrific sense of foreboding. Bruno's a magician."

"Great DP," Vail agreed, moving to the door.

The relief Fletcher heard in Vail's answer alerted him that something was wrong. His reaction was, as usual, to press the point. "Hey, Vail, what do we have here—an honest difference of opinion?"

Vail surrendered. "Fletcher, I guess that's right. Yeah, I saw the picture, and there're many good things in it." Patsy, behind Fletcher, was waving "no, no," at Vail.

" 'Many good things'?" Fletcher repeated, dumbfounded. "What the hell does that mean?"

Vail avoided Patsy's angry stare. "You're one of the best, Fletch, but it just didn't work for me. I never believed that guy was in a jungle, let alone actually engaged in a hunt for his brother. I just didn't care about him. But, Fletch, plenty of people will."

"You mean the indiscriminate know-nothing moviegoer?"

"It wasn't your fault, Fletch," he said, getting excited, getting engaged. "You lost Martin, you lost the picture. It works on some levels, the cartoon levels, it just isn't what I thought it would be, and it probably isn't what you set out to make. Sorry, I got to run." Vail opened the door.

"You stay here," Patsy said to Fletcher. She followed Vail into the hallway and down to the elevator.

"You had to do it," Patsy whispered.

"I didn't do anything," he hissed back. "He forced it out of me."

"Couldn't you just compromise a little—if not for Belinda's sake, then for mine?"

"I know he's the answer to a prayer for Lindy—"

"Forget Lindy! How about me? I'm in a terrible position here with Fletcher."

"I didn't want to mention it, for Chrissakes! Fletcher never knows when to quit!" The elevator appeared and he jumped into it.

"You come back here!" Patsy shouted at her husband.

Vail saluted. The doors closed.

She went back into her office. Fletcher began ranting about Vail's prejudices. "He's absolutely out on the edge," he yelled, stamping about the office. "He's talking about my best work! He's so fucking wrong, it's laughable!"

"Sit down," she said, roughly. "There's an important player who wants to fly you to England to consult with him. Geoffrey Venner of Venner Broadcasting."

Fletcher stopped stomping. "That damned *Crossing* thing."

"Venner's optioned it."

"I'm not making his picture."

"He just wants some advice, to hear how you might approach it."

"Oh, well, sure," Fletcher said. He'd often been asked to consult on various projects, and he liked doing it. "But I'm not going to make that book into a television movie."

"Not even if we talked him into letting you produce?"

"You can't be serious—me do television?"

"Times are changing fast, Fletch. Let's just keep an open mind. What's Belinda think of all this?"

"Oh," he said, waving an arm, "she loves it—it's her dad's book! She wants me to do it."

"Would you do it for her?"

"Are you kidding?" He laughed. "Make a major career move just for her?"

Patsy looked down at her desk top. "Spoken like the man I've always known you to be, Fletch."

Neil was sitting at Vail's desk when Vail walked into his office that afternoon. "I thought you were having lunch with Patsy," Neil said, startled.

"We changed our minds. What's up?"

"Nothing much. Don't have to snap, Vail," Neil said, getting out of the chair.

Vail touched the edge of the desk, ran his finger along it as he walked around the desk and sat down. "Sorry. Just on edge today. You need something?"

Neil started out. "No, just trying to piece together what you said in the screening yesterday. Part of my education. You're the most, Vail."

He went out, closing the door behind him, satisfied that he had handled Vail's surprise entrance well. He'd been looking for Sandra's transcription of Vail's reactions to *Force Field*.

Schurl was standing in the outer office, looking at him. "Vail's back," Neil said.

"Has Vail seen this?" Schurl asked, holding up a letter.

"Oh! Jeepers, Sandra asked me about that," Neil said. He took it from Schurl and marched back into Vail's office. Schurl followed him.

"Vail," Neil said softly, "Sandra wanted to know if she should write the usual reply." Neil glanced over the sheet of paper. "The letter's about Sky. Another request for some merchandising rights around a fan club." Neil looked at his shoes. "I just thought I'd help Sandra out a little."

Vail was the executor of his sister's estate. Though Sky had been dead over ten years, people were still drumming on him for everything from documentary rights of her life story to autographed pictures. "Who's it from?"

"Ah, a Patrick O'Mara."

"Patrick O'Mara? Jesus Christ! Gimme that!"

Startled, Neil handed over the letter.

"I thought he was in prison," Schurl said, lowering himself into the couch.

Vail glanced at the letter. "How can that son of a bitch be out?"

"Who?" Neil asked.

"He's the psycho son of a bitch who murdered Sky!"

"That guy wants to start a Sky fan club?" Neil asked.

Schurl suppressed a smile. "Now that's chutzpah."

"Maybe he says he's sorry in the letter," Neil said to Schurl with a grin.

Vail jerked his head up and viewed Neil coldly. "Do you think I'd let my sister's killer start a Sky Wyman fan club?"

"No, Vail." Neil straightened his face.

"I'm going to dictate a letter to Sandra that'll curl her hair. Where is she?"

"Out to lunch."

"Get me what's his name, the DA," Vail shouted at Neil.

"Vail, what are you going to do?" Schurl asked.

"I'm going to be outraged and incensed."

"One DA coming up," Neil said as he scurried out.

Schurl folded his arms across his chest. "Vail, let the O'Mara thing rest."

The telephone chirped. Vail snatched the receiver. "Bob, I'm not going to start with a lot of pleasantries. I'm calling about how you guys are letting the killers out—"

"Now, Vail," Bob Morrissey, the district attorney, began in

his best campaigner's voice, "we just make the cases, we don't make the sentences. You're talking about O'Mara."

"You're damned right I am. I can't believe that convicted killer is back on the streets!"

"Streets are full of criminals," the DA said. "But we didn't have anything to do with O'Mara's release." Vail heard Morrissey rattling papers.

"How's O'Mara walking around loose?"

"Good behavior!" Morrissey shouted, exasperated. "A model goddamn prisoner. He didn't get the death sentence, Vail! I'm sorry he's out. One of my guys says he's rented an apartment in West Hollywood. Looks like he's nice and quiet. I don't like him being out any better than you do, but there it is."

"What are you going to do about it?"

"There's nothing I can do. And don't you do anything, either. We're watching him. You leave him alone. He's a free man. That's that."

"Fucking shades of Dan White," Vail grumbled.

"C'mon!" Morrissey exclaimed. "That guy shot the mayor and a councilman and got out in *five* years. At least O'Mara spent twelve years in the slammer."

"You wanna tell my mother that her daughter's killer's out?"

Morrissey sobered. "No, pal, I don't. I feel for you."

Vail held the receiver away from his ear. "Is this justice?" he shouted.

It was a clear, sunny summer day. The downtown streets of Beverly Hills were crowded with shoppers. Even the palm trees looked scrubbed and shiny as Vail's car, driven by a muscular ex-surfer he'd hired, glided into the hills.

The coolness between Vail and his mother since the argument about Eddie's schooling had decreased, but it had not gone away. It made telling her about O'Mara harder. I'll tell her before we have dinner, he thought. No, I'll tell her after dinner, that's better. Should he have a doctor there in case she had a heart attack? No, there was Harry, the doctor next door. But maybe he should make sure Harry was home tonight. Yes, he'd do that. Vail took off his glasses and rubbed the lenses with his handkerchief. He did this several times a day, a gesture that was now as natural to him as running his hand over his thinning hair. But his glasses did nothing to improve the narrowing field of his vision. He was waiting for the avalanche to engulf him. Behind it came Seeing Eye dogs and white canes and darkness. But most of all, he worried about the moment that Patsy and Eddie found out he was going blind.

He told Patsy about O'Mara before dinner.

"I was thinking about putting off telling Mother," he said, trying to find a pen he'd had in his hand a minute ago. He thought he'd put it down on the table.

"We can't put it off, Vail. God, this is so shocking."

"Maybe a bus will hit him. Maybe he'll move away. Why leap to tell her?"

"Honey, you know you have to. What if he showed up on our doorstep?"

Vail and Patsy waited until Eddie went out with some friends, then showed his mother back into the study.

"Mother, I have to talk with you. Something's come up."

Her look raked him. "Very well," she said, "if it's important."

Patsy sat down next to Diana on the sofa. Vail paced. "Mother, something awful has happened and just let me say that if there were anything we could do, we would have done it."

"What is it, Vail?" Diana asked, steeling herself.

"It's about Sky."

"Sky?" It jarred her. She was sitting rigidly, her powdered, wrinkled face with its upswept silver hair contrasting with the dark blue wall behind her.

"Patrick O'Mara has been released from prison."

Diana's arms flew across her chest tightly in a self-proclaimed hug of protection and a high, whistling moan escaped her. "No . . . !" She pitched to one side stiffly, her head hitting the padded arm of the sofa. Patsy leaped up, trying to take one of her hands, but it was wedged beneath her other arm across her breast. Vail hovered. Diana lay on the sofa, bent at the waist, her feet still pointing toward the carpet. Vail poured a glass of ice water from a carafe at the bar and offered it to her but the old woman shook her head. She moaned continuously as if she were being tortured. Vail was about to call Harry when suddenly Diana unlocked her arms and, pressing one hand into the sofa, she pushed up to a sitting position.

"Why is he alive and Sky dead?" she said in a strong, clear voice. "Why is he alive and my baby *dead*? It's unconscionable. I won't tolerate it! What are you going to do about this?" she demanded of Vail. "She was your sister; she was closer to you than anyone. I demand that you call the authorities and have something done about this. What are you going to do?"

Vail struggled, describing his conversation with the district attorney. Patsy found herself surprised at the depth of the pity she felt for the aging woman. Nothing was worse than outliving a child.

"But, Vail," Diana pleaded with him, "what are you going to do about this?"

"There's nothing we can do," he finally said simply. "He's been released and he hasn't committed any crime."

"Not committed a crime? How can you say such a thing?" Diana shouted. "You act more like *his* brother than Sky's!"

Patrick O'Mara was making himself a chicken sandwich and humming "The Age of Aquarius" from *Hair*. He carefully stuck the chicken slices into the mayonnaise on the bread. He was wearing a fire-engine red shirt, blue slacks, and a yellow ascot. He looked like a paint box.

As a young actor working with Sky and Sara, Patrick had been elegant in a lazy sort of way and fun to be with. But now his bright blue eyes were more gray than blue, the flesh on his face sagged, his once yellow hair was an undistinguished hay color mixed with gray. He was in his early fifties and he looked older.

He took the sandwich and a cup of coffee into the dining room off the living room, sat down at the table, and brushed out his paper napkin. The high, atonal, repetitive chords from *Hair* replayed in his head. He licked a drop of mayonnaise off his little finger, then opened the letter from the publishing company and smoothed it out beside him. He smiled at it and he could see the type and print smiling back. "You wait, Vail," Patrick said softly. Vail's letter had been vitriolic. But hearing from a publisher made Patrick O'Mara feel better.

He couldn't remember when he'd last seen Vail—years ago—before the messengers had come and the voices about Sky. He remembered seeing Sky's daughter, Lindy or Linda, practicing diving in the pool. Sky had been sprawled on a chaise, wearing a big sun hat and tinted blue glasses. The girl had been about fifteen, he thought, slim and small like Sky, but without her mother's raven hair.

Patrick was going to write his memoirs. He was comfortably situated to do that since his mother, unlike his father, had put a chunk of her fortune in trust for him shortly before she'd had a stroke. She'd gone to her grave believing utterly in his innocence.

The words in the letter from the publisher were separating, grinning at him. And why not? He'd paid his debt to society, right? So it was his prerogative, even his duty, to tell his story—and Sky's. He bit into the sandwich. It would be easy to sell, for it was the real story, and he was going to leave nothing out. He didn't care about the money—he would do something for Sky with it—maybe start a scholarship in her name.

He checked his watch: a writer the publisher had suggested working with him on the book was due in half an hour. They would have a drink. Well, the writer would have a drink; Patrick didn't drink anymore. Maybe the writer was in AA—many were. But Patrick was cynical: they were all drinking mineral water in public and Scotch at home. He'd bet on it.

Patrick devoured his sandwich quickly, dabbing at his mouth with the napkin. He picked up the plate and rinsed it off in the sink.

He went back into the sparsely furnished living room and sat down in a black leather chair. In the sunlight, its color had reminded him of Sky's glossy black hair. He was sorry about Sky; if he wished for anything, it was to bring her back whole. He looked down at his hands. *They* were the enemies; *they* had strangled the woman he adored. He was very sorry.

He took the Bible from the shelf of a small table next to the chair and opened it at a marker. He looked across at a matching chair a few feet away. "We're on the Book of Saul, Sky, and the Witch of Endor. Do you remember her? A fast piece of baggage . . ." He began reading aloud, sitting alone in the huge chair in the low-ceilinged room whose walls were studded with posters of Sky's films, theater cards, and photos of her, some blown up to three feet. Her remote, exquisite beauty choked the chamber. The room was a tomb, a shrine, and an offering.

CHAPTER 12

SEPTEMBER 1988 to FEBRUARY 1989

Geoffrey Venner had more money than anyone could spend or use. His kind of fortune could feed Africa, support the Russian switch to a free market, or replant the Amazon basin. To the astonishment of many who knew him as a hard-line, bootstrap Reagan conservative, Geoffrey Venner had started contributing heavily to environmental salvage efforts. It was a sea change that boded no good, his friends said, signaling deeper alterations, which they distrusted.

One of his newest interests had coincided with the Galway Plate in Ireland and had caused him to meet Victor Oliver. Now, a few months later, Geoffrey Venner was sitting at a table on his luxurious private jet, flying from San Francisco to London. A neat stack of legal documents sat in a chrome basket beside him. He was going over his attorneys' comments on the expansion of his television universe. He stopped reading only to make brief margin notes in his tiny, precise script.

Guy Venner, as he was universally called, had a proud head with an arched nose and a jutting chin. His slender mouth was framed on each side by a single vertical line. His blue eyes were shielded by thick well-shaped brows, which, when raised, gave him a look of delighted surprise. He was a man who loved challenges. He had been brought up to ride well, speak well, dress well, live well. He saw no reason to be dissatisfied with any part of himself or his life.

Venner was a home-grown American media king. He'd inherited one fortune from his grandaunt, Faith Venner, of the San Francisco Venners who'd made their first towering profits from railroads. Guy was a brilliant player in the hot, high-roller, leveraged buy-out atmosphere of the eighties, concentrating on media, buying up film libraries and expanding his hugely successful cable TV operation. He operated on a daring principle: hire first-class people and give them creative freedom.

Guy liked to think of Venner Broadcasting as a happy organization. He'd started it by acquiring a television station in San Francisco, his personal and corporate home base. KVCG was a real dog, last in the market. But in the mid seventies, media growth ballooned—cable, pay TV, satellites which had caused him to pay more attention to this orphan TV station lost in the matrix of his other concerns. He'd put the station on the satellite, which made it air nationwide in rebroadcast on other cable systems. His people fanned out, stalking national advertisers. He'd bought into other cable systems. He'd installed salespeople and programmers and had directed them to "take on the networks." He'd instituted hip, experimental shows. He'd gloated as the studios became more calcified and entrenched, and their theatrical film budgets ballooned. He'd celebrated as the television networks lost 40 percent of their audience. Cable ate up what they squandered. In 1986, he'd bought a studio film library and started showing packages of old films on his television station. The debt from the library purchase threatened to cripple Venner Broadcasting. Columnists said he was dead in the water—an overreaching upstart. But by 1988, his media group was in the black. He'd expanded again, creating an independent film production unit to produce television movies and series, documentaries, even commercials. The budgets were lean and mean, like the rest of the organization. He'd acquired major shareholders from immense corporations with whose presidents he consulted and dined. Guy Venner was building a global communications network—a media force to be reckoned with. And like Ted Turner, he did believe in colorizing old black and white films—it was the wave of the future. He was fifty and divorced. He was enjoying the prime of life. Gambling was his first strength—on horses, properties, deals, or pictures. And he was lucky.

What had changed along the way was his perception that he couldn't just take out: he had to put back in, too.

Diana was obsessed with Patrick O'Mara. He brought her bitterness and disillusionment. He made her ill. How could he be free as if he'd never killed her Sky? It was intolerable.

She was weeping again, and it wouldn't do. For months, she'd prayed for death, but she woke up every morning. Eighty-eight years old outside, a lonely enraged child inside; in this crucible Diana longed for the mother she'd never had.

On this September morning in Los Angeles, she sat down in a chair, her hands in her lap, and stared at a tiny, leather-bound, gold-stamped book by Carlyle. It was the only physical object of her mother's that she possessed. She'd been farmed out—abandoned—to a minister's family in Oregon. She'd been beaten and neglected. But at age ten, Diana had found out by accident that her real mother was Faith Venner, and that she was alive. In her child's heart, she knew her mother would come for her, she would save her.

She never did. Diana knew that her mother was a wealthy and prominent woman. And when, after years of searching, Diana finally found her, an old woman shut away in a San Francisco mansion, Faith Venner had denied her. She'd had a white toy poodle in her lap and Diana, though she'd been in her forties by then, had wanted with a direct and overwhelming emotion to be that dog.

Diana didn't make snap decisions, but she was fully capable of acting on the tide of emotion. She picked up the telephone and dialed. "Zip, this is Diana. I want to talk to you. I need some advice."

"What's happened?"

"I don't want to say over the telephone, dear. But I—I really think I'll go mad if I don't talk about it."

The Bel Air was unchanged. The wide banana trees were draped against the clapboard walls; the swans drifted in the pond. It was comforting to everyone but Diana.

"You're upset," Leonora Lytton said to Diana with some alarm.

"Zip, dear," Diana whispered, "I simply cannot handle this."

Leonora couldn't believe her ears. Haughty Diana asking for help? "Tell me why you're so agitated."

Diana started to speak, then stopped; she took her handkerchief from her sleeve and forgot to use it. She twisted her pearls and tugged at her ruby ring. "My daughter's murderer has been released from prison. He's walking around Los Angeles right this minute. And, he's writing a book of memoirs about Sky. I simply cannot stand it!" Her fury and her sorrow were immense, immeasurable.

Leonora's nostrils flared as she inhaled. "I don't know what to say," Leonora admitted. "A book?"

"Yes."

"How do you know?"

Diana turned a ring on her hand violently. "From Vail, Vail heard about it."

"I suppose there's nothing you can do about it." But Leonora, who had fewer moral reins than Diana, was thinking.

Bright pink spots appeared on Diana's cheeks. "That's what everyone says," she murmured, tightly. She seemed to sink into herself, collapsing inwardly. But then, abruptly, she rallied, reared back in her chair, and wailed, "Am I never to be rid of this man or this act?"

A startled waiter, staring at them across the room, rattled a tray of cups. Diana, so conscious of social niceties, didn't even notice.

Fletcher saw a woman and two men in their fifties coming toward the table at Morton's, a private club with wood paneling and soft lighting, on Berkeley Square in London. Fletcher had accepted Geoffrey Venner's invitation.

"My dad's the one in the dress," Belinda said.

"Don't tell me, nut cake. I wanted to pick him out myself," Fletcher muttered.

The woman was sleek and angular, her pale hair swept up on top of her head in hard curls. Fucking her, Avery thought, would be like scaling Everest. The trio stopped, the woman kissed the air toward the man on her right. He was over six feet tall with a quick step and a quick smile. His graying ash blond hair was combed straight back from his forehead. He had the polished, buffed-up air of success. Unmistakably Venner. The woman walked away and joined a table of people by the wall.

"Great," Fletcher said, relieved. Venner waved at someone. The man with Venner was elegantly dressed, but his creased, angular face had seen action in the streets. "Victor," Fletcher said, putting out his hand to this man, "I'd know a tough writer anywhere." Vic smiled tightly, introduced them to Venner. They all sat down.

Venner had a deep, resonant voice. "I saw *Force Field*," he said to Fletcher. "Great picture. You oughta get an Oscar for it."

"Over ninety mil at the box office," Fletcher said, "and still going strong." Only Vail and a couple of others had panned it.

"Guy!" A clever-looking, muscular man had separated himself from a small group by the entrance. He was approaching Venner's table with a no-nonsense strut.

"Don, I didn't know you were in London," Venner said, warmly. "Everyone, this is Don Regan, better known once as President Reagan's chief of staff. The hatchet in the velvet hood." Venner introduced his table.

Regan had seen *Force Field*. "It gives us a new gander on the MIA situation," he said as he left, briskly tapping Venner on the shoulder.

Guy Venner knew presidents and cabinet officers, business luminaries and stars, and he told discreet stories with relish.

"How did he really feel about Mrs. Reagan's horoscopes?" Belinda asked when Regan was safely out of earshot.

"Spitting bullets is too mild," Venner replied. He ruled the table, turning his sunny smooth face with its merry blue eyes on each of them.

Victor had a lot riding on this meeting. *Crossing* could be a smash or a dud, but his career's salvation lay in a television production of it. With Belinda's help, and Patsy's, he'd done an end run around Fletcher. The hidden agenda now was to interest Fletcher in Venner's plans enough so that he'd take on the direction of *Crossing*. But it was a wild shot. Fletcher was perfectly capable of saying he didn't give a rap about *Crossing*, and that any production would run twenty-five million, which would close off Guy's interest.

"Yes, I see a family resemblance," Guy was saying of Victor and Belinda. Guy was struck by the hard intelligence of Belinda; she was not the pretty zero he'd expected.

When they were into dinner, Venner launched into a description of his new production arm and then outlined *The Crossing* as a two-hour pilot for a dramatic series, starring the American diplomat in the book. Fletcher began to listen up. Successful series were extremely lucrative.

"The power of television," Venner was saying, "is simply not to be believed. Why do we still cling to the idea that a first-rate picture had to play in theaters to be important? What's more important than an audience of millions in a single throw?" If he had been counting to ten, Venner's mellifluous voice would have compelled attention. "I want first-class directors and producers." He named people now developing movies and series for his company. It was quite a list, seasoned with two big feature directors. "Fletcher, I know you're not able to do something like this right now but give me an idea of how you'd approach it—because as far as I'm concerned you're the best." Venner grinned, his eyebrows shooting up.

The Crossing story was simple: public and political forces were at work to break down the wall between East and West in Europe, a movement which conflicted with British and American arms manufacturing interests which saw the end of the cold war as an end to their powers. Three people were caught in the middle: a charismatic Hungarian political figure, an American diplomat, and, crucially but tangentially, an American translator.

"First of all," Fletcher said, "it's not a studio piece. You've got to shoot in Hungary, got to get a sense of that light and those streets on the screen."

"Shooting in Budapest," Venner said, raising his eyebrows at Fletcher. "Jesus, you can only Xerox from one to three in the afternoon over there. Fletcher, what would you do with a budget of fifteen mil?"

"That's not enough." Fletcher started to talk about the story, and the more deeply he got into the translation of it to the screen, the more he realized that he wanted to make it. They talked production details and story all through dinner, then moved for coffee into another high-ceilinged room that resembled a private library. A fire in the fireplace warmed the book-lined walls and the green and scarlet leather chairs.

Crossing had finally been left behind. Victor and Fletcher were talking sports, and Venner was talking to Belinda about plutonium pollution of the Irish Sea. "We can't go on behaving like children," he was saying, "just discarding or changing whatever we like to suit our immediate needs. What gets me is the lack of imagination."

Belinda kept her eye on Fletcher. He was fitfully engaged in the sports roundup with Victor, but she knew he was thinking about *Crossing*. She'd seen that look of distraction on the set as he listened to actors' complaints with one ear while he planned how to skewer them into a new emotional risk.

Fletcher broke into the conversation. "I've changed my mind," he said to Venner. "I'd like to direct *Crossing*, but only under certain circumstances."

"And they are?" Venner said, composed, interested, waiting.

"I produce and direct with full creative control. And it's shot in Hungary."

"Only if you hold the costs to fifteen mil."

"Twenty-five."

"Fifteen, tops. It's a pilot, not a feature."

"You talk numbers with my attorney," Fletch said.

Venner admired his brandy. "Fifteen," he said casually. "With a four-week shooting schedule."

Fletcher groaned dramatically. "Call my lawyer."

"And," Venner said, "if *Crossing* goes over budget you'll be personally liable."

"Talk to Patsy." Fletcher waved the conditions away: he felt lucky, and he cared little about the business end of his deals. Patsy handled all that.

"Since we're staking the property, I get the second unit," Belinda said. It was a risky and unusual move but it didn't match taking on a psych-tech or Quake.

"Huh?" Fletcher was astounded. Venner chuckled.

Victor said, "Hey, Belinda, slow down."

"You heard me," she said.

"We'll talk later," Fletcher said.

"I want a yes or no." Belinda smiled broadly.

"Okay, fine, yes," Fletcher said in a rush.

Venner stuck out his hand. "I know we'll get together on the numbers, Fletcher, and I know it's going to be a great television first. Welcome aboard."

Victor, sitting next to Belinda, put an arm around her shoulders and kissed her cheek. "It wouldn't have happened without you," he said to her. "Not in a million years."

On the way back to their hotel in the cab, Fletcher was livid. "I've never heard such shit in a negotiation! Where do you get off?"

"Fletcher, I'm not a camp follower and this isn't a new conversation. We've talked about me directing the second unit before. You just conveniently forget it."

"It's mighty forgettable."

She laughed and moved closer to him. "I'm going to hold you to it. You promised and it's mine. What do you think I'm knocking myself out for, to be second assistant assistant assistant? C'mon, Fletch, get real."

A few months later, in February, Fletcher was nominated for an Oscar as best director for *Force Field*. As soon as she heard the news, Patsy walked into Sid Niden's office.

"He's going to be big again," she crowed to the senior partner.

"I'm glad you're winning, Pat," Niden said.

"You are keeping up with Venner Broadcasting's promotional apparatus, aren't you?" she pressed on. The publicity people were building Fletcher's coming production of *Crossing* as a new age television first.

"I know it's been rough for you. But, Pat, I think you like sailing close to the wind."

"Not that close." It had been a terrible year of cancelled lunches, minimal cooperation, of being interrupted in meetings by other partners, of sly looks, and crushing pressures. There were few positions more lonely than losing, or seeming to lose, status in a law firm. The jockeying for rank and money was incessant, and even close associates, seeing the possible vacuum she might leave, had moved in to pounce.

Niden leaned back in his chair. "One thing about Fletcher's work, it always has some moving human truth buried in all that adventure shit. If *Force* hadn't had that, no one would have remembered it at Oscar time." He winked.

"Thanks for your vote of confidence," she said.

Patsy was high on triumph and she didn't want to fence. She and Fletcher had beaten the odds. Even though Belinda was living in L.A. and not conveniently abroad, even though Eddie was older and would soon be asking questions, even though her husband was irascible and contentious and she didn't know why—despite everything, Patsy was confident she could handle whatever came. She hadn't felt that way in a long time.

*   *   *

Fletcher wasn't hot—he was red-hot. Everything changed with the nomination. He responded by leasing a three-thousand-square-foot house in the Palisades and a suite of offices in The Courtyard on Wilshire, complete with a full kitchen and a lavish entertainment room choked with video, film, and CD gear. The telephones rang constantly; requests for media interviews flew in on a windstorm of acclaim. In the midst of it all, Fletcher's production of *Crossing* climbed into high gear.

"I thought we were producing this thing from London," Belinda said. "I don't want to be in L.A., Fletch."

"Are you crazy? We can't leave now," he said, pacing his new space energetically. "You want *Crossing* to come alive?" he said. "You want your second-unit slot? You're here to stay. And get out of barrio Berendo," he ordered. "I'm a hot director again." He paced up to her and hugged her hard.

Belinda put her head on his shoulder. "Do you think about Buttons?"

Fletcher pressed his lips into her cheek. "Yes. A lot."

Belinda didn't realize it until she saw the slight, dark-haired figure coming through the door to her new office how much she'd missed her or how much she needed her now.

"The woman from Hong Kong," Belinda cried.

Yvonne Duret, looking chipper and trim, held up one small hand. "No applause, please. I just dropped in to congratulate Fletch on his nomination." She glanced around the large, airy office. "You're coming up in the world."

"Tell me all about working in Hong Kong," she said, waving her to a leather and aluminum chair.

"Ah, the Hollywood of Asia." She sank into the chair and curled her feet under her.

Since the early seventies, Hong Kong had been a prolific film center and profitable industry. "We have big stars and producers working out of big studios over there," Yvonne said. "Most of the films are exported to Japan and Korea—escapist entertainment. We even have *auteurs* over there, and women directors. But I'm just off a ghost story, a very popular genre in Asia."

"What's going to happen when the British leave in 1997 and the Chinese take over?"

"Who knows? People are uncertain, so lots are making as much money as possible like there's no tomorrow. Listen, pal, I'm looking for a place to live. I'm coming back to the States."

"Great! Stay at my place."

"I don't want to dislocate you and Fletch."

"No, I mean *my* place. I have an apartment here."

"I thought you were living with Fletch."

"I am. This apartment is separate. I meant to give it up, even though I haven't lived there since *Force* began shooting, and I'm not living there now."

"Why didn't you give it up?"

"I don't know. It's like a sanctuary, a place that's all mine. And now it can be yours for a while. Come this afternoon."

"Well, great. Now, tell me what's happening here." Her dark blue eyes, lit with mischief and glee, bored in on Belinda.

"It's a madhouse, what with the nomination and preparing to shoot in Hungary. Know anything about Hungary?"

"Nope."

"*Crossing* is different from Fletcher's other productions. It's for television, so there's not as much money. It's got to be shot fast, but it's cumbersome, international. It's going to be hard."

"Everything's hard," Yvonne said, happily.

"Here's the bottom line. Producing is not Fletcher's big strength," Belinda said. "We're late with the pre-production, we're scrambling to make up the time, but we're never going to do that."

"Isn't it crazy to shoot over there now?" Yvonne said. "Eastern Europe's in an uproar."

"People *are* shooting there, Yvonne. And you know what? Vic's book is going to be really big when it comes out."

"Boffo."

Belinda fell silent and looked at her friend for a long moment. "Would you consider coming aboard as associate producer?"

"No. It'd have to be full producer credit or nothing."

"We'll talk to him."

"What's *your* title?" Yvonne asked.

"Servant to the production—"

"Be-lin-da! What's the matter with you?"

"Wait a minute. And, I'm doing the second unit. Now, let's go see Fletcher, start the wheels rolling."

All that afternoon, she, Fletcher, and Yvonne talked production and agreed in principle to a deal: Yvonne would get the title of producer and handle the line work of organizing the production, while Fletcher retained the real power over *Crossing* as executive producer.

Later, Belinda went back to Berendo Street. The neighborhood seemed more crowded, the graffiti more aggressive. The apartment was musty. She took out a dust mop and some spray polish and started to work, thinking about how good it was to have a friend like Yvonne. Her return made everything better.

"Is my rental car safe out there?" Yvonne asked as she came in the door.

"Probably. Enter."

"Well, you are full of surprises," she said, looking around at the plain but decent furniture, the bay window, and the huge cushions. "Does Fletcher know about this place?"

"He thinks I gave it up. Come in the kitchen—I have some Cambodian food from the restaurant down the street."

"When did you get so interested in directing?" Yvonne asked.

"A long time ago. Before *Force*. On the ill-fated *Guardians*, I asked Fletch to give me the second-unit job. He found that laughable. He split his sides."

"Other people would have helped you," Yvonne said.

Belinda shook her head. "I wanted Fletcher to admit my worth. Yvonne, you have to understand that we'd fight all day and then fall into each other's arms at night. It was a very intense period."

"So why's it going to be different on *Crossing*? Has he changed or what?"

"He's agreed to it." Yvonne looked skeptical. "He's promised."

"Have you heard from Buttons?"

"No."

"I feel guilty about him," Yvonne said, sitting on the kitchen stool. "I chose the site, my location manager made assurances, I accepted them—"

"Take it from me, guilt is a killer. Forget guilt. But you and Buttons never got along," Belinda said. "All you did was snipe at each other."

"That just vanished in the operating room that night." Yvonne took the glass of wine Belinda offered her. "And now, here's *Force* nominated—I mean, that's Buttons's film more than anyone else's."

"Then go and see him."

"My god, Belinda, you're practically running the place now!" Fletcher shouted the next day. "Besides, I already hired the guy."

"It's outrageous," she said. "Unhire him."

"Listen, we'll work something out. I want you to be happy."

"You *promised* me that second-unit spot."

Fletcher was uncomfortable but stubborn. "It's too late. It's a done deal."

"You went back on your word or you just didn't care—which is it?" Belinda demanded.

"Oh, good, a happy shoot." Keith Llewellyn was standing in the doorway, lifting a battered Panama hat from his head with one hand. The other held the leash. At the end of the leash was Bob.

"Keith!" Fletcher said, rising. "Ladies, our scriptwriter. Keith, this is Yvonne, our line producer. Keith is a writer who understands production."

"Fletcher likes writers," Keith responded, "which means he isn't *too* hostile to us." He was decked out in his usual casual style: jeans, T-shirt, sloppy jacket, messed up hair in need of a cut. "This is Bob," Keith said.

"Great," Fletcher said, patting the dog's head. Bob held up one paw. "Smart, too."

"Sit, please, Bob," Keith said. The dog sat down, then lay down and put his big golden-brown head on his paws.

"Ladies," Fletcher said. An elfin smile punctuated his rough face. "You'll have to excuse us. We have to talk script."

It was as if all the air had been sucked out of the room. Belinda said, "God knows what *my* job is but *Yvonne's* your producer."

"Fletcher," Yvonne said, "let's not start this way. It's too soon."

"Hey," he snapped, "this is my show and don't you forget it."

Color was seeping into Keith's dark Welsh face. "I don't like to work this way," he said to Fletcher.

"Ah, what way, man. C'mon, sit down, let's talk script."

But Keith wasn't sitting down. "No, I always work with the team. Makes things easier later on."

"Goddamnit, a million bucks for a script you get one time and it really goes to your head," Fletcher said, still jovial and aggressive at the same time. He was a master at the combination.

"Okay, we'll all sit down," Keith said.

It was now a contest and Fletcher strode up to the line. "Nah, the ladies are leaving."

Keith stared at him. Hard. He was sure Fletcher had been kidding when it started but now he was forcing it and Keith knew he wouldn't back down.

"I'm not leaving," Yvonne said.

"I'm not leaving," Belinda said. Insurrections brought out the worst in Fletcher. She waited for the explosion.

"But I'm leaving," Keith said.

"Goddamnit, what's going on here? What's the big deal? I want to talk with my writer."

Keith's face had changed. The bleak humor in it was gone, and what Belinda saw replacing that was passion.

"No, not talking with this writer," Keith said.

"What?" Fletcher demanded. "You're going to let them do this to you?"

"No one's doing anything except you, Fletch," Keith said.

"Then you can fucking get out," Fletcher shouted, certain that Keith would do no such thing.

Keith said in a deep quiet voice, "Fletch, I respect your work, and I've often defended you."

"I don't need *your* protection, buster."

"And I don't need your film." Keith came to life, his face slipping back into its jaunty rough lines and colors. He walked to the door. "But you *do* need my protection, Fletcher. You need friends." He picked up the end of Bob's leash, and he left.

Fletcher was floored. "Get out of here," he sputtered to Yvonne and Belinda. "I've got work to do."

They moved slowly and casually out of the office, closing the door behind them, then raced into Belinda's office. "Wow!" Yvonne said. "Is this show going to be a roller coaster or what?"

Keith and Bob stood in the doorway. "Got time for lunch?" Belinda asked him. "You could leave Bob here in my office."

"Okay. Meet me at Musso's."

Keith fit himself into the hard, austere booth at Musso and Frank's restaurant in Hollywood. "I won't eat anywhere else unless I'm forced," he explained. "I don't like posh restaurants." He looked around. "If this were Paris, I coulda brought Bob. Paris loves dogs."

Belinda was furious with Fletcher but she put it aside, partly out of loyalty to him, partly because a temper display wouldn't bring Keith back. "You know, this thing with Fletcher can be fixed," she said.

"I don't want to fix it."

"Why'd you quit?" she asked, exasperated.

"I think you know."

"No, I don't know."

"C'mon," he said, "you're acting like my sister."

"You know what Fletcher's like, you knew going in—"

"I guess I forgot. Let's drop it."

"Then why take the script in the first place? You're not getting the money you make now—the budget's not that big."

"I wanted to work with Fletch, as I told you. He's an important if unstable artist. I wanted to write it. I can afford to write what I want. Great way to live." He started in on the bread plate.

The waiters in Musso's were hard men who'd spent decades taking orders. They didn't put up with any nonsense. One of them came to the table and slapped down glasses of water. "What?" he asked them. Belinda expected the barrel-chested writer to order steak or a big slice of fish, but Keith ordered a salad. She ordered one too. The waiter left.

"Please, change your mind, Keith. Come back."

"No." He bit into the chewy bread. He looked at the ceiling, then at a faded hunting mural on the back wall, then at her.

"Did I ever tell you that my father was a writer?"

"No," she said, "I thought he played soccer."

"It was after that, after he became world famous in certain circles and married the daughter of a New York playwright. He went to Hollywood in 1950, at Mom's insistence, and he became a writer by dictating his fantasies to secretaries. Kinda amazing, isn't it? His scripts were wonderfully visual, loaded with trite emotions—crowd pleasers. He always said that when the back of his neck itched he knew he was doing something wrong. If I recant, I'll have to live with the itch. I don't like living that way."

The waiter slapped their salads on the table.

"My ex-wife," he said, "didn't understand that."

"I didn't know you were married."

"And divorced. No children."

"Keith!" A statuesque woman in a trendy white leather outfit was passing their table. "What happened to you last night?" She was touchingly beautiful, all eyes and perfect features and major hair. Keith introduced her as a writer.

"I just didn't feel like a party," he said.

"Don't you do that to me again," she scolded him, going off with a group of friends.

Belinda wasn't going to give up. "Look, we're having a big dinner tonight—Venner's in town."

"I've met Venner," Keith said happily. "He's someone only the eighties could invent."

"What do you have against him?"

"He's okay, a little smooth for my taste. But you know what? He's serious about the oceans and the rain forests, he's spending real money, not play dough."

"Well, terrific."

Keith smiled his crooked smile.

"You're not real interested in what others think, are you?" Belinda asked.

"No."

"Fletcher isn't either."

"Yes, he is. Within his own directing group. That's okay." He moved a wavy hank of dark brown hair away from his eyebrow. "I want the respect of my fellow writers, too, but I don't care what some able sitcom writer thinks."

"So, what about the dinner?"

"Belinda, I don't want back on board." He watched her sink into herself, frustrated. "Still water runs deep. That's a great description for you. So much beneath the surface. I was on a lake once somewhere in Washington state. It was dead still. I was in a canoe. The surface was broken by I guess a dozen tree trunks sticking up at angles. I paddled up to one, a huge tree, its roots splayed out in the air some three feet above the water, and I looked down and the trunk, massive goddamned thing, disappeared into the dark water till I couldn't see it anymore. It made me feel—uneasy, the surface of that water like glass, really beautiful, and those monster trees below. I couldn't figure out how they'd got there—uprooted—couldn't see the bottom. What lived down there? How big were those trees? Did some of them stand on the bottom? Was the bottom crowded by a dead forest? It was beautiful but there was so much hidden, only hints on the surface." Thoughtfully, he put the tip of his thumb against his teeth. "Like you."

Belinda was touched. She leaned against the hard booth, suddenly aware of it.

"I want to tell you about a script I wrote a while ago. It's called *Indictment*. Another pass at the justice system. Would you like to read it? Just for fun, no proposition." He realized that there were parts of Belinda in his main character, Chicky.

"Sure. I'd like to read it."

"Belinda, can I give you some advice?"

She didn't answer. He went ahead.

"You're better off without Fletcher now."

Belinda narrowed her eyes.

"In the last couple of years, you've become Fletcher's untitled associate, his alter ego, his amah, his undeclared wife, the handmaiden behind the throne. The word is out: if you don't have the juice to get to Fletcher directly, you go through Belinda Oliver." He checked her face for a reaction. "You can work on your own. Don't overstay with Fletcher."

"You've got a lot of nerve loading off all that stuff on me."

"Fletcher will not stay with you. And you're not happy with him."

"It's a very lively and challenging relationship. You wouldn't understand."

Fletcher bumped into Keith and Belinda in the office hall as he came out of the men's room. "Where've you been?" he demanded.

"Canoeing," Belinda said, gaily.

"Having second thoughts?" he asked Keith.

"No. Came back for Bob."

Fletcher grunted. "I want you to see someone," he said.

Guy Venner was towering over Yvonne in Fletcher's office.

"The writer," Guy said to Keith. "It all starts on the page, doesn't it?"

"Yes, but I'm not working here now," Keith said, shaking Venner's hand. "Fletcher made me an offer that I could refuse."

Venner turned to Fletcher. "What's this?"

"He had another offer and we lost him."

"Hell, really?" Venner said. Keith nodded. "Well, come for dinner anyway."

To everyone's astonishment, Keith accepted and sat down on an Italian chair.

"And you're the one who'll hold it all together," Guy said to Belinda with his smooth, playful charm. He expected to captivate everyone.

Belinda saw her chance and sprang for it. "Yvonne's going to glue it all together. I'm trying to convince Fletch to give me some directing responsibilities."

"Ambition," Guy said, checking his cuffs. "I like that. I remember you saying something about that. Not many women around can handle directing."

"Anything she wants," Fletcher bellowed, wrapping an arm around Belinda.

Keith was grinning and Fletcher hated it.

"I've always believed in letting my people bite off as much as they can chew," Venner was saying. His smile was contagious, his charm sunshine in the dim beautiful room. But behind the words, behind the enthralling power of the man, Keith heard the clank of traditional and rigid mores. "After all, we're not solving the Beirut crisis here, are we?"

Fletcher said, "Guy, this is a big international production. It'll be like Patton's Third Army out there."

"We're all kids playing in the attic," Venner said. "That's the fun of it. Never lose sight of the fun. When do you leave for Budapest?"

CHAPTER 13

Fletcher Avery's production team for *The Crossing* arrived in Budapest in July 1989, and found themselves in a city teeming with East German refugees. Budapest was the bellwether for a historic shift that would alter the face of Eastern Europe. Two months before, in May, Hungary had been the first East European country to open its borders to the West by removing the fence that separated it from Austria. The wall had cracked; everyone waited for the break.

The ancient city of Budapest, which dated back to Roman times, had seen migrations before. Buda was on the west bank of the Danube, and Pest was on the east bank. They had been separate cities, officially joined in 1873, but they were still separate—in looks, in interests, in manners. Buda had the air of ancient medieval Europe, hilly, cobblestoned, narrow streets leading upward to the castle and to revered old churches; Pest, on the flat land, was governmental and industrial and younger.

Fletcher had not won the Oscar. The demands for interviews, the invitations, the sudden heated attention had ceased. The morning after the Academy Awards ceremony, the telephones in his office had been so quiet that Belinda thought they were out of order—until one call came in, from Keith, inviting them all to lunch. It had been the only call that day.

Fletcher's disappointment, far deeper than he allowed anyone to see, was soothed by the reception the Hungarian and Eastern Bloc filmmakers gave him. For them, Fletcher's cachet as the "bad boy–enfant terrible" of American pictures outstripped the loss of an Oscar. He, his cast, and crew were plunged into celebrations that ranged from long intense dialogues cored by Hungary's seasoned respect for cinema aesthetics to boisterous declarations of the country's new political reality. Every night after dinner the first week they were in town, Fletcher, Belinda, Yvonne, and many crew members went to the Hungaria coffeehouse, an artists' hangout in Pest. Under ceiling frescoes, chandeliers, and towering marble columns, they pulled tables together and embarked on a shouting, laughing dissection of cinema and politics, Hungarian style.

For some months, Hungary had been in the middle of its own moral revolution against the totalitarian indifference and corruption that had looted and mismanaged it. New political parties were springing up, and a movement had started for free press, a constitution, minority rights, free enterprise. But only the old Communist party had money, cars, or phones. Sitting at the coffeehouse table were members of the Academy of Theater and Film Arts, the head of a Budapest film studio, assorted poets, musicians, a television director, and, usually, a writer who was working for the Free Democrats Party. Hungary loved American movies and American music. And Hungary loved Fletcher Avery.

This jubilation contrasted with the opening two weeks of Fletcher's shoot: the crew was not a unit, the rental gear wasn't working, the Hungarian actors' English was hard to understand, the locations were more difficult than anticipated, meticulously researched sites were regularly dropped from the script, the writer rewrote, actors learned lines only to have them replaced on the morning of their scene. Fletcher's directorial instincts had been off since they arrived, and he was suddenly unwilling to share with his crew the results of his conferences with his DP. By the end of the first week, Fletcher's communication with his crew had broken down. By the second week, he had become a maniac, personally and professionally.

"Here's the list," Belinda was saying to Yvonne. They were seated in Fletcher's hotel room with the art director and the Hungarian location manager, Miklos. "We're still looking for the carnival sequence—"

"We'll shoot it in Mohacs."

"Okay. The spa thing's at the Gellért Hotel, we'll use the Chain Bridge for the chase across the Danube, but we need a riding school, a leather shop, an industrial site—"

"Maybe Miskolc, grim town . . ."

"Are we putting off the grasslands sequence?"

Fletcher was sitting across the room with Gloria Griffin, holding her hand. She was an arresting American actress of thirty-five who hadn't made a picture in five years. Her part as Kat, an American translator having a short affair with the hero, Hammond, wasn't large, but it was crucial. Her key scene had been set in a spa where her betrayal at the hands of another American turned the hero's fate around and sent the film's action sailing in another direction. Gloria's depiction of Kat was a fulcrum of *The Crossing,* the kind of role that could create or reawaken an actress's career.

Gloria was quite aware of this. But Gloria was a woman in turmoil: she had kicked her coke habit, but she'd just learned that her estranged husband in the States had kidnapped their child as soon as she'd left for Budapest. Fletcher was spending a lot of time with her.

When the art director and Miklos left, Yvonne tipped her head toward Fletcher, who was still huddled in a hushed, intimate conversation with Gloria. "Fletcher, the charming confidant, is emerging," she whispered to Belinda.

Fletcher seduced secrets out of his actors, then disclosed them at key moments during production. Nothing was sacred. "I'm sure Gloria knows what's what," Belinda said.

"She's drinking vodka," Yvonne said quietly.

"This is her big rebreak," Belinda said. "She's not going to blow it and her sister knows where her kid is."

"Keep an eye on her. I'll get John to help her," Yvonne said, referring to John Harcourt, who was playing Hammond, the hero. He was forty, credentialed in both films and theater. Gloria had worked with him before, and of everyone in the cast, she knew him best. Had things been different, Gloria could have expected support from John, but he was going through a highly publicized paternity suit: whether they shot in a coffeehouse or at a horse farm twenty miles outside Budapest, the set was swamped with international reporters and TV camera crews, stalking Harcourt. He dodged them, he fled, he hid, he ate in his trailer.

Adding to the disorder, a grade-school buddy of Fletcher's was making a documentary about the filming of *The*

Crossing. He and his video camera were always underfoot, circling Fletcher or Gloria or Harcourt, bumping into reporters, unsettling the crew. And somehow, he always ended up next to Fletcher on the set.

The hotel room was suddenly full of assistants reworking the schedule around actors' children, Harcourt's court appearance in New York on his paternity suit, unscheduled political rallies in squares, crowds of East German refugees.

"There are no telephones in this country!" Belinda moaned. "How does anyone get anything done?"

Miklos, the Hungarian location manager, was a graduate of the state film school. "You always keep appointments," he said, smiling thinly, "because you can't reach anyone to change them."

Belinda shook her head. "I don't get it. How can anyone run a political campaign without a telephone?"

"We hold meetings. Everyone attends."

"Fletch," Yvonne called out, "about the grasslands."

"I'm not giving up the grasslands," Fletcher said through his teeth.

"You're going over budget, mister." Yvonne was always pushing him about the budget. "Any overage comes right out of your pocket. Guy's going to be here soon. He's not like Jerry, Fletcher. Guy'll see it. He sees everything."

Fletcher stormed back to the bridge over the Danube where they were shooting a scene with Harcourt and his nemesis— a high-level Hungarian diplomat.

"The sun's out," Fletcher yelled, grateful.

"It's only a light test," the camera operator replied.

Above, on the hilly Buda side, the Bel Air of Budapest, the suddenly rich were building huge houses. "Bel Air prices and Ethiopian wages," Yvonne said of the building boom. Down on the streets by the bridge, in an engulfing mist of exhaust, the sound of heavy traffic pounded around them— horns and squealing brakes and heavy trucks. Jackhammers bit into pavement; streetcars rattled past students with rucksacks, women with shopping bags, sour-faced businessmen. Undisturbed by the thunderous traffic, pudgy women from the country were selling embroidered clothes at the end of the bridge. An organ-grinder with a fake parrot on his shoulder, and dressed in a crushed top hat, checked jacket, and a fake beard played "Mack the Knife." Farther off, downtown, buildings were covered with scaffolding, the grime-cleaning brigade.

Flocks of extras—sidewalk artists, musicians, workers, and shoppers—stood around drinking coffee, speaking mainly Hungarian, but plenty of German, too.

"C'mon, c'mon, c'mon!" Fletcher shouted. The crew worked; makeup was summoned; problems mounted: someone cut his finger, the group of taxi drivers were moving too much, lines were flubbed or mixed up, Harcourt was walking too soon, the diplomat was looking at the Danube instead of at Harcourt, the extra in clown makeup carrying the flute was unintelligible, the taxi driver forgot his line.

"I don't feel any sense of horror from you," Fletcher said to Harcourt. "You wouldn't stand close to someone who's scaring the shit out of you."

Belinda was shouting: "Get those students back. Yes, they can watch, but get them back!"

Fletcher shouted, "Action!"

A cloud of pigeons swooped into the shot.

"Those fucking pigeons," the AD grumbled. They'd wrecked shots all day long.

Fletcher yelled, "Cut!"

"Organize those pigeons," Belinda screeched, loving the chaos. "I want every one of them in formation and on cue!"

Patsy and Vail were on a vacation that now included a trip to Budapest. They were coming out of their hotel in Munich, headed toward the train station, when the concierge stopped them.

"This package was delivered for you early this morning," the concierge said.

Impressive stickers and warnings were affixed to it. Vail put it under his arm, and he and Patsy hopped into a taxi.

"God, how I hate trains," Vail said to Patsy. "I won't let you talk me into this again. We had everything planned! And now this miserable side trip to Budapest. Why can't Gloria take care of herself?"

"It's not Gloria, sweetie, it's Fletcher."

"It is Gloria. Former stars are such difficult people. You said he said she was drinking again."

"I think Fletcher's exaggerating." Gloria Griffin was also Patsy's client; and when Patsy had seen her a month ago, had been excited about playing Kat for Fletcher. Now she was threatening to leave the production. "Fletcher asked me as a personal favor to drop over and try to work something out with her."

Vail started to open the package. Idly, Patsy looked away from the window to glance at it. It was a time bomb sitting on Vail's knees.

"Who would send such a thing to us on our vacation?" Patsy demanded. Vail mumbled the name of his attorney. "I'll have him shot when we get back."

Lying in the wrapping paper was a copy of Patrick O'Mara's bound book galleys, *Sky and Me: The True Story of the Star and Her Killer*.

Guy and Victor arrived in Budapest on the same day but from different directions. That evening, they were waiting for Belinda on the terrace of the Forum Hotel that overlooked the Danube. The Chain Bridge, strung with lights in the warm night, looped across to the Buda side of the city.

"There she is!" Victor said as Belinda dragged in. She dropped into a chair beside them. At one end of the terrace three Gypsy violinists were playing "Lara's Theme" from *Dr. Zhivago*.

"What I shall always remember," Belinda said to them, "is a ceaseless torrent of musical schmaltz. And I'm going to nuke the next violinist who plays that song." Victor immediately signaled the head violinist, pressed a bill into his hand, and received a solemn promise that "Lara" was scratched from the evening's card.

Victor was on a great high. Guy, sitting across from them, seemed dour and composed by comparison. A large leather file was open on his knees. Her father talked on, about *Crossing*, about looking forward to seeing part of the shoot the next day, about being back in Hungary.

"When were you here?" Guy asked him, not looking up from the beautiful leather file.

"After the war. First stationed in Austria, aide-de-camp to a NATO chieftain who did a lot of traveling. I don't know why we were in Budapest—it was just before the Soviets moved in. This city was wrecked—Castle Hill was in ruins. Today, just walking down a street, I saw bullet holes in the concrete of some of these buildings." He sipped his coffee enthusiastically. "You're too young to know it, Belinda, but it's hard to believe what's happening here. I remember when the wall went up and now I'm seeing it coming down."

Belinda smiled at his excitement. "Yes, Victor. And *Crossing* is timely as hell."

"It's incredible, isn't it?" Victor said, afraid to believe the good fortune that had suddenly blown his direction.

Working closely with the script from the book for months, Belinda was deeply, newly aware of the violence and complexity of its story. Victor's savage streak was safely and acceptably emitted through his characters, through the prism of his imagination. But on the surface, he seemed gracefully masculine, a flexible and cordial fashion plate. Sitting on the terrace in the warm Hungarian night, looking at the reflection of the bridge lights in the water, she compared Victor's safety valve violence to her own. Her ferocity had come spurting out in action, ripping up her life. But it seemed far away now. As long as she kept on the move.

"I've got to get some faxes off." Guy was rising, a sanguine, supremely confident man. "I'll meet you for dinner."

Belinda checked her watch. "No fax now, Guy."

"Don't be silly."

"Hungary doesn't fax by night."

Unfaxed, they walked outside, across the wide bridge to Buda heading toward the Vadro'zsa restaurant to join Yvonne and Fletcher. A thready, martial rendition of "Hang On, Sloopy," drifted across the water to them.

"Even at night, this city smells like an underground parking lot," Guy said. "Worst smog I've seen since Mexico."

"Yes, but Budapest's fascinating," Belinda said. "It's sort of like a cross between Italy and Mexico with a heavy Austrian overlay." Guy laughed, a deep rolling melody. He fell into step beside her. Guy Venner was cool and analytical and confident. But Fletcher was hot, aggressive, and intuitive. Venner enjoyed a reputation as a playboy; Fletcher did not. To Guy, creativity could be used to buff up new sales or programming. To Fletcher, creativity was all.

"Where is this restaurant?" Guy asked in his resonant voice.

"Up the hill," she said. "We'll get a cab over there."

The Vadro'zsa restaurant was set in a private house and garden in a residential area of Buda. They were shown to a table outside in the garden where dim lamps shone and the air smelled of flowers. Fletcher and Yvonne were not there.

Victor ordered the local eau-de-vie, *barackpálinka*, apricot brandy. He looked across at Belinda, the daughter who had changed his life, the daughter to whom he felt closer than anyone.

Even in the forgiving candlelight he could see the dark circles under her eyes and the fatigue lines around her mouth. "How's everything going?" he asked.

Guy said, "Yes, how do you like second-unit work—getting some great inserts?"

"Love it. And the whole shoot's going well, too," she added loyally.

"Yvonne says it's over budget."

"Not much."

Guy said nothing.

"There's a lot of press about Harcourt's paternity suit," Vic said. He began filling the silence by reciting gossip he'd heard about their shoot, most of which was untrue.

Venner wasn't listening. There was something about Belinda that thoroughly intrigued him. He wondered if he could get her into bed. He was pretty sure she'd duck. The more he thought about it, the more appealingly the moves arranged themselves in his mind.

"What do you plan on doing when this wraps?" Venner asked her.

She shrugged. "Life after Budapest?" She was so embroiled in the daily emergencies she hadn't thought of normal life in weeks. "I'd like to direct my own picture."

"Go for it," Victor said.

Guy contemplated her. "So you don't want to be a satellite," he said.

Belinda looked at Guy's smooth face, his shrewd eyes. He had precisely identified her discontent.

"We're going to put ten films a year into production," Guy said, slicing off a corner of fresh goose liver. "I'll give you a chance to direct if we agree on the script"—he said, laughing—"and on everything else."

"Money, producer, location, et cetera?" she said.

"That's right." He popped the goose liver into his mouth.

"Quit kidding. I'm too tired."

"I'm not kidding." He spread another minute slice of bread with goose liver and handed it to her. "There are people who've directed features without much more experience than you have. I know a guy who wrote a novel, adapted it to the screen, stood around on the set, wrote a second script, and got himself a directing deal. I know the kind of job you're doing. I'm not talking about a thirty-million-dollar shoot in Tangiers. I'm talking about a nice two-hour movie in a domestic location. Do you want to do it or not?"

"Is this on the level?" She distrusted the offer and started mentally listing other reasons it was being made.

"Try me."

"I will," she said.

Venner smiled flat into the astonished look on Victor's face. He raised his glass to Belinda to seal the bargain. He felt it needed no words. He would fund a film for her, and she would be, if he wanted, receptive to him.

"Goddamn," Vail muttered, "you won't believe this! Unconscionable!" His heated mumbles had punctured the iron miles all the way from Munich. "That son of a bitch!" Vail slammed his fist into the open book.

Patsy wasn't paying any attention to him as the train rocketed east from Munich through Austria to the flat, late summer plains of Hungary. She was thinking about Gloria and Fletcher knotted together on a shoot she had finally counseled against if Fletcher was both producer and director. But Fletcher had been high on the Oscar nomination, high on his own sense of rebirth, high on Venner's publicity. Patsy prayed her misgivings were mistaken.

"A bald-faced lie!" Vail shouted.

Patsy rose, steadied herself against the roll of the train, and took the book out of his hands. "Don't spend our vacation reading that trash," she said. "You can't do anything about it."

He took it away from her. "It's worse if I don't know what he's written."

She sat down and stared out the window. Her husband was a most annoying and surprising man. He swung from pettiness to generosity and compassion; he was loyal to old friends, cynical about and distrustful of the public taste, excitable and, sometimes, not very nice. But he could cut right through to the bone of an issue, a deception, a work of art, a human being. She smiled at him fondly, at his finely drawn face, his narrow eyes that turned up at outer corners and gave him a quizzical, playful look. Vail's noise was all an act. Inside, he was soft and vulnerable.

She'd met him in 1960 on what they'd later called a psychedelic bus, the most prominent design feature being a huge lightning streak on its side. She'd been just seventeen when she'd heard the siren call of the last of the Beats and the first of the flower children. She had left her mother, a blackjack dealer in Reno, and had run to San Francisco with the idea of being a singer in a jazz and poetry club. Her new connections there had landed her on the bus touring the west, living life as it came. And then Vail and his Korean war buddy, Bondy, had jumped onto the bus. Vail had had a come-hither eye, and a ripe, hilarious laugh. He and Bondy were Kerouac devotees who'd been on the bum for a while. Quite a while. Patsy had gone over to them and asked for a smoke, and, receiving one from Bondy, she'd sat down in Vail's lap, put her hands around his neck, leaned her head against his.

The train was slowing down for a little town with an unpronounceable name. Patsy McAulis was locked in the past, a respite from the present. "You were so cute on the bus in Colorado," Patsy said, with a sly smile.

Vail, reading, waved her memories away impatiently. "You were an uneducated beat chick," he muttered.

"Yes, I was. What fun." She'd panhandled for Bondy and Vail, and every afternoon she'd combed Vail's hair and made him iced tea. "Oh, lord," she sighed, "were we ever that young?"

Vail was so angry at Patrick's book that the scar on his forehead, won in the Korean War, stood out like a tiny crescent moon, chalky white. "I'm going to put out a contract on him," Vail shouted. "My sister never slept with him, never!"

Patsy couldn't help laughing. "Don't worry, Vail. When Diana reads it she'll kill him herself." Vail shut his eyes at the thought of his mother reading Patrick's book.

Patsy put her head against her seat, looked out the window, and let the train roll her. But Patrick and the book had become part of the trip now. She thought about Belinda and Patrick. The difference between them was that he had been loon crazy, and he had killed in the grip of it. Patrick, crazy, hadn't been sent to an institution but to a jail. Belinda had not been crazy, but she'd killed and had been sent to an institution, then to a mental ward. Justice in action. Killing had always been part of the American way of life; the murder rate in the U.S. outstripped that of other nations. Why had Belinda killed Archie? Patsy had felt like killing a lawyer once but she hadn't. There was fear in murder, and there was self-loathing. Belinda had spoken often about changing her life, but Patsy wondered if people ever really changed.

A few minutes later Patsy noticed the way Vail was reading. His glasses were propped on his nose, he held the book close to his face, tilting it toward the light of the window and the lamp above his head. Every second or so he would blink. He'd been reading for almost four hours but he'd only turned a few pages.

"Vail, why are you blinking?"

He looked up. "What?"

"Blinking. You're blinking as you read."

"Drops," he said immediately. "I put drops in my eyes. Strain."

"Strain? From what? You've only read about twenty pages."

Again, he waved her away imperiously. But Patsy watched him covertly as his head traveled down the page—a twenty-minute distance. She tried to remember when she'd last seen him reading anything. He'd given up the newspaper in the morning because, he said, he was sick of seeing everyone "reinvent the wheel and pass it off as brand-new," a dictum he applied to everyone from the State Department to the city planning department. She assumed that Sandra cut out reviews and other items for Vail to read at the office. She remembered the audiotape of the Updike novel she'd found in his car. The book had just been made into a film, which he had reviewed, comparing the novel to the picture. But Vail had no drive time to speak of; his office was a couple of miles from their home. It was much easier to read at home than get snatches of audiotape in the car.

She took off an earring and tossed it under his feet. "Vail, honey, my earring just fell off. Help me find it."

He immediately put down the book. "Where?"

"Over there somewhere," she said. It was a heavy and solid gold orb, not a hoop, and she could see it clearly resting against the angle between the floor and the berth. He peered down, pressing one finger against the bridge of his nose to keep his glasses from falling off. Then he raised his head and started to feel around the baseboard with his hand. "Can you see it?" he asked, getting down on his knees.

"No," she said, watching him. He held his head as if he were looking for it, but his hand was still sliding along as if he had no visual clues at all. She got down on the floor with him. "Vail," she said, "what's wrong?"

"I can't find it."

"No! What's wrong with your eyes?"

His head snapped up. "Nothing's wrong with my eyes."

"Don't tell me that." She reached across the space between them and snatched up the earring. "Here," she said.

He reached out for it, but instead of simply taking it from her, his fingers landed on her hand, an inch short and to one side of the ornament. He dropped his hand.

"I don't see very well anymore," he finally said.

"For how long? Did you go to a doctor? When did you first notice it?"

"Yes," he snapped, "I saw a doctor. I noticed it about two years ago."

"Two years? Why didn't you say anything?"

"It's not important. Everything's fine."

"But you can't see. You couldn't see my earring."

"I was just horsing around."

"You weren't! Tell me what's going on."

"I did. I don't see very well. It's age, got a lot to do with age."

"You're not telling me the truth."

"I am."

"I want the facts," she wailed. She pitched forward, putting her arms around him, pressing her face to his.

He pushed away from her. "The facts are that I have an incurable problem and I'm going blind." He moved to the other end of the seat, away from her.

"What?" She put her hands to her head. "Blind?"

"Yes. That's it in a nutshell. Called retinitis pigmentosa, a narrowing of vision until it narrows out."

"Oh, Vail," she moaned, sitting down across from him. "Why didn't you tell me?"

"I don't want anyone to know," he said fiercely. "Once people know, I'm finished."

"Oh, honey, that's not true," she whispered, aghast at what was happening to him. "It's not true of me!"

"Maybe not," he said grudgingly, "but it's true of anyone else, and you know it. A blind film reviewer—what a joke!"

"I'm having a hard time getting used to this," she murmured. "I'm sure there are things we can do. Have you—"

"I don't want to discuss it."

"But Neil, he could—"

"Neil and Sandra are already watching the movies for me, though they don't know it yet. I can still see enough to know what's going on." He was rising, and she reached out for him. "Quit that!"

She sank back on the upholstered ledge. The train was now shooting over a flat stretch of bare countryside. Blind? How could he be going blind? She looked at his face, set and sullen. He was afraid of appearing weak in her eyes, of being dependent and disabled, of losing her love to pity. She felt calmer, realizing that. "Okay, Vail," she said, "so go blind and don't ask anyone for any help. At least it will keep me out of the divorce courts."

"What?"

"Blind men don't have a lot of adulterous affairs."

An unwilling chuckle came out of him. "On the contrary, making love blind is the best way. The only problem is finding the door of the motel room."

She opened her arms. "Find these."

He lurched across the space between them, tumbled into her arms, stretched out beside her. "I was scared I'd lose you," he whispered savagely. "It was the worst nightmare. I'm no good to anyone blind, I can't face it, I can't deal with it, I know I've made a mess of it, I meant to tell you, but it would make it all real. . . ."

She stroked his hair. "Shush. I was good at panhandling, don't you remember? We've always got that to fall back on." She kept her voice light and buoyant.

Fletcher was trying to guard against what he called question overload, a form of director's mental fatigue. His feet felt as if he'd walked fifteen miles since noon, and they weren't even halfway through what he'd planned to do that night. His crew was unhappy: they didn't like night shoots but that was the only time they could shoot in this hotel spa. In a corner, one of his actors was preparing for his scene by the Method, breathing hard, going back in memory, weeping at childhood woes, performing gymnastics. "Fletch," he asked, "I'm trying to figure out if my character would wear his towel over his shoulders or rolled around his neck like a jock. Whaddya say?"

"Shoulders," Fletcher said, spotting Patsy standing behind a knot of extras in bathing suits. Vail was with her. He went up to them, grinning. "Patsy, you're here! Marvelous! Welcome to our set. Gloria, look who's here."

They were shooting in the Gellért Hotel's spa, a baroque, cavernous, thermal water-fed pool. A domed mustard-colored glass ceiling flew above giant, ornately carved columns, washing them, thanks to the lights, in a golden sheen. Branching out from the columns on the second story, bulbous balconies overlooked the vibrantly green blue pool below.

An hour later, the sound man was shaking his head like an old horse in front of the glue factory. Fletcher, distracted, didn't want to hear anymore about the hard room that was playing havoc with the sound. Gloria, wrapped in a terry-cloth cape, was standing with Patsy by the edge of the pool and sipping from a paper cup. Above, on a center balcony, a sinister-looking Hungarian character actor was leaning over, trying to hear something Belinda was saying. He wore a cheap suit and striped tie, carried a viola case.

"Everyone shut up!" Fletcher roared.

"Quiet," his AD repeated.

Harcourt, in a bathing suit and towel, stood under the overhang on the pool level beside the flamboyantly decorated entrance. "Harcourt, you just come here, to the mark," Fletcher said, winded, "and watch her swimming. She's all alone. And that's when you know it's a setup." He turned to the sound man. "No dialogue here. Sam! Shoot over his shoulder, come up over his shoulder and pick up Gloria in the pool and just follow her."

"But we start on Harcourt's profile, slip over the side and out, right?"

"Yes. Just glide past him. He's not moving."

"Sound rolling. Speed."

"Scene number one hundred fifty, take four."

"Action."

It went smoothly.

Gloria got out of the pool, her dresser threw a robe over her, makeup rushed out of the crowd and patted her face. She sipped from her cup. Fletcher went up to her; he knew she was drinking vodka. "Fix her eyes. Bigger. She knows what she's about to do. Gloria, got to see everything in your eyes. When you turn at the end of the pool you see Harcourt, and you know he knows. The camera will be in tight, then we'll move out and we see Stanos slipping back from the balcony up there like a cat. Let's try it once."

But Gloria was tiring. The evening wore on, take after take. "Honey!" Fletcher said loudly, "the look on your face goes from indifference to horror and each one is more forced than the last."

At eleven o'clock that night, Gloria was out of the pool, drinking, and looking for a scapegoat. Extras and crew muttered uneasily. Patsy went over to her.

"C'mon," Fletcher said, moving Gloria away from Patsy

toward the crew strung out along the side of the pool. He said in a normal tone of voice that echoed along the tile and marble: "Just think of what your mother did to you when she read in your diaries about you and your brother, think about the horror and the shame. You felt like a worm, an enraged worm. You've never gotten over it, you're still carrying that humiliation—"

Gloria darted backward, her outlined eyes huge, her face twisted. "You bastard!" she snarled, hurling the paper cup at him. "How dare you bring that up?"

"Get in there and do it, yes, just like that," Fletcher yelled. "Do it now. Give us the shame and the fury—"

Yvonne, on the second story, heard them as clearly as everyone else, and cringed. She leaned over the balcony. "Fletcher!" she yelled, but she was too late.

"You immoral son of a bitch!" Gloria shrieked, running down the tile corridor. Patsy broke out of the stunned extras and went after her.

"Okay, so it backfired," Fletcher said aggressively. "Sometimes I go too far, I know that. But I had to cut through her defenses. Actors have masses of them. I had to find her vulnerability. Damnit, we'd still be there if I hadn't—"

"Don't give me that," Patsy said. "You were deliberately callous. You have a death wish, Fletcher. You've caused a major problem—you haven't solved anything."

"If I hadn't cut through," he bellowed, overriding Patsy, "she'd never respond emotionally. Gloria's got a lot of inner rage."

"That's exploitation. You know how frantic she is about her child. You know this is the first job she's handled in years—and you slam her with incest in front of everyone!" Patsy spun around tightly. "If I hadn't heard that myself I would never have believed it—even of you. What's the matter with you, Fletch?"

"Cut to the chase, Patsy."

"She's going back home. She can't face the crew and she won't work with you. She means it."

Fletcher was suddenly quiet. Patsy, Yvonne, Belinda, and the AD were ranged around him in his hotel room. It was three in the morning. He got up and poured another large glass of apricot brandy. Gloria's big scene with Harcourt was to be shot the next night in the spa.

"Nah, she doesn't mean it. I'll get her back," he said. "I'll grovel and plead and apologize."

But by noon the next day, after Gloria had screamed at him, and slammed the door in his face, Fletcher knew he'd have to change his shooting plan until she was under control. He sent Patsy up to calm her while he stayed in his room with his team going over their dwindling options. The mood was morose; the ferocious logistics controlled their choices. Fletcher would have to film the crucial spa scene that night or change the script and shoot it in some other location.

"The hotel is not moving," Miklos said. "You get one more night in the spa and no more."

"I don't want to lose that spa," Fletcher said. "Anyway, the hotel'll come around, if not now, later. Offer more money."

"It's not money," Miklos said.

"It's always money."

"No, it's got to do with the tourist season—the spa is the hotel's greatest attraction."

"Cast someone else," Yvonne said.

Fletcher looked at her angrily. "What a stupid idea."

"It's not a big part."

"It's an important part!"

"Budapest is full of fine actors," the AD put in.

"Oh, God," Fletcher moaned, "cut the crap."

"Get Gloria ready to work by tonight," Yvonne said, "or change the location and do it with her later." But that meant changing a whole string of locations and everyone knew it.

The telephone rang. Belinda picked it up. "Patsy," she said. Everyone looked at her. "I see. Okay." She hung up. "Gloria's quit. She's leaving tonight."

"Ah, that's just talk. She's drunk."

"Patsy says she's packed and comparatively sober."

Once again, Fletcher went up to Gloria's room to beg her to stay. But it was useless.

The hotel hallway looked as wide as a boulevard. "Patsy," Fletcher said as they walked away from Gloria's room down toward the stairs, "what am I going to do?"

Patsy waved her arms, frustrated. "I don't know."

They came to the stairs. He looked down them, slowing. Patsy started down. Fletcher stopped walking. "I've got it!" He stood at the top of the stairs, stunned by his own brilliance. "Belinda."

"Belinda what? Oh, no, Fletch," Patsy said, realizing the rash course of action he was now contemplating, "that's no good at all. She has no acting experience—"

"It's a small role. There's only one big scene, and even that one's short—"

"But it's a tough scene, and she's got no experience."

"I can get it out of her. She'll be just fine. I mean, Patsy, God has sent this to us. We're not doing an Oscar film here, we're doing a television thing. Belinda can handle it, she knows all the lines—"

"If you're going to start picking people out of your crew, why not the script supervisor, why not one of the extras?"

"The extras don't know the lines and half of them are unintelligible Hungarians. No," he yelled, more convinced than ever, "this is it."

It was three o'clock in the afternoon when he and Patsy returned to his hotel room. Belinda was stretched on the sofa, Yvonne was on the floor, talking into the phone, the AD was drinking coffee and eating sweet red peppers from a dish. Miklos, location manager, was slouched in a chair, his eyes closed.

"Sit up," Fletcher said, nudging his leg. "We got a plan." Patsy sank into a chair and looked at the carpet. Fletcher sat down on the floor and put a hand around Belinda's ankle. "You're going to play Kat. We're shooting at eight o'clock tonight." He turned to his AD and the location manager. "Get it going. We're going to be back on track." Astonished, they both rose.

"What else are you smoking, Fletcher?" Belinda asked, stunned. She looked over at Patsy. Patsy smiled confidently. The AD slammed out of the room with Miklos. "Are you *crazy*?" Belinda yelled, leaping to her feet. "I've never acted in my life! I can't do that part."

"Yes, you can." Fletcher was actually smiling.

"No, no, shut it down, we'll get another location later,

maybe Gloria will be back. I'm shooting the bridge inserts tomorrow with the second unit. This is nuts!"

But Fletcher seemed calm and happy. He took her wrist and pulled her down. "No, it's not. I don't have those options, and Gloria isn't coming back. But you can do Kat."

"Patsy, for Christ's sake, I can't do this."

Patsy rose, smoothing her wrinkled skirt. "It's your choice. He thinks you can. He has all the reasons why you can. But it's up to you. Would you like me to leave while you two discuss it?"

"No. And I'm not discussing it." She turned to Fletcher, shaking his hand off her wrist. "I can't do it. Yvonne, talk to him."

He put a finger over her lips. He looked at her face, his gaze caressing her. "Yes, you can," he said, softly. "You'll do it for me. You know all the lines. I'll walk you through it. All you have to do is show me on your face what you're feeling. You have such powerful feelings right under the surface. You know what it's like to love, you know what betrayal's about, you've been afraid—who hasn't? We've never talked about this, but you know what losing is, too. All I'm asking is that you show your feelings truthfully in Kat, and I'll walk you home." He ran a hand down her cheek. "Please, honey, help me. I can't get out of this box without you."

Under the spa's high glass dome ceiling, Belinda faced the head gaffer, prop man, Fletch, the focus puller, camera operator, the DP with the contrast glass around his neck, the camera grip, the boom man, and, behind them continuity, Yvonne, the AD, and the sound recorder. They all looked like strangers.

Fletcher said: "You've just had this big scene—with Stanos. You think he's left the pool. You know you've been used, sucked into betraying Harcourt and you've got to tell Harcourt in order to save him. You love him; you know he doesn't love you. Don't let him sidetrack you. Action."

Belinda pushed off from the side of the pool, swimming smoothly toward Harcourt, yelling the character's name: "Richard!" He was turning away. "Richard!" She leaped out of the pool, raced toward him, slipped on the tiles, spraying water everywhere.

"Keep going!" Fletcher called out. "What do you want to

tell him? Tell him!" The lines tumbled out of her.

"Cut!" Fletcher yelled. "Harcourt, don't let her—you don't want to hear about it. You don't want to believe it. Can't be true! Get away from her. Belinda, don't let him get away. He doesn't want to hear you—tell him! Tell him! Pick it up from the edge of the pool. Action!" He let her get three lines into it, then interrupted. "Belinda, force him to listen to you. If he won't listen, he's dead. Keep rolling, goddamnit. Harcourt, don't let her, she's going to weigh you down with something appalling. Get away from her—watch your fucking marks! Get away, get away or she'll tell you . . ." Finally, he let them get all the way through it without breaking.

Belinda emerged from the housing of her terror astonished: acting was freeing. As she pursued Harcourt under Fletcher's relentless directions, following him around the side of the pool, tugging and pulling at him, she saw not the actor she'd known for weeks but a different man behind his eyes. She felt her own personality inside her shifting. She was out of the prison of herself. She wasn't Belinda. She was Kat. These were her feelings but they weren't coming from the same place inside her, they were precise, not diffuse, and she wasn't responsible for them, only for the truth of them.

"Cut! Print!" Fletcher bawled, his voice echoing in the spa. "Great!" He trotted up to Belinda and threw an arm around her.

Harcourt said, "You're good, Belinda. Congratulations." Privately, the grumbling crew, solidly against Fletch by now, thought it was probably the only scene in the film that would work.

"Sit here," Fletcher said, motioning at a bench at the side of the pool. He put a towel cape over her shoulders.

"Did it really work?" she asked him.

"You saved it," Fletcher said in a confidential voice. "You never looked better. Just beautiful. Now we got to shoot the other two Kat scenes, get a bunch of reaction shots . . ." He was thinking aloud. The prop man was hovering, the AD was hovering. "Leave us alone a minute, will you?" They stepped back reluctantly. The camera and lights were being moved for the next setup. The noise in the room was horrendous. He clasped her waist and kissed her. People were still hovering impatiently. "I suppose you want to be an actress now."

"Don't make me laugh."

"That's good. Just keep that same high energy for Kat in the next scene. It's a rough scene, hard to do—" He put both hands on her shoulders, holding her apart, holding her gaze. "You've acted before, haven't you? Why didn't you tell me?"

"No, I haven't."

"Something . . ." His dark intense eyes examined her intimately.

Belinda was high, perfectly in tune with herself, as if she could make no mistakes, as if anything were permitted. "Maybe it runs in the family," she said. "Sky . . ."

"Sky Wyman?" Fletcher said softly, deliberately, his eyes caressing her, completely focused on her. "Of *course*—Vail's sister . . ." He took her hand. "You're not related to Patsy, but to Vail, right? How secretive you are," Fletcher said, amazed and then, in rapid succession injured and angry. "Why haven't you told me before? Did anything happen between you and Sky? You've never ever talked about her!" He clamped both hands on her shoulders. "Did Sky embarrass you, did she—?"

"Fletch—" the AD tried again.

"Can't you see we're talking?" Fletcher hurled at him. "Scram!" He turned back to Belinda and immediately picked up the intensely intimate exploration. He no longer seemed angry but elated. "What do you remember most about Sky?"

On the other side of the pool, Yvonne was watching them. Fletcher was tense in a new way, the strain reaching deep inside him. It's not fun for him anymore, she thought. She'd seen him browbeat and abuse actors, protect them and court them, but he'd been way off the line with Gloria and she suspected it was desperation that drove him because he knew the film was not working. She started walking around the pool and reached them just as Guy Venner came up.

"I heard about Gloria," Guy said, exuding confidence and sophistication. "Too bad, but I must say, Fletcher, you punt well. Who'd have thought about casting Belinda in the role?"

Fletcher looked up but didn't move from Belinda's side or take his arm away from her waist. "Had to have someone in six hours who knew the lines and looked enough like Gloria so we could cheat some of the old stuff."

Guy beamed at Belinda. "You never know—you might like acting over directing. There I was," he went on to Fletcher, "making her an offer to direct a film, and what does she do? Jumps into acting."

"What film?" Fletcher asked, looking up from two folk masks the prop man had just handed him.

"We're going to handle several productions a year for the next two years," Guy said, checking his watch. "Belinda wanted to direct, and I told her we're open, depending on script. When she gets home. Damn, I've got to get to the airport."

Fletcher burst out laughing, his arm falling off Belinda's waist. "Oh God, not *that* again. Please, directing's a man's world." He rose, looking around at the people carrying lights and flags and mikes and makeup, the scurrying horde.

"That depends, doesn't it?" Guy replied indifferently. "I'm off," he said to Belinda. "See you back home."

"Let's do one film at a time," Yvonne said. She had recognized Fletcher's mood and it was extremely dangerous. It came from fatigue and frustration and fear. She'd seen it once on *Alms* in an unforgettable and now legendary episode when he'd exploded at an actor in an orgy of egoistic, maniacal recriminations. The actor had been talking about his next role, instead of concentrating on the work at hand.

Patsy, just back from seeing Gloria off at the airport, came up to Fletcher. Someone was asking him about the location shoot on the Hungarian grasslands. "All right!" Fletcher snarled. Vail, beside Patsy, saw Fletcher launch into an argument with the prop man about the masks. Something had changed, something big, and Vail knew he was about to see the Fletcher Avery he'd always imagined was there, the shadow Avery, the dangerous Avery.

Others picked it up, too, and were backing away. "Aren't we ready to shoot yet?" Fletcher roared. "David, get rolling!"

The sound man, talking to himself as he approached, was aware of none of this. "Most of Harcourt's lines are gonna have to be dubbed. This fucking tile, man, is killing us."

"I'm shooting in five minutes!" Fletcher was yelling. "Get on the balcony," he ordered Belinda.

Yvonne went with her. "It'll be fine," she said.

"What's the matter with him?" Belinda asked as they went up the stairs to a balcony.

"Fear. Afraid the picture's no good, afraid he can't rescue it, tired to the center of his bones. Don't let him get to you. He'll try. Just do the part, just shut him out—"

" 'Shut him out'? My God, Yvonne, I can't do this without him. I don't know what I'm doing."

"Belinda!" It was Fletcher, below on the tile by the pool. "Hit that mark on the balcony!" She did so. "Now go back, farther, farther, camera's following you here, okay there, back there, then run forward around the pool up there, and hit that mark!" She did that, stopping just before the railing. "Stanos!" The Hungarian character actor waved from the opposite balcony. Fletcher repeated the same action with Stanos, coming forward from the shadowed overhang onto the balcony and stopping. "Now, Belinda, when you see Stanos you've got to give us everything—this man is going to kill you and you know it, you freeze, and that's when I want a look of submission and horror and triumph. You know that by dying you can save Richard."

"Oh, God," Yvonne whispered to Patsy. "That's hard enough for the most experienced actors."

"I know, I know," Patsy said.

"She can't do that," Vail muttered. "He's crazy, that son of a bitch."

It went on past midnight. The look on Belinda's face was never good enough, she was panting from the short run, she wasn't panting enough, she was faking, she was not on the mark. "Can't you do this simple thing?" he screamed at her from the floor. After the fourteenth take, Belinda was crying and the tears showed. Fletcher threw up his hands. "Well, ladies and gentlemen, I guess she can't do it. Honey, you're a real piece of work. How long have we been together? You've always given me what I want—why stop now?" He looked at his crew. They looked at the floor. "Let me tell you, Belinda, if you can't do this, you can't direct. She wants to direct! Can you imagine that?" he shouted to the silent crew. "The arrogance of it! Why is it that the amateurs come in and think they can do everything better than the pros who've done it for years? Hey, Belinda—maybe you can run sound in a few years." He whirled back to his crew. "Would you ever have guessed that's a relative of Sky Wyman up there acting like a schoolgirl, mugging and indicating and faking?" He let that one sink in, then turned around to face Belinda. "I guess genes don't give us anything after all. You're pathetic. I shouldn't wonder you didn't want anyone to know—"

"Fletcher!" Patsy screamed. "Cut it out!" Vail jumped; her nails were digging into his arms.

Belinda was looking down at Fletcher from the balcony, hearing his voice echoing against the tile walls and floors. The blood thudded through her. She gripped the balcony rail. She wanted to kill him. The shooting, mushrooming craving seized her. She'd done it before; she recognized the appetite as loaded and unstoppable as a convulsion.

Fletcher was completely out of control. She'd seen prisoners like that, girls who snapped, exploded right in your face. She could escalate the mad flight, ride it into violence, or she could let go, calm down. In the crowd behind him, she saw Patsy and Vail, looking at Fletcher with shock and anger, she saw Yvonne waving her to come down. Fletcher was still shouting, the colors in his voice sliding from sarcasm to contempt to a phony appeasement. But no matter what he said, he wasn't as tough as the girls in the school.

Rage drove sound out of her. "You've gone too far and you will never get back again!" Her voice, panicky and full of desperation, reverberated around the pool. "Do you want the scene or not?" She let go of the railing; her hands ached, her fingers felt broken. Fletcher had shut up and was staring at her. "Stanos, get ready!" she shouted, and to the cameraman: "Roll it!" She spun away from the railing, back to the far end, then ran forward, hit her mark, took a beat, and jerked her head up. Stanos, from a dead run to make it in time, crashed into his railing, cracking his knee, the pain shivering across his morbid face. In the loony bin, she'd seen pain like that shake across another face as the head psych-tech cracked an iron bar across a girl's knees.

Belinda jerked backward from the waist, her eyes still on Stanos, whose pain made him look even more threatening. He growled. She had fused in the role. She looked up and down the tiled spa for escape, then realized she needed none because she would not escape. She knew she was acting, but it didn't feel like acting now. The man Kat had loved was gone. Fletcher was dead, too. It was over. She herself would soon be dead. Belinda and Kat held still for a beat, knowing she'd locked everything on her face, knowing they had it.

"Cut," she said. She turned from the railing and walked away feeling as high as she once had on Haldol, walking on cushions, walking on the quaking bog, knowing nothing for her would ever be the same again.

CHAPTER 14

DECEMBER 1989

"It's just like the old days." Patrick O'Mara chuckled. He was looking into a wall-sized mirror, remembering his former life as an actor. A makeup man flourished a powder brush across his face, looked distastefully at O'Mara, and left him sitting in the makeup room. But Patrick didn't notice; he was keyed up for his first television interview about his book, *Sky and Me*.

Patrick was facing Juan Ramondo's reflection in the mirror. Ramondo, the host of a popular Los Angeles afternoon talk show, had dark eyes and shiny, vinyl-black hair. He held a copy of Patrick's book in one hand. With a short smile at Patrick, Ramondo turned away to talk with his secretary. A large monitor in the corner revealed the studio audience laughing at the heavy labor of the warm-up man. It was countdown to airtime.

Ramondo's secretary left. On the monitor, the warm-up man cracked a final joke and retreated to boisterous audience applause. Music was coming up from somewhere.

Juan Ramondo was studying Patrick, who held his hands in front of him like long bony paws, not useless, exactly, but not useful. There was something creepy about the aging man.

"You don't like me," Patrick said to the mirror image of Ramondo.

"I don't have to like my guests," Ramondo replied in his soft, Latin-accented speech.

"Think of your ratings. My book's been out a week and it's already on the best-seller list."

"I *am* thinking of my ratings."

A harried but cheerful woman put her head into the room. "One minute!" she said to Juan.

"Get ready," Juan said to Patrick. He ducked out of the room, went down a narrow hall, turned a corner, opened a door, and stood behind a huge curtain. Ramondo put on his television face as the audience on the other side of the curtain stilled. He got the sign, curtains parted, and Juan, his television face alight, charged onto the stage, arms up. "What a show today, folks!" The audience applauded wildly, the music soared—a hard-driving, no-fooling beat. Juan tried to speak but he was drowned out. Finally a hush descended on the audience, punctuated only by little cries of adoration.

Juan said: "Going to be talking about infatuation and murder. What happens when love goes too far. And our guest today is none other than the man who killed Sky Wyman, who has served his time in prison and has written a best-selling book . . . Patrick O'Mara!" A second set of curtains opened and Patrick, his shoulders rounded, his smile fixed, a phony expression of, at once, sheepish bewilderment and excitement, stepped out.

In her sitting room at the top of Vail's house, Diana Wyman watched *The Juan Ramondo Show* without moving. Sara, in a wing chair, shifted constantly. She'd come to talk to Patsy about the anonymous letters, which she had in her purse. But she'd been ambushed by her mother and the televised Patrick.

"But, Mr. O'Mara," Juan Ramondo was saying, "you must have known when you were going to kill her—"

Diana winced.

"Mother, don't watch this," Sara said.

"I *was* her," Patrick was saying. "She was me. I wouldn't kill myself, would I?"

"Plenty have."

"It was when I became convinced that she was an impostor, that she'd taken Sky's place, taken my place in destiny—you see, that woman walking next to me in her body was an impostor—that's what I thought then—it was crazy," Patrick said disarmingly. "I was crazy. But I was right, too. She was so famous that she was like a public relations forgery of herself. She wasn't the Sky I'd known."

"He's right about that," Diana murmured.

Sara poured herself another cup of tea. The latest anonymous letter had said, "Lindy and I are one . . . She and I have had the same experiences in different ways. That's why I know she has to pay, why I must be her executioner. . . ." It had been chilling. Sara had to talk to someone.

Patrick was saying, "I knew I had to kill her. And I will have to live with that until I die."

"And live pretty well," Juan interjected. "Your book's climbing the charts; you're going around the country promoting it—"

"The money's not for me," Patrick said, intensely. "It's for Sky. I've set up a scholarship in her name at UCLA."

"A scholarship?" Juan asked, surprised. "You come from a wealthy New York family, don't you?"

"Yes, but my father cut me off when I insisted on acting as a career."

Sara remembered the father—a bullet-headed man with a military bearing who'd greeted her in a vast marble foyer. It had been 1961. Sara had arrived for the weekend. Sky had refused Patrick's smothering attentions but Sara had been flattered, not realizing she was his substitute for her sister. It was hard to believe now that she'd once been in love with Patrick, that she'd had sex with him in that Long Island mansion, that he had, in his ecstasy and despair, called her "Sky."

Sara closed her eyes, still powerfully humiliated by that moment in bed with Patrick, naked, stripped, less. He'd been the first man to show her the length of the shadow Sky cast across her life. But not the last.

Sara looked at the television screen. Patrick had been a vibrant, elegant youth. Now he looked gray and washed out and old.

"How did your father react when you were arrested for murder?" Juan was asking.

"He died before that. But Mother always understood," Patrick replied quietly. "She left me well off."

Juan was on his feet, springing toward the audience. "Questions? How about some questions?"

A woman in a blue suit and a nervous mouth waved her hand. Juan thrust the mike toward her. "Yes. I want to know if he took anything of Sky's?"

"What do you mean?" Juan asked her.

"Well, after he killed her. Did he take anything from her, like a ring—a little memento-like thing?"

"No, of course not," Patrick said, startled. "See, I was a sick man back then, sick in the head. I was thinking that as soon as she was dead, she would be the real Sky again. And I looked down at her, lying there, and she *was* Sky again and I was me again."

"Mother!" Sara cried. "For god's sake!" She felt soiled by the ugly, silly glare of Patrick's book.

"Do hush up, Sara Bay," Diana said, not looking at her daughter.

A woman in beige with large, heavy eyes was standing in the audience, demanding: "Are you sorry?"

The camera moved in for a close-up of O'Mara's response. He looked thoughtful and sad. "For releasing her from the impostor? No." The audience gasped. A few applauded. O'Mara looked straight into the camera. "For killing her, yes, and for the pain I've caused her family. I want them to forgive me." Sara shivered, transfixed by his tone. Patrick was nuts, but his desperation was human, and he was sane enough to be sorry. "Mrs. Wyman, if you're watching today, please forgive me." His chin trembled and his eyes filled with tears. "Please, Mrs. Wyman . . ."

Diana clicked off the television set. "Never. Never," she hissed at the set. "I will not put up with it."

"I'll bet you're not against capital punishment anymore," Sara muttered.

"I most certainly am," Diana replied. "But they shouldn't have let him out! He's mad—mad then, mad now, only *now* he has more company—the system of justice in this country that can let someone like that out."

"I'm sorry I brought it up," Sara said, exasperated, "but don't hide behind the issue. You're always doing that."

Diana Wyman's old face was suffused with an unnatural rosy tint. Her voice echoed in the room—strong, injured, pulsing. "Just what do you suggest I do, Sara Bay? Debate him? Sue him? Kill him?" Her anguish spilled out of her in a sudden tormented sob. Her grief was huge, dreadful, obliterating. "Leave me alone! You can't know, none of you can know!"

Patsy and Eddie were seated in an air-conditioned Westside coffeehouse, drinking chilled coffees, when Juan Ramondo's television show slapped onto the TV screen in the large cheerful room.

There was no middle ground in the public's carnivorous appetite to hear Patrick explain, over and over, how crazy he was, how he'd killed the screen star, how he'd adored her, when he'd slept with her. Some people in the audience spoke of Sky as of their own sisters; others spoke of her in the possessive, remote tones they might use about public property.

"This is so weird, Mom," Eddie said, watching the monitor.

"It's one of the penalties of being in the public eye," Patsy replied. Eddie was growing up. Almost eighteen, he was a tall, relaxed, laid-back, California blond with a winsome smile.

"That's really the guy?"

"That's the guy."

"Jeez, why did I pick this place?" Eddie mumbled. He'd chosen Espresso Con as a treat for Patsy's forty-ninth birthday.

"We can't hide from it, honey. He's written the book and a lot of people are talking about it." She looked around at the marble-topped tables with their ice cream parlor–style chairs. "I like it here," she said.

Eddie was looking at the screen. "Mom, I was thinking about Fletcher the other day. Why did he and Belinda break up?"

"I don't know, Edward. Love is hard sometimes. You know that."

"Yeah," he said, with feeling, thinking of Zoe, a girl he'd been crazy about. But Fletcher was a film director and he wasn't missing a hand so it didn't seem like a real comparison to him.

"What's happened between you and Zoe?" she asked.

"She turned out to be shallow, Mom."

She reached across the table and squeezed his shoulder. That's what he said when he broke up with a girl and it usually meant that she had not been able to get past his missing hand. "You'll find someone wonderful when the time comes," she said.

"The relationship just wasn't working," he said. It wasn't working because they weren't having sex, and they weren't having sex because of his hand.

"You're sure you don't want to try a super, deluxe, electronic computer hand?" Patsy said.

"It still looks fake."

"Edward, good friends don't care. You could have a green hand attached to you—"

Eddie frowned. "Okay, Mom, I've heard your green hand speech before. Enough." He nested his stubby wrist in the palm of his right hand.

"I understand, Eddie." Her thoughts went to Fletcher. He'd returned from Hungary, demanding and miserable, asking her to intercede with Belinda. Patsy had refused; he'd threatened to change attorneys, and she'd actually hoped for a while that he would, but he started editing *Crossing* instead.

Ramondo was still taking questions from the audience. "You should have been executed," a woman in a black suit said. The audience applauded.

"I agree," Patrick said, dolefully.

"What was Sky like?" Eddie asked. She seemed mythic, unreal.

"She was very kind," Patsy said. "I always liked Sky. But she was self-destructive. I don't think her life was very happy."

On the screen, a man in a wrinkled jacket was asking, "Aren't you just doing this as a stunt?"

"No. I owe it to Sky to tell the truth," Patrick said with a pout.

"Sickening," Patsy said.

"C'mon, Mom, we're getting out of here," Eddie said.

The sunshine and the heat baked the street, warmed them up like a flame.

"Was Sky alive when I was born?" Edward asked.

"Yes." She slid into the driver's seat of her car and waited for the next question.

Eddie shut the door on his side. "My—other parents," he said, "can I ask you a question?"

"Yes, dear," she said softly.

Across the years, the whispered argument between Patsy and Vail about his real mother came back to him with force. She'd committed a terrible wrong, or she'd caused it to be done. And out of the whispers had come his feeling that he, by being born, maybe by being born without a hand, marked and different—had it been part of whatever his mother had done? His questions about her and his father were always with him like the sound of traffic, like his skin.

"Edward . . . ?"

He had a sudden sense of dread. He didn't want to know.

"Ask whatever you want," Patsy whispered.

"Maybe some other time, Mom. God, start the car, it's broiling in here."

Patsy started the car, turned on the air-conditioning. A hot wind from a vent hit her face. She felt cowardly. She wanted to press him to ask; she wanted everything out in the open. But she held back because of Vail. As his vision decreased, and his secrecy about it grew, he became more desperate about everything, especially about Eddie.

"I wanted to ask about Dad," Eddie said in the silence. "Does he seem upset to you these days?" He tried a laugh. "I mean more upset than usual."

"He's under a lot of pressure over the Patrick thing," which was true, but by no means all.

"You and Dad are arguing a lot lately."

"It's a tense time, honey. Vail's not getting any younger." She sighed.

"What, Mom?"

"Nothing. Just thinking of all the things life throws at us that we don't expect."

"Does every creep in this country have a fucking book inside him?" Vail yelled at Schurl. It was four o'clock in the afternoon, *The Juan Ramondo Show* had just wrapped up.

Schurl's office reflected his enthusiasm for the American West. Vail called the decor "rancho roundup." A lariat and an antique set of spurs, pictures of Indians, knotty pine paneling, a cracker barrel, rough wood chairs, and a send-up poster of Custer's last stand.

Vail was sitting on a horsehair chair beside the desk; Schurl was standing at the mirror of his dressing room off the office, putting on a clean shirt.

"Do you know how many requests for Sky this and Sky that I'm getting?" Vail said. "That son of a bitch has brought it all back."

"Hand me that other cuff link, will you, Vail?"

Vail saw it on the corner of the desk. He stabbed his hand toward it, looking up as Schurl shut the dressing room door.

When Vail looked down for the cuff link, he'd lost sight of it in his narrow field of vision. "Shit," he muttered.

"Vail, toss the link." Schurl was tying his tie.

Vail strained to scan the desk. Then he spotted it! But he didn't dare toss it. He carried it over to Schurl.

Vail was living in a world of denial. His vision was now so limited that the screen looked like a petri dish or a special-effects iris-in: a circle of visible action on a field of black. He could not see what happened outside the circle. Reading was slow and difficult, but his system at screenings worked well with Sandra taking notes and typing transcriptions, which Vail pretended to read. But after everyone left for the day, Vail lifted the audiotapes out of her desk; it was from these that he slowly wrote his reviews on his computer. Vail was certain that neither Neil nor Sandra suspected anything. He didn't think about being exposed or about the first time someone would call him blind.

Schurl picked up a dart and flung it into the dart board. "Bull's-eye, almost," he reported. "I hear that Belinda Oliver broke up with Fletcher."

"That's right."

"It's hard to step out of a relationship like that," Schurl said, firing another dart. "You know, being connected to some-one as well-known as Fletcher, and then disconnected. Life changing."

Vail was sorry it had ended mainly because it meant Lindy was a loose cannon again. She wasn't occupied with work, distracted by marriage plans or another child. But she had kept her word over the years; she hadn't interfered with Eddie.

"I'm off," Schurl said.

"Wait, look at this." Vail fumbled in his jacket pocket, pulled out a jeweler's box. "See?" He opened the lid to show Schurl the earrings he was giving Patsy.

"Very nice. Are you okay?"

"You're not used to seeing me happy."

"You don't look happy."

"I will be by the time I get home."

Belinda was not watching television. It was the warmest December day in history, and she was lying on the sofa in her apartment on Berendo, an ice pack on her head, a bottle of aspirin on the floor beside her, a pillow behind her. The room was stifling. She had no idea how long she'd been lying there since the heat had driven her out of the bedroom. She felt like wreckage. She'd left Fletcher.

She'd come off the Hungary shoot determined to prove Fletcher wrong, determined to do what he'd shouted to everyone she couldn't do: direct.

That had been four months ago. She'd had energy then. She'd connected with Keith and had sent *Indictment* to Venner; then she and Keith had enjoyed a hilarious dinner plotting how they'd film it. Venner had not responded. His people said he'd been in New York, then in Argentina, then England. Weeks passed. *Indictment* came back with a note: "Belinda, no thanks, not right for us. I'm off for a few weeks. Let's talk soon. Guy." She'd called Keith; he'd been in France on location.

Since then, she'd tried to get on as a second-unit director. The town was full of them. She'd looked for work as a production secretary. As the weeks uncurled, she knew she didn't have the heart. Free of the demands of production, the emotional cost of leaving Fletcher poured in. He'd brought her legitimate excitement, as opposed to notoriety. Even though he was nuts, he'd brought her a way of life everyone in her family had approved of, and she was shocked to feel alone, unclothed, without it.

The telephone rang, and her answering machine beeped. It was Fletcher. He was in the editing room; wanted to see her, have dinner with her, wanted her. She listened to the growly voice, loving him, wanting to give in, forcing herself not to.

"Belinda, I know I treated you hard," he was saying, going on, getting irritated, "we were all uptight, you know what the pressures were, but why didn't you quit me after the spa scene, why'd you hang on just to leave me after we wrapped?"

"I'm no quitter," she mumbled from the couch, not moving.

"Why don't you talk to me, Belinda? God, babe, I miss you."

The final days of the shoot slammed back. Everything changed when they'd moved into the grasslands.

The Hungarians called the flat grassy plains in the center of Hungary *puszta*. It was a wild and strange place where human arguments and concerns, their strengths and defects, dwindled at the border of the dreamscape. It was a steppe and a pampas and a plain controlled by herders and horsemen and wind.

All the pettiness and panic of the production faded. People began helping each other out, laughing at breakdowns, hugging, being inventive, keeping their tempers, staring into the horizon. The country held onto its old-fashioned ways; people rode bikes, hauling produce in big carts; dapple gray horses pulled plows; lines of men in the fields hoed and scraped at the earth, and trudged home to their thatched houses. It had been there that Fletcher had finally apologized, humbled by loneliness, by the austerely flat land, by the sea of grass. Standing alone with him in the wind on the plain, it was almost as if they had not been speaking—there was no one to hear except themselves and the grass ocean. Words were insignificant there.

"I am sincere," he'd said.

"I know."

"I *do* love you," he'd said.

"I know, in your way. But you're toxic."

"No!" He had clung to her, wrapping her in his arms, the wind blowing his long hair back from his face.

She had shut him off. She was good at that after the years inside, shutting off the girls and the noise, shutting out fear and boredom.

It had been on the plain also that she'd realized she had no perspective about men. She'd spent almost all her life with women—how could she know anything about men? Survival tactics in the school had prepared her not for understanding, but for advantage. Everything had seemed inconsequential on that ocean of grass, and it had allowed her to face the link between Archie and Fletcher. It disgusted her. It defeated her. She wasn't going forward; she was going backward. If she hadn't known Archie, she wouldn't have loved Fletcher. The wind swept the grass in waves like breakers, building and depressing acres at once.

"Take it or leave it!" Fletcher shouted over her answering machine. "Damn you to hell!"

The machine beeped. Over and out.

Belinda lay on the sofa, sweating. She felt bound to Fletcher while angrily struggling to be free. She didn't want to live with him; she didn't know how to live without him.

She put the ice bag on her throat. She had to get up and pretend. Victor was in town.

Victor's publication party for *The Crossing* was held in a garden courtyard of a new hotel. Most of the guests were knotted under a trellis of vines and closely spaced olive trees where it was marginally cooler. A huge banner displaying the words, "The Crossing," sighed above the area in the faint baking breeze. An artfully staged stack of books framed the area like a wall. Everywhere there were reminders that *Crossing* was soon to be a Fletcher Avery film for Venner Broadcasting.

Victor was wearing a cool-looking sand-colored jacket with a red handkerchief rising from his pocket. His white hair was combed back, his dark blue eyes moved restlessly in their nests of lines and creases. His book was a hit but Victor still had trouble believing he'd escaped the biting creative problems that had trailed him for years like wolves. He scanned the babbling crowd, looking for Lindy, feeling at his best, wanting her to see him now. He had a ticket for her to join him in Ireland, and, through Sara, he'd quietly made production contacts for her in London. In a year, he was sure, Lindy would look back on Fletcher as an indifferent encounter.

Belinda arrived in a pale blue dress, beads, heeled sandals, no stockings. The effect was simple and alluring.

"How nice you look out of uniform," he said.

"Yeah, no jeans," she replied. "Vic, I can't stay. Birthday tea for Patsy today, then Yvonne Duret is flying in from Hawaii tonight—I haven't seen her since Hungary."

He drew her aside, separating them from the crowd which was managing to speak in spite of the heat. "I thought we were having dinner," he said.

"I got my dates mixed up."

Victor readjusted. "Breakfast tomorrow? I've got a surprise for you." Her face showed no curiosity. He plunged ahead. "Tickets to Ireland!" He slipped them out of his pocket.

She was already shaking her head. "Got some things working here, Vic. Thanks anyway."

He steered her farther away from the jabbering crowd into a long, covered outdoor corridor used by the waiters to ferry food and drink from the kitchen. "You're not still—it's not Fletcher—?" She shook her head. "Thank god. I felt you and Fletcher—sort of like oil and water. Once something ends, it's best to let it go."

"I just don't want to leave L.A. for a while. It's got nothing to do with Fletcher."

"But I'm setting it up for you to go to film school in London."

Suddenly, she felt invaded and breakable. "What makes you think I want to study in London? I'm not a thing to be moved around."

"Lindy, without you, *Crossing* probably would never have been on film. You did me a great favor. Let me help you."

"I don't mean to sound rude, but right now I don't need any help."

"But I thought film school—"

"I have my own life, my own plans."

Victor, taken aback, sputtered and was aware of it. "I thought you wanted to get into directing."

"I don't know what I want to do. I need some time to figure it out. I'm fine," she said, lightly. "Quit hounding me."

"Hounding you? You're my daughter."

"I'm sorry, but—this feels like pressure."

"I'm concerned about you."

"Well, don't be."

Her face had set; it was the marble look he knew well from her time inside. "But I thought that we were closer."

"We are." All her bitterness was coming out, but she couldn't stop. "I'm an adult, not a teenager, Vic. Don't try to make me dependent. I don't trust that."

Vic saw himself at thirty, a bitter young man without prospects, angry at the world, barely hanging on, spitting back an offer of help, rejecting everyone.

"You can't do it by yourself," he said.

"Yes, I can. I'll see you in a few days—you're going to be around that long, aren't you?" He nodded. She squeezed his arm, an apology, and walked away from him.

Victor slumped against the wall of the corridor. He knew so well what it was like to feel alone and in danger, what it took to survive. He wanted to make things easier for her. Her skirt whipped around her legs, she was walking away so fast. Vic pushed off the wall.

Patsy's birthday tea party for the family had degenerated. Diana was standing by the huge arched window overlooking the garden. She wouldn't let anyone forget Patrick.

"That man had the effrontery to ask my forgiveness right there on television, shedding his crocodile tears," she said. "Is this to be the end of my daughter's life, dragged through the mud by that man on that toadying show?"

"Mother, please stop," Sara said.

Belinda remembered Patrick from her childhood when he'd given her artfully wrapped picture books, a music box, and dolls. Sara had been staring at Belinda since she arrived. "Why are you doing that, Sara?"

"What?"

"Staring at me?"

"No one will buy the stupid book, Grandma," Eddie tried. His grandmother's tremendous grief had taken over the room. "I mean, there isn't anything we can do about this guy's book, is there?" Eddie demanded, upset.

"No, dear," Patsy said.

"I won't put up with this, having her name ruined by that man," Diana said, still not looking at any of them. "I'm eighty-nine: I don't care what happens to me—I want him stopped." She faced them. "Why is he out?"

Eddie shouted: "You're ruining Mom's birthday!" And he stomped out.

"Eddie," Patsy called, "please stay."

"Why is that man out?" Diana repeated to Edward's back.

Belinda caught Sara glancing at her again. Like me, Belinda thought: Patrick and I are both out. That's what Sara's thinking. We both killed the people we loved. I don't feel like a killer—does he? His act had been premeditated, hadn't it? But what difference did that make? Of course, Patrick *was really crazy*, she thought, but was I sane? The doubt was always with her. She slid away from it, she buried it, and she pretended it wasn't there, but, like winter, it always came back: can you kill anyone and still be sane? The irony of it jabbed her. She was a reflection of Patrick. They were both out but which one of them was nuts? Belinda laughed.

Everyone looked at her.

"Really, Belinda, control yourself," Diana said. "This is no laughing matter."

Vail came bouncing in, a straw plantation hat clapped on his head. Edward was with him, trying to be upbeat. Patsy began pouring the tea.

"We were just talking about Patrick here," Sara said grimly to Vail.

"Oh," Eddie groaned. "Let's forget him."

"Right, Son. I'm not going to let the man ruin my wife's birthday."

"Way to go, Dad," Eddie said.

Vail leaned in to kiss Patsy but she was distracted by the tea pouring, and she shied away. "Can't I kiss the birthday woman?" he said. Mercurially, typically, his thin, desperate cheer vanished, his anxiety flared. He mashed it down but it always ballooned out again: he could not control his fear that Patsy's love was fading now that she knew his blind future. She would be kind to him but she would have affairs with other men. The thought of it turned his insides to jelly. His fears were crazy, an inner voice said, Patsy loved him; they were a team. But his fears continued to dine on his guts anyway.

He looked at Patsy, Diana, Lindy. A terrible calm fell over Vail like an envelope. He saw them with the wide clarity of perfect vision. He felt a rush of joy. He could see again. The joy broke off. Lindy was falling from a great height—he heard the sound of her hitting the pavement, a melon cracking open. He saw his mother serving tea to Patrick, extending a fine china cup.

"Vail!" Patsy screamed. He was groaning, swaying. And then he collapsed.

Vail succeeded in passing off his fainting spell as a result of the heat.

"Dad," Eddie said, "you sure you're okay?"

"Yes. Yes," Vail said. But he was shaken and pale. He hadn't experienced anything like that for years. Had dealing with that wretch Patrick brought it on? Seeing Lindy again living at loose ends? The last time he'd had one of these horrors had been about—what? Sky! He'd come to Sky's house. On the landing of the stairs, a round window framed the fat fronds of a palm tree outside. He'd been drawn to the landing and had looked out the window. Lake Hollywood shimmered in the California afternoon. Behind him, at the bottom of the stairs, Sara and Sky had been chattering and laughing. They'd all been, what—twenty-five, twenty-eight? He couldn't remember. He'd just come off a long, drug-filled trip around the country; he'd been feeling really low and out of it. Behind him, Sky had said: "Vail, come on down here! Nothing out there but that fake lake and the path!" A dizzying sensation had swept over him. Two people now stood on the path around the lake. The man seized the woman. Her arms had flown out. The man was strangling her. Vail had gripped the molding around the window. It had been like watching a hideous private movie. The woman was falling; the man was kneeling over her. Vail had put his forehead down on the cool windowsill, sweating, sick. When he'd looked up, the path was empty. "Vail!" Sara had said. He'd jumped. She'd been right behind him on the landing. "*What* are you doing?"

He had ignored the vision. Years later, Sky had died on that path. Could he have saved her? Was Patrick bringing it all back now? This time he would not ignore the vision.

When Belinda got home, there was a message on her machine from Buttons Botsford. "Remember me?" his clever voice sailed in on her tape. "This is the legless wonder from *Force Field*, the shoot you'll never forget, you dear thing." He laughed sharply. "Neither will I. Yvonne's plane is going to be three hours late. I'm picking her up at the airport—I've learned to drive those cars with levers—quite the most superior way to go at it, let me tell you. We'll come straight to your place from the airport. Have the Singapore slings ready."

Her apartment depressed her. Three hours, she thought. She picked up her purse and went out into the fiery, unseasonal streets.

A few blocks away on Melrose Avenue, an upscale restaurant-cum-singles spot, the Sombrero, was frequented by people from the nearby studio and its lab. It served free food at the cocktail hour, and, when Belinda arrived, it was revving up for the night. She sat down on a stool at the cool marble and metal bar, relieved to be in a recreational place where no one knew her and where nothing was demanded of her.

It was as she looked up at the music videos flashing on a TV monitor that Belinda recognized Maisie Short. She was sitting beneath the hiss-pop-shout of the video monitor at the other end of the bar, observing the crowd in the room with eyes that did not see. Dressed in a tight pair of pants, a sheer blouse, fashionably rumpled linen jacket, and a sweatband. She was twirling a strand of blond hair around her forefinger. Maisie Short, wise and vicious, had helped protect Belinda in the school, but not for free.

At that instant, Maisie saw her. Her face registered neither surprise nor pleasure, only recognition as they stared at each other, the school and its ghosts, their only common bond, hovering between. A drink in her hand, Maisie slid off her stool and came around the bar.

"Lindy, girl. What's happening?" Maisie asked in her hard nasal voice. She sat down.

"Nothing much. What's with you, Maisie?"

"No complaints. Have a drink," Maisie offered.

In the school, few said no to Maisie. Belinda ordered a white wine.

"Why not a champagne cocktail?" Maisie had a sly but pretty smile. "Ain't that more to your taste, little buns?" Maisie could speak good standard English as well as anyone, but when she was comfortable, or when she needed it for effect, she fell into the language of her childhood.

"Cut the crap, Maisie," Belinda said, "or I'm outta here." It was the first time either of them could, at will, physically and totally get away from the other.

"Aw, I don't mean nothing," Maisie said with her cocky smile. Maisie had virtually run the school from the inside: she'd controlled drugs, cigarettes, discipline and, to some extent, sex. She'd been the toughest white girl on the block.

The bartender delivered the glass of wine. "What are you doing these days?" Belinda asked, taking a swallow of wine.

"Sort of consulting for some of the production outfits around the corner."

Belinda felt sure she was supplying drugs.

Maisie's thin mouth opened once again in a wise smile. She had small even teeth. "You know, I was just thinking of you the other day," Maisie said, opening a new conversational gambit. "I was down on a set where they were rehearsing a scene, and what do I hear but a girl yelling her head off—it was in the scene, y'understand, she wasn't really having a fit—and I say to myself, 'That girl sounds just like our Lindy back that day. Remember? Your folks and your kid were visiting, and Lindy, you were downright rude, told 'em to get out. And then, just like you, you go on and have a change of heart and you was weeping to have that kid back. But ol' Betty Boop—you remember her, the guard?—she'd had enough of you, and you couldn't have him back—and you started carrying on. We could hear you all over the school." She sipped her drink. "Actually, I think you took on a lot louder than that actress in the scene. But she was pretty loud too."

Having a drink with Maisie was like being thrown back in time and space. Part of Maisie's power inside had been her ability to talk her way into or out of almost anything. She'd always been a talker and she proved no different now. She resented interruptions except nods or murmurs of agreement.

"Ruby's dead," Maisie went on, speaking of the girl who'd run the black dorms in the school. Maisie mimed a hypodermic with her fingers against her arm. Ruby had scared the hell out of Belinda until Maisie had come along. " 'Member Sandy?" Belinda nodded, feeling weights added to her shoulders with each name. "Back in the can. That girl was forgin' checks again," Maisie said in a low voice.

Belinda found herself thinking of Archie—not the early, hot, eager times, but of her hatred for him, which had been fresh her first months in the school.

"Sandy was doing something else besides forgin' the checks. I think it was mail fraud," Maisie said. "But, hell, most of 'em was in for drugs, except Sandy. I guess we can say she was special."

Belinda could feel again her rage and sorrow when she'd discovered Archie was seeing another girl about her age, another "patient." The accusations, the shouting fights, the twisting sex afterward were all coming back to her as Maisie talked on. And under it all ran a stream of her awareness at the time that it was wrong to be secretly and intimately connected to him. But she'd needed Archie. He was an emblem. He'd proved something about her. She carried Archie around with her, the ecstasy of first being with him, the decay, the disastrous aftermath. That was like Fletcher now, a thing gone sour. And she hadn't scraped Archie off her back.

Maisie's total recall of the school was like someone recalling halcyon college triumphs. "You know what happened to Betty Boop? Heart attack. Right in the front office. Great, huh?" She had a laugh like a honk.

"Maisie," Belinda said, "who framed me?"

"Wasn't no frame, pretty girl." Maisie finished her drink.

"Don't give me that shit. I didn't kill that girl. Who did it?"

Maisie tugged delicately at her nose, then lit a cigarette and blew the smoke out of the side of her mouth. "Ruby. She overstepped herself, as you'd say. Wasn't nothin' I could do, sweetmeat. Betty Boop and Ruby and them had it sewed up for you to take the fall."

"Betty made a deal with them."

"Well, you gotta admit you fit the bill. Why would a rich girl like you kill someone if you wasn't nutso? It was easy for them to turn you into a nutso. Get it?"

"Ruby killed her," Belinda said.

"Yeah, sorta by accident. Betty was there, so I heard. So Betty hung it on you and Ruby helped make it stick. Ruby hated you. You was getting out, you was white. You'd only been in about two years—she'd been in for three. She wanted to get on home and see her kid. But if Ruby was involved in the death, she wouldn't get out." Maisie's flat gray eyes regarded Belinda. She smiled and showed her tiny teeth. "I hated losing you to the county jail and then to the nuthouse, all your soap and cigarettes. Had to shut down my store, almost."

Belinda had long suspected Ruby of killing the girl, and it had probably been over drugs. Maisie's old power and the months they'd spent together felt like a deadweight. "I got to leave," Belinda said, putting some bills on the bar. Maisie clamped her hand around Belinda's wrist.

"You was always dumb, Lindy," she said quietly. "You think it matters who did what in there?"

Maisie's touch was like ice. "It does matter. Let go."

Maisie showed her tiny teeth and shook her head. "We're out here. I can make you a shit load of money if you'd smart up."

"Let go," Belinda said again.

"You oughta pay attention here, Lindy," Maisie said, coldly.

Belinda's free hand took a fork off the counter and pressed it against Maisie's soft middle under the level of the bar. "If you ever recognize me again," Belinda whispered, putting her elbow on the bar and leaning close to Maisie as if they were exchanging confidences, "if you ever say so much as hi, or involve me in any way with what you're into, I'll fucking kill you. You got that?"

"Don't kid me, sweetmeat," Maisie said, but her eyes looked cold and dead.

Belinda put the fork back on the bar. She dragged the weight of the school and Archie through the café to the outside double glass doors.

She was shaking. She walked back to her apartment in the heat. The streets were swarming with people off work, cranky, irritated, disappointed, relieved. But she wasn't really aware of them. She was back in the school with Maisie and Ruby, waiting eagerly to be released, feeling it coming closer to her, and then being dragged into offices, being accused of "being responsible" for the death of a new girl, one she hadn't even known, being transferred to the county jail, a hellhole unlike anything she'd experienced, being tried and convicted in a nightmare and sent off to Patton State Hospital for a sentence of five to ten years but with good behavior, maybe three years, and hearing a new set of iron doors shut behind her, and facing a giant called a psych-tech, a nurse, who had arms like tree trunks. It was really an indeterminate sentence because no one could get out until cleared by the chief psychiatrist. She was at the mercy of a whole new set of thugs.

So began her "junior year" of college, the loony bin. At the school, she'd been a petrified freshman and a wiser sophomore familiar with the system. Without that training, she would not have survived her upper-class semesters at the nuthouse. The nurses were worse than the patients. The nurses hated their lives, hated their work, were jealous of her good looks, education, and status. One of them gave her a black eye the first night. To the confusion and conflict drug stupors, she tried kicking back and then withdrawing. Finally she used her heart and her head. She tried to be strong and kind when she wasn't flattened out by Haldol. She tried to be smarter and cleverer.

Belinda hadn't fit in the state mental hospital and everyone knew it. It made her a target; it made her find ways to survive. What angel had told her they wouldn't beat her as much if she'd been abused by men? She'd been in the dayroom: one of the psych-techs had made an offhand callous remark about Ghost, a skeletal woman who went around talking to herself. Ghost had started yelling and another nurse had twisted Belinda's arm in passing. Belinda had shrieked a challenge to her: "You don't do it as good as that son of a bitch Archie, and I killed him." The psych-tech let go of her arm. From that moment on, Belinda had defended herself by buttering the techs up, by making up stories about Archie's cruelty, by running errands for them, by buying cigarettes and giving them away. She wanted out in the worst way; by the time she'd been in there a year, she still wanted out but she feared getting out.

The phone was ringing when she got back to her apartment. Her machine clicked on and Fletcher's voice came rolling toward her. Why wasn't she responding to him? he demanded. He hadn't done anything to hurt her. She sat down and listened to the growl and rumble in his voice. He was bad for her. She wanted him. Finally, he stopped talking.

She felt breakable, as if she couldn't deal with him or anyone anymore.

She was sitting in Archie's garden on a cold October night in San Francisco, waiting for the girl who'd gone in an hour ago to come out. She'd taken a wide plastic hair clip out of her hair and was breaking it into pieces when she saw the girl leave. "What are you doing with her?" she'd demanded of Archie when he answered the door. He was in his bathrobe and slippers. He'd denied everything. She'd cursed him. He'd bottled up her fists in his arms, rubbing his whiskers against her face, lying and soothing, stripping off her blouse and jeans, lying some more, his fingers like fish, darting in and out of her, his tongue a third lip, nipping. She broke away. He pushed her head down on his erection, held her there, seized her hair and lifted her head away, then he'd fallen on her on the floor of the hallway, licking her breasts, pushing his fingers into her mouth, rounding himself over her, poking and invading and groaning. He'd picked her up and stood her against the wall, flattening her, impaling her, and coming in her frantically, his big blond head raised above her, the forbidden strain of the act stretching his features. And above his profile, in the dark spiraling stairwell, she'd seen a flicker—someone moved. But the image had vanished in Archie's ravenous groans as he jerked and shuddered against her, free and trapped.

Belinda, on her sofa, was crying with shame and hatred. She put her hands behind her head, felt the tears slide down the sides of her face, and through the window at the end of the room, watched a dark gray cloud line turn red in the western sky. Then she got up.

At the time, it didn't seem like a big decision. She remembered walking into the bathroom, pouring the pills into the palm of her hand, clapping her hand to her mouth, and swallowing a glass of water. Then she walked back to the living room which was still cooler than the oven of her bedroom. She lay down on the sofa.

CHAPTER 15

Belinda thought she was still in the hallway with Archie when she woke up. Was it morning? It was light. Where was Archie? She was in bed. Her throat was raw and sore; her ribs and jaw ached. She felt beaten up. She didn't recognize what she was wearing.

Yvonne was sitting in a chair beside the bed. Her eyes were closed. Her black hair was rumpled, her shoes were off.

Is this a dream? Lindy, shocked, tried to speak; her throat was too raw. She felt drugged. She shut her eyes. It had to be a dream.

She opened her eyes. Yvonne was staring at her.

"Good, you're awake," Yvonne said in a no-shit-now voice.

"I've made some tea for when she—" Dr. Suico came through the doorway carrying a tray. "Oh, you're awake." She smiled professionally, put the tray down. "How do you feel?" She sat down on the edge of the bed, took Lindy's wrist in her cool hand, felt for the pulse.

"What are you doing here?" Lindy asked her in a hoarse whisper.

Dr. Suico looked at Yvonne. Yvonne looked at Lindy. Dr. Suico said, "What do you remember?"

Belinda shook her head. But mentally, she started stepping backward. She'd been lying on the sofa in the drenching heat, watching the cloud wisp. "I was waiting for you," she said to Yvonne. The pills! She saw the basin, the running water, her cupped hand full of pills.

She groaned and lay back on the pillows. She had hit the gravity belt after a walk in space. She had not escaped. She was trussed up in the net with Archie and Fletcher and the family. She would have to fight on.

"I'll leave you now," Dr. Suico said. "But later, Belinda, you and I will have a chat. That was my prescription, you know. In this state, attempted suicides are taken very seriously. You will have to see a therapist. And I," she said, rising, "will make sure you do."

When she'd left, Yvonne took hold of Lindy's arm and fluffed pillows behind her. "C'mon, sit up."

"When did you get in?" Lindy asked.

"About ten. Buttons and I came over here to pick you up thinking we'll all have a late supper. We get here and there's no answer. Now, I can't believe that just because I'm late that you'd go out without leaving a note or anything. So I keep ringing the bell, and then Dr. Suico comes along and lets me in. Buttons was down in the car. She says she'd seen you come in and she didn't think you'd left. So we bang on the door. And we get nothing. I had the crazy feeling you weren't okay. I couldn't shake it. We were about to break your door down when I found it was open! You didn't lock your door. You—you wanted to be found." Belinda turned away, pressed her head into the pillow. "You were half dead. Dr. Suico and I carried you down to the car, Buttons drove us to her friend's clinic. She got your stomach pumped. But Dr. Suico made promises to her friend, another doctor. These things are supposed to be reported. You don't remember any of this."

It was like remembering an unedited film. In one shot, Lindy saw people bending over her, putting something down her throat, forcing her mouth open. In another shot, she was vomiting. In a third, someone was shouting at her. But they were disconnected shots, a rough assemblage, out of order, not her own memories, something she'd seen happening to someone else. "No," she said.

"Why did you do it?" Yvonne suddenly cried.

Belinda tried to figure it out. It had not seemed important. "I ran out of steam. I couldn't fight anymore."

"We all fight."

"There's a lot you don't know about me."

"Like what?" Yvonne asked.

"Fletcher was the first man I loved—since Archie."

"Who's Archie?"

"I didn't take the pills because of Fletcher." She felt light-headed. "Maybe because of Archie. I don't know. For a while, with Fletcher, I thought I was in love. I thought I'd put the past behind me, but I was duplicating the past—since I've been back here—it just hit me—the whole thing with Fletcher—God, I don't feel real anymore."

"Who's Archie?"

Belinda clutched the sheet folded over the top edge of the blanket. "Archie. He was the first man I ever loved. I was seventeen and he was about fifty, I guess. Well, cut to the chase. I shot him, Yvonne. And I killed him."

Yvonne blinked. "You killed him?"

"Yes." She saw Yvonne pulling back. "I had a hearing before a judge and I pleaded guilty to manslaughter. I was sentenced to an institution for juveniles."

"A prison?"

"They called it a school. What a place."

"My God."

"I didn't mean to kill him. But the gun was there and I did it—I acted on—on—passion and hatred. I did it, I did it." She couldn't stay in the bed. Shakily, she climbed out, but she had nowhere to go. She knocked her stiffened arms against her sides, then sat down. "That one moment—blew up my life." She was crying. "I'm not sorry he's dead—I never will be—but those places, that school was—I mean, talk about Darwin, it was Darwin backward—survival of the *least* fit. Only the mean and the clever survive there." She was pulling on a pair of jeans, grabbing at the material with both fists, tears streaming down her cheeks. Yvonne didn't try to stop her. "It didn't teach me how to love, but somehow, after all those years, I fell in love with Fletcher. Remember me telling you in the car in Malaysia how surprised I was? I never thought I'd feel anything again. Oh, it was so good to feel something hopeful, something good." She sat down on the edge of the bed.

"Are you glad you're alive?" Yvonne sat down next to her. "Are you?"

"I'm not sure."

The doorbell rang, a quick, short jab. "That's Buttons," Yvonne said softly. "Do you want to see him?"

"I don't know. Sure. Why not? Next, it'll be my dad, god forbid." Belinda was calming down.

Yvonne walked down the short hallway. She stopped beside

the front door, and leaned against the wall until the sound of the bell pulled her back again.

Buttons wheeled to a stop at Belinda's bedroom door. Yvonne stood behind him.

"Hiya," Lindy said.

"Hiya yourself." He stared at Belinda. She was sitting on her bed, dressed in a T-shirt and jeans, a wadded ball of tissue in her hand. "You better take a long look at yourself because you're never going to be so low," he finally said. "You can go up, or you can slide on down from here. I know what I'm talking about. I've been there. Which is it going to be?"

It was night. They had talked for hours. "Okay, you want to see it?" Belinda asked them.

"But I don't get it. When did you make this documentary?" Buttons asked, rolling his chair to a stop in Belinda's living room in front of her television set.

"Between the time I was let out and the time I showed up at my family's house."

"But weren't they concerned?" Yvonne asked again. "You keep dodging that. I mean, you're let out and you disappear."

"I wrote them; I let them know I was alive. But I couldn't see them. I was my family's skeleton. I liked being with other family skeletons. I went home when I felt I could handle it."

They thought about this. Then Yvonne said, "What did you do for all that time?"

"I worked on film productions, nonunion stuff in Texas, in Maine, in Montana—even Hawaii once. Production assistant stuff. I was hiding. And for two years, off and on, I worked on this documentary." Belinda shoved a videocassette in the VCR.

"Hold it," Yvonne said. "You started to say something earlier about Venner? What about him? Remember, I was there when he talked about you directing a picture."

"He didn't mean it."

"Have you talked to him?" Yvonne said.

"No. I sent him a script. He sent it back. Do you wanna see this tape?"

"Okay. We'll talk about Venner later."

Belinda pressed Play. The title bounced onto the screen: "The Mental Patients' Liberation Project."

"It's about how mental patients have rights, too," Belinda said, shyly. "You don't have any idea what it's like in there."

Guy Venner angrily turned his back on the man standing behind him. They were fifty floors up in Guy's San Francisco office, overlooking the bay. Bill Hatfield was a short, muscular, balding man in his fifties. He had known Guy all his life, and, as a chief of Venner Broadcasting, a subsidiary of Venner Enterprises, Bill ran the outfit Guy considered his best and proudest.

"I asked you to keep an eye on my daughter, not have dinner with her at a quiet candle-lit boîte," Guy said, his resonant, deep voice rising. He turned around. "And then, you go into her hotel room—"

"Guy, for Chrissakes, it wasn't like that." Hatfield couldn't believe what he was hearing. He'd looked up to Guy like a brother since college. "It was raining, we ducked in to talk about the next day—"

"You're not going to make any time with my daughter!"

"Now, look here, Guy, I don't know who told you a crazy story like that—"

"You aren't good enough to shake her hand!" Guy roared.

Hatfield stared at his friend, hurt, dismayed, furious. "I'm the man who stuck with you at the very beginning. Someone's been feeding you lies—"

"Get out of here, Bill, before I knock you out."

"You're a real bastard," Bill said, turning to leave. "All my life people have warned me what a snake you can be, but I never saw it that way—"

"Out!"

"If you think you can hold on to Cynthia like this, you're dead wrong!"

Hatfield slammed the heavy door. Guy whipped around and faced the bay again.

Hatfield *had* been with him since the beginning. He'd helped create Venner Broadcasting. Guy had gambled big, defying everyone, and only Hatfield had stood solidly beside him. "Shit," he mumbled, "what's the matter with me?"

Venner had grown up knowing he could be whatever he wanted. As he looked back on it, he'd wasted his twenties "running around," as his mother said, "fucking every woman under sixty," as his father said, "traveling," as Guy and his friend Bill Hatfield told it. Guy had been on his own since he'd turned eighteen in 1958, except for the men his father sent after him—guardians, companions, spies. His father had always reminded him of a teddy bear given to sudden temper tantrums. Guy thought him not smart, a man who hadn't reached high enough. His mother had been a small, compact society woman with a sense of fun. Both were conservative people, aware of their positions in life, protective of them.

Guy had stopped screwing around and started in business when he realized that some friends from college were already successful: one was a self-made millionaire at thirty, another was a nationally known painter, a third was an architect changing the face of San Francisco. Even Bill was a successful businessman. Guy was suddenly envious: what they could do, he could do.

Guy Venner turned back to his broad, shiny black desk. He sighed deeply, thinking of Hatfield. "Shit." He strode out of his office into a huge foyer. He turned left and pushed open the door of Bill's office. Bill was sitting on a couch, his feet up on the coffee table. He was smoking a cigar.

"I'm sorry, Bill," Venner said. "I'm a real asshole. Forgive me."

Fletcher was in a Los Angeles editing room, watching scenes from *Crossing* go by on the screen. The airdate was putting him and his editor under a lot of pressure to finish.

"Oh god, this again?" Fletcher groaned.

The editor nodded. "Can't put it off. I've made some selections, Fletch. See what you think."

The spa scene. The strange thing about Belinda on the screen was that her face softened and became more mobile. But it was hard to watch her. He missed her and it cut like a knife. He'd tried to talk to her, but in his gut he knew it was over: Belinda was one of those women who didn't look back. But Gloria had come back, maybe Belinda would, too. Nah, she wouldn't. He knew it.

The footage rolled on. Belinda was standing on the balcony over the spa's pool. He saw a family resemblance to Sky Wyman, but, more important, he saw the emotional resemblance of the actor: the barely checked emotions, the vibrant intensity.

Tears sprang into Fletcher's eyes.

"She's good, isn't she?" the editor said.

Fletcher nodded. "Yeah, whoever woulda guessed?"

"Not as good as me!" Gloria had come into the room behind the console where they sat.

"You blew it," Fletcher muttered.

"There'll be other parts—better parts," she said. "Listen, Fletch, I got something for you." She was twisting a sawed-off straw between her fingers. She leaned over and whispered, "Some really good blow, Fletchie."

"I'll be back in five," he said, rising. The camera was moving in for a close-up of Belinda as he ducked out the door.

"I didn't have a successful relationship with the last shrink I knew," Belinda said to Dr. Anita Durbin, a middle-aged African-American woman who sat across from her on an overstuffed chair.

"Oh?" the woman said. "And who was that?"

"Dr. Archibald Moberly. I shot him."

Dr. Durbin didn't miss a beat. "The last patient who said that to me was talking about photography. I have a feeling you're not."

"Bet your ass I'm not," Belinda said quietly.

It was the second time she'd met with Dr. Durbin in the clinic office. Dr. Durbin didn't look especially hip, but she was. She wore bright clothes, red being the predominating color, large earrings, and hats. She exuded warmth and unruffled common sense. Nothing seemed to shock her.

"Do you remember shooting him?"

"Not really. I remember the fight before, and being fingerprinted after. How many times do you think I'll have to come here?"

Dr. Durbin shrugged. "Tell me about your father, Victor."

"He helped me a lot once, and then I helped him, so we're even. He's okay, kinda distant. Wants to be perfect."

"And you are none of those things."

Belinda laughed.

"Do you think there is a connection between Archie and your father?"

That hit too close to home. "Archie was a blond. And I didn't know Victor too well, then. He was in Ireland, he wasn't around." She wasn't telling the complete truth and she knew it. Victor had been there for a while. "I told my father I was pregnant; I remember doing that."

"And what did he say?"

Belinda laughed. "He was confused. He told me to see my mother."

"Maybe that was the best advice he could manage."

"Yes, it was. I like Vic. We had a meeting of the minds a year or two ago—he really leveled with me. We became really close. Then *Crossing* was made." She looked away. "I was a shit to him a couple of weeks ago, I—I think he sensed I was falling apart. He wanted to help. I just shoved him away."

"He won't hold it against you. He's your father—he's got that role for life. But when you were young, you had no father. So you found a substitute."

"I wasn't screwing my father," Belinda said.

"You were a bright student, but you had a liaison with a man old enough to be your father—"

"Plenty of precedent."

"And then you got pregnant. Why didn't you get an abortion?"

Belinda had often thought about that. "I'm not sure. I was lonely. I hate to admit that. If it was now, I'd have an abortion and leave Archie, sure. But I just couldn't let go. I guess I wanted something good to come out of all the bad."

"The bad?"

"I knew it wasn't right, me having this affair with Archie, my mom's shrink. He was jealous, we fought and argued—he had another girl, a patient, he called her. I don't mean his daughter, she was living with him—I mean someone else."

"So we have this middle-aged man with an appetite for young girls. What kind of a picture does that make? A man who feels powerless deep inside. A man who cannot form adult relationships."

"We were having an affair." Belinda looked at Dr. Durbin's red jacket.

"I don't think so. You're drawing a picture of a man whose appetites are out of control. That's not an affair. He meant *more* to you than a lover who didn't want to be a husband, don't you think?"

"No."

Dr. Durbin leaned forward in the comfortable chair and knit her fingers together. Her sharp warm eyes studied Belinda. "Why did you pick a fight with your father—that day of the book signing?"

"Oh, I don't know . . . I'd like to be close to him, but I don't know how. He began playing the same old tune—come to Ireland, study film in Britain, do this, do that . . ."

"Why not?"

"Why not?" Belinda repeated, nonplussed. "I don't want to be trapped with him off in Europe somewhere."

"Why?"

"Because—" Belinda stopped pacing. Because it was like being with Archie, she thought, astounded. Because he was linked somewhere deep inside her with Archie. And Archie was dangerous. "I guess we're not as close as I'd like because I'm afraid of it. I guess it's not Victor's problem." Belinda turned, staking her hand on her hip. "See? I can be sane and insightful."

Dr. Durbin sighed and sat back. "So you give birth to your child, and your aunt and uncle raise him, give him a good home, but now you're a mother without being a mother. Do you want Eddie to—what do you hope your relationship will be with Eddie?"

"Well, first, that he doesn't grow up and be like Archie. He won't—he's a really swell kid. Next, I don't want him to know about me. Last, that we can be friends. I can handle that."

"But he knows he's adopted, doesn't he? He'll want to know more about his parents," Dr. Durbin said. "That's inevitable."

"His mother's dead! That's all he needs to know," she yelled. "Lay off."

"That's not my job."

It was not until Belinda had entered Guy Venner's office that she fully remembered the smooth, energized grace of the man. He looked like a man who'd never washed a plate, the kind of man some other man shaved every morning. Power oozed out of his pores. "It wasn't as hard to see you as I thought," she said.

"Of course not. It's been too long." He made no explanations and gave no excuses. "Would you like anything?"

"A deal."

He laughed shortly. "How about starting with coffee? I make it myself," he said. He went to a decorative, built-in buffet that housed, among other things, an espresso machine. When he'd handed her a cup, they settled on a pair of dove gray slipper chairs near the acreage of his desk. One wall held a bank of inset television monitors.

"Your call was timely," he said, his deep voice in perfect harmony with his confident manner and his expensive clothes. "I was going to call you."

"You were?"

"Yes, I saw a cut of *Crossing*—you're very good. I think we ought to talk about casting you in a new series we've got coming up."

This she had not expected. "I'd rather talk about *Indictment*, the script I sent you last fall."

"We'll discuss both," he said. "You first." He glanced at his video telephone when it purred; it wrote out for him who was calling. He made no pretense about clocking it.

"I know you didn't think it was right for you but I have a different proposition. Keith wrote this script a few years ago before he got rich and famous."

Venner beamed at her. "Oh, make no mistake, we'd like to have a Llewellyn script."

"This one's perfect for television—a punchy story about corruption, disillusionment, and it ends in triumph," she said. "Do you remember it? The leads are women—a public defender, a defendant, a local prosecutor, and a bagful of great local characters." It was about something she knew: courts, prisons, capture, survival. "I still want to direct it," she said. "I want to pick up from where you and I left off in Hungary."

Venner eyed her engagingly. "Much has changed since we talked about directing."

"I'm the same."

"You were with Fletch. He would have looked out for you

on a shoot, backstopped you. It's different now."

"It's not that different."

"You're untried."

"You'd let Keith Llewellyn direct *Indictment* if he wanted."

"He's been around."

"He's been around a word processor."

"You know what I mean. Look, I regret this, Belinda."

"You make low-budget movies—"

"But no one's going to hand one of them over to a beginner. You understand."

"I'm not a beginner. But I admit there's some risk." Venner was sitting there waiting for her to sell him on it. "You like risk, I know you do. And, directing, per se, with a good crew, is a rather straightforward process. The gift is something else again."

"The gift?"

"A gifted directorial eye, a gifted director with actors that makes a picture stand out."

"Ah, yes."

"You'll get a competent film out of me," she said. "I can't guarantee a gifted film." She paused to let that sink in. "I have a package offer for you. Yvonne wants to produce *Indictment*. Her associate is Burton Botsford—Buttons—he's worked with Fletcher for years. Lots of experience there, lots of backstop."

Guy was amused. "I know Yvonne Duret's credits."

"That's not too risky. Besides, you've taken chances on people before." How different this man is from Fletcher, she thought, so smooth and restrained.

"Yes."

"On people like me. I know I can do this picture," she said intensely. "It's about fighters and survivors—I understand women like that. And we don't often get to see them on the screen."

Guy was enjoying himself and her compelling combination of the delicate and the savage.

"There's something else," Belinda went on. "This script needs women directing and producing it. I know Keith agrees with that. Women are the main characters and there are nuances— shades of meaning to get in the performances that a man might not see. Men let us into their stories and adventures all the time. Let's open a door onto the female world. What are your stations' demographics? Lotta women, I bet." She smiled, a beautiful smile.

Guy's telephone unit beeped politely; he looked at it, pounded a "not now" back to his assistant. "Okay, you bring Yvonne in here, and we'll talk. If we go ahead with this script, it's got to be done for five million."

"You'll get it under budget and on time," Belinda said.

He chuckled. "Well, we'll see." Guy Venner wasn't being candid. He was vitally interested in the Llewellyn script, and he'd been furious at its summary return while he was out of the country. But when he'd talked to Keith to determine its status, Keith had said he wouldn't sell it unless Belinda directed it.

What surprised Venner about the meeting with Belinda was her gritty passion. It would be entertaining to see what she made of her chance.

Patsy was in her office reading a financial report when Belinda telephoned her.

"Patsy, I want you to represent me on a project with Venner Broadcasting." Belinda set out the details and Patsy listened carefully but without enthusiasm. "I need you to go to bat for me, Patsy. I'm serious about this. Will you do it? Can I come over?"

"Wait a minute." Patsy put Belinda on hold. There was a new note in Belinda's voice. She was sounding like someone on the way up—a tone that Patsy had heard before. Something had changed. But Patsy didn't want to be her lawyer or be tied to her developing career. There was too much old business between them.

She punched her telephone. "Belinda, I'd love to help but I am just crammed full of commitments—"

"Patsy, you must do this. I don't trust anyone else. I need help. I need a leg up."

"I'll recommend someone."

"No. I want you."

"Belinda, just think a minute, we have a lot of unfinished business—" Why horse around, Patsy thought. "Eddie."

"I'm not talking about Eddie," Belinda said. "I'm talking about me. Please. How about this? You help me on *Indictment*, and then I'll move on to whoever you suggest. Is that a deal?"

Patsy reluctantly agreed. But when she hung up, she didn't like the feeling of being in business with Lindy, no matter how temporary the arrangement.

Belinda's near death had changed her. She could feel it inside, a shifting, a sorting out. She was telling Dr. Durbin about it.

"Close escapes often do that," Anita Durbin said. She was wearing a cherry-red suit.

"Buttons was right: it's go up or slide down. I'm determined to go up. I only have one life. I can give it away, I can ruin it, I can hate it. Or I can use it. I've done all the others. This time, I think I'll use it."

Dr. Durbin smiled. "Good. But therapy's not over yet."

"For a while it is. I'm going into production."

"I recommend you see me when you're out of production, Belinda. Did you write your father?"

"Yes," Belinda said, "but he's stuck in Ireland for a while, as usual."

"He's got a life of his own. Did he ever thank you for what you did around his book?"

"Oh, yes," Belinda said.

Dr. Durbin was looking at a tablet in her red lap. "Then let him help you, too. Did you like acting in the film?"

Belinda looked at the ceiling. "There was a moment before all the shit hit the fan when I felt I'd lost myself in someone else. Everyone's always saying something like that but it's true, and it felt good. It was like flying. I felt like a bird— no gravity, not weighed down. Free."

"Better think of doing some more, yes? That's a good feeling." She consulted her tablet again. "Let's see if you can remember some more about the night of the shooting."

"Oh, not again."

"What did you feel?"

"You want to know if I felt remorse." Belinda smiled without warmth. "That's what everyone wanted to hear afterward. I knew that. I said I was just lathered in remorse because I knew everything would go easier on me. But I'm not sorry I shot him. I'll never be sorry."

"It's hard to be sorry until you feel your own life is worth something."

* * *

The writer sat at a large table, watching the pen move over the paper, forming the words effortlessly.

I am dread and retribution. You can't protect her. All of the guilty will be discovered and I will bring you to justice. She isn't worth anything. She will be carved and quartered. She doesn't deserve to live . . .

The scratch of the pen filled the room.

CHAPTER 16

MARCH 1990

Belinda didn't like being in San Francisco, but she was there with Yvonne, spotting locations for *Indictment*. The picture, now a fact, was part of their lives and it would remain so for at least a year.

It was a gray March day. Yvonne, in a raincoat, was leading the way up a flight of stone steps to get a view of the marina. She carried a bag of corn chips in one hand, a clipboard in another. Belinda, behind her, in a blue hooded rain jacket, was packing a camera and a leather notebook.

"Guy wants us to drop in on opening night at the film festival tomorrow night," Yvonne said, dipping into the corn chip bag.

"We don't have time to attend film festivals."

"This isn't just any festival and you know it. Play the game."

San Francisco, home of the radical documentary and the experimental feature, was hosting a noncompetitive film festival retrospective. It was sponsored by various corporations, arts organizations, and by the city. It was the centerpiece of a spring arts festival.

They came to the top of the climb and rested against a low stone wall. Beneath them, the marina bobbed with boats. The clouds were low and thick on the misty horizon.

Belinda looked at her friend. "Yvonne, nix on the film festival."

"What's the matter with you? You've been in a lousy mood since we got here. Venner Broadcasting has given the festival a big grant. Guy has strongly suggested that we drop in. Now, to anyone else with half a frontal lobe, pal, that means we go. Are you reading me?"

"Okay, okay." She looked out at the gray boats and the

clouds. Yvonne rattled her corn chip bag. "I don't want to shoot the film in San Francisco."

"What?" Yvonne said, amazed.

"Keith's script only said an urban setting *like* San Francisco," Belinda said. "I don't want to do it here. I hate this city."

Yvonne popped another corn chip into her mouth and chewed thoughtfully. "Belinda, be sensible. We'll get a lot of support here from Guy. He wants it set here. That's one of the things he liked about the script. It has a San Francisco flavor."

"I want us to think of some way out of it."

"Oh, no!" She balled up her corn chip bag.

"This was Archie's city," Belinda said. "This is where everything ended for me."

"Guy's joining us for breakfast tomorrow morning." Yvonne said, "We can talk to him. But it's a big mistake to move locations."

The next morning, they were sitting in the hotel coffee shop. Belinda was glancing through the *San Francisco Chronicle* as Yvonne went over a new version of the *Indictment* budget.

"Jesus. Sara's part of this festival," Belinda said, scanning the column. "She's showing her latest film and two of her early ones. There are panel discussions."

"I'd rather be shot out of a cannon than listen to a panel discussion," Yvonne said, taking the paper from her. "Does anyone up here know she's your mother?"

"No, and let's keep it that way."

Yvonne scanned the column. "My, my, this *is* an effervescent recital of events and gossip," she said. "Sara's got an interview . . . and, she says, among other things: 'My films are my real children,' " Yvonne read.

"I can hear her saying that," Belinda said. The quote hit her hard and that surprised her. Had she not caused her real child to be released from the loony bin? Or had Sara only gone through the motions with Victor out of duty and guilt?

"Ah, there you are!"

Guy Venner and an attractive young woman were coming toward them. "I'd like to introduce my daughter, Cynthia. These are the talented women I was telling you about, my dear," he said, in his rich, full-toned voice that carried without trying. "And they both worked on Fletcher Avery's last film." Guy was in an expansive mood, taking time off to be with his daughter. He was wearing a handsomely tailored summer suit without a wrinkle in it. His gray blond hair was combed straight back from his brow in thick waves. His keen eyes picked out the people in the room who interested him.

Yvonne glanced at Belinda who silently acknowledged that discussion of a location change would have to wait.

"Do you go to school here?" Yvonne asked Cynthia.

"No, in France. I just returned."

"Ah," Yvonne said, "my father was French. Duret." She began speaking French to Cynthia who replied without effort in a tony Parisian accent.

Cynthia was about eighteen. Her auburn hair was pulled back from her lightly freckled face, falling in a flip just above her shoulders. Her hazel eyes reminded Belinda of Vail's, lifting at the outer corners, giving her face a gleeful cast. She was a sheltered girl, Belinda judged—bright, assured, poised—but she didn't seem snobbish or vain. Nothing bad had ever happened to her. She's like I was before Archie, Belinda thought; she'll grow into the woman I could have been.

"You'll be going to college here?" Yvonne was asking.

Cynthia laughed. "Dad and I disagree about that. I'm thinking about law or journalism. Dad wants me to keep studying in France."

"It's a very fine school for young ladies," Guy said.

"It's a great school if you just want to get married," she said, winking at them. But there was an edge in her voice. "Dad sees me as a San Francisco socialite." She hugged his arm.

"Oh, I do not," Guy replied, laughing. "Of course I'd like to see you well married, what father wouldn't?"

"Dad's a little overprotective," Cynthia said airily.

"What kind of law are you interested in?" Belinda asked. Guy frowned at her.

"Public interest law, maybe international human rights— something different." She laughed, a pretty, harmless sound.

"Being a lawyer is fine," Guy said, gravely, "but why not aim high? There are superior legal firms in San Francisco."

"I don't want to do the wills of the rich, Dad. Actually, now

I'm leaning more toward a career in television news."

Guy sighed and looked around the room. Belinda, wondering how she could smoothly bring up a discussion of her production, said, "Terrific," and Yvonne looked at the top sheet of her budget.

"Cynthia's been working on the festival with the steering committee," Guy said.

"The whole idea," Cynthia responded dutifully, "was to prove that San Francisco has been at the center of American films—we just haven't gotten enough credit. Think of the films that have been set here: *Guess Who's Coming to Dinner?* and *D.O.A.* and *Petulia, Barbary Coast, The Glenn Miller Story*. Even *Run and Hide,* Fletcher Avery's first film. He was only a student then, too. We hope he's bringing his director's cut of *Crossing* up here—Dad's put the squeeze on him for us. What a coup that would be."

Belinda rolled her eyes. "Sure will be great seeing old Fletcher again."

A waiter appeared and Guy turned away to order breakfast.

Cynthia leaned toward Yvonne. "I hear Avery is stressed out with some 'personal problems.' Are he and Gloria Griffin an item?"

Belinda had heard about Fletcher and Gloria, a duo that reminded her of nothing as much as a match in a live ammunition depot.

"Oh, dear, I've made a dreadful gaffe," Cynthia said, glancing at Belinda.

"That's okay," Belinda said. "Fletch and I are just friends." That'll be the day, she thought.

"What are you talking about?" Guy said as the waiter left.

"About the festival, Guy," Belinda said.

Cynthia gave her father a quick smile that breached all the differences between them.

"I would like both of you to be my guests tonight at the screening and banquet," Guy said.

Belinda smiled, and the warm, rapid lie that came out of her astonished Yvonne. "Thank you, Guy, we'd love to but we're going to be up near Stinson Beach, checking locations. Early tomorrow—"

Guy waved away production duties for one night.

"But, Guy," Belinda said, still pumping, "we didn't bring anything formal, we'd look—"

"Wonderful, I'm sure," Guy said with vigor.

Yvonne saw that he was enjoying this. "Let's take a break," she said to Belinda.

"Sure." It was hopeless. It was settled.

Cynthia began talking about who would be at the festival. "Major filmmakers based here—like George Lucas and Francis Ford Coppola, or people who shot a famous film here or people who were born here like Sara Wyman. I saw her picture, *Winter Wheat*. Kinda dark and moving, but really emotional. Sky Wyman, her sister, was in it. Have you seen it?"

"I saw it when I was a teenager," Belinda said, remembering a scene of Sky's on a train that had made her cry with pride for both of them.

"Sara Wyman's great, isn't she?" Cynthia said enthusiastically. "Did you see what she said in this morning's paper? That her films were her children? On the surface, that's so cool. I can't wait to meet her."

Guy Venner was thinking of ways to pilot his daughter into law and away from television reporting: it just wasn't good enough for her. When she'd been young, before and after his divorce, he'd tried to shape Cynthia's interests, stimulate abilities he cared about. Now he wondered if he'd done it all wrong. She was a considerable heiress—she had responsibilities. The school in France had given her poise and learning. But she'd always had a rebellious streak, a stiff-necked unwillingness to be led. It was common and mulish. He didn't want it to lead her into passions or situations that were beneath her.

He looked from his daughter to Belinda Oliver, struck again by the mysterious combination of qualities he felt in her, the savage and the delicate. Her beauty came from her slightly arched nose and her deep-set unusual eyes. Her mouth was generous but not sensual. Belinda's small chin nestled deeply in her cupped hand—a gesture he would have criticized in Cynthia. Yet, it rather suited Belinda, speaking of her need to state her attention fully without holding back. That's the duality he sensed in her: she didn't hold back and yet her rather remote face advertised restraint.

He became aware of his erection slowly. He shifted in his

chair, drew closer to the table, crossed his legs. He saw Belinda and Fletcher, that wonderful tyrant, tussling like bobcats. He was sure that Fletcher had discovered her savagery, that with him—*for* him—she had let it out. Would she show it to him?

The cocktail party before the kickoff screening that night was held in the foyer of the hotel banquet room. It was a distinguished room with marble columns and a soaring ceiling. Under it, a flock of society guests, supportive of the arts, chattered noisily and gaily. Waiters with trays moved through the crowd, and two large tables at either end offered mountains of canapés, cheeses, fruits, and pâtés.

Cynthia had adopted Yvonne and Belinda, introducing them around, and for several minutes Yvonne and Belinda shook hands, missed names, agreed with statements they couldn't hear, prayed to be elsewhere. But through the haze and the noise, Belinda was aware of the way Guy, who was with them, was treated: the women flattered him, leaning in toward him; the men listened alertly with respect and interest. No one interrupted him. He was more than a successful man with business acumen, he was more than handsome and striking: he was one of them, part of the upper crust San Francisco society. He was a man of good birth who was also, in his own right, wealthy and powerful.

"Oh, *mon dieu*," Cynthia breathed, "there she is."

It was Sara, and Eddie was with her. He's all grown-up, Belinda thought with a sudden sense of loss and pride. He's a man and he has style. Someone had locked him into a tuxedo. It made him look taller and older than his eighteen years. It made him look like a very young version of Victor.

"Oh, Miss Wyman," Cynthia said brightly, "I'm with the festival committee. I'm so honored to meet you."

Sara glanced at Belinda, then turned to Cynthia. "Thank you." Sara was dressed all in black, her bronze-colored hair a wide frame around her narrow face. "I was misquoted in the newspaper this morning," Sara said, making an apologetic gesture to Belinda, "and it made me mad—I've been trying to locate that reporter—"

" 'My films are my children,' " Cynthia chirped.

"I never said that," Sara said pointedly to Belinda.

"Oh. I'm sorry, Miss Wyman," Cynthia said. She started

introducing herself, fairly shouting over the noise in the crowded room.

"Eddie," Belinda said, shaking hands and feeling the light of his smile, "you're looking very handsome."

"And this is my father, Guy Venner," Cynthia was saying.

"Venner?" Sara said.

"That's right," Guy replied. "I'm a big fan of yours, too. Edward, good to meet you."

"The San Francisco Venners, by any chance?" Sara asked Guy.

"Afraid so, yes. Originally in railroads—that's what brought us out here."

Edward was gazing at Cynthia attentively, trying not to let the full force of his admiration show on his face. "You go to school around here?" he asked her.

"What?" She pointed to her ear. He stepped closer to her. "You look like a California surfer," she said.

"What?" he yelled, smiling.

She stared into his round appealing face. "I can see you on a surfing board."

Edward put on his most open and honest expression, but he felt a sensation he hadn't had for a long time: he felt deformed. He didn't want to test her about his missing hand; he wanted to hide it. His body betrayed none of this. He kept his left wrist in his pants pocket, his shoulders back, gesturing with his right hand occasionally.

Cynthia bent toward him and said: "You want to get some food?"

"I want to get out of this tux, if you want to know the truth. But food will do." He followed her into the crowd, noticing her beautiful carriage.

Sara barely noticed their departure. She was face-to-face with Guy Venner who, she was sure, was related to Diana, and hence, to Archie. Sara remembered an antique-filled room with a worn Aubusson carpet and a tiny old woman, Faith Venner, sitting in a tall chair holding a white poodle on her lap. Miss Venner was cackling, pointing her skeletal finger at Diana, ridiculing her.

In the theater across the street for the screening, Sara sat next to Belinda, and whispered: "I'm so sorry about that stupid thing in the paper. He really did misquote me."

"Don't worry about it," Belinda said.

"I've never felt remotely like that."

"Don't sweat it, Sara." She didn't believe her mother; the quote had sounded just like her.

"I hope we can talk later," Sara said, keeping her voice low. "I was shocked by the quote because I knew it would hurt you."

"I'm all right."

Sara looked away, hurt by her daughter's coldness. "How's your film coming?"

"Fine."

"If I can help, let me know," Sara said.

"Sure."

"You know," Sara said, deliberately changing her tone, "Guy Venner is probably related to us. Diana's mother, Faith, was a Venner."

Belinda turned. "Well, there are lots of Venners." The house lights went down, the crowd stilled.

"Not San Francisco Venners, Lindy." She looked at her daughter's profile in the darkened theater. "I'm sick of talking to you like a stranger," she whispered. "It's time for some truth between us."

"I don't want to talk about Eddie," Belinda whispered back. "Or those stupid letters."

"You know how I feel about Eddie. I've got other things on my mind."

The banquet after the screening was held in a huge *belle epoque*, over-decorated hall lined with giant stills depicting areas of San Francisco preserved forever on film.

Sara and Edward were seated at Guy Venner's table, along with Belinda and Yvonne, two award-winning technicians from Industrial Light & Magic, George Lucas's outfit, one of the coordinators of the festival, and two San Francisco filmmakers who had both won Academy Awards. An orchestra was energetically rendering themes from movies that everyone could recognize.

Edward shifted uncomfortably in his chair. As soon as the dining began, it would be hard to hide his missing hand. He leaned across the two empty chairs between them and said to her, "Does that podium up there mean we have a long program ahead of us, speeches, and all that?"

"No, no. This is supposed to be a party—with dancing. You want to dance?"

"I'm a rotten dancer," he said. "We'd have to give you first aid afterwards." Most of the people on the floor were dancing close together to the syrupy movie theme music. But Eddie, without a left hand, could not hold a girl's hand in his. This was usually no problem because most dancing he did was to rock and roll.

"We won't do anything ambitious," Cynthia said, rising.

Eddie followed her onto the floor and assumed a nonchalant, debonair stance about two feet from her, one hand in his pocket, the other making graceful gestures in time with the music. Fortunately, the slow tempo of the music picked up, making it less ridiculous for them to be gently gyrating in front of each other. He reached his right hand out, caught her left and spun her, then separated and jiggled in place.

Cynthia waved at a closely knit couple, skimming past. "I suppose this room's jammed with high society," he said, talking across the space between them.

"Yes. San Francisco's first families, all out for the arts."

"People like your family?"

"Yes, we're all bluenoses. You got an attitude about that?"

"No." He twirled her again, then stepped back before she could close in.

"Your dad's Vail Wyman, the critic, isn't he?" Cynthia asked, dipping and bending in front of him, her arms out. "I'll bet you get a lot of flak when he gives a bad review to a really popular film."

"Nothing that can't be handled," he said. "My mom's an entertainment attorney."

Cynthia heard the pride in his voice. "You have a really special family," she said. "I mean, your dad, and Sara being your aunt—"

"What do you do at that school in France?" he asked.

"We learn to be extremely well-educated ladies. Ask me anything about place settings." She giggled, and flipped a wing of auburn hair. "I'm kidding! It's demanding, big on arts and history."

"Must be lonely in another country."

She didn't answer. He spun her in tight with his right hand, then out again, then he put his right arm around her waist, putting his left behind his back, and walked in place with her to the music.

"I'm not going back there," she said, jiggling away from him. "I've already stayed an extra year. My dad doesn't know that yet." Her cheeks were pink. She bobbed in front of him. "How did you know it was lonely over there?"

He shrugged, danced back a few feet, then forward. He felt the sweat forming at his hairline.

"How about you?" she asked.

"I'm going into prelaw this fall," he said, looking at all the other couples dancing close on the floor.

"That's great." She flipped her hair back from her face again. "Do you really do any surfing?"

"Yeah," he said, "but there are some things I can't do." He was edging into the truth about his missing hand and it made him extremely nervous.

"I don't believe that," she said.

Edward stopped dancing. "I got this little problem and I don't want you to be shocked," he said. "But I can't hide it much longer." She stopped dancing. "Let's get off the floor," he said, taking her hand. He nodded at a corner near the first tier of tables. But then he realized they'd look silly standing there when everyone else was either dancing or beginning their meal. "Guess we better go back to the table," he said.

"Is anything wrong?" Cynthia asked.

They were edging around crowded tables toward their own, the dance floor on their left. "Take my hand. But I'm warning you, it's not a hand."

"What is it? A hook?"

"No." Gently, feeling the intimacy of the gesture intensely, he fit his stubby wrist into her palm. She stopped and looked at him, then looked down. "Let's not stop and examine it here," he said. "Keep walking."

"Oh, okay," she said, holding the soft rounded skin and bone appendage that ended at the wrist. "How do you eat?"

"With one hand, just like everyone else." Irritated, he took his wrist away from her and put it in his trouser pocket. "Usually I'm cool, but in public with a lot of people, it's— I mean, when they catch on, a lot of people stare."

"I wouldn't stare." She frowned. "I don't think I would have." They were back at the table. "Dad, I have to pick up something for the committee and take it to the press room and I've asked Edward to help. We'll be right back." She turned to him and whispered. "C'mon. Outside."

Eddie smiled. "Smooth move," he said. He followed her toward a pair of double doors at the back of the noisy dining hall. Outside, in the reception room, a few members of the committee were holding fervent, low conversations, and a couple of reporters were arguing about tables. "Out here." She was heading toward a door at the side of the room that led into a small courtyard. The night air was fresh and it smelled of the sea.

"Now," she said, pivoting to face him.

"This is embarrassing," he said. "Will you show me your hand, too?"

"Cut it out," she said.

"Let's just forget this, okay?"

"Sure." She started back toward the door.

"Wait." He went over to her. He wished he hadn't started this, but he knew he had to get past it. "Here." He took his handless arm out of his pocket.

She glanced at it cursorily. "Hmm, no hand. Sort of ends at the wrist."

"Excellent observation, Cynthia, head of the class."

She ignored that. "There are little indents here."

"Where the fingers would have been."

"Five of them. Well, okay, no hand. Lucky you have another one, isn't it?" She smiled up at him. "You must be right-handed." She took his arm and began walking. "Do you spend a lot of your time hiding it?"

"No. But I didn't want to—surprise you in front of every-one."

She stopped walking but didn't drop his arm. "You wouldn't have embarrassed me, Edward."

After dinner, while coffee was served, Edward and Cynthia got up to dance again. Belinda changed her place at the table to sit down beside Sara.

"How is Guy related to Grandma?" Belinda asked her in a low voice. Guy was standing a short distance away.

"I don't know, Lindy."

"It's all past history, anyway."

"You had to be a triplet, had to have Diana for a mother," Sara said, "to know how much the Venners colored our lives." She was watching Eddie's stylish rendition of the twist to the orchestra's rendition of "Mrs. Robinson." She didn't seem interested in Belinda's questions.

"What did you mean about telling some truth?"

"I meant that I'm tired of the family lies. I'm not going to be part of them anymore."

"Miss Wyman? Belinda?" It was Guy. "A whirl around the floor?"

Belinda pushed back her chair and collided with a woman passing behind her.

"Oh, I'm sorry!"

"Francine!" Guy said to the woman. "I was looking for you."

"A little trouble outside with the reporters," Francine replied in a warmly cultured, but tight voice.

"Belinda, this is Francine Cheney," Guy said. "She works with me so you'll be hearing more from her."

Francine Cheney was a tall, trim, athletic-looking woman of about Belinda's age. Her dramatic blond coiffure, pulled tightly back from her face, made her look even taller. She was wearing a strapless rose silk gown that showed off her strong, rounded shoulders.

"Francine's done more for this festival than anyone," Guy went on, introducing her to Sara. "I don't know where she finds the time."

"Oh, Guy, please, I didn't do anything except show a little support," Francine said, widening her large brown eyes and smoothing back a wisp of hair that had escaped. "You know Boo and Tick did all the work." Francine's jaw did not move much when she spoke, which gave her speech a delicately affected sound.

"Francine is my administrative production liaison," Guy said. "She watches the money. She's also a big supporter of the arts here."

"Fine arts, Guy. I confess the movies never thrilled me as they do you." She smiled at Venner with respect and tolerance.

"But you're working with Guy—" Belinda started to say.

"Yes, but I watch the budgets. I'll be watching yours, too," she replied.

"Oh, this is Fred Zwick, the columnist," Guy said, introducing the man who'd been standing behind Francine.

"I have a bone to pick with you," Sara said over the hubbub in the room.

"Me?" He laughed, the fingers of one hand flying to his chest. Zwick had runaway sandy hair and dark, curious eyes.

Francine Cheney was signaling a friend and pointing to her watch. "It's time we got this show on the road. People want to get home." She had a strong, driving but polished manner. "That Mr. Avery is so irritating," she went on to Guy. "He promised he'd be here tonight."

Guy had joined the discussion between Sara and Zwick. Belinda asked Francine, "Are you from San Francisco, too?"

"Yes, all my people are from there." She smiled politely. "Like Guy's."

There was something about Francine Cheney that tugged vaguely at Belinda, something in the combination of face, hair and eyes, or perhaps the woman's carriage, like a gymnast or a dancer—erect, poised. But she couldn't place it. She was distracted by a sudden change in the music, and a drum roll. Sara and Guy turned back to Francine.

"Oh, there he goes. We'll start any minute now," Francine said. She looked at Sara. "I'm sorry, I didn't hear your name."

"Sara Wyman."

Everything about Francine Cheney came to a complete stop. "Yes, I see." She shot a glance at Guy, turned, and stalked away. Fred Zwick said something in a hushed voice and followed her.

Guy looked after her. She was like a galleon under full sail. "She's under a lot of pressure," he mumbled. "She takes on too much, always has, full-time job, hours of volunteer efforts. But she's doing some wonderful things for the arts. Her husband, Charles Cheney—he's quite a bit older than she, a splendid fellow, and also very supportive of arts. They have a great art collection."

"Oh, please, don't bother apologizing," Sara said, grandly. "Some people don't like my films."

A festival organizer came for Sara and she was swept away.

Yvonne was at the table, talking with one of the filmmakers. Belinda and Guy sat down. Cynthia and Eddie were dancing like a couple, not apart. Belinda watched them, trying to figure out what looked different. And then she realized that they had reversed the traditional close dancing position so that Eddie could wrap his handless arm around her waist, and hold her left hand in his right.

Francine Cheney was mounting the steps to a platform. Guy leaned close to Belinda and said softly, deeply, "Francine's a crackerjack. You'll find her a big help."

"How so?"

"She'll be overseeing your production for us. Yours and half a dozen others. I've known her for years. After my divorce four years ago—she's been perfectly splendid to Cynthia," he went on, "always interested in what she was doing, you know the sort of thing. Actually, Francine's a distant relative of mine. Her father was a man named Arch Moberly."

Belinda's head shot up. Francine was on the podium, talking to a man who stood under a banner decorated with the festival logo.

"Old Arch was shot, years ago," Guy went on, his resonant voice hushed. "Quite a scandal, though the family hushed most of it up. I don't want to sound ungenerous—and don't ever tell Fran this—but that man was a joke. I never liked him."

Belinda sat very still. She wasn't sure which shocked her more—that Francine Cheney was Archie's daughter, or that Guy considered Archie a fool and a fake.

She looked across the hushed room at Francine, the daughter, in whose face she could now see the uncanny, distant likeness to the father. She'd only been about eleven when her mother had died and she'd come to live with Archie. And how old had she been when Belinda had first met her, fifteen? Francine Cheney started to speak in a clear, tight voice, the adult configuration of Francine, the teenager, who'd once been the pale, shy girl Belinda had met on the stairs. The full weight of Archie, dead and alive, came rolling back on Belinda.

CHAPTER 17

Fletcher had given the two men from his office the slip, and he was now sitting in the backseat of a taxi. One was his assistant director and the other was a Venner executive flunky whose sole job was to bird-dog him through editing.

Fletcher was more drunk than coked up. He felt loose and sharp simultaneously. The editing on *Crossing* would be finished in a month, pre-production on his new film was already under way, and in three months he'd be in Berlin, shooting. It would be commercially successful—he could pump out all the reasons like bullets. Fletcher's friends and associates hailed him, predicting a fortune in respect and in money from his new picture. Only Fletcher felt *Crossing* had no "bottom." Only Fletcher felt he'd lost what he'd started out with, that crisp shiny truth. Belinda would have understood, he thought. The taxi sped over a raised stretch of freeway and slid down to street level, swishing by the bay and its twinkling lights. Wherever he went, Belinda went with him, next to his arm, through doors, under the sheets with him. She was even sitting next to him in the cab, and he expected to hear her sweet, rough laugh. But she wasn't there. Instead, he heard her warning in the spa that he'd gone too far and would never get back.

After the welcoming speech, after the band resumed playing and after conversation at the tables boiled high again, Belinda saw Francine everywhere, the tall shapely woman in the rose silk gown, her broad, contoured shoulders and strong bare arms visible like pieces of moving sculpture under the lights. She moved gracefully but always with purpose, like a cat. Belinda wanted to bolt but fascination held her. She was locked in place by the deadly secret only she knew.

The crowd began to thin out, but the band kept going, sliding into laundered versions of rock and roll.

Edward sat down, startling Belinda. "Sorry," he said, "I guess you were lost in thought."

"How are you doing, Eddie?"

"Great." He sighed.

"So I've seen. Cynthia. She has character and looks."

"You said it."

"How'd you get roped into coming up here?"

"Sara asked me as a special favor. She didn't want to come alone, and Vail couldn't make it. Something's really eating at him these days." He'd tried to find out what was bothering his father, but Vail kept saying it was Eddie's imagination.

"It was nice of you to take his place, Edward."

He cocked his head back and smiled. "I'm a nice guy."

"Vail's probably working too hard," Belinda said.

"Nah, it's something else. But I don't know what."

Belinda looked away from Francine. "You're all grown-up now," she said. "You look smashing."

That pleased him. "Thanks," he said. "I hear that you're going to direct a film." She nodded. "That's really cool. How'd you do it? I mean, did you have a lot of experience?"

"Most of it's being in the right place, at the right time, with the right script, with the right attitude."

"Uh-huh. I've heard that before. I'm in my spring vacation mode," he said, "cooling out." He was still checking the room for Cynthia. "There's Avery!" Edward gestured at the center double doors where a crowd was forming. "You want to go see him?"

"Not especially."

"Yeah, Dad's down on him, too. You're not with him any more, are you?"

"No. We split." She saw Francine Cheney approaching Fletcher.

"I can get behind that," Eddie said solemnly. "He's great and weird."

"Yeah, that's Fletch." She didn't want to see him but she knew she couldn't stay parked at an empty table with Eddie.

"Do you think he'd remember me?" Eddie asked.

"Can't say. Iffy," she said. "Let's go."

Fletcher Avery was standing just inside the doors. He wore jeans, a rumpled white jacket, no tie, and his long hair was in disarray as if he'd been running hard. His dark eyes, under the ledge of his brow, were looking at Francine Cheney and Guy Venner with a kind of wicked glee. Francine had an expression of anxiety and contempt tacked on her face. Fletcher's voice was loud and his gestures were too big for the emptying room which was not a set he controlled. People stood around him, shaking his hand, murmuring about his films, wanting to be close. The band, located on its own planet, was playing the theme from *Splendor in the Grass*.

Belinda said to Eddie, "Fletcher's drunk or high or both."

"Don't sweat it, Guy, old boy," Fletcher was saying boisterously. "The cut's fine."

"You're running out of time," Guy said, affecting nonchalance.

Fletcher eyed Venner malevolently. "It's not ready. I won't show it till it's right."

At this point, Fletcher caught sight of Belinda. "There she is," he bellowed. He strode through the little crowd of well-wishers to Belinda's side and folded her into a fierce hug. "Oh, my Christ, how good you feel," he sighed close to her ear. "I only came up to this dog and pony show to see you."

Belinda tried to break away but he wouldn't let her go. Suddenly, Yvonne materialized beside them. "Fletcher," she said with remarkable cool, "there's a phone call outside for you. It's Gloria. She's having some kind of nose attack."

"Huh?" Fletcher loosened his grip on Belinda. She broke away from him.

"Hi, Mr. Avery," Edward said. "Remember me?" He stuck his hand out.

Fletcher only glanced at Eddie. "Yeah, sure, the kid with the kite. How're ya doing?" He turned his back on Eddie. "Belinda, we gotta talk. You gotta take pity on me. I'm justa big oaf who done wrong." Fletcher swept an arm around her waist and began to pull her toward the doors.

"Stop that," she muttered, wrenching away. She saw Francine Cheney's face twist in a look of cold outrage.

"He's going to create a scene," Francine's companion said, looking nervously at Guy and then at Fletcher. "Heavens,

the publicity!" Francine glanced at Fred Zwick, the magazine writer who was standing nearby and watching carefully.

"The telephone, Fletcher," Yvonne cried, taking his arm.

"Fuck the phone, Yvonne. Get away." Again, he grabbed
Belinda.

"Let go of me," she said.

"Fletcher," Venner said, coming up to him, "outside." He
was taller than Fletcher but not as thick and broad and young.

"The fuck I will." He glared at Venner. All motion in the
room ceased, all talk died. The band sounded loud. "You
wanna make me?"

"You want a scene?" Venner shot back. Then he laughed,
full of high spirits. "Not a good plan for a great artist like you,
Fletcher. Come up to my suite and have a drink."

"The hell I will," Fletch said, staring at Belinda.

She saw his suffering, the longing mixed with hatred in his
eyes. She felt the look palpably on her skin. "I'm not going
with you, Fletcher."

Fletcher's strong, crude face collapsed, and Guy Venner
relaxed. He knew he'd won. "Fletch, do yourself a favor.
Meet some of the people who admire you so much."

"You bitch," Fletcher said to Belinda.

Belinda felt Edward tense beside her. She put a hand on his
arm. Venner promptly stepped forward, opened one arm, and
drew Fletcher aside by pressing the air around him but never
touching him.

"Okay, okay, Venner, I won't break any china." Fletcher
cast an ugly, sad look at the crowd. "I'm certainly not breaking
any hearts here."

"Let's meet in the morning," Venner said, still walking the
air around Fletcher to the doors, herding him forward.

"The fuck we will, Venner." Fletcher pushed through a door
and was gone.

Guy Venner literally snapped his fingers. Two men came
out of the crowd, and Guy said in a deep, pleasant voice,
"Let's make sure he gets to his room all right." The two men
left. Venner turned to the little crowd. "Dreadfully sorry. Too
much to drink tonight, I imagine. High-strung. Are you all
right, Belinda?" He cut between Eddie and Belinda and put a
hand on her arm.

Cynthia came up to Eddie. "Wasn't that something?" she said, clearly excited. "Is he always like that?"

"No. He was really great, once," Edward replied. He had been deeply shocked by Fletcher's performance and surprised by Belinda, who hadn't given an inch during the crunch, and she wasn't relaxing now, either. Her narrow pretty face was set like stone and her eyes glittered: she was really angry.

Francine Cheney was annoyed. "And I don't want to see one word of this in print, Fred. Not one word. Are we together?" She pressed her long square fingers to her temple. "Guy, I'm leaving. You understand."

"Yes, my dear. Artists are difficult, we just have to understand that. Wait till you see *Crossing*. It'll be worth this little disturbance."

Her glance said that she doubted that.

Guy said: "Yvonne, you were wonderful. Poor fellow, he's driving himself too hard. Good lord, where's Sara?"

"She went up to her room, Mr. Venner," Eddie supplied.

"Before Fletcher came in?"

"Yes, sir."

"That's good. Well, you and Yvonne and Belinda come along to my suite. We'll have a nightcap and try to forget this nonsense."

Cynthia slid her eyes toward Edward and smiled. She didn't think it had been nonsense. She obviously thought it had been thrilling.

In Venner's top floor suite, Eddie was sipping a Coke, watching Cynthia and her father wrangle happily about Fletcher Avery. The two Venners were very different, and yet it was obvious they were very close. Venner had expectations for his daughter, and Eddie wondered what they were and how much Cynthia agreed with them. But as Venner went on and on about forgiving artists their outbursts, the man's condescension irritated Eddie: it was bullshit. You might forgive what Fletcher had done, appearing drunk or high, making a scene like that, but you didn't camouflage it with this thinly veiled derision as if Fletcher were a toy or a kid. He was a great director who was out of control. But why was he out of control? Because of his picture? Because of Belinda? Belinda was sitting at the end of a huge sofa, looking tightly curled, talking too much. One of her earrings had fallen off and she was trying to reattach the hook. She puzzled Eddie but he liked her because she wasn't phony.

The suite reminded Belinda of the ones Sky had stayed in when she'd traveled: anonymous and luxurious, removed from real life even though back then the comfort had seemed like real life to Belinda. Cynthia and Guy reminded her of her life before "the war," before the nuthouse, before everything. Growing up with Sky, Belinda's life had been furnished with luxuries she'd taken for granted and packed with expectations. It was time to start enjoying them again and put the old war to rest. She didn't need what she'd learned inside to survive now. She didn't need Maisie or Ruby—or the psych-tech she'd bought off with Victor's money. She, Belinda, needed to get back to the good times.

The two men who had escorted Fletcher somewhere came into the room. They nodded at Venner, who expressed elaborate concern for Fletcher's well-being.

Yvonne made a graceful exit, and soon everyone was leaving. As Eddie went out the door, Guy said: "Belinda, may I have a word?" Belinda waved to Eddie. The door closed.

"I know you're tired," Guy said, "but I just need a minute."

"Of course." She walked back into the suite's living room.

"Dad, I'm on my way to bed," Cynthia called out. "See you in the morning, Belinda."

When she'd left, Venner indicated the sofa. "I hope you're not too upset—about Fletcher," he said.

"No."

"Are you nervous about the production?"

"Keyed up, let's say. It's a new lease on life."

"Was Fletcher drunk or high?" Belinda shrugged. "I think he was high," he said, lifting an eyebrow.

"I don't know."

"Poor fellow. I suppose he's one of those who has to go all the way down before he goes back up." His announcer's voice went all the way down.

Belinda didn't say anything.

"I know it's none of my business, but I feel—protective. Did you love him a great deal?" He stared into her delicate face, hunting for a way to crack the facade.

Since her suicide attempt, she'd made a pact with herself about the truth. In all cases, at all turns, when she could face the truth and tell it without hurting others, like Eddie, she would. Now she said, "Yes. A lot. And—it's none of your business."

He lowered his head. "I hope it won't interfere with your work."

"Are you kidding?" she replied. "I'm aware of the opportunity and I won't blow it."

"Good! Well said! Stay and have one drink," he said. "It would please me. I can't sleep yet, I'm a bit of an insomniac." He was up on his feet pouring her a glass of wine, glancing around at her. "Yes?"

"Okay."

"Belinda, you're a damned tough combination," he went on, his voice full and rich. He handed her a glass. "Utterly fascinating, too, I might add." He raised his glass. "Here's to *Indictment*. May it bring on a long and happy collaboration." He sipped. "I like seeing newcomers succeed," he went on. "You and Yvonne will make a good team."

They talked for half an hour, ranging from *Indictment* and the work plans for it to the global communications explosion. At one point, he said enthusiastically, "You know what I believe in? Living well, doing right."

"You believe in power, Guy."

"Hmm, yes. But powerful people are lonely. They can't confide in anyone."

"That's your choice, isn't it?" But Belinda was conscious of something else in the room straining the air between them. It wasn't being close to a man like Guy Venner that reminded her of her former life and its solid securities. There were other emotional motes in the air, and they all came from Guy.

They fenced enjoyably, getting to know each other. "I like stimulating new work," he said, "new expressions, combinations. That's the heart of business, you know. *Indictment* is going to change your life, you know that? You won't be able to go back, but you won't want to. Think of the stories you can tell if this one works." He was standing by the sofa, grinning at her, his sharp distinguished features lit from below by the lamp. "You can call your own shots, travel all over the world, get to know the people of your time who make a difference, make changes, work with the best people. There's no life like it, believe me, Belinda."

"You sound like my Mephistopheles."

Venner laughed fully. "But you are no Faust. You're too pragmatic. I know you."

She knew he did not, but his picture of her future moved her and tempted her.

"You think I don't believe what I'm saying about your future?"

"Well, who knows?"

"Believe it." He sat down near her. "Where do you start shooting in this town?"

"I was going to bring that up next," Belinda said. "I think the San Francisco setting is clichéd. I want to play the crime story in *Indictment* against the grain, set it in a town in the northwest, someplace that looks pretty, where we don't anticipate gangs and overworked public defenders—a place that says the people have moral values and trees and bottle laws."

He was shaking his head. "There's plenty of values in San Francisco—we're a value town!"

"Guy, it's a little film. We can only make it bigger by keeping it small. If we force it bigger, it'll lose its power, its—well, its universality. It'll get smaller." She squinted at him. "Does that make sense?"

He nodded. "You creative people have your own language, that's for sure, but that's damn smart, what you say."

"Don't con me."

"No. I think you should shoot it here."

"You've got Yvonne buffaloed about San Francisco—she knows Venner Broadcasting and Venner Everything can smooth over a lot of rough spots here. But it's bad for the picture to be shot here."

In repose, Guy's long handsome face with its prominent nose looked dejected. He rose, took the glass from her hand, refilled it. "Tell me more." He put the glass down on the table before her. She ignored it.

"I want to shoot in Portland—it's charming, full of art and fountains and parks, and you know what? Right under that skin, they have a drug and gang problem up there that won't quit."

His manner changed abruptly. "You don't want to shoot here and it's got nothing to do with the picture."

"Why are we arguing?" she said, smiling disarmingly. She rose. "You don't give a damn where the picture's shot. But I do, so let me do it my way." She started toward the door.

He studied her, testing the temperature of the room. He followed her. "Relax. You're always ready for battle. I don't run my business that way."

At the door, she turned. He was right behind her. He opened his arms and embraced her. "You have too little comfort in you, Belinda. You're hard as agate and soft as silk. Let me give you some comfort. Stay with me tonight." He was kissing her cheek and her hair, holding her tightly against him, ignoring her stiffness. "You won't be sorry, Belinda, not for a moment. Let me take care of you a little."

Archie, she thought. Archie had said, "I know how to make you feel good." She looked up at Guy's proud face, elastic now with anticipation. The sloping eyes beneath his brow watched her.

"I'm not interested in pleasure," she said.

But his arms felt good. There was toughness, ease, and confidence in this man, but she sensed no war in him. She didn't feel the astonishing flood of appetite she'd felt with Fletcher, but she felt a longing for comfort and sensual human contact. He would do her no harm.

She relaxed against him. His whole body seemed to swell up against her. He pressed his lips to her throat at the base of her jaw, moved to her chin and cheek, and came to rest on her mouth. "Come with me," he murmured.

One entire wall of the bedroom looked over San Francisco. The city lights punctuated the darkened room—a glittering diamond array. Venner's trembling fingers were slipping the straps of her dress from her shoulders.

When they were naked, she put her arms around him, smelled his sweet skin that had been buffed and scrubbed and massaged by hired hands all his life. She wanted to be consoled by this clever and opulent man. She reached out for his face and drew his lips to her breast. His mouth was warm and wet. He breathed on her nipple, cooling it. Desire skittered through her. He seized her hand, twisting his fingers through hers. "Come," he whispered.

They stood in one corner of the huge tiled shower, sheathed in soap lather. Guy's muscles were lean and long. She ran her hands over his thighs, his erection, his chest, until they were both white with foam and slippery as fish. Guy Venner was playful, clapping a mound of lather on her head while he nuzzled one soapy leg between her thighs. He seized her waist but she darted away from him: she did not want him in the shower. She danced out of the cubicle and plunged into the churning hot tub. He followed, jubilant and frisky. They wallowed, bumping up against the jets, splashing and delaying, until she put her head back against the rim, and drew his mouth down to hers. When the kiss ended, she pushed him away, jumped out of the tub, ripped a big towel from the rack, and skipped into the bedroom. He followed, dripping water and soap, as she flung herself on the bed and opened her arms.

Tenderness invaded play. He moved over her with discretion and a kind of solemnity as if a critical bargain had been made. His head came to rest next to hers as he fitted himself into her, his eyes never leaving her face, never breaking the pact that was being consummated.

Belinda soaked in familiar sensations, a spiral that wiped out hunger. Archie and Fletcher approached, then receded. Her pact in this act with Guy was built more on avenging pain than on pardon or pleasure.

It was exorcism. She arched her back and made it real.

The following afternoon, Sara was sitting in a coffeehouse down the street from the hotel, waiting for Belinda. She was in a pair of bright green jersey slacks and a matching jacket. She'd wrapped a scarf around her head, a wide band of color against her wiry bronze and silver hair.

"Sorry I'm late." Belinda perched on the seat across from her at the tiny coffeehouse table. She looked cheerful. Her face had a rosy color, her eyes were bright. She'd fastened her hair in a ponytail, but a strand of it had escaped and drifted down the side of her face.

"I liked *Weathervane*," she said about Sara's new film that had been shown that morning. "But what a reaction." It had been greeted as disturbing and controversial.

Sara smiled smugly. "Debate in panels after my films is

always hot. What did you think it was about?"

"Fathers and daughters, and I didn't think it was antifamily at all." She'd watched it as a newcomer who could learn from the mother she did not know. "I watched it for composition, for acting and character, for movement, for pace. It was really good."

"You sound surprised."

"Well, I guess I am."

Sara said, "There's something different about you lately, Belinda. I don't know what it is."

"Delayed maturity!" Belinda shrugged.

Sara made a sudden decision. "C'mon, let's walk. I have cabin fever."

Outside, a cable car crowded with tourists had stopped at the corner. "Run for it," Sara said gaily. Belinda darted after her, realizing she'd never seen the kid in her mother before. Somewhere, deep inside, Sara was younger than Lindy.

Surprisingly fleet, Sara caught the grab bar as the car started moving. She and Belinda sat down on the outside bench seat, facing the street. The cable car climbed noisily up the hill.

"What's this all about? Where are we going?"

"I don't know," Sara said, puffing. "Maybe the wharf, maybe Golden Gate Park—does it matter?"

Sara had come to an end of the duplicity, the half-spoken thoughts and feelings, the omissions. She was going to say again all that was in her heart and if her daughter couldn't handle it, Sara would live with that. Oh, she'd spoken out before, but all her life she'd wanted Belinda to accept her, and anxiety about her daughter's reactions had kept her from being completely honest.

"I was thinking about that scene in your film," Belinda said over the noise of the cable car as it ground uphill to California Street. "When the family's in the forest for the picnic, and the father refuses to let the daughter eat the birthday cake because of spoilage. I mean, he's really talking about the family, isn't he, not the cake?"

"That's right," Sara said. "A kind of rot sets into some families and keeps infecting the members down the generations."

"How does a family repair that?"

"I suppose every family has a different answer, but mine is honesty. Being honest. We haven't done a very good job of that in our family." She paused but Belinda said nothing. "I've always felt guilty about you, Belinda, but I can't let it run me anymore. I don't want it to run you, either. I want to have a long talk."

They had crested the Powell Street hill; people were piling on and off. "I don't think a cable car is quite the place."

"I think it's perfect," Sara said. "I was thinking about Guy Venner and Archie and the past." She had never discussed Archie with Belinda.

"I don't want to get into all that, Sara." The cable car jerked forward, heading downhill toward the bay.

Sara was holding onto the bar, her head up. "I've given up wanting you as my daughter. I've even given up wanting you as my friend. But I still feel responsibility for you. I want to tell you what I know to be true. What you do with it is your business."

Belinda shut her eyes briefly. "I don't want to get into this today."

Sara only smiled.

The cable car hurtled down the hill and made a creaky, rapid turn. Belinda wondered where she could pick up a cab and get back to the hotel.

Near the marina, the car came to a rest. People jumped off. It was a beautiful day with a bright cool sun. The salty breeze snapped at two fishtail kites engaged in mock combat, held aloft by two Japanese boys who ran along a parklike green field. Belinda looked around for a cab. Some of the tourists were headed toward a famous old coffeehouse down the street. Sara was headed toward a park bench.

"Sara . . ."

"Sit," Sara said, sitting. "What do you have to lose?"

Belinda sat and watched her mother watching the silvery kites.

"Belinda," Sara finally said, "I made *Weathervane* with you in mind—for you and for me, too. Secrets mar relationships. That's self-evident, but it took me a long time to know it." Sara turned away from the kites and looked at her daughter. "You're right—that family in the film has been infected, and it's disintegrating. That family is our family. Secrets ruin relationships. Your grandmother will never admit it and Vail says everything right out; he never had any secrets except one from Eddie—you."

"Oh, god, we're back to that. I'm not going to tell Eddie—"

Sara laughed shortly. "You do what you want. It's your choice. I just want you to know what you're choosing."

"Sara—"

"Just hush up and listen!" Sara barked. "You owe me that." The look on Sara's face silenced Belinda. "Families have a way of camouflaging discomfort and shame. Every family does some of that, but we've done a lot of it. I started to tell you about your great-grandmother, Faith Venner, last night. She had a brother, and I think Guy is that brother's grandson."

"He is. He told me."

Sara was surprised. "What did he say?"

"Just that."

Sara took a cigarette out of her purse. "Faith had two children," she said. "One was Diana, very early, from an affair with a man her father despised. Her father sent her away to have the child—Diana, as it turned out. Years later, Faith married and their child was Archie. He was about fifteen years younger than Diana."

"Guess I was screwing my uncle," Belinda said.

"Flippancy will not protect you. If you want to keep hiding with the rest of the family, just leave."

But Belinda did not leave. "I knew that Archie was related to Diana, but it seemed, well, remote compared to the deeper connection I had with him. Where did Diana grow up?" she asked, wanting to get off Archie.

"Vail and I know only pieces. Your grandmother never talked about it. But I know she suffered terribly as a child. At some point she overheard her foster parents talking about the money her mother was supposed to send to support Diana, about how powerful her real family was. And from that day on, Diana found her reason for being—she would prove herself worthy of her real family, she would educate herself, raise herself up—"

"Poor Grandma." Belinda found herself unaccountably close to tears. She looked up at the sky and the kites swimming in air.

"Diana spent our entire childhood looking for her parents, and when she found Faith, that awful old woman threw her out. Mother tried so hard to be, as she said, worthy of her important family. Worthy! It was a cruel joke."

"Weren't they important?"

"They were thieves," Sara said with passion. "They robbed California, sacked it, built a fortune on the backs of the Chinese, the Mexicans, the Indians. Let's let the scales fall from our eyes on that one." She finally managed to light her cigarette by cupping her hands around her lighter. "Diana's search and that ghastly disowning of her shaped my childhood, and Sky's and Vail's. This is one of the things I want you to know— if Diana hadn't kept trying to win her mother, Sky wouldn't have raised you and Archie wouldn't have entered our lives, and what happened to you—wouldn't have happened."

Belinda felt her heart beating too fast. She inhaled a deep breath of the sea air.

"Diana insisted that Sky raise you because she was still hoping that her mother would accept her, she was still trying to make a pretty family picture her mother would admire. But I didn't make a pretty family picture. Vic had left me, I was studying acting in New York with a little baby on my hip. You didn't do things like that in the fifties—single parents were not only rare, they were a disgrace. I finally gave in. I let Sky raise you. I thought it would be better for you. The problem came from the lies, letting you be raised as Sky's daughter—that was the deal. It was not spoken of when I gave you up, but subconsciously I knew that was the price. And I did it anyway. Your grandmother and Sky could live with the lie. I did, too, but it marred every connection I had, every relationship—the most important one being with you. I couldn't live with the rot, and I don't think you can either. But it was there long before you formed your attachment to Archie."

Belinda watched the kites dipping and climbing. "Thanks," she said in a low voice. She felt gently liberated. It was not her single sin anymore. She stared into Sara's face, at the wrinkles around her narrow foxy eyes, at her full mouth and high cheekbones. She couldn't remember when she'd ever really looked at Sara.

"I'm glad you're going to make that film," Sara said. "I just wish a Venner wasn't involved."

Belinda was remembering Sara in the morning panel. Her mother was a pro, fielding some hostile questions, never ducking. It took nerve. "You like being a director, don't you?"

"Can't imagine another way of life," Sara replied, putting out her cigarette. "You'll like it, too. It's thrilling."

"I don't want to be a carbon copy of you—"

"Couldn't be if you tried. You and I—we're very different."

"Were you very nervous before your first shoot?"

"I vomited. I tottered onto that set on rubber band legs. As I recall, I had a very nice crew but I thought they were testing me. Lindy, be easy on yourself, trust yourself more. I feel you're always testing yourself, are you tough enough or good enough?" Sara put her hand over Belinda's and for the first time, Belinda did not move away. "C'mon, I'll buy you a gin fizz."

The coffeehouse was warm and full of sunlight. Round oak tables were stationed along one side, the bar was on the other. Locals in jeans, boots, and mackinaws, and tourists in pastel polyester were hunched over omelets and fizzes and designer coffees. Belinda and Sara took a seat at the back.

"Sara," Belinda said when their fizzes arrived, "I understand from Patsy that you and Victor played a fast hand of poker with the loony bin chiefs and got me released."

The lines in her lively face deepened, and Sara said, "Yes, it was all I could do. It was the least I could do." Sara's eyes filled with tears. "Shit," she said. Belinda realized with a jolt that Sara was human. She'd never acknowledged that. Sure, she was emotional, dramatic, often loud, even brazen. But for this instant she was uncrowned, another human woman who had physically given birth to Belinda just as Belinda had given birth to Eddie.

Sara was fishing in her pockets. "I never have a handkerchief like normal people," she said, sounding deeply annoyed.

"I don't either."

Sara looked up, and then she laughed. "Good," she said, a punctuation mark. "Why prepare for every catastrophe?" Fresh tears came into her eyes. "Oh, god, I thought I would die when they sent you to that place. I thought I would die." She looked sideways at her daughter. "Victor was magnificent. He's so—

canny for a kind of wastrel of a guy, you know? He's such a
lovable man, but so vain and—and—well, wonderful. I always
liked him but I didn't admire him until that time. He knew right
away what to do. You must thank him sometime."

"I'm thanking you. I'm grateful." She wanted to feel inun-
dated with feelings for Sara, but she had no connections of
trust, no bonds. The absence overwhelmed her suddenly. "I
can't get past this," she murmured.

"What?" asked Sara, alarmed.

"I don't know you, I haven't any faith in you, no history
with you, and I know it'll be the same with Eddie and me
and I can't get past it." All the consequences of her glib
arrangements with Patsy and Vail, the "Eddie's yours, I gave
him up," rushed at her in the coffeehouse. "I'm so angry that
any of this is so."

Sara leaned across the table. "Change it," she said, intensely.
"Tell Eddie."

Belinda shook her head. "Never. I'm enough of a fruitcake
without having him see me as one." She drank her gin fizz.
Her face smoothed out, she cracked a hard smile. "Let's not
argue about it anymore. It is what it is, right here in the real
world. Deal?"

Sara was uneasy. "You're very emotional, Lindy. A minute
ago, you were furious and frustrated, and now"—she narrowed her hazel eyes at her daughter—"you're ready to have
lunch."

"I learned not to let my emotions run me in the school,"
Belinda replied.

Sara ordered two more fizzes. She was steeling herself.
She lit another cigarette. "I'm still receiving anonymous letters." She watched her daughter carefully. "I'm only the con-
duit."

"So you've said."

"These letters aren't meant for me, but for you." I hope
that's true, Sara thought, I hope you're not writing those
letters. She felt tears in her eyes. Lindy's face was still as
stone. A wisp of her hair fell over her forehead; she didn't
touch it. "The writer doesn't know where you are or who you
are because Lindy Wyman doesn't exist anymore."

"I've told you what I think about those letters."

Sara seemed to ignore that remark. "In the beginning, they

were quite ugly and threatening, but they're less so now."

"Maybe they'll stop soon," Belinda whispered.

Sara looked at her searchingly. "Do you think so?"

"Well, I don't know, do I?"

Sara crushed out her cigarette. "I'm getting a picture of this person. He or she isn't crazy, but driven and divided."

"Maybe it's Patrick," Belinda quipped, feeling profoundly uneasy.

"I knew Patrick well once. It could be him but I have a hard time believing it."

The air between them felt thick and infected. All the lightness was gone, sucked out. Belinda sat still, staring over her mother's shoulder. Is it you? Sara wanted to ask her daughter, dear god, is it you?

CHAPTER 18

Angular, modern lamps glowed in Guy's San Francisco office; the wall of inset television screens was dark. A month had passed since the film festival. Francine Cheney sat in a chair by Guy's desk, her long muscular legs extended, a folder open on her lap. Other folders rested on a small glass table beside her with an empty coffee cup. Guy, at his desk, bent over a computer printout, concentrating. His shirt collar was unbuttoned; his tie was loosened. He'd kicked off his loafers underneath the desk. Rain streaked the huge plate glass window behind him.

"The numbers look good," he said. His golden voice rolled into the silent room.

Francine smiled. Numbers had no gray areas or oblique directions—they went up or down.

"But being without your assistant," Guy went on, "means you'll have to watchdog these production costs for a while. Keep extra close tabs on the Oliver production," he went on. "They're—"

"New," she said.

Guy didn't like having his sentences finished but Francine always interrupted. "Not new individually, but it's their first as a team," he corrected her.

"Why are they shooting in Oregon?"

He didn't answer. He glanced at a computer list. "Can you oversee all these productions without what's his name—"

"My assistant?" she broke in. "Yes."

"Don't want you to get all tired out, Fran."

"I never tire, you know that."

Guy was a shrewd judge of human behavior and he knew exactly what he had in Francine. She was not a whirlwind or a bright, cheerfully occupied executive who delegated well.

She did not have those graces. Francine was a locomotive. She could always do more. Socially and professionally ambitious, she was always phoning, talking, noting, or checking, and, in addition, she was always volunteering—to fill in at Venner Broadcasting or to fill a need for an arts program or a local women's media group. She belonged to a string of organizations. She postponed living for events or duties. She used involvement like a shield to protect her from looking at herself, though Guy had no idea why her extreme energy might be an act of suppression, nor was he interested. Her various occupations fueled her personality, consuming humor and domestic enjoyments, leaving her an intensely busy but dull person. Occasionally Guy wondered what would happen when the fuel gave out. But Guy liked Francine because she was competent, smart, and intensely loyal.

He watched her straighten the printout pages in her file and note the date of this meeting on the file tab. Her blond hair was pulled tightly back in a French twist, her eyes fixed on her task. He couldn't imagine Fran in bed with her husband, Charles, or with anyone; she couldn't lie still for the thirty minutes it'd take poor Charles to get warmed up.

Francine looked up suddenly. "I'm off to the squash courts," she said, gathering up the computer sheets with an air of importance. "You want to hit a few?"

"No, not tonight, Fran." He rose and followed her toward the door. "Fran, meant to mention this earlier. Why did you bite that filmmaker's head off at the festival that night?"

"Which filmmaker?" Her brown eyes widened, a look of concern crossed her face.

"Sara Wyman."

"I can't imagine," she said, opening the door. "I certainly wouldn't mean to do anything like that."

Guy laughed. "Fran, I've known you since you were a kid so don't con me. When you do something, you mean to do it."

"This time you're wrong, Guy. Did I—was I rude?"

"Oh, it doesn't matter," he said, dissatisfied. "Forget it. Have a good weekend and say hello to Charles."

He watched her go, standing in his stocking feet at the door. She had a brisk, no-nonsense walk. She was trim as a filly. She'd go down to the squash courts and slam that ball around and then swim a hundred laps in the pool. Her trainer came to her house three times a week at six A.M. to put her through her paces. Guy was in good physical shape, too, but if he'd worked his body out at thirty like Francine, he'd probably last all night every night with Belinda. But, he thought, closing the door, how much more fun would he have?

"First you move my script from San Francisco to Portland," Keith was saying to Belinda, "and now you want to change the title." He was stretched out on an old couch in her Los Angeles office, a copy of the script tented over his face.

"Take that off," she said. "It looks like you've died."

Keith removed the tent. His face, rugged, warm, decent, capped by his slate-colored hair, emerged. He sat up.

"I don't like messing with this script," he said.

Keith was an important writer, much sought after, and Belinda realized this; but in another way, the man in the jeans and the jacket across from her was old Keith, the guy with the Mustang and the Santa Monica apartment and the dog.

"The title—"

"Don't screw with my title," he said, irritated. *"Indictment* is an ironic title; it doesn't mean the legal accusation against Chicky, the gang member, it refers to the system itself." It was a quarry that Keith Llewellyn had worked before. Chicky is accused of murder and indicted. While in jail, without bail, her parents leave town, abandoning her. Untrusting and untrustworthy, she finally learns she can't fight the whole system without a margin of faith for the public defender.

"Okay, Keith. On to other matters. It's my humble opinion that the Phyllis and Ken characters aren't right."

"Ah, let 'em alone, they're fine," he said.

"They're just neighbors, so where's the tension between them? And the college demonstration doesn't work," Belinda said.

"My god, woman, I thought you liked this script."

"I adore it. How about making the Phyllis character an animal rights person, a real tiger, so to speak?" She smirked at him.

"Is this your director persona?"

"Guess so."

"Why do directors like to rewrite so much?" he asked her. "Why is that?"

"Well, can't we discuss these things?"

Keith tacked into another wind. "I'm noticing how often our illustrious leader, Guy Venner, comes down here to Sodom from heaven up north. Like the fallen angel." He smiled craftily like a fox, waiting.

"He has a lot to do in Los Angeles."

Keith blew out a lot of air, wrapped his arms around his middle, and mimed a horrible mirth. "My dad used to say that all you could do in the face of a huge lie was laugh big."

"What a card he must've been." She'd expected a happy collaboration. This wasn't it. "Phyllis's predicament with Ken. What if she raids the local medical school and springs the chimps and the cats?"

"That's a lousy idea, Belinda, second-rate."

"Then you fix it! God, you're so exasperating."

He lay back on the couch. "Oh, make her an animal radical, I don't care." He sat up. "You're seeing a lot of Guy Venner, I hear. He can be stingy—with money *and* affection."

"Stay out of my private life, Keith."

He knit his hands and frowned as though confronted with an insupportable problem. "I know you're tough—it's charming. But, Belinda, just keep a few things in mind. One: he may say his production chief makes the final decisions over there, but he doesn't—Guy does. Everything comes from the top in Venner land. Two: no matter what he says he isn't really interested in you or me or this production. He's only interested in big pictures—I mean global power, not high-budget films."

"I can take care of myself."

"I'm sure you can."

"Are you finished?" she asked.

"Yes. Yes I am."

But he was tempted to tell her she would have had a much harder time punching through as a director with Venner had it not been for his help. He hoped she wasn't close to Venner, close enough for confidences. She'd hit the ceiling if Venner told her at the wrong moment. Keith himself had tried to find a way to hint that he'd had the confidence and respect in her to give her a hand, but they were now too far along for him to drop that kind of message on her. Belinda would be shooting in three weeks.

"Phyllis. If she's in animal rights, she could be mounting a raid . . ."

"All right, all right, it's not a bad idea." They slogged through the rest of the script. Belinda's phone rang constantly, attended by one of Fletcher's original muses, Jane Weyfield, in a cubbyhole off Belinda's office. She was an auburn-haired young woman with a relentlessly upbeat manner. Belinda's assistant director was an intrepid and resourceful man recommended by Buttons Botsford. Opal Douglas had agreed to do the casting for a minimum fee which had surprised and pleased Belinda. "You got outta that thing with Fletcher pretty well," Opal had told her when she'd signed on. "Not many do."

Yvonne opened the door and strode through it. Her hair was longer, her color was high, and her blue eyes bright. Buttons wheeled in behind her. Pre-production with Yvonne was like the busy and contented buzz from a hive. Yvonne launched into a detailed outline of the schedule.

Buttons sat quietly, gazing at Yvonne until he caught Keith's eye on him. He rearranged his expression.

After Yvonne and Buttons left for a lunch, Keith said, "They're in love."

"Who said?"

"I say. Eagle-eye Llewellyn says."

Guy's whole body felt slippery with sweat. He braced himself above Belinda, combing out one wing of her hair with his fingers.

She looked up into his strong calm face. His sharp eyes were lazy with pleasure. She slid her hands down his arms to his flared hands propped on the bed, felt the pulse beating in his wrists. A drop of sweat from his face fell on her breast. She moved, twisting slightly, feeling good, feeling a long-delayed connection, feeling conscious. His lips separated, exposed his beautiful teeth. He turned his head up, angled away, groaned, a long sound, part pain, part bliss.

His arms collapsed. He fell beside her, breathing deeply, reached out, drew her near, smoothed her hair back from her forehead. She went to him easily, liking and enjoying him, feeling every day comforted and wooed, closer to him. Where

Fletch had been hot, aggressive, intuitive, Guy was cool and analytical and confident. But being close to Guy brought back to her wonderful trace memories from the time before the war. It wasn't like being with Fletch, wildly in love—surprised, addicted. With Guy, she felt merged with no danger of war. She was keeping her head, learning to trust his judgment, his experience. Despite what Keith said, she didn't find him at all stingy.

Guy pulled Belinda closer, felt his body slip and slide against hers, glossy and damp. "Are you happy?" he whispered in his satin voice.

"Yes." She was happy. He didn't ask her questions about her childhood or her youth, he seemed only interested in her present, possibly her future. She mistakenly felt he was uninvolved, since he made few demands on her, only that she be courteous and somewhat remote when they were out together. He was a shrewd judge of human behavior, reciting discreet examples from Venner Broadcasting or from his lobbyists in Washington: how people overplayed their hands, engaged in political blackmail, warred for turf, or just plain lied when only the truth would save them. She curled against him, closed her eyes. "Yes."

Guy liked to think that he had no conflicts in his life which couldn't be solved, and on the surface, he had none: his business was public and challenging, his daughter was intelligent and graceful, his ex-wife was quiescent. He pressed his cheek against Belinda's hair, holding her. He felt they shared a mutual tolerance and vigor. He felt he could tell her anything: she was smart and ambitious—he trusted ambition; she gave him wonderful sex and companionship without the difficulties of marriage or other demands. He squeezed her flank and kissed her ear. But he knew he was approaching an edge; he couldn't believe the chasm that was waiting for him. It humbled him. He wanted Belinda's life to revolve around him.

He rose on one arm and stared at her. Her mystery and her strength had invaded him. She was more important to him than he'd ever meant her to be. But he couldn't crack her. She always held back. His wealth didn't impress her; his power didn't intimidate her. Yes, she was fucking him but she wasn't his and he knew the difference.

"Belinda," he said.

"Mmmm?"

"Am I important to you at all?"

She opened her eyes, alert. "Yes."

His mouth twisted into a smile that verged on mockery. "Good." He put his palm on her belly, tapped her gently, then leaped out of bed. "We're dining out."

"Guy, Francine Cheney telephoned today. I'm afraid we don't see eye to eye about the script changes."

"She's a bit of a stickler," he said, pulling on a robe. "But she's my rep to the productions, so don't duck her."

"I wonder if someone else could—"

"She's it. Get up. I won't feed you in bed," he said, leaving for the bathroom.

She looked at a wall mural that resembled a Navajo sand painting, angular and strict. Her life was working for once, she felt. But talking with Francine Cheney on a regular basis made her uneasy. It was like having Archie back, looking over her shoulder.

Eddie rolled on his bed, imagining Cynthia beneath him, beside him, on his face, kneeling. He writhed and exploded and pushed his head into the pillow. Cynthia had done a number on him. Cynthia had swept him away.

He flopped over on his back, panting and hot, and rolled his eyes around his room. He'd kept a wall of maps; another wall held his bulletin board on which he tacked the best Polaroid shots of his fights. Clothes were strewn about, singly and in heaps. Music videos pounded out of the television set in the corner. But Eddie was reliving the last moment with Cynthia as he shook her hand by the elevator in San Francisco. Her hand was hard, flat, and cool, and he could still feel the pressure of her grip. He'd relived every syllable of their conversations at the film festival at least ten times. Her stories about her family were daunting in their detail. God, she knew everything about her people ten generations back. She'd asked questions about his but he didn't know much of anything. He didn't know who his father was or how he'd died; he knew Vail and Patsy had disapproved of him—it was in the air, something disreputable. He knew his real mother had been Sara's daughter, but he'd never had the guts to ask about her in any direct way, he was afraid questions about her would hurt Patsy's feelings. But what, finally, had happened to her? What had Vail and Patsy been whispering about? What had she died of? Where was she buried? Well, he didn't want to know the morbid stuff. But it was his family, after all: he hadn't been taken out of a home or anything; his mother wasn't a stranger—she'd been part of the family. Maybe he could frame all his questions to Vail in some other casual way, like—like what? Victor, the trashy author grandfather! Maybe he could start the ball rolling with Victor.

He looked out the window at the benign street, waiting for his father to come home. Edward got up, turned up his TV set: the Beastie Boys' "Shake Your Rump" injected the room with a music video blast.

"Belinda, do you have a minute?" It was Buttons.

"Sure, come on in. Don't tell me you've also had words with Francine Cheney about the script changes."

"Nothing like that." He reached behind and shut the door. He parked in front of her desk. "I got a problem and I want you to give me a straight answer."

"Okay."

"I'm in love with Yvonne and I don't have the guts to tell her."

Canny Keith, she thought. "What's the question?"

"You know me. Do you think—and I want a straight answer—that there's any hope?"

Belinda picked up a pencil and began to doodle. "There's only one person who can answer that. And it's not me. You've never suffered from cowardice. Go out there and ask, tell her how you feel."

"This is different."

"How long have you felt like this?"

He thought back to the moment months ago when he'd felt the wonder of loving her. "Seems like a long time. I've been thinking about it a lot but . . ." He fumbled for a cigarette and lit it. "I'm crazy to even be thinking about this!" He blew out a jet of smoke. "I just don't think that Yvonne could love me."

A lot of questions occurred to her, the main one being "Why me?"

"Buttons, remember during *Force Field,* about a month after I met you. You were sitting on my desk and you said that on

Fletcher's sets there was always a sense of danger, and you talked about being in the whirl? Well, I think you lived with a sense of danger with Fletcher for years and then you got blown up and then you had rehab—you've been in your own whirl so long you don't know what it's like to float on a lagoon and let things happen." His sharp, agate eyes moved from her face to his hands and back again. He stabbed out his cigarette. "Just tell her how you feel and see what she says. That's all you can do. You already know that. What are you doing in here anyway?" she asked, dramatizing it, giving him an out. She threw an entire file into the air. It rained paper.

Vail was sitting in the broad, air-conditioned backseat of his chauffeured car with his prop file open beside him. He called it a prop because he couldn't read it but carrying it, people believed he could. He was on his way home. That morning, he had screened *The Crossing*.

He was not doing an official review; that wouldn't be ethical since members of his family were involved in it. He'd screened it out of avid and natural curiosity. Neil had already written a review of it for the show, but he'd asked for his comments informally, and Vail had drafted his thoughts.

Vail was stupefied by Lindy's brief but powerful performance. She was going to be noticed as soon as the movie was aired in a couple of weeks. He didn't know whether to be glad for her or sad for her, because it was a fork in the road. Unlike many of the men in the business, being an actress/director really wasn't open to her. She would have to pick one or the other.

Since Patsy's birthday, he couldn't think of Lindy without seeing his vision of her. He'd replayed her fall from that building, trying to recognize the part of the city around it. But all he could see was the corner of the building jutting up against a rosy afternoon sky. The image kept returning to him like an indelible memory. He shuddered. He prayed that with time it would go away.

Except for the clear vision inside his own head, Vail's eyesight on the real world was narrowing. It was becoming hard to locate something right in front of him, for if he looked away, he lost it and had to hunt it up all over again. It was like looking through a telescope the wrong way: on a page, like the file beside him, only a small circle of print was visible.

"Hiya, everyone," Vail said to Patsy and Sara as he carefully entered the kitchen. "Didn't expect to see you here, Sara."

"Visited Mother. We trashed politicians."

He watched his footing as he went to the table where they were sitting. "I've got some good news and some bad news. *Crossing* is great. I just screened it. Fletcher's pulled it out of the fire one more time." Patsy smiled. He turned to look at Sara. She was smiling too. Vail ran one hand proudly over the marble surface of the table, checking where the chair was, and sat down. "The surprise is Lindy. She's tremendous," he breathed. "She's like Sky."

Sara groaned. Patsy said, "In what ways?"

"In the acting sense, the vulnerability, the sense that she's strong but capable of being terribly wounded. In her concentration—magnetic. I mean, you can't take your eyes off her."

"But she doesn't look that much like Sky," Patsy said.

"I'm not talking about looks. I'm talking about her manner, her style! And, in a way, on screen, she does look like Sky in some of the shots."

Sara groaned again. "The press will have a field day. They won't rest until they find out everything about her." She reached across the cool marble table and put her hand on Vail's. "Vail, it's only a matter of time."

"Well, she'll be noticed, she'll get some press, she might even want to go on acting. But everything will die down."

"No, everything will come out," Sara said, squeezing his hand.

"Sara, you're being hysterical."

"I'm not hysterical. I think getting everything out is a good idea. *If* she's as good as you say, *if* she'll remind people of Sky, you've got to tell Eddie everything now because some reporter will start digging."

"You're always flying to conclusions!" Vail shouted.

"I agree with her," Patsy said.

"What? What?" He leaped from the table. "I don't believe what I'm hearing!"

"Vail, the big lie has to come to an end."

"I suppose the two of you have been sitting here hatching this thing to spring on me—"

"Vail! We haven't seen *Crossing*," Patsy said, "and we haven't been hatching anything. Sara was telling me about San Francisco when Eddie was with her up there. Eddie mentioned something about knowing that Vic was born there."

"Which I confirmed," Sara said. "I told him you and I were also born there. His information about the family is patchy, to say the least, but he wanted to fill it in."

"You never know about children," Vail said. "You think they know that their grandmothers came from Bulgaria and then one day they say they never heard that. Selective memory."

"I want to tell him soon," Patsy said, "or he'll feel betrayed."

"You're defecting!" he threw at her, and indeed he saw her reversal as a defection, as a way to distance herself from an increasingly disabled husband. "Don't you care about Eddie or me?"

"For heaven's sake, Vail," Patsy cried, stung.

"I'm not even going to consider this. Thanks a lot, Sara, for your role in this."

"She's giving us her opinion just as she always has," Patsy said.

"Take her part! What else do I expect? Just abandon me! I'm right about this, you'll find out—"

"You're not right," Patsy said. "You're afraid of losing Eddie and it's making you crazy."

"I'm not going to lose him. He's my son! But how about you? Have I already lost you?" He turned too suddenly and bumped into the edge of the stove. "Damn shit-faced stove!"

"Vail," Patsy said, "come on now, be sensible. We've got to talk about this."

"I'm not talking about it." He started for the door.

Eddie had reached the top of the stairs as his father came slowly down the center of the hallway. His head turned from side to side in quick, birdlike motions to which Eddie, in the past year, had become accustomed. He saw his father's hand reach out for the banister oddly, and had Eddie not anticipated so greatly what he wanted to discuss with Vail, he might have understood the gesture and all its implications.

"Dad, can we talk?"

Vail, startled, cocked his head and looked up. "I'm not in a good mood right now. Can it wait?"

"Don't think so, Dad."

Vail followed Eddie into his room. Music videos flashed mutely and aggressively on the television set. Eddie's chamber was not a place anyone sat down in to have a chat. All the surfaces were covered with clothes, books, CDs, tapes. Vail aimed for a spot at the end of the bed, moved a batch of CDs, and sat.

"What?" Vail asked, still wrestling with everything that had been said in the kitchen.

"I want to see the trashy grandfather," Eddie said, trying to make it light.

"What?"

"Victor. Wanna see him. Figure I should, after all this time."

"See him? What for?" Vail was now alert to the present, to Eddie.

"Well, Dad, gee, I know I'm adopted—"

"Victor hasn't anything to do with it. Where was Victor when you needed something?"

Eddie backed off. "What do you mean? Food, clothes—?"

"Right!" Vail said, knowing he was forcing himself into a corner. But he couldn't stop. "Did he ever write and say, here's a ticket to wherever, come and meet me?"

"No, Dad, but I just thought—"

"He abandoned Sara, he can't write worth a lick, he's a clotheshorse, he even wears a pinkie ring. What do you wanna see him for?" Vail was shaking his head, trying to sound bewildered and outraged and superior, hating himself for the act. Vail had always said that he had no time for someone like Victor because he'd left Sara and wrote bad books, but that wasn't true. He was afraid of Vic. Victor was a grenade waiting to be detonated. It was inevitable that Eddie would meet and talk to him. There was no way Vail could prevent Victor from telling Eddie about Lindy, about everything.

"I just think," Eddie went on earnestly, "that I should learn more about my real mom and dad."

What Vail had avoided for years fell upon him full force. He looked at his boy, at the outline of his thick blond hair shooting up from his head, at his round face and broad shoulders, his bare chest and flat stomach. He saw a blurry image of his kneecap sticking through a fashionable rip in his jeans.

"Why now?" Vail asked. "What brings this on now?"

"I met someone. Cynthia. We were talking about, well, families, and I just realized that I didn't know much about mine—"

"Cynthia?"

"Yeah. Met her at the film festival in San Francisco." Vail put a hand over his eyes. "Dad, I've been thinking about this a long time. I've been wondering."

"But Vic's in Europe. He—"

"He's right here in Los Angeles, Dad," Eddie said, hurt. "It's his book that Fletcher used to make *Crossing*. He's out here on a promotion swing."

"I didn't know that."

"Ah, c'mon. He's going to be on television plugging it." He peered at Vail. "We're going to the premiere, aren't we? They've got a lot of hype behind it. Aren't you reviewing it?"

"Yes, yes. Yes." It was hopeless.

"Why don't you want me to see him?" Eddie asked.

"This isn't a very good time," Vail muttered without hope of reprieve.

"*When's* a good time, Dad?" There was a new note in Eddie's voice, a note of challenge.

Vail knew that he had to reach across the eighteen years he'd spent with Eddie and pull on the thread of mutual trust that he'd always assumed was there, stretching between them. And when he tugged at it he would know, irrevocably, if that connection existed, or if he'd only made it up.

"Edward, have I ever lied to you?"

"Not that I know of, Dad."

"I'm telling you that this is not a good time. I want you to trust me. I'll find Victor and I'll set up a time and a place for you to see him, but you have to wait a little bit. Will you do that for me?"

Edward thought this over. Except for avoiding drugs, unprotected sex, and booze, as long as he could remember his father hadn't asked him to do anything for him.

"Okay, Dad. But how long do I have to wait?"

Vail couldn't clearly see the features on Eddie's face but he heard the resentment. "Not long, Son, I promise."

Vail's outer office was crowded with new deliveries of movie promotional junk from the studios' promotion departments—posters, foldouts, flyers, a stand-up Batman left over from that campaign, windup toys. The predominant gizmos this week were from *Die Hard 2*.

Schurl wouldn't let any junk in his office. It would pollute his rancho roundup, American West decor. Schurl was standing at his rolltop desk, trying to make a windup Ninja turtle work. It was supposed to scoot across the floor. It wouldn't move an inch.

"Can I come in?" Neil asked from the doorway.

"If you can make this work," Schurl said. "I gave this thing to my sister's kid."

"My rap for summer releases for the teen crowd, and a draft of Vail's review of *Crossing*," Neil said, handing him a few sheets of paper. He looked dubiously at the motionless turtle.

"Vail isn't reviewing *Crossing*," Schurl said, giving up on the toy.

"They're notes. I think he wanted to steer me."

"What? That's not like Vail. What do you mean?"

Neil flashed his boyish smile. "Well, I think we're lucky he took it upon himself to do these notes. There's something we have to talk about."

Schurl was getting into his coat and pulling his ponytail out from under his collar. "I don't know what you're talking about."

"Vail's recap of the action is wrong," Neil said.

"Wrong?"

"Have you seen *Crossing*?" Neil asked.

"No, not yet."

"You know how much I respect Vail," Neil said, shifting his weight from one foot to the other. "I'd do anything for him."

Schurl looked up. He hadn't heard Neil sound like a hypocrite before, but he knew he was hearing it now. Neil had a habit of smoothing back one side of his blow-dried red hair with the flat of his hand. He did this now. "I had some choices and I didn't know what to do," he said to Schurl. "You know the way we've worked. Sometimes I still sit in on his films with him, but Sandra takes notes now, transcribes them, and he writes his reviews from the notes, from his research, all that. I wasn't around when he saw *Crossing*, and Sandra said she had a couple of calls so for a few scenes, she wasn't making any notes."

"What are you getting at, Neil?"

"He's misread one of the key scenes. I went back and watched the film over to make sure."

"So what? He isn't reviewing the show."

"It's bigger than just this one show," Neil said with an air of reluctance.

Schurl sat down. He had the feeling that Neil had rehearsed what he wanted to say. "How bigger?"

"I don't think Vail can see details on the screen anymore. I don't think he can see very much at all." And in that second, hearing the words, Schurl knew Neil was right. It explained so much: Vail's hesitancy going down stairs, which he'd blamed on an inner ear infection that disturbed his balance; his increasingly powerful glasses which Schurl, thinking they were his own, had mistakenly picked up one day, and had been amazed at the magnification; Vail's reliance on Sandra, Neil, and the transcriptions; the fact that Schurl hadn't seen Vail reading a script in the office in a year or more.

"I'm sure Vail's eyesight is as good as mine," Schurl said, trying for a natural tone. "Have you mentioned this to anyone?"

"Now, that's why I wanted to discuss it with you. My girlfriend's father is Mobil Oil's CEO—"

"Our main sponsor?" Schurl cried, springing out of his chair. "You little shit, are you blabbing unfounded gossip to sponsors?"

"I'm *on* this show now, Schurl, and I do talk to sponsors."

"Have you checked our ratings? We're in a slump and I'm working night and day for new formats, a bigger budget—"

"They're interested in *my* ratings for *my* segments. I get good ratings."

Angrily, Schurl slapped a file he still held in one hand down on the desk. Neil jumped. "Get out of here before I throw up. You're just a fucking disloyal little rat, you know that, Neil?

You can't hold a candle to Vail Wyman. He thinks the sun rises and sets on you—"

"I know," Neil said with a slight smirk. "But Vail doesn't know what audiences want to watch."

"And you think you can fill his shoes?"

"I'd never do that," Neil said, fawning. "But I've put how many proposals to you to boost this show, bring it into the marketplace, jive it up? You never have time to sit down and discuss them with me." He straightened. His voice grew bolder. "I'm not Vail Wyman's assistant anymore. I have good ideas. You should take me more seriously." His smile, a masterful combination of the toady and the snake, swept across his face as he turned and slowly left the room.

Patrick O'Mara was not having a good day. He was sitting in a Harvard chair in an office on Sunset Boulevard near Gower, facing a man who had egg on his tie.

Patrick didn't want to be there with this man who wanted the world to know he was a Harvard graduate, probably because no one would have otherwise guessed it. But Patrick felt it was his own failing that had put him in that chair: last night as he'd been imagining his conversation with Sky, she'd again refused to tell him where her daughter, Lindy Wyman, was living. But he had to find her, talk to her, force her to forgive him.

For his part, Raymond Halsey, the investigator, was calculating how much real money he could obtain from O'Mara. The man was wearing a great herringbone jacket and a white Boss shirt. O'Mara's book was still in bookstore windows, testament to the public appetite for all the sad, juicy details about his crime. While people like me, Raymond Halsey thought, who've managed to keep from killing people or robbing them, have to fight for every dollar.

" 'Lindy' sounds like a nickname," Halsey said. He was a short, muscular man with closely set, unflinching dark eyes.

"It's the only name I ever heard."

"Okay," Halsey said briskly. "I'll check the birth records in L.A. County. Know who her father was?" O'Mara shook his head. "Makes it harder." Halsey squinted at his new client. "Celebrities can cover their tracks, y'know." O'Mara was looking at the corner of the desk. "Scandal—you say there was something with the daughter, some scandal."

O'Mara took his gaze away from the desk corner and nodded. "Arch Moberly . . ."

"Oh, right." Halsey whistled. He remembered it. "Okay, I'll check that out. So I'll find her, and what do you want—just the address?" O'Mara nodded again, staring at the desk. His eyes weren't blinking. Fucking crackers, Halsey thought. He coughed loudly, wetly. O'Mara's head came up. Blank eyes were staring at him. "That's two thousand for openers," he said.

Patrick wrote out the check and rose. Halsey was holding a ballpoint pen between two fingers like a stick, snapping it back and forth.

"Mr. O'Mara, you understand this will not be an easy job. Celebrities' kids have a way of disappearing. They get threats, they don't want attention," Halsey said, making things up as he went along, "the memories, the comparisons. Gonna cost money." He walked him to the door, shook his hand. "Thanks for the autographed book." Patrick nodded again, and left. Halsey watched him go down the hall. Prison shuffle, he thought, loony tunes.

Patrick stopped in a coffee shop on the corner of Santa Monica and Vista. It was a plastic anonymous place in a shopping center. His table was sticky, the coffee greasy. He was thinking over the interview with Halsey when he decided to shortcut everything.

Outside, there was a pay phone coated with graffiti. The directory had been snipped off at the wire. He dialed Diana Wyman. When she answered in her calm upper-crust voice, he tried to speak but couldn't get any words out.

"Hello?" she said again. "Is there someone there?"

"Mrs. Wyman. It's me. Patrick."

There was dead silence.

"I'm just calling because I have to find Lindy, and I wanted to ask your forgiveness for—"

Click. She hung up. He kept the phone receiver to his ear because he was embarrassed at being hung up on, and the man at the next phone was looking his way. "That'll be fine," Patrick improvised. "I'll call you next week." He replaced the receiver. He would try again. He was going to find Lindy. He was going to be forgiven.

*   *   *

Usually, Vail would have told Patsy that Eddie wanted to see Victor. But Sara was still sitting in the kitchen with Patsy and Vail couldn't face them both with the proof that they'd been right.

Vail left Eddie's room with its howl of MTV, went down the stairs, and paused in the foyer. Patsy was on the telephone in the study.

"He's upstairs, Schurl. I'll get him. Is it . . . ?" There was dead silence. Vail, alert, hesitated. *"What?"* he heard Patsy gasp.

Vail tensed. "I'm here," he said, going into the study. She handed him the phone. "Yes?"

Schurl said, "Vail, something's come up. We have to talk."

"So talk."

"No, not on the telephone. Can you come down to the office?"

"Not right away. What's it about?"

"Crossing."

Victor Oliver stayed at the Beverly Hills Hotel on Sunset Boulevard. Vail had not paid any attention to Victor's being in town, though he was well aware that Venner Broadcasting's promotional machinery for *Crossing* was gearing up for an all-out assault on America's television viewers. Guy Venner was going to make America pay attention to his media empire and *Crossing* was only the opening shot across the bow.

"I'm on my way up to San Francisco on this damned tour," Victor said over the house phone.

"This is about Eddie," Vail snapped, "and it can't wait."

He walked over to Victor's bungalow, picturing Eddie with Victor and worrying about what Schurl had just said to him. What could possibly be wrong with *Crossing* that would make Schurl want to meet privately?

The peach and green bungalow was cool and shaded. A neat set of Louis Vuitton bags sat just inside the doorway.

"What's wrong? Is he sick?" Victor demanded as Vail stepped inside. Victor was wearing an Albert Nipon jacket and cream colored slacks. He would always look like an overdressed rancher to Vail.

"No, he's okay," Vail said. "Eddie wants to see you."

Victor was overwhelmed. He backed into a chair and sat down. He turned the pinkie ring on his finger.

"And I want you to refuse," Vail said.

"Vail, Jesus Christ, I won't do that. Goddamnit, I won't do that!"

"Vic, just for a while. Just till things settle down. I want to prepare him, about his mom, I mean, about Lindy."

"No. That's final."

"Vic, I'm begging you."

"I don't bear you any malice. In fact, you were real good to me when Sara and I were trying to date back then." He smiled. " 'Way back then. But your exclusive time with Ed is up. It's his choice, now. He's a man."

"He's not a man—he's a boy of eighteen!"

"That's grown-up!" Victor shouted.

"It's not! He's a kid!"

"You think of him as a kid because you want to keep him a kid. Let go," Victor said with strength and some compassion, seeing loss and hostility shift across Vail's sharp features. "Lindy and I don't have a real father-daughter relationship, though we both work at it. And I don't expect to have a real relationship with Ed, but I'd like him to know that I'm in his corner, you know what I mean."

Vail sighed and sank into another overstuffed peach chair. Victor moved like a man who'd been around, a man for whom life had not always been easy, as all those creases in his face exposed. Vail sighed again. The problem with Victor was that, despite everything, Victor was hard to dislike. In his way, Eddie would be drawn to him.

"You know, Eddie and Lindy are sorta friends, have been for the last few years," Vail said, watching Victor turning his pinkie ring again.

"I know that," Vic replied, glancing at his watch. "Lindy's spoken about seeing him, writing him."

"You going to tell him Lindy's his mother?"

"I don't think that's my right," Vic said promptly. "But if he wants to know what his mother's like, I'll tell him."

"And Archie? He doesn't know anything about Archie, who he was, what happened—"

"You can't plot this out like a movie or a book, Vail. Maybe he just wants to talk to me about me, about where I came from, all those Russian immigrants, very fashionable now, about how I write or why I write." He got up and moved across the room. "I'd like to see him today but I'm due in Seattle. I'll be back here in a few days. You tell him I'll call him and we'll set a date. I leave it in your hands."

Vail leaned his head back on the chair. "God, everything's changing so fast."

The next day, Los Angeles was baking under a sizzling spring heat wave. But Schurl and Vail were sitting in an elegant, windowless screening room completely cut off from the elements.

"Pal, we go back a long way," Schurl was saying in his tough-love voice. "Bear with me."

Vail was irritable. "What are you doing with my *Crossing* notes?" he asked, peering at the yellow pages in Schurl's hand. Vail wrote notes and first draft reviews on yellow, second on blue, final on green. It was the only way he could tell at a glance which draft someone was holding.

"Were you thinking of reviewing this show, Vail?"

"Christ, no."

Schurl was relieved but not surprised. "That's what I thought. Neil seemed to think you wanted to review it and, failing that, wanted to put your words in his mouth."

"No, I was just going to sit there like a stick and watch it for my own amusement," Vail said, sarcastically, "but Neil asked me for my thoughts as part of his ongoing seminar, his learning experience. He'd already written his review."

"Okay, now listen to this." He shifted the draft papers.

"I know what it says. Jeez, I don't have time for this. I've got a lot on my mind, Schurl, and Eddie's at the top of the list this week."

Schurl read: " 'A contemporary television movie that changes the rules. Our hero kills his heroine—a truly doomed woman in this case, and—' "

"For Chrissakes, Schurl. I know what I wrote."

Schurl put a hand on Vail's arm. "Can it. Stick with me here." He picked up where he'd left off: " 'The role of Kat is too small a part to qualify as a heroine, yet it was large enough to attract, at one time, an actress of Gloria Griffin's stature . . .' No, it's further down. 'Adapted from an able book . . .' " Schurl looked up. "That was generous of you, Vail, considering how much you dislike Victor. Ah, here we go, the scene with Belinda. 'Don't underestimate the punch of this small role,' " he read on, " 'Kat's love for the hero is elegantly understated and she positively blooms in an astonishing and dramatic scene when her lover repays her by killing her. . . . The show is full of such surprising twists. It's a nineties' take on love and international intrigue.' " Schurl bent down and pressed a button to speak to the projectionist in the booth. "Roll it, please." Up popped the scene in the Budapest spa bathed in Bruno's golden light. "Now watch this, Vail."

"I've already watched it," Vail said.

"There's Belinda, running around the pool toward the balcony," Schurl said, conversationally. "Here she comes, closer. There's the close-up of Harcourt, our hero, below, at the end of the pool. There's the full shot of the spa, showing Belinda up top, and below, stage left, is Harcourt. He's turning and leaving. She reaches the balcony railing. She looks across— and there's a full shot of Belinda on one side, and this guy on the other side—on the balcony opposite her." The man facing her across the pool was leaner and older than Harcourt, the hero. Both wore shirts and slacks, one had light hair, one had dark hair. "Hold it there," Schurl said to the projectionist. To anyone with normal eyesight, the contrast between the scene on the screen and Vail's review was painful.

Schurl turned to his good friend. "Who is that guy, Vail?"

But Vail could only see a small field of each full shot. Walking through the scene step by step, he knew how big an error he'd made: he hadn't been able to see Harcourt leaving in the first wide shot, and he'd assumed the man on the balcony was Harcourt. Vail covered his mouth with his hand, then rubbed his cheek. "Not Harcourt."

Schurl spoke to the projectionist, "Okay, Jay, thanks. That's all." The picture dropped from the screen, the house lights came up dimly. "You going to tell me what's going on?" Schurl asked quietly.

"I made a mistake! Didn't you ever make a mistake?"

"Forget that shit about making a mistake. Level with me. I'm the guy on the front line here with the ad boys and the network. What if it had been on a show you reviewed? What if you'd been on the air? I want an answer to what's going on."

Vail looked off at the white blurry space that was the screen. He bit the inside of his cheek. "I can't see worth shit." He closed his eyes, sighed, opened his eyes. "It's called retinitis pigmentosa, but the bottom line is my eyesight's all fucked up. I shoulda told you, but I thought I had it wired—Neil and Sandra and our setup."

"Neil. Let me tell you about Neil, my friend. He wants your job. He probably got sick of waiting around for you to make a big mistake on the air. He's the one who brought me these notes. He's forced my hand. He's telling, Vail. He's probably got a dozen copies of this. Jesus, if you'd only told me, we coulda engineered something, we coulda made a graceful exit. Now we got bubkes. It's going to be all over the business and there's not a goddamned thing I can do about it."

Vail shrugged and looked away. "I couldn't face it."

"Little shit Neil." Schurl punched a glancing blow off Vail's shoulder. "Remember that creep we caught informing to the FBI during the Berkeley strike back in 1964?"

Vail smiled wistfully, acknowledging other landmarks in his long friendship with Schurl. But his smile faded, he stared at the blank white screen, weighed down by the crush of losing his work. Even more awful was his fear that he might lose Patsy. And how about Eddie? Tears rolled out of his eyes. He brushed them away angrily with one hand.

"Guess it's time to go," Vail said, hoarsely.

Schurl squeezed Vail's arm. "We'll go together, Vail. I'm not producing a show for that little fucker."

Vail was on his feet, one hand on the back of the seat. "Get a print of that frame in the spa for me, Schurl. I wanna hang it in the john." He pretended to tap up the aisle with a cane.

"Wait up," Schurl said, "I'm coming, too."

"Think I want to walk alone for a while," Vail said, pushing through the doorway.

He knew the building well. He walked carefully but steadily down the hallway into the lobby where the weekend guard waved. "How's it goin', Mr. Wyman?"

"Great, Mike," Vail said in a robust voice. "Let me outta this dump."

The guard unlocked the door and Vail walked into a sheet of hot sunlight. He stood still, letting it sink into him, getting his bearings. Then, confidently, he struck off down Doheny, through the glare and the sound bullets of cars in the street that he couldn't see. He was going to walk to Trumps where he'd go in and pretend life was great, that he could see the whole menu, that he recognized the waiter. But as he walked in the tunnel, past the surprising shapes of trees heaving like ships in front of him and falling into the black void on either side as he moved, all he could feel was despair. Like a scaffolding, the pretense on which he'd constructed his life for the past five years, collapsed.

CHAPTER 19

WARDROBE TRANSPORT CASTING CREW . . . INTERVIEWS PRAYERS HAIRDRESSER UNINSURABLE ANAMORPHIC LENSES NOT NOW BRUTES RENTALS LOCALS NEED FOUNTAINS PARKS COURTS JAIL ROSE GARDEN WATERFRONT GENERATOR ONCE MORE VOUCHERS CATERING TENT DOUBLES IS THIS FOR REAL?

Indictment was a modest shoot compared to Fletcher's, but it had its own momentum, governed by the same basic physics of movement, direction, and collision.

The production office was in a building near the Heathman Hotel in downtown Portland. The outer room was crowded with Belinda's small staff, with crew members, and with locals looking for jobs as extras. Smaller rooms, fanning off the central area, were for the accountant, a local production manager, local casting, Belinda's assistants, Yvonne's personal staff—the engine of the production.

The day before shooting was to begin, a windblown Keith Llewellyn threw open the door of Belinda's cramped office. From the outer office, Lindy heard the camera operator say, "The test film's scratched. Gotta check everything." Someone else was shouting, "I don't get it—are we digging a moat for this or what?"

"Shut the door, Keith," Belinda said, without looking up. "I don't want to hear those problems. I've given up trying to control anything." She was bent over papers on her desk, making sketches of the camera positions for the shoot.

"You are surprising," Keith said slowly, catching his breath. The door flew open. "We're meeting downstairs with the crew in thirty minutes," Yvonne said. Belinda nodded. Yvonne shut the door.

"You have that last scene done?" she asked Keith.

He put it on her desk, then stood back, his arms folded comfortably across his broad chest. Belinda had changed since he'd met her at Vail's five years ago. From a brittle, secretive woman locked in private struggles, she was now a crisp, first-time director who didn't even seem particularly nervous. "You can't be as calm as you seem," he said.

"Are you kidding? I'm damned terrified." She went on sketching. "Got your plane ticket?" she asked. "Bet you're glad to get out of here, back to some real sunshine. I'm sorry I rode you so hard, Keith. About the rewrites."

"Belinda. The *New York Times* television guy is writing a rave review of *Crossing*."

"That's good." She drew a camera placement. "That shoot seems like some other life."

"He speaks very well of Fletcher, and there's a paragraph about you. You're a hit."

"Me?" Now she looked up. Her face was pale, a curl of thick brown hair trailed over her forehead. "It was such a little role."

"But meaty," Keith said.

"But costly."

They laughed.

"You're called a new actress who will be noticed." He raised his bushy eyebrows.

"Who said?"

"My friend at the *Times*."

"It'll blow over. I can't think of that; I've got too much to do up here."

"Don't you care?" he asked.

"No."

"It's airing in two days."

She started sketching again. Keith knew that if the publicity mills began grinding in earnest, he might not see her again as she was today. She was going to be talked about, the attention might change her; he'd seen it happen before. Some people recoiled from the sudden light, others swelled to fill it, and some, in its heat, grew addicted to its burn.

He stepped around the desk, leaned down, and kissed the

top of her head. "Call me when you want to talk to someone real," he said. She barely looked up.

He went outside. The sky was bubbling, a moving, shifting, dark and light gray canvas, but the air was warm and fresh. The maples along the street swayed slightly. He wondered if he'd been right not to tell her exactly what the review said. But he hadn't wanted to be that messenger. Belinda had never reminded him physically of Sky Wyman, in fact, he couldn't really remember what Wyman had looked like. But the reviewer had seen a similarity between them, more in style than in features, and the reviewer was printing it.

Keith buttoned his coat and walked. Portland straddled the Willamette River, a deep-water port; but timber had built the city, and timber had built the state—Douglas fir and Ponderosa pine, giant spruce and spicy cedar. Even now, in downtown Portland, the aroma of pine and cedar permeated the damp gray air. As he cut through the park blocks in the center of town, a wave of seagulls flew overhead, landing like sparks on the grass. The location manager, a Portland native, said it meant there was a storm at sea a hundred miles to the west.

Keith walked down to a pub on Third Street, hoisted himself on a stool, and ordered a Pellegrino.

"Oregon water's better," said the bartender.

"Okay," Keith said, "give me some Oregon water in some—what do you all drink up here?"

"Besides water?"

"Yes."

"Bourbon, mostly, maybe some rye. Scotch is too fussy, too eastern, if you get me."

"Put some Oregon water in some bourbon," Keith ordered.

Keith tried to think back. Patsy had introduced Belinda as a cousin, but whose cousin, he wondered—hers or Vail's? He'd always assumed Patsy's but maybe not. Vail had been Sky's brother, maybe Belinda was Vail's cousin. He sipped the bourbon and water. He couldn't taste the water.

After a while, he slipped off the stool, walked around the block, and landed in a little park. A bronze elk held center stage along with a bubbling, antique, four-spouted water fountain. He'd seen them all over town, those fountains. A state rich in water and boasting of it. But it was great water, better than designer water.

The researcher in him stirred. Maybe he'd call that big Los Angeles gossip who collected old Hollywood lore like other men collected baseball cards. Maybe he'd go to the library and look up Sky Wyman.

Suddenly his instincts told him to hang around Portland for a while. He walked back to his hotel and rebooked his room.

Belinda could not sleep. In the last few months, she'd crammed herself with information on lenses, lights, cameras, unions, costs, and the minutiae of production while she navigated rehearsals and casting, line readings, problem solving, and camera tests. She was thrilled and challenged and afraid of failure all at once.

Still wide awake at four in the morning, she dressed and walked, mentally rechecking her shots and setups, thinking of Fletcher and how he'd walked each morning. Though it was the beginning of summer, the streets smelled of rain and mist and leaves. There was only one other person on the street, a man in a jacket looking at statues in the park blocks. He was about a block behind her. The gray and black sky was turning oyster pink when she sat down opposite a statue of Teddy Roosevelt; the other walker sat down in another section of the park. Was he following her? Suddenly, she couldn't concentrate on what she needed to remember for the first setup. Paranoid, she thought. She strode up the park blocks in the gray dawn, east down Salmon Street, looking behind her, not seeing the man. Good. She went south on Fourth, turned east again on Salmon to the river. It was after six in the morning.

Two huge equipment trucks were stationed in a turnaround, their bellies open, disemboweled of gear and cables. Crew members in their jeans and sweatshirts were setting up on a grassy waterfront park edged on one side by a cement and brick wall, and, at the other end, by the Willamette River. After the walk in a strange town, trailed by a strange man, she felt she was among old friends. Her cameraman waved, talking about the light, about angles. The sound man, six feet tall and lean as a stick, said, "Nervous, huh?"

"Yes," she replied.

"First day sweats."

The local location manager had a broad Scandinavian face. He was a serious, forthright young man with a lot of low-key energy. He'd been born and raised in Portland, where the people smiled and asked how you were and actually listened for a reply. No one rushed about, even in the rain. They were used to the rain. But it was a beautiful day, sun-splashed, breezy, and blue.

"Keith! What are you doing here?" Belinda asked.

"I came down to cadge breakfast, what do you think?" He took a cup of coffee from the catering truck. "This is the first day. Firsts are important."

"Oh, thank you," she said, running a hand down Keith's arm. "I'm glad you're here."

They were standing by a wall beside the river. "Wow. You starting with the tracking shot? The shot Yvonne doesn't like?" he asked.

"Yes, starting with controversy," Belinda said.

Affixed to the wall was a tile mural by a Northwest artist, George Johanson. Yvonne felt that the bright, complicated images of the mural, depicting Portland history, would detract from the actors' action in front of it. But Belinda wanted to use the mural as counterpoint to the dialogue.

Everyone was arriving. The actor playing "Bill," the local district attorney, was sitting with his co-star, who was cast as "Nell," the public defender. An unknown actress was playing "Chicky," the gang member accused of murder in the script; "Nell" and "Bill" were experienced, looking for their breakthrough picture. When the actress playing the much enlarged "Phyllis" role arrived, everyone perked up: she was a prankster everyone liked. Peaked eyebrows and a heart-shaped face gave her the look of a cat. Keith said he expected whiskers to sprout from her cheeks.

The tracks for the camera that would follow "Nell" and "Chicky" along the wall had been laid, the lights and reflectors were set, the cast was in place, the crew was standing around. It was time.

Belinda was scared shitless. She hadn't felt this petrified since the iron door on the third floor of the nuthouse had closed behind her and she'd come face-to-face with the psych-tech, a massive woman with large, cold eyes. The crew and actors massed around her now were as unnerving as the immovable psych-tech with her confrontational eyes.

Keith gave Belinda a thumbs-up. She felt sick. Then Belinda saw Yvonne, who was standing behind Buttons, slip her hand along Buttons's shoulder. It was a gesture of kindness and affection that erased Belinda's fear. Buttons grinned.

Belinda nodded at her AD. "Let's do it."

"Sound rolling." The take was read, the clapper struck.

"Action," Belinda said.

"Nell" and "Chicky" walked along the mural, pausing for their lines at set points. It was a dead scene. Belinda let them get all the way through it. "Cut."

"Chicky, you've got to be here for the 'I never done it' line." She pointed to a spot in the mural where light from the open doors of an isolated barn silhouetted a small lonely figure. Above the barn a clouded moon hung in the dark sky. "Chicky" made a sour face. "And, Nell, when you first start here, get all the way through your first lines before you move on. Take a beat there, too, then move." She pointed at the far left of the mural where moonlight glinted off a dark choppy river overhung by a roiling, lightning-lit, black sky. "See, Chicky, here's where you start really lying your head off." Belinda knocked her knuckle against the tile rendition of the electrically charged sky. "You're in deep shit and you think you can fake your way through it, just as you've faked your way through everything." Like Maisie who'd faked it all the way. "Okay, everybody, let's do it again."

Afterward, Eddie couldn't say how he'd come to lie so hugely to Patsy and Vail in order to get to San Francisco. He had few secrets from them, he more or less did as he pleased, but leaving Los Angeles and flying to San Francisco without telling them was not what he'd been raised to do. But he'd done it three times to see Cynthia, returning the same day. The first time, they'd had a Chinese dinner and had gone to a movie; the second time, she'd invited him to a party. Now, his third secret trip, he was lying next to Cynthia in a bedroom of Venner's Nob Hill home.

Venner's luxurious scale of living surprised even Eddie who'd witnessed the excess of movie stars, TV directors, art collectors, studio brass—he'd gone to school with their kids.

But Venner's money was old money, and there was a difference. As he put his arm around Cynthia, he was afraid every second that Venner would come in. But Cynthia didn't seem concerned. Her skin was smooth and warm, her thighs moist. His heart was going to jump right out of his mouth. "You've done this before," she whispered into his ear, then licked it with her tongue, sending a spasm of wonderful pain through him. He had in fact "done this" before but not regularly like some of the guys. He thought she'd done it, too. From the moment he'd kissed her for the first time that evening, out in the gymnasium she called the sitting room, there seemed to be no barriers between them. He rubbed his handless wrist between her legs and she moaned. Another exquisite spasm thrilled him. "Put it inside me," she whispered. It seemed to be as natural as everything else they were doing, which was to say unnatural—new, alien, unexplored, permissible, and forbidden all at once. She was groaning; the whole house would wake up. He was caressing her, kissing her, and she was opening up— legs, arms, mouth, fingers—everything was spreading out like a flower shot in slow motion. He withdrew his handless wrist from inside her and slid on top of her, grateful for the condom because if it hadn't been there he'd have come instantly. She was hanging onto his shoulders with her head thrown back, and he couldn't believe the huge feelings washing inside him, so much bigger than the excitement with Zoe or Brenda, because he loved Cynthia and there was no going back and he looked at her arched throat and put his fingers high between her legs and that's what did it because she screamed, a deep wonderful cry that positively collapsed her insides against him, shook her walls and squeezed him, an embrace and a punch all at once.

"I'm going to have bruises," she said, showing him her upper arm where his fingers had dug into her.

"I'm sorry," he said earnestly.

"I'm not."

Her hair was very fine, like shiny reddish cobwebs. He pushed a wing of it back from her face. He felt perfectly in sync with her, with himself. "I love you," he said. "I've never said that before."

"I think you really know how to love, Eddie," she whispered, moving even closer, hugging him tightly.

"Eddie" never sounded so good to him.

He held her close, her head on his shoulder, his handless arm cast around her, his hand stroking her breast. She took hold of his wrist and kissed it. He never thought he'd feel that. He shut his eyes as her tongue licked the indentations of the fingers that were not there. Tears slipped out of his eyes, down his temples, into the pillow.

Later, they were talking.

"I'm adopted," he said.

"Were you left in a reed basket?" She propped herself up on her elbows. He pushed her head back down on his shoulder. "It's okay to be adopted," she said.

"My real mom died somehow, violently, I think. My parents don't like to talk about it. I used to think that she'd given me up because of my hand." Cynthia said nothing. She pressed closer. "I used to think—oh, all kinds of dumb things . . ." He frowned, remembering his baby's dread. "Stupid things," he said out loud. "Kids are cruel."

"When you're adopted," Cynthia whispered, "you know you're wanted. It's a conscious decision, don't you think?"

"Yes, I do." He buried the fears of childhood in her soft, pink skin.

After a while they got dressed. "Your parental unit will be here soon, right?"

"I suppose so." She was putting on some kind of under blouse, not a bra. Her nipples pressed into the silk. She smiled slyly at him. "Just where are you supposed to be tonight?"

"At a really slamming party in L.A. that won't end until three A.M. It gives me enough time to get back from the airport." He didn't want to leave at all. If he touched her again, he was lost.

When *Crossing* was aired, no one working on *Indictment* gave it a second thought—except Keith. He hunkered down in front of the television set in his hotel room. Everyone else was looking at dailies.

The Northwest Film and Video Center had rented them a cool windowless room for this ritual. Belinda sat between her editor and her cinematographer. Yvonne and Buttons were in the back; the cast was scattered around.

Take after take bounced over the screen. Except for "Chicky"'s cynicism, the atmosphere of the shoot's cooperative adventure was being established, and that first night of dailies confirmed the collaboration: "Nell," the public defender, "Phyllis," the madcap animal warrior, and even "Chicky," gang girl, were coming alive. The group laughed at the flubs—at "Chicky," who had a way of staring deadpan into the camera when she forgot her line, and at "Nell," who winked and sang a scale. Other moments made everyone groan. One scene was so bad they watched in silence, waiting for it to end. "Chicky" put her finger in her mouth, simulating the heaves, then said to Belinda, "Now maybe you'll let me do it my way."

They stopped at ten o'clock. Yvonne and Belinda walked outside into the park blocks, into the cool and peaceful night.

"It's going too well," Belinda said.

"Let us not look a gift horse in the mouth," Yvonne said cheerfully. "Remember Malaysia?"

Belinda smiled, remembering the nightmare shoot, and that reminded her of "Chicky." "I don't know what to do with her," Belinda said. "Did you hear her today, shouting about her wardrobe?"

"People skills are not her strong point. But she's talented. That Francine Cheney's arriving tomorrow night," Yvonne said.

"That's all we need," Belinda said, hating the thought of Francine.

"She says she's on her way to Canada and is just dropping in to say hello."

"The financial people like Francine *always* say that. Are we in budget trouble?"

"No. She's just a tight ass. Belinda, can we talk about something else?" Yvonne said.

"Sure."

"Buttons wants me to marry him." They had come to a block lined thickly by trees.

"I didn't know people still did that."

"What? Marry?"

"No. *Ask* other people to marry them. Sounds formal." Belinda was thinking about Francine, the camera moves in the next day's first scene, about how to control "Chicky," how to keep her sourness from infecting the other actors. "Are you?" she asked Yvonne.

"Marry him? I don't know. I'm really torn about it."

"Do you love him?"

"In a lot of ways, yes." Her forehead wrinkled up, and her small pert mouth pulled down. "He's wheeling around as if whatever I say doesn't matter, but for him he's sitting on the edge of a cliff waiting for someone to push him over or pull him back."

Their positions had reversed. Belinda realized Yvonne had always been the one to whom she'd gone for advice, even for comfort, though she would never have admitted that then. Now Yvonne was asking her for help. "I don't know anything about marriage, Yvonne."

"What if Guy asked you?"

"That's not what we have together. It's like a sexy business partnership—with affection. Guy isn't in a wheelchair, either. And Guy isn't ten years younger than I am."

"Age doesn't matter," Yvonne snapped. "And Buttons is pretty independent. Actually, he's amazing."

"Just tell him you have to concentrate on the shoot and you want to think it over. He'll understand."

"I did that. Give me some credit," she replied, sharply. "I don't want this problem right now—"

"Don't take it. Don't let him—"

"I'm not taking it. It's there!"

"Hey, do I have a producer or what?" Belinda demanded. "Damnit, everything's cool."

"Well, keep it cool."

Yvonne stared at her. "Boy, I know you're tough but I thought you'd take one minute to talk—"

"We are talking."

"No, we're not. I'm sorry I bothered you with these minor personal problems."

"Yvonne, don't do that. C'mon, we'll have a cup of coffee—"

"I'd rather not, thanks," Yvonne said coldly. They were near the hotel. "I'll see you in the morning." Yvonne walked away, her heels rapping on the pavement.

Belinda stood on the sidewalk, her eyes following Yvonne. "Yvonne, wait!" She ran up to her. "Yvonne, I'm sorry. Stop."

She reached out and pulled Yvonne back from the door of the hotel. "You're the best friend I ever had. You're the only friend I've ever had. Please don't walk away." Yvonne's eyes were full of tears. Her arms were folded across her chest. "I'm so sorry. Sometimes I'm only half a person. I'm afraid to be close to anyone. I didn't mean to be cold to you but it's my first reaction—to be too harsh. I won't let it happen again, I swear. And I apologize. Please, forgive me."

Yvonne embraced her, putting both arms around Belinda's waist, hugging tight. Her head only came up to Belinda's shoulder. "Of course I forgive you. You're the fastest draw in the west." She pulled away, but kept a hand on Belinda's shoulder. "You're my best friend, too. Don't forget it."

All the way up to her room, Belinda felt lighter. As she put her key in the lock, she found herself humming. It was good to be alive.

That evening, in Los Angeles, Diana and Leonora were having dessert after a supper in Diana's newly redecorated apartments on the third floor of Vail's home.

"Apple green," Leonora said, gazing at the walls. "I like this color better."

Diana was in no mood for decorator talk. They had just watched the first airing of *The Crossing*. She'd read the reviews in that morning's paper which had compared Belinda's style on the screen to Sky's. Though no one had yet made the connection between Belinda Oliver and Sky Wyman, Diana feared that someone soon would.

A serving tray held slices of angel food cake and almond cookies. Leonora helped herself to a cookie. "I really shouldn't eat these. My doctor says my cholesterol is two forty-eight. I could pop off at any moment."

Diana put a sliver of lemon in her tea, began to stir it, then abruptly put down the spoon and clasped her bony hands together. "That man has been calling me."

"What man?"

"Patrick O'Mara! I won't talk to him, but he keeps calling."

"Oh, him." Leonora sipped her tea. "I tell you, dear, sometimes the things we have to face are almost unbearable."

Diana was not in the mood for commiseration. She was on her feet, the fingers of one hand closed around her napkin tightly.

"It isn't enough that they let him out of prison. It isn't enough that he wrote a book about my daughter and her terrible death. It isn't enough that all of America is reading it."

"Diana, calm down!" Leonora said.

"Now I have to put up with his incessant, cruel pestering!" Diana whirled around. "I'm afraid, Zip. I'm afraid he'll do something to Belinda."

"Why?"

"I'm afraid he'll put it together, that Belinda Oliver is 'Lindy,' the Lindy he knew here. He's calling me and demanding that I tell him where Lindy is! He calls her Lindy!" Diana was literally wringing her hands. "It's intolerable." Her eyes were full of tears. "I feel I have to do something."

Leonora went to her friend and put an arm around her. "But what could you do?"

"Zip, I wouldn't tell this to another living soul but I want—" She hesitated. "I want to kill him," she whispered, breaking away from Leonora. "I won't do any such thing. I'm being foolish, but it's with me every minute. I can't sleep." She sat down, took her handkerchief, and dabbed delicately at her eyes.

Leonora had never seen Diana Wyman so distraught. "Let's talk about it. Then you'll feel better." She sat down, put another almond cookie on her dessert plate, and paired it with a thin slice of cake. "Of course, you wouldn't want to do anything messy. Such a lovely room." She waved her linen napkin at it.

"I've made an absolute fool of myself," Diana murmured.

"No, you haven't. You're depressed and you feel helpless."

Diana cut a tiny corner off the end of her cake. "Do you remember that painter who put LSD in Sky's tea—he just popped it in and stirred. Sky went off on a twelve-hour trip watching the cushions move up the wall and the plants turn into snakes."

"Didn't she know she was drinking LSD?"

"No. Not a clue."

"But, dear, the LSD didn't kill her," Leonora said with finality, reaching for the teapot.

"No."

"Isn't this naughty of us, talking like this?" Leonora said with a wicked grin. "It's like being back on the boards in a new play." She bit into the cookie. "I suppose arsenic is out because that could be traced," Leonora went on gleefully, getting into it.

"I wouldn't care. I'm almost ninety."

"Maybe there's some kind of drug overdose," Leonora offered, "so it would look accidental. Drugs are easier to obtain than poisons these days."

"I wouldn't know where to get anything like that," Diana said.

"My grandson would, Justin would."

"Heavens, Zip, is Justin on cocaine?"

"They call it crack, my dear. No, he isn't, but I'm sure there are people at the studios . . . well, you know. But is cocaine poisonous? Isn't it a stimulant? And how much would we need, dear?" She was excited.

Diana was staring at the plate of cookies. "Perhaps a mush-room salad?" she said, hiking one eyebrow mischievously.

"Yes! Or lettuce mixed with azalea blossoms. Azaleas are quite poisonous."

"Are you sure?"

"I've always heard that," Leonora said. Silence fell. "I feel we're going around in circles. We need research here."

"We don't need any research for rat poison," Diana said with a new energy. "Anyone can buy rat poison."

"Bitter. He'd know if it was mixed into the jam tarts." Leonora glanced out the window at the shed where Diana raised her prize delphiniums. "Or you could take him down to show him your flowers, lock him inside, and set the place on fire. I don't think it would spread to the house. We could call the fire department after a while. It would be a terrible accident," she said, rehearsing. "Dreadful."

"Heavens, Zip, you should have been a screenwriter!" Diana laughed. "You know, you were right. I do feel better."

Leonora was looking down at a poinsettia tree. "Now those are really poisonous, poinsettias . . . you wouldn't really . . . ?" Leonora turned to face her friend's ivory, wrinkled face.

"Don't be silly, dear. But I loathe that man being alive and my Sky being . . . gone. And now he's asking about Belinda— we don't know what someone like that might do."

Leonora helped herself to another slice of angel food cake. "It's really terribly hard to kill someone if you're a law-abiding citizen, isn't it?"

The next morning, Belinda was filming in the southwest downtown area around the Ira Kellar fountain. Taking up an entire block like a plaza, the monumental fountain was cut out of the sloping ground. The high end, backed up against Fourth Avenue, was planted with pine trees and grasses. From this greenery, water rushed over a series of descending stone slabs, sheeting them, lightly filling the pools below on each tier. To one side, steps led down, edging the fountain's various areas to the wide pool and apron below that faced Third Avenue. Extras were sitting on the edges of the tiered pools, holding prop bag lunches. A few children in shorts played in the water. "Phyllis" sat on the edge of the lowest pool near Third Avenue, eating a prop sandwich.

"Here," Keith said, striding up to Belinda before the first shot and handing her a newspaper. "Your reviews."

"What?" she replied. "No, I can't."

He leaned in close to her. "You were terrific."

"Good," she said, distracted. "Chicky, you run around the fountain like this, straight past the camera and out over there. Phyllis! Lunchers!" she called out to the extras. "When she runs past, you've got to really notice this. People don't run for their lives around this fountain—and Phyllis, you recognize her—got it? Now you," Belinda went on, going up to one of the kids. "You remember what we're doing here? She's going to knock against you, knock you right into this pool. Okay? Just like we rehearsed?"

"Miss Oliver!" A stranger from the sidelines was waving at her.

"That's the reporter I told you about," her AD said. "The guy who wants the interview with you about *Crossing*."

"No, no," Belinda said. "Who are those other people out there?"

"More reporters. *National Enquirer*, too."

"What?"

They saw her looking in their direction. "Miss Oliver! What are your plans?" They began flinging questions at her. "How did you feel—?" "—working with Fletcher?" "—more roles or more directing—?"

"Get tough," she said to the AD. "You're resourceful. Control them. Ask Keith to help."

"Belinda." It was the prop man with a problem. She heard him with half an ear. There were a lot more spectators today than yesterday. They were filling the space around the fountain.

"Get those cops to clear this area back. We can't move in here. What?" Belinda said to wardrobe who was holding a child's pair of shorts in her face.

The first take was a disaster. "Chicky" didn't have enough room to run in, and looked like she was loping past the fountain. The boy who was to have been pushed into it ducked and dropped in before "Chicky" even reached him. "Phyllis"'s sandwich fell in the fountain and she spent crucial seconds fishing for it rather than recognizing "Chicky." The crowd was growing. As soon as Belinda called "Cut," the reporters started yelling questions.

"For god's sake, what do they want?" Belinda cried to Yvonne, exasperated.

"It's *Crossing*. The whole town seems to know you're filming here. They saw you on TV, and now they can see you direct at this goddamned fountain."

"God, this is a sideshow." Belinda turned around and collided with Keith.

He took her arm and walked her away. "Stay calm, general," he said. "Your minions will handle press, but I warned you about *Crossing*, didn't I?"

Flowers from Guy arrived that afternoon with a nine-page fax of glowing reviews. And the crowd grew, boisterously following the production from one setup to another. When they wrapped for the day, two police officers escorted Belinda and Yvonne back to the hotel. They were trailed by a dozen fuming reporters who bawled questions and waved cameras and microphones. As one policeman eased Belinda through the doors of the hotel, a reporter screamed: "We'll get your life story—" Belinda bolted inside. "What a ghastly thought," she muttered to Yvonne, "my life story on national air."

In the lobby, four violinists energetically struck up "Lara's Theme" from *Dr. Zhivago*.

"My god, what next?" Belinda cried.

"I see Fletcher's hand in this," Yvonne said. She was right; Fletcher had sent them. The front desk had dozens of messages for her.

At last, in her room with Keith, Yvonne, and Buttons, Belinda collapsed on the sofa. She looked at the telephone messages. The *Los Angeles Times*, the *New York Times*, *TV Guide*, two television news stringers, two magazines, four messages from Patrick O'Mara, one each from Patsy, Sara, Vail, Vic, Fletcher, eight people she'd never heard of, and Guy.

"This is wacky," she said. "What is going on?"

"God, don't you listen to me?!" Keith handed her a fax of the review from *Eye* magazine, the *National Enquirer* of the film world.

" 'The new face in *Crossing* was apparently a last minute replacement,' " Belinda read. " 'Belinda Oliver in the role of Kat gives a gripping if brief performance. It's her intensity that makes this old movie fan remember Sky Wyman, film actress *extraordinaire*, who was killed in 1975. In her roles, Wyman had a way of at once retreating from and exposing emotions which the new Belinda Oliver also shows on the screen. We think Belinda Oliver just may be a real comer. This reviewer can't wait to see her again.' " Belinda stopped reading. "Somebody fix me a white wine with lots of strychnine in it."

Buttons said, "It's unusual, drawing attention to you by comparing your acting to Sky Wyman's."

Belinda distastefully and fearfully read the rest of the review. It didn't say she was Sky's daughter or related to Sky in any way—that morsel had not been discovered, yet. But the reviewer noted in passing that Belinda's eyes were "icy hot, like Wyman's." Though her identity as Belinda Oliver remained in place, the review's praise had torn away her anonymity.

"You'll need to get some security," Buttons said, "some guys who know what they're doing."

"Belinda, do an interview," Keith said. "What's the problem? Get them off your back." Belinda waved this suggestion away. "But they'll just stay there—"

"I'm not interviewing!"

Nobody liked that answer, but everyone backed off.

"Are the other reviews like this one?" Belinda asked.

"Run-of-the-mill raves," Keith said, surveying her.

Yvonne was pouring everyone a glass of wine. She said without thinking, "Nothing to be concerned about, no disclosures." She turned around, a glass in each hand, and saw Belinda looking at her.

"What disclosures?" Keith asked.

"Have a drink, Keith," Yvonne said. "It'll all die down," she went on to Belinda.

"It's not going to die down," Buttons said.

"Let's wait and see," Yvonne said.

"Wait and see what?" Keith demanded.

The telephone rang. The bellman arrived with more huge flower arrangements from Guy and Fletcher.

"Wait and see what?" Keith repeated.

Belinda knew Keith wasn't going to let go. "Sky raised me," she said. "I thought she was my mother for many years."

"Oh," Keith said, "is that all? Why hide it?" Belinda shrugged. "You don't look like Sky," Keith said, peering at her theatrically. "Anyway, who cares? So Sky took care of you when Victor left. Where was Sara, in Italy?" Belinda nodded. "Well, I don't get it—why are you all so jumpy?"

"I'd just rather keep my personal life personal," Belinda said.

Downstairs, in the lobby, Francine had arrived. But the hotel had lost her reservation. They were filled, the clerk said hastily, they would find her another hotel. While they searched for a room for her, they offered to buy her a drink at the bar. Irritated, Francine picked up her briefcase and went into a small cozy room off the lobby. Tiny tables hugged the walls; the bar looked antique, gleaming wood and brass. Above it, a television set played quietly. The bartender looked like a farmer's son, open and wholesome.

"What'll you have?" he asked her.

"Vodka martini with two olives," she said, sitting down on a stool.

Keith had come down from Belinda's rooms to the bar a few minutes before. He glanced at the woman who perched on the stool next to him: it had been a while since he'd heard anyone order a martini.

There were three other people in the bar: a man in a suit sitting next to a woman in a fur coat, and a second man in a wrinkled sports coat.

Francine was looking at Keith. "You're from Los Angeles," she said to him. She was proud of her memory for people's faces and occupations. She measured this man's height, his broad chest, his mustache, and bushy eyebrows. "You're Keith Llewellyn."

"That's right," Keith said, neutrally. The man in the wrinkled sports coat looked up.

"Francine Cheney." She held out her hand. "I'm with Venner Broadcasting."

"Oh," he said with more interest. "Up here for the shoot?" She was a good-looking woman, almost as tall as he was, and even in the dark bar, her blond hair shone.

"Yes. I thought I'd say hello."

"Un-huh." He laughed. "That's what you all say. Isn't it kinda early in the shoot to be worried?" He pegged her for a numbers person, maybe head of accounting.

"No one's worried."

"Congratulations on *Crossing*. Great show. I meant to call Guy. Is he in the country?"

"He'll be up here tomorrow or the next day. We're going to some meetings in Canada."

Sport Coat, sitting near Keith, had an authoritative voice. He ordered another drink at full volume.

"Belinda's shoot is going well," Keith said, watching Francine drain her martini and order another one.

"Glad to hear that," she said, smiling a little. "Rewrites added costs into the budget."

Yup, Keith thought, numbers woman.

Sport Coat said, "Couldn't help overhearing." He was a man of forty, Keith judged, with a twinkle in his eye and an easy manner. "Aren't you with the TV movie that's being shot around here?"

"In a way."

"Well, in what way?" the man said.

"Writer."

"Yeah, you're Keith Llewellyn," he said in his friendly but aggressive fashion. "I've seen your stuff." He held out his hand. "Burton Harris with *Eye*. But don't take it the wrong way," he added hurriedly. "I'm no smear guy."

Upstairs in her room, Belinda was on the telephone with Vail.

"I wanted to tell you what a great job you did in *Crossing*," he was shouting. "Suppose you have some press up there because of it."

"Yeah, reporters all over the place. How do I get rid of them? Why does anyone care? It was such a little part."

Vail cackled, a mirthless sound. "What role does everyone remember from *Judgment at Nuremberg*?"

"Oh, Christ, I don't know," she said crossly.

"That Montgomery Clift part."

"It was only seven minutes long!"

"I rest my case," he said. "The only *other* thing people remember in that film is Spencer Tracy's white hair."

This was not helpful. Patsy came on the line. "Lindy, much might change."

"I'm in the middle of my first shoot. It's hard enough."

"We'll get some security up there for you," Patsy went on calmly, "but some enterprising reporter is going to dig around and come up with the story of Sky's daughter. 'Belinda Oliver' won't shield you for long. Lindy, have you heard from Patrick O'Mara?"

"Yes. What's going on with him?"

"He's been pestering Diana by telephone. Keep your eyes open. I truly don't think he's dangerous, but we don't know."

"Jesus. Is this really happening?" Belinda's hand on the receiver started to shake. "What should I do?"

"About Patrick, just keep alert. About the press? Do some interviews and set the ground rules for them. Tell them you'll talk about the role, about Fletcher's directing, about your picture up there, but you won't talk about personalities or Sky."

"How's Eddie?"

"Fine. He saw *Crossing*, thought you were terrific. So did I." Patsy paused.

"Yes?" Belinda asked nervously.

"Eddie wants to meet Vic."

Belinda sat on the edge of the bed. "I see." Her whole body ached. "Everything happens at once, doesn't it? It's over, isn't it?"

"I think so. Vail has talked with Vic."

"Should I come down?"

"No, we'll hold the fort here. You finish your shoot."

Belinda hung up knowing she'd have to tell Eddie everything, maybe as soon as she got back to Los Angeles. She wanted to hide in her film, delay, duck. She didn't want to be Sky Wyman any more than she wanted to be Lindy.

In Los Angeles, Vail watched Patsy hang up the telephone. He was sitting across the room from her in one of the corner chairs, glowering. "You sound as if everything's just great down here in Hollywood," he said.

"I can't tell her everything over the telephone, Vail. And what's she supposed to do about it?"

"For a mother who's about to be unmasked, I'd say you were pretty nice to your natural enemy," he said.

"Unmasked? What are you talking about? Eddie knows I'm not his birth mother. I've tried to be a good parent, the best way I know how, and I'm nervous about all of this—about Eddie. I've spent years being ambivalent about Lindy—sometimes I wished she'd never come back, but sometimes I felt more sorry for her than for anyone."

"You've hidden the truth from Eddie."

"And you're a bystander?" She inhaled deeply to calm down. Living with him had become a trial—he was nasty, cantankerous, self-pitying. "Vail, I know you're upset about your—the show." She couldn't call it his work because it was his life, it was his identity. She'd been appalled at Neil's duplicity, miserable about Vail's lame withdrawal from his program, a ragged end to a distinguished career. His publicist had hastily erected "contract disputes," "disagreements," all couched around hints of retirement and plans for travel. Publicly, not a word of his blindness had been printed; privately, half the town knew it.

"How can you be so great to a woman who can ruin everything you have with Eddie?" Vail demanded.

Once Patsy would have gone over to his chair and kneeled down on the floor beside him. But not now. She started out of the room. "There's no way she can do that," she threw over her shoulder. "I'm late. I'm going to the Women in Film meeting."

"Sure," he sneered. "I know you're lying. You're going to meet some lover. Have a good time."

She spun around at the door, amazed, furious, and stung to the heart. One of her clients, a writer, had that day passionately declared his desire for her and had proposed a weekend at a resort hotel in Laguna Beach. Before she'd turned him down, she'd actually considered it: she'd felt the embrace, the tenderness, the heat and the closeness, compared to the increasing chill at home.

She strode over to him, grabbed his tie and yanked it hard. "You are really a shit these days, Vail. Do you know that?"

In the bar, Keith noticed that Francine's hands never touched her face. She did allow the knuckle of one finger to touch the base of her chin in an attitude of listening, but he suspected the gesture really signaled that she was thinking of something else.

She was on her third martini. Keith was on his second bourbon and water. Harris was talking to the woman with the fur draped over her shoulders. The hotel had found a room for Francine, and they were readying it. She and Keith had drawn together, excluding Harris. She was telling Keith about the party Guy had given to mark the airing of *Crossing*.

"Everyone was there," she said, overstating it with relish. "Guy had the big screen up and there were sets all over where people sat in groups to watch it. Of course, most had seen it at the screening." Keith smiled falsely; gush did not suit this woman.

"Oh, turn that up," Harris boomed to the bartender with a big friendly wave. A nationally aired program on entertainment news had popped up on the television set.

Francine scowled at Harris and at the TV. "I detest that man," she said conspiratorially to Keith, nodding at the television set. Victor Oliver was being interviewed about how *glasnost* had affected the thriller genre and about the filming of *Crossing* in Hungary.

"But Venner Broadcasting produced *Crossing*," Keith said, baffled by her remark. He wondered how drunk she was. Francine tossed her head, ignoring him, staring at the screen with distaste.

"*The Crossing* was a real TV first," Harris said to Francine in his warm big voice. "You got Avery doing TV for a first shot, that little actress everyone's talking about that's up here directing her own thing. You got this guy." He flapped a broad hand at the TV set. "Publicity heaven."

"Victor Oliver stinks," she replied.

Jarred, Harris said, "Maybe so, but he writes great books that make great television programming." The wheels were turning: he wondered if he could get a story about Oliver out of her.

Francine felt dizzy as she heard Victor describing how entrenched elements of the Soviet bureaucracy wouldn't welcome *glasnost*. The bar receded. She was a young girl again, sitting at a desk in a sunny room, reading minimal press reports of her father's death, reports that raised more questions than they answered. But Victor Oliver, writer, had come through clearly as Lindy Wyman's father and she could still remember picking up a fountain pen, unscrewing the cap, and scratching his name on a pad.

The bar came back again. Victor was still talking about *glasnost*. When Francine had first heard that Venner Broadcasting was going to produce a show adapted from Victor's book, she'd fought Guy about it. It had been clear from the outset that Guy was committed to it. She'd backed off and had not been involved in the production, had avoided it, and, except for Avery, she hadn't met anyone connected to it. Whenever the financial sheets hit her desk, she'd glanced at the trouble spots and turned everything over to her assistant. Since that moment in her youth when she'd scratched out Victor's name with the fountain pen, he'd become one of the reminders of her father's death.

A bellhop came into the bar. Francine's room was ready.

She slid off her stool. "About time," she said.

Harris was an enthusiastic purveyor of rumor and information. He loved connections, entertainment-family histories, who was part of the scene, who wasn't. "You know that Belinda Oliver?" he said. "She's Victor Oliver's daughter."

Francine Cheney was reaching for a napkin from a stack on the bar. Her face paled; her extended arm froze. In the middle of her shock, she condemned herself for not ever having connected the two Olivers.

Keith heard Francine whisper, "*She's* Lindy Wyman?" She was shaking her head as one hand was clawing at the bar for support.

Keith reached out for her. "You okay?" Her waist and back were hard muscle and bone. "Who's Lindy Wyman?" Keith asked. Francine looked stricken.

Harris noticed nothing and hadn't heard what Keith and Francine were saying. "I'm tellin' ya, that Belinda Oliver's gonna be big, I kid you not. Listen, Llewellyn, how about helping me out, fixing me up with an interview with her?"

Francine put one hand, fingers splayed, palm down on the marble bar top. "I have to sit down," she said to Keith.

"How about it?" Harris pressed.

"In a minute," Keith said. He helped Francine to a seat in the lobby, away from Harris and the noise from the television set. Keith sat down opposite her. Francine's face was completely white. She lifted her head and stroked the fingers of one palm down her throat. "Do you want some water?" he asked.

"A brandy, if you wouldn't mind."

He went back into the bar and ordered the brandy. Harris said, "How about it?"

"You're up here to do a story on Belinda Oliver," Keith said as conversationally as he could manage. "Wasn't Victor married to Sara Wyman at one time?"

"Oh, yeah, that foreign director. Sky Wyman's sister. Yeah, that's the family. Probably one of the reasons she's so good on the screen. It's in the genes. There's something else about her but I can't remember it," Harris said, shaking his head. "Got a little gal in clerical checking on it. A trial or something." He looked up. "You know her—you're working with her, for Christ sakes—what's she like?"

"The greatest," Keith said immediately, taking the brandy from the bartender. "But shy. I don't know about an interview. Publicity will be real hard on her," he added, pointedly.

"Yeah," Harris said, hanging his head like a sad dog, "press can be rough."

Out in the lobby, Francine was sitting bolt upright, powdering her face. "Thanks," she said, taking the brandy from Keith. She downed it in a gulp. "I'm fine now." She stuck a smile on her face. "Just got dizzy there for a moment."

Despite his own uneasiness, Keith found Francine fascinating. Her manner swung between a snappy, spoiled bitch exec and a pathetic, lost child. "I'll walk you up to your room."

"Oh, there's no need of that," she said, rising. "I'll be fine." She put down the brandy glass. She looked like she needed another.

He went over to the elevators with her. "I guess you know Belinda pretty well," he said.

Her head turned toward him suddenly; she looked anxious. But her voice was perfectly calm. "No, I only met her around this production."

The elevator arrived, she stepped into it, gave him a business smile, and pressed the button for her floor. The doors closed on her handsome, upright figure.

Keith went back to the bar, but Harris was gone. He checked the front desk; Harris wasn't staying there. He went to the lobby telephones and called Belinda, but she didn't answer. He retreated to his own room, wondering how many people was this Lindy Belinda Wyman Oliver? She was obviously not Patsy's cousin. She was much closer and there was a reason why they'd all hidden it. About midnight, he called Vail.

"Oh, shit," Vail said when Keith told him of the exchange in the bar. "Shit."

"Can you be a little more specific, Vail?" Keith asked him.

CHAPTER 20

Francine wanted her father to come and free her from the confusion of her soul.

She was crouched on her bed in her hotel room, fully dressed. The universe had squeezed down to Lindy and herself. Her memory of the dark hallway and the spiral stairs of years ago nudged her.

She'd never connected Belinda—the short, rather delicate-looking woman she'd met at the film festival—to Lindy, the seventeen-year-old girl in San Francisco. Did Lindy know who she, Francine, was? Did she have any idea what they had shared? Francine threw herself on her back and stared at the ceiling. No, there was no way Belinda could know.

Francine's mother had derided Archie, but Francine had always defended him, and she'd adored him—until she'd come to live with him. Her mother had died of a heart attack, teaching Francine the startling finality of such things: her mother had been at home for breakfast; she'd been somewhere cold and far away that night.

Archie had flown her out to San Francisco. She'd been eleven. In the first months, Archie had been solicitous, understanding, had urged her to take her time, to go easy on herself. He said they'd get reacquainted. She had wanted that, too. Francine flipped over on her stomach. She didn't want to think of that time.

When had she first met Lindy? She'd been about fourteen or fifteen, she thought. One rainy night, about six o'clock, she'd come home from a dance class and had found the two of them coming out of the study, straightening their clothes. He'd introduced Lindy as a patient, but Francine knew it was a lie. This girl, only a couple of years older than she, was not a patient. There had been other girls, but this one was different.

Francine had tried hard to forget all of it. Sometimes the years she'd lived with Archie, from age eleven to fifteen when he'd died, seemed like a dream. But it was real and pieces of it always came back. She'd be somewhere ordinary and innocent, and the corner of a bed, a stairwell, a look or tone of voice would strike a deep reverberation in her, sending out minute waves of memory. These she rigorously suppressed.

Tonight the pictures were tidal.

Another night, months later, broke upon her. She saw Lindy pressed against the wall in the dark hallway, and her naked father holding her there, his bathrobe in a heap by his feet, his legs bent in a massive plié, his broad body pounding against her. A fountain of evil gratification had shot through Francine, instantly followed by repulsion and anger. Lindy was robbing her of her father. Francine Cheney had never cut the tension of disgust, relief, and rage all knotted together that those minutes in the dark stairwell had delivered.

She jumped off the bed in her hotel room, fell on her strong, beautiful arms, and pumped push-ups until she lay on the carpet, exhausted. She thought of her husband, Charles; she tried to recapture the feeling of gratitude she'd once felt for him. Before Charles, she'd avoided men who, she'd felt, might take advantage of her. When Charles asked her to marry him, she'd accepted immediately. He was wealthy and admired, but she now knew him to be cold. She couldn't feel any of the bright emotions for him anymore.

It didn't matter. Living in the light and shadow of Archie's link with Lindy, every feeling, good and bad, seemed pale by comparison. She sat up. Archie and Lindy . . . and the child! Lindy had been pregnant; she and Archie had been arguing about it the night she killed him. What had happened to that child?

Patrick was desperate. He knew where Lindy was now; the press note had helped, but the investigator with the dirty tie had really done it. Now, Patrick felt it was even more urgent that he talk to her—she was Sky's true heir. But Lindy, like Diana, wouldn't take his calls. Sky had been very specific: he was to beg her pardon as well as Diana's; he was to beg and receive forgiveness.

It was evening. He was sitting in his black leather chair in his still sparsely furnished living room. The bookshelf now contained, besides his Bible, a well-thumbed copy of his own book, *Sky and Me*. He looked across at the matching chair facing him, but Sky wasn't there. It was empty. He glanced furtively, almost pleadingly at the pictures and posters of Sky on the walls, forever youthful. He felt old and wrinkled and dry compared to her exquisite beauty. I'm trying, he thought, trying as hard as I can. But he knew he wasn't good enough, he'd never been good enough, and that was why Sky didn't come to him anymore. He would have to do something right away to bring her back.

As Victor pushed through the door of the Hard Rock Café that evening, the magnitude of his misjudgment hit him like an ax. When, forty-five minutes later, he and Eddie were finally seated at a table, Victor felt he was sitting in front of the amps at a Billy Idol show. Waiters Eddie's age, carrying loaded trays, virtually chased around the room, yelling, accompanied by the percussive crash of a thousand thick china plates and steel utensils. Diners screamed to be heard. The hardwood floors and the high steel-beamed ceiling amplified the thundering din of monster music.

Eddie tapped his foot to the beat; Victor drank a martini straight up. Making conversation was out of the question, though Victor tried by firing questions at him about school. Their dinner arrived in record time.

"I don't want to talk about anything heavy, Victor," Eddie shouted at him, dipping into his fries. Keeping his eyes trained away from Eddie's missing hand, Victor asked him about starting college, about his interest in maps, about sports, especially soccer. They talked about Victor's house in Ireland, about his youth in San Francisco, about his stint in the army after World War II.

Finally, Victor threw forty dollars on the table and rose. "C'mon, Eddie, we're getting out of here."

Outside, the four-lane boulevard, jammed with cars at the intersection with La Cienega, a major artery, looked serene, and the roar of the traffic sounded hushed.

Across the street was the Ma Maison Sofitel hotel, the kind of place Vic was used to. "C'mon," Vic said. They sat down at the edge of a lobby bar in soft chairs. The roar of the rock still sounded in Victor's ears like surf. "What do you want to drink?" Victor asked him.

"Diet Pepsi."

Victor ordered. The luxurious backwater where they now sat was only a few yards from the Hard Rock: it was like the other side of the moon. But the difficulty of communicating in the Hard Rock had spared both of them the uneasiness of their first meeting.

Eddie looked at the deep creases in Victor's lean face, his leathery skin, his unruly white hair. He looked tougher than his pictures on the jackets of his books. He looked like he knew his way around. "Sara," Eddie said in the silence. "Was she always like the way she is?"

"What's that?"

"Dramatic, like an opera star."

"Sort of. But sweet, too." Here it comes, Victor thought. But Eddie veered off, started talking about soccer again. Victor was relieved but he wanted to seal his value with Eddie. He wanted Eddie to like him, to confide in him. He wanted to leave some mark on the boy.

When they had fully mined out soccer, Eddie said: "Guess you knew Vail and Patsy before they were married."

Victor considered this. "No, they were already married when Sara and I crossed paths again. Diana didn't want Vail to marry Patsy."

"She didn't?" Eddie asked with interest. His right hand was wrapped around his glass; his left was in his lap.

"Very determined woman, your grandma Diana."

"I guess you knew everyone," Eddie said.

Victor waited, but Eddie said nothing more. "You get a lotta shit about your hand?" Victor asked suddenly.

"Used to. Not now. One girl, first day of fifth grade, screamed in class. I mean, she just bawled out and I was so mad that I put it—" He lifted his stump from his lap and touched Victor's cheek with it. "Just like that. Like I burned her, she jumped back, screaming and waving her arms, and two of the guys jumped on me and ripped my clothes, so I put my stump right in one guy's eye. It was quite a morning."

"What happened?"

"I got a new classroom. See, each year I'd have to get past

it with the new kids in school but I figured if they couldn't handle it, it wasn't my problem."

"Sorry you had to have that," Victor mumbled. "I suppose you've looked into artificial hands."

"I've had them all—hooks, knobs, hands, harnesses; we even talked about implants. Grandma found me an attachment that had a fork on the end of it—can you believe it? A *fork*, as if I couldn't hold a real fork in my right hand." He slipped his left wrist into his pocket. "I know she meant well, but I didn't like it. Did your dad have all his fingers and toes?"

"Yup."

"Triplets had all of theirs," Eddie said, frowning. "And my mom? How about her?"

"Yes." Victor felt his stomach tighten.

"And my dad? Did you know my dad?"

"I only met him once."

"He had all his fingers?"

"Yes." An image of Archie's big, meaty but well-shaped hands came back to Victor. His right hand lay on a white tablecloth, his left was under the table—patting Lindy's leg, Victor had imagined at the time. "At lunch, I met him once at lunch."

"What kind of a guy was he?"

"Nice fellow," Victor said. "Calm, good-natured. He was blond." Archie had been mighty embarrassed at that lunch because Lindy had told Victor outright that she and Archie were seeing each other.

"Blond, like me. Well, I get the feeling from Patsy and Vail that they didn't like him." He didn't wait for a reply. "He's dead now, isn't he?"

"Yes."

"But you thought he was all right, huh?"

Victor sipped the last of his drink. "Yes. But I didn't know him. Neither did Patsy and Vail, for that matter."

"And my mom, was she nice?"

"Yes. Real nice."

"That's good." Eddie could see Victor was uncomfortable. He wasn't sure that he himself wanted to pursue it with this man who was a stranger. "I've read all your books," he offered.

"What do you think?"

"Good. *Crossing*'s the max. So was *Devil's Deal*."

"Did you see *Crossing* on TV?"

"Oh, yeah! Very fine. I know Belinda Oliver. I thought she was fresh. Really good, but I didn't know she was an actress. She's directing a TV movie of her own now, up in the northwest. I met Fletcher Avery a couple of times."

They were skimming home on a good wind. They talked about Fletcher's films, about some of Vic's characters that repeated from one book to another, about the cities he'd written them in.

Victor dropped him in front of the house in Beverly Hills. "I think you're great, Edward."

"I was on my best behavior. Wait till you get to know me." He laughed, liking Victor, and shook his hand.

Victor clapped his grandson on the shoulder. He drove away reluctantly, but he felt a pure, unalloyed, uncontested happiness. It took the heat off his worry about being close to Lindy. It didn't make it less important to him, but less urgent.

When Eddie entered the living room, his father was sitting alone listening to hit songs from the fifties. "How was it?" Vail asked.

"He's not so bad. We talked about soccer."

"Come in and sit down, Son. We have something to talk about."

"I'm beat, Dad."

"This is important."

Eddie, uneasy, sat down on the couch across from his father. The music came to an end. Vail looked at Eddie, then at the arms of his chair, then back at Eddie. "Son, there are some big changes coming up. I won't be reviewing anymore."

Eddie frowned. "Jeez, Dad, why not?"

The front door opened and closed. High heels sounded on the tile of the foyer. "Patsy?" Vail called out.

"Yes." She sounded remote and grim. When she appeared in the archway, she looked it. Her pert, triangular face had no happiness in it. "Your father and I had a big fight," she announced to Eddie, "and I'm still mad."

Eddie brushed all this aside. "Mom, Dad says he's not going to review anymore."

Patsy's face softened. She came into the room, tossed her purse in a chair, sat down, and waited. Eddie began to feel afraid; something big was up. His mother wasn't analyzing and explaining and helping. His father wasn't cracking jokes; he wasn't blowing his top or pacing around. He was just sitting in a chair looking sad and uncomfortable.

"What's going on, Dad?"

"Son, I can't review anymore. I'm going blind."

Eddie couldn't take it in at first. "Aw, Dad, c'mon . . ."

"That's right," Vail said. "I'll be blind as a bat in a year or so."

Now a collection of small gestures and incidents fell into place for Eddie. Most of all he remembered noticing and ignoring the way his father moved his head, tilting it to one side alertly. How long had he been doing that? "Can't they do anything?" Eddie asked. Vail shook his head. "They must be able to do something! Mom, what's happening?"

Patsy rose, went across the room, and sat down on the big arm of Vail's chair and put her arm around his shoulders. She knew that it had taken Eddie's dinner with Vic to force the truth out of Vail. She hoped tonight he would at last tell Eddie everything. "Your father's been very stupid and very brave," she said, leaning her cheek on the top of Vail's head. "He didn't want to worry us. But he has a progressive disease and it can't be cured."

Eddie looked at his parents, bewildered, miserable. "Oh, Dad," Eddie moaned, tears forming in his eyes. "Jesus, I feel so bad for you." He stuttered and swallowed hard. He understood the fact of disability. "I feel so bad."

"Nothing to do about it, Son." His voice broke. Patsy hugged her husband.

"Dad, can you see now?" Eddie asked.

"Some. I can get around." As if to prove this, Vail rose and marched over to a water pitcher on the little bar table, tilted his head, surveyed the table, and picked up a glass and poured himself some water. "I don't want this to change anything around here. I'm not bringing home a bunch of Seeing Eye dogs. We're just going to go on with our lives."

"But, Dad—"

"Tell your mother about your dinner with Victor," Vail instructed him.

"Yes, how was he?" Patsy asked, still perched on the arm of Vail's chair.

"Fine. Seems like an okay guy," Eddie said, distantly, watching his father.

Patsy looked pointedly at Vail; he turned away. "Where'd you eat?" she asked Eddie.

"Hard Rock Café."

Patsy smiled at Eddie. "Sort of birth by fire, wasn't it?" she asked.

"It was his idea, not mine," Eddie replied.

"Poor Victor." Vail still wouldn't look at her. Damn you, Vail, come on, now's the time, she thought. But Vail said nothing. "Eddie," she began, "there's something else you ought to—"

But Eddie was rising, going over to his father. "Dad," he was saying, trying to sound on top of distress, "take it from me, having a physical problem shouldn't get you down. You can't let it, right, Dad?" He put his handless wrist against his father's arm. "It's like, I mean, like another kind of bond for us." He tried a laugh. "No eyes, no hand." He had never felt closer to Vail and he knew Vail needed to know it.

Patsy saw Vail turn away from the table and decanter, open one arm and fold their son into a hug. "Right, Son," Vail said, his voice thick with emotion. "How can anything ever go wrong for me when I have you?" Edward put both his arms around his father and squeezed tight.

Across the room, Patsy watched her two men cry and hold on to each other. There would be no other revelations this night.

The next morning, Francine felt that the agonies of the night had been brushed aside like cobwebs. It was a clear sunny day, and from the window of her hotel room she could see across the Willamette River all the way to the snowy peak of Mt. Hood. She stared at the mountain, drawing strength from it, the strength to deal with Lindy Wyman.

But the local newspaper carried an article about Belinda Oliver, "a fresh new star in *The Crossing*, currently filming in Portland, the city of roses." Minutes later, Guy's office called Francine from San Francisco, preening about the media splash on Belinda and *Crossing*. Venner Broadcasting was pressing it for all it was worth. "We're pumping up fresh publicity," Guy's assistant told her, "for the rebroadcast schedule. And Fletcher Avery will be up there in a few days—we're sending up a crew to shoot a half-hour documentary of him with Belinda."

The news disgusted Francine. Belinda didn't deserve all this praise. Did people think she was a great actress? Was she going to end up like Sky Wyman, adored? It was the last straw. She wanted to expose and humiliate Lindy. But a familiar, less strident, much less welcome voice inside her wanted to recognize Lindy. *She saved you*, this voice said, *you owe her*.

Francine stood in the middle of the beige room and screamed, "Why can't I just forget?"

She canceled her meeting with the *Indictment* production accountant, turned on the TV set, and got into bed. A telephone call from San Francisco awakened her that afternoon: Guy was arriving for the night, and he was expecting Francine to accompany him to the meetings in Canada the next day.

Francine was stretched out on the floor doing leg lifts, feeling the sweat and the pain. A jab of euphoria shot through her. "What am I waiting for?" she said out loud. Anything she did was justified because Lindy was being rewarded instead of punished. Excited, she stopped exercising and strode into the bathroom. She turned on the shower. I'll confront Guy with everything I know about his toy director, she thought, this murderess he's sleeping with. She closed her eyes, let the water run over her face. The high was fading. She leaned against the tiled wall. She wouldn't do that. She started to weep. Lindy was the only woman in the world who could understand her.

Absently, she began to rub a bar of soap over her arm. She screamed. She was still wearing her nightgown.

"Belinda, dear, it's Diana."

"Yes, Grandma, how are you?" Belinda said, surprised. She checked her watch. Her car was waiting in back of the hotel to take her to a nineteenth century Portland mansion where they were shooting interiors.

"I'm fine. That dreadful Patrick called me again. I'm concerned about your safety. Who are your security people?"

"Vail got them for me." Her grandmother's tone was maternal, the same she'd once used with Lindy years ago when she cautioned about swimming on a full stomach, about forgetting her galoshes, about the sort of boys who brought the wrong corsages.

"Is he telephoning you?"

"Yes, Grandma."

"This is not bearable," Diana said, her voice shaking. "You ought to be back here with us, with everyone."

Belinda hadn't heard that in many years. Tears flooded her eyes, ran down her cheeks. It was with the greatest effort that she kept her voice steady. "I'll be fine, Grandma. I've got dozens of people around me every day."

"You call me each night."

Belinda smiled. Yes, general, she thought. But when she hung up she was so touched by her grandmother's call that she sat on the edge of the bed and wept. She couldn't face her people for half an hour.

In Los Angeles, Diana was still seated by her telephone, nervously trying to sew on a loose button. Her hands shook, she pricked her thumb. A tiny drop of blood fell on the pale cloth. She put the whole thing down, needle, thimble, material, picked up the telephone and dialed.

"Belinda called me, Zip—about the fuss about her role in that film of Mr. Avery's." She was not aware that she'd reversed the facts of the call to Belinda. "The press is hounding her."

"You mean about those comparisons they're making," Leonora asked. "About Sky?"

"Yes."

"Reporters," Leonora said energetically. "They get hold of something and worry at it like a dog's bone. It's exasperating."

"Belinda was concerned lest I think she'd been trying to imitate Sky. Wasn't that kind of her?"

"Considering she's shooting a film, yes."

"I assured her I thought no such thing." Diana's tone changed. "That man has found her and he's calling her." She rapped her bony knuckles against the arm of her chair. "Insistently calling her."

"What man?" Leonora demanded.

"Patrick O'Mara! What if he tries to harm her?"

Leonora sighed as if she didn't want to cover the same ground again. "Doesn't she have the proper security?"

"You and I both know it isn't foolproof." Diana was literally wringing her hands. "I can't sit back and lose another one . . . Zip, I want to go ahead with our plan."

The elaborate High Victorian Gothic mansion in the west hills of Portland had been built by a lumber magnate in 1885. It sat on a sloping piece of real estate. Vigorous and sharp, it bristled with finials and crockets and leaded glass. Behind it, a string of equipment trucks beside a huge sugar pine had been emptied out for another day of shooting.

Inside, pointed arches, spacious rooms, and dark wood paneling settled a cathedral calm on the workers. No one was shouting. Even "Chicky" was calmly walking through her moves up and down the broad central staircase. She muttered a line, slowly raised and lowered her arms, getting into character. They were about to shoot "Chicky"'s big scene after her acquittal.

"But, Belinda, I have to talk to you," Keith said again, following her around the base of the staircase.

"Can't now, Keith," she replied.

"This is really important—"

"It'll have to wait." She started toward "Chicky." He followed.

"How about dinner tonight?"

"Can't."

"Then after dinner?" He looked cross and anxious.

"I don't think so."

"Listen, since all this broke about *Crossing*," Keith said quietly but urgently, "you're just out to lunch. You don't give interviews to the press, despite the advice from the publicist Patsy sent up here; you've boxed yourself into the shoot; you ride in an old Cadillac limo with shaded windows that doesn't fool anyone; and now I'm asking for an hour of your time and by God I expect to get it!"

"That Patrick O'Mara is still calling you," Belinda's production secretary, Jane, said, coming up to them. "He's very insistent."

"No way, Jane. I'm never in to him. He'll stop."

Jane fussed with her papers. "Guy's arriving today. He's sent word that he'll wait for you back at the hotel."

Belinda began talking to "Chicky."

"Belinda!" Keith said, taking her arm.

"Later, Keith, and I mean it."

"The hell with you," he said. "Why am I even sticking around?"

"Yes, why don't you go back to L.A.?" She glared at him.

"Chicky" said, "I think I ought to take a couple of beats after I come down the stairs, don't you, Belinda, and then start the monologue?"

"Yes, fine," Belinda replied. "Jane, isn't Francine Cheney around today? Wasn't she supposed to be here?"

Jane said, "I heard she's got the flu. Sticking in her hotel room."

"I saw her," Keith said.

"*You* have? When?"

"Last night. That's one of the things I want to talk about. Now may I have an hour of your time?"

Belinda looked at him warily. "After we wrap today. I'll meet you at the hotel."

When they shut down late that afternoon, Belinda's limo drove her past the reporters to the back of the hotel. She rode up in the service elevator. The phone was ringing as she came into her room and, without thinking, she picked it up.

"Lindy, it's Patrick." Belinda felt every muscle in her body contract. "All I want is your forgiveness," he said in a rush, his voice climbing. "Sky wants it, too. Just let me talk to you for a moment. Is that too much to ask?"

Belinda hung up. She unwound her hand from the receiver, flexed her fingers, felt hot, then cold. She remembered Patrick well from her childhood, the tall, happy, rather languid man in the red sweaters. But as she'd grown into a teenager, he'd become grayer and crazier, and his drunken, demanding appearances at Sky's front door had been unnerving.

The phone was ringing again. She had to get out of that room. Guy. She'd go to Guy. She raced down the hall to the service elevator, punched the penthouse button, leaned against the cool steel wall. She'd never felt so tired; her legs and feet ached as if she'd walked five miles. She probably had that day.

Thank God it was Saturday and they all had tomorrow off. She thought about the calls she still had to make that night, about the problems she still had to solve. Monday, they were moving to Multnomah Falls, a few miles outside Portland where, from a crack in the granite walls, a narrow torrent of water shot down for six hundred feet into the ferns and the pines. She forgot all about meeting Keith.

The elevator stopped. She left the service area and went along a short corridor to the penthouse door and rang the bell.

"Hello there," Guy said, cheerfully, glancing at her dusty jeans and sweatshirt. He opened the door wide.

Across the room, Francine Cheney was standing by the brightly lit windows, facing her.

For a half hour, they'd all been sitting on the off-white and plum colored furniture, chatting stiffly. Guy was at his courteous best, though he wasn't offering Francine a second sherry. She seemed permanently fixed to one end of the sofa, talking about her husband, Charles, and the preservation of an 1870s house on Franklin Street in San Francisco. "It's not the Comstock House, of course, but it's an adorable Queen Anne and they want to clear it for another ghastly parking lot."

Francine's fair hair was swept tightly back from her face; the lower half of each exposed ear was studded with a large gold earring. When she gestured, two heavy gold bracelets jangled dully. Her suit was neat and sharp, her blouse frilly and immaculate. She was the picture of a young woman without a care in the world.

But there was a current beneath her convivial manner that made Belinda uneasy. Francine was playing with them. Belinda wanted to say, Listen, I know who you are and someday you're going to know me, too, so let's cut through all this shit and talk about what happened. But she didn't. Francine chattered on. It was one of those grueling social situations which numbed the will.

Finally, Guy said, "Francine, you'll have to forgive us, we've made some dinner plans and we really must be going."

"I don't think so, Guy," Francine said. She felt a rush of panic and excitement.

"I beg your pardon?" he snapped, astounded.

"What I mean is, you're going to be late." She gazed at Belinda.

"What on earth are you talking about?" Guy demanded.

Belinda felt the blood rushing into her face. It's here; she knows, Belinda thought. But how does she know? Had there been some exposé in the paper? How? How?

Guy looked irritated; his mouth had thinned. He has no idea what's coming, Belinda thought. She glanced back at Francine.

Francine's expression was twisted—in pain or exhilaration, it was impossible to tell. Her large eyes had deepened, and except for two rosy spots on her cheeks, the color had drained from her face. Her carefully shaped brows seemed higher, drawing her face up in an expression of cunning. Her mouth also lifted but in a parody of a smile: it was a grin of revenge.

With one finger, Guy was lifting his cuff to check his watch. He had missed the transformation of Francine Cheney.

"Guy," Francine said, unable to keep the triumph out of her voice, "Belinda is a fraud! Her real name—the real name of this—this—person you're sleeping with is Lindy Wyman. Guy, she shot my father."

"What in god's name are you talking about?" Guy was straightening his cuff and stopped in mid gesture.

Francine rose unsteadily from the sofa, her voice full of ecstasy, a tone Guy recognized. "When the clandestine affair ended, this woman shot him! You're sleeping with a murderess."

Guy's face was stony. He stared first at one, then the other woman.

Belinda felt she was sinking in a dark, flooded cave. She would never find her way out. "It wasn't like that," she heard herself saying.

"Of course it was like that!" Francine snapped, her low voice trembling with passion.

"God, why are you doing this, Francine?" Belinda shouted. "We were both so young. I wanted to marry Archie—"

"Marry him?" Francine laughed. "He'd never have married a little whore like you!"

Guy shook his head and he smiled in a bewildered social sort of way. "Francine, have you lost your mind?"

She drew herself up to her full height. "I know exactly what I'm saying."

"Now, give me a little credit here, Fran. You're making a lot of unfounded charges—and that's quite unlike you." A warm, condescending smile appeared on his face.

Francine had not expected to be patronized, and his indulgence felt like an amputation. "It's true!" she screamed. Her eyes narrowed, the bright spots reappeared on her cheeks, her strong, trim body tilted toward Belinda. "She murdered Archie. I can prove it. Get rid of her. And if you don't, count on it— I will!"

Francine surged forward, brushing past Belinda, who felt the rush of her fury like a hot wind. She was deeply afraid of this woman. She steeled herself for blows, received and thrown. But Francine was actually gliding across the room and remembering to pick up her coat and bag. She paused at the door melodramatically, sending out a final triumphant smile. The door closed. The click of the lock behind her seemed deadly.

Belinda collapsed on the sofa. She couldn't believe Francine had simply left. Her body, energized for emergency, for bloodletting, collapsed. She put her face in her shaking hands.

Guy poured some whiskey in a glass. "Amazing," he said. "Absolutely amazing."

Belinda raised her head. "Don't you believe her?" She felt in disarray, adrenaline leaking through her, shaking her.

He handed her the glass. "Oh, yes, I believe her. You did shoot Archie, didn't you? *You* were the one." His narrow eyes under his bushy eyebrows fixed on her.

"Yes."

He swung away to pour himself a whiskey, then stood before her, one hand in his pocket, the other holding his glass. He studied the ceiling, rocking slightly on his heels. "I never liked old Arch," he said casually. "Did I tell you that?" He looked down at her, examined her. "This explains so much about you, my dear." He grinned. "You're a very enticing mixture of opposites. I've been curious about you. And now here you are with a sordid, tragic past—a challenging past, we could say. Actually, I'm indifferent to the past. I live in the present. And you are the pleasure of my present." He smiled again, a charming, wide smile of respect.

"For god's sake, Guy, get real. Don't you give a damn what I did or why?"

"Yes," he said gently, sitting down next to her, "and I hope you're not going to apologize."

"No."

"Good. What a rogue he was." He sipped his drink. "If we'd had an election in the family, everyone, except Francine, would have voted for his quick demise. But Fran was always nuts about him. His own wife left him, you know, just a couple of years after they were married. She never said why. You probably did the state a favor, because god knows where he would have ended up."

"Don't you feel anything?"

He cocked his eyebrow. "Yes. I feel sorry for poor Francine, who must have been lonely—my wife thought so. I feel sorry for you, a young girl of what—eighteen?"

"Seventeen."

"Being used by a sick man like that."

"He didn't seem sick."

"That's because you were so young, my dear. You wouldn't have known. At least you—took action. God, so bold." He leaned back against his end of the sofa and surveyed her with admiration.

She felt disconcerted. "It was wrong."

"Well, yes—and no. It was wrong, but it wasn't *that* wrong. How did you meet Archie?"

"At Sky Wyman's house, my mother's house." She waited for that to sink in. She pointed at her eyes. "See, I have her eyes." She knew she was misleading him but her past felt lurid, soiled. She didn't want him to know all of it.

"You *are* a bundle of surprises. So, there's some truth to all this press."

"My grandmother and Archie were related through Archie's mother. After Sky had an accident, a bad one—this was when I was about fourteen—Archie, being a doctor, I mean a shrink, began to, well, I don't know, consult with her. Anyway, he was around a lot."

Guy Venner was aware of feeling a deep and emotional partnership with Belinda. It surprised him. "I must confess," he said, "that I'm envious of you. There were a couple of men I'd gladly have shot if I'd had the chance." But he also felt warned. He never thought he'd be sleeping with a woman who'd actually killed someone. He rose. "Why didn't you run?"

Belinda thought about that. "It never occurred to me. I could have, but I'd shot him—I was responsible. At the same time, I didn't believe any of it had really happened."

"But you could have—disappeared, couldn't you?"

"Yes, but I was pregnant."

"Ah. Too bad. What happened to that?" he asked.

"Eddie."

"Eddie?" he repeated, startled. "The boy with Sara at the festival?"

"Yes, he's mine. He doesn't know it, I don't ever want him to know it. A few days after he was born, Patsy and Vail took him home. They raised him. I was sent to a prison for young women on their way down."

Guy Venner turned away again, staring out the windows, then turned back. "I'm surprised that they sent you away at all, a girl of your education, family."

"I survived."

"Ah. The toughness—that's where that comes from." He approached her.

"I wish I could go back to that study and speak the truth and not kill to hide my—fear, I guess it was. What I did was so bad it was unpunishable. They didn't really punish me. That was left to me. And I was very hard on myself."

"Regret changes nothing," he said, sitting down next to her.

"It wasn't regret."

He was aroused. He pushed aside a lock of her hair, moved her chin with his hand, and kissed her passionately on the mouth.

"No, Guy." She pulled away.

He wanted to feel her flattened and naked and damp beneath him. He put both hands on her waist and kissed her throat. He couldn't remember when he'd felt more excited. "Calm down," he said, "you're like a wildcat."

"Guy, please."

His lips pressed against hers and his tongue butted against her teeth as his hand slid up her leg. His breathing was husky. The more urgently he touched her, the more she resisted. He gripped her shoulder hard and pressed her back. "I have to have you," he hissed. "You can do this, you can do this . . ." He was pulling at her blouse with one hand, while his other pinned her shoulder to the back of the sofa.

A throbbing vein she'd never seen before bisected his forehead. "Guy, this is mad. You'll bring us both down—don't do this . . ."

But he was blinded by inflammation. His hands shook and reached and squeezed; his mouth, trailing saliva, roamed over her face and neck; his knee landed between her legs as he was trying to force her to lie down. Yet, instead of fighting, she felt strangely calm as she witnessed whatever was working inside him lessen and devour him. He was submitting to its teeth. She could easily get away from him; he wasn't as ruthless as the psych-tech. But she still couldn't bring herself to strike out. She couldn't believe that the controlling, sunny man she'd known was aroused on his deepest plane not by love but by the nearness of power over death.

"If you do this, it will be the finish of us," she said, twisting beneath him, facing into the sofa, her back to him.

His hand between her thighs stilled. Slowly, in stages, he lifted himself away from her. He smoothed his hair and punched his shirt back into his trousers. She sat upright, then rose, straightened her clothes. As she walked past him, he grabbed her hand, quickly, submissively. Then let go.

She saw Keith at the end of the corridor, sitting outside the door of her room writing in a spiral notebook. As she approached, he got to his feet. His smile was ragged and tired. She stopped in front of him and sighed. His green gray eyes under their dark brows, his dingy jacket housing his barrel chest, his faded jeans seemed familiar and intensely trustworthy. In the silence as they stood facing each other, a shift rocked them. He opened his arms and she fell inside them, leaning against him so hard that he had to take a step backward. He held her tightly.

"C'mon," he whispered, "we're getting out of here."

The mighty Columbia River, north of Portland, cuts a channel through granite walls on its rush to the sea. Belinda and Keith were speeding along the highway beside the gorge, heading east.

"I drove up here yesterday to clear my head," he said. "It's gorgeous."

"It's too dark to see anything," she muttered. "Where are we going?"

"To a roadhouse up here. They have loud music and great chops and beer."

She put her head back on the seat and let him drive.

The roadhouse had no loud music, but the aroma of great chops filled the room. Patrons past had carved benign graffiti in the wood surfaces of the booths—initials, hearts, arrows, stars. Every red plastic stool at the small noisy bar was taken by men in lumber jackets or by women in denim skirts. Keith moved Belinda to a back booth. "This is my kind of place," he said, "real down-home."

They ordered a beer. "You look like shit," he said, "but you'll improve."

"I know you're trying to be nice. I'll improve when this shoot is over."

"I'm not talking about the shoot. Belinda, how about being real straight with me?"

"How about shutting up?"

"Yeah, that's the way you'd like it, but we're way past your lies. I tried to talk to Vail but he wasn't really forthcoming, either. So I'm looking to you for honesty."

"I've been pretty honest with you."

"Ah, come off it! You're not even honest with yourself!"

"All right," she stated, "get in line. Just what is it that *you* want to know?" She thought of Maisie who had taught her well.

"Last night I was sitting in the hotel bar, minding my own business, when along comes this woman called Francine Cheney who works for Venner Broadcasting." Belinda put a hand to her forehead. "Wait," he said, "it gets better. So we're sitting there and down the row a bit is a guy named Harris who works for *Eye* magazine when lo and behold, up comes your dad on the TV doing one of the interviews he's so handy at about *Crossing*. Harris is one of the loudest guys who's wanted an interview with you." She shrugged. "So there we are, watching Victor doing his thing on TV, and Harris wants to tell us everything he knows about Hollywood history. He says that Victor's your dad. No flash to me, but it hits Francine Cheney like a Palestinian rock."

"So?" said Belinda, not a muscle moving in her face.

"God, I love the way you get all involved in our talks. Know what happened next? Ms. Cheney says *you*, Belinda, director and actress, *you* can't be Vic's daughter because some girl called Lindy Wyman was his daughter."

"I see. So that's how she put it together."

"What do you mean?"

"I've just come from Guy's room where Francine told him everything she knew about me. It was quite a scene."

"What's she got to do with all this?"

A geyser of laughter shot up from the bar, good-natured and full. "I knew her once for about ten minutes. We were teenagers."

"So what? Tell me!"

"Your timing's rotten, Keith, I wish you'd drop it."

"I won't."

"I don't have to tell you anything!" They were shouting, people were turning around.

Keith lowered his voice. "Who cares who your father is?"

"What difference would it make if I told you?"

He stared at her. "Screw it," he said, disgusted. "Beers are on you." He slid out of the booth and left.

A heart and arrow were carved into the table. She couldn't put her thoughts and emotions together. When she looked up, a man at the bar in a red checked shirt was gazing at her speculatively. He had beefy jowls and thick legs. She looked away. She felt no hurry about calling a cab or leaving and hitching a ride back. She had reached a fountainhead where all she'd done or been had coagulated and burst. The appetite for Fletcher and for Guy, the appetite for intimacy and sensation which had given her a measure of value now felt like a patina, an excrescence, a nasty way to conceal the disorder of who she was beneath. Even the work that challenged and excited her seemed like a frantic diversion from the main artery that drove her. And that current was fabrication. For an hour, Belinda Oliver simply sat in the old wooden booth and let the years of deceit fall away.

She paid for the beers and pushed through the door to wait for the taxi in the fresh air.

Keith's car was still there, and she could see a figure sitting at the steering wheel. She went over and opened the door and slid inside.

He did not welcome her. He did not deny her. He sat at the wheel, facing front.

"Scared?" he said.

"Yes."

They drove back along the river. The night was cool and fresh. Belinda opened a window and smelled the pine trees.

"I killed someone named Archie—Francine's father," she said, dully.

"By accident?"

"No, by murder."

Keith swerved the rented car to the side of the road. When he turned to face her, she was smiling at him.

CHAPTER 21

She was back in the room of the killing.

"It's funny, when I think of Archie now, I see him in that one room, that dark study. He just never gets out of that study."

Archie's study had been on the first floor of the huge old San Francisco house. The walls had been covered in a dark, narrow-striped paper; a green-glass shaded lamp glowed from the desk and cast its light on an oil landscape in a gilt frame and on the carved leather furniture.

Archie had been a big man, blond and broad, with lively brown eyes. He'd sat on the sofa, teasing her, calling her Dr. Wyman because she was at his desk. He'd said how girls her age always survived "little agonies like these."

"I was pregnant. He didn't want to marry me. He wanted me to get an abortion," she said.

They'd been fighting about it, he by turns laughing, serious, or condescending. She'd wanted the child, and his indifference to it astonished her. Last month, she'd been adored; now she was a problem. "He accused me of using my pregnancy to play the martyr. That struck home. I did feel sorry for myself. I felt abandoned."

She'd been playing with a letter opener on his desk, but as the argument escalated, she'd started opening the desk drawers. "I'm not going to let you make me the fall guy on this," he'd shouted at her as she opened another drawer and saw the revolver nesting inside it. "I remember he yelled that at me, I saw the gun, and I looked at him squarely and I said, 'I want you to be a proper father and marry me.' He laughed out loud, told me it was over, told me I should get used to it and grow up."

Through Sky, Archie had built an illustrious clientele. "I'll tell Sky everything," Belinda had said, "all the different kinky ways you like to make love." Sky was her mother; Sky would be appalled that her fifty-year-old shrink was screwing her seventeen-year-old daughter. It would wreck Archie's career.

The dark, lamp-lit room had glowed, waiting with its century of secrets. "Don't be stupid!" he'd shouted. "She won't believe you!"

"She will! She's my mother!"

"She's not your mother!" he'd roared.

Everything had stopped. They'd stared at each other across the rim of the golden light.

But once the secret was out, the secret Belinda had never known until that moment, the momentum seized Archie. He'd become reckless. "You think your mother's the revered Sky Wyman? You've enjoyed that, haven't you? It's a fraud! Sara's your mother—an Italian porno queen who spread her legs for all the pizza boys—"

"You're a liar!" she'd shrieked. He was robbing her, and even today she could feel the size of the theft physically. She'd seized the gun; he'd lunged for her; the gun went off and flew out of her hand.

"The sound, the sound was so loud."

Archie had staggered back, falling heavily to the floor. "He looked astonished. He was holding his throat and blood was seeping out between his fingers."

Belinda had picked up the gun, aimed at him. He'd waved his arms at her, gasping. She'd fired again.

Keith had parked in a turnaround at the side of the road. Below, unseen, the river, immense and indifferent, roared. The dark Oregon night closed in on them.

She sat on the seat with one leg curled under her, living in the night that had changed her life. Keith was staring out his window. "What did you do then?" he asked her.

She looked up, startled. "I fainted. I woke up on the floor."

"How long was that?"

"I don't know, a few minutes. The police arrived—I guess someone had heard the shot . . ." Her throat felt dry. How could she have been sane and have killed him? Had she been sane one moment and insane the next? Was she sane now? Keith was looking away from her. Was he offended? Probably. "What are you thinking?" she asked.

He turned. "I don't know how you survived it, being so young."

"You can survive anything if you want to bad enough."

He looked away. "Tell the rest."

After a long silence she said, "Something was worked out between the district attorney, the judge, and the lawyers—Patsy was one, just starting out in criminal law. We waived a jury trial, I pleaded guilty to manslaughter, and I was sentenced to the Ventura School for Girls. Sounds like a finishing school, doesn't it? My child was born—" She stopped. "No, *Eddie* was born—"

"Eddie?"

She shut her eyes. "Yes, Eddie! Eddie's mine!"

In the dark, Keith reached out and seized her wrist hard and didn't let go. "Go on."

"Well, Eddie was born and then I was sent to the school for young thugs for two years. But just before I was about to be released, I was implicated—framed—for the death of another inmate. I had nothing to do with it. But let's face it, I didn't have a lot to recommend me in the record department. I was tried and convicted again of manslaughter, but this time they sent me to Patton State Hospital, the loony bin. Now that was really rough. I spent three years there, and then Sara and Vic got me transferred to a private institution. I think the nuthouse let me go because they didn't have any space. They were letting a lot of poor wackos out." Her heart was beating fast and hard. "Still are."

"How long did you spend in the private place?"

"About six months."

"So, you never met Francine till now."

"I barely met her then, Keith—she was just a little white face on the stairway. I'm sure she hates me for what happened. I feel sorry for her, running to Guy that way like a kid, yelling and demanding."

His fingers, around her wrist, slipped down and wound between her fingers. "Where was she when Archie—died?"

"I don't know."

He stirred, turning slightly toward her on the seat. "I want to hold you but I'm not sure you want that."

She put her other hand over his. "This is fine." After a moment, she leaned her head against his shoulder. He shifted back against the door, put his arm around her neck, bending the elbow in front of her, sealing her against him gently.

"Just rest," he said. He felt scarred.

In her room the next morning, Belinda awoke at dawn. It was Sunday. She dressed, took the stairs down to the lobby, and looked around for reporters. It was empty.

Outside, the light was a shiny pale gray. The air was chilly and damp; it smelled of cedar and salt from the sea. But they were miles from the sea. She started walking east, toward the river. She listened to the click of her heels on the pavement. At the river, she looked up and down. Bridges called Ross Island, Hawthorne, Morrison, and Steele looped across it. She stared down at the deep gray water. She hadn't told Keith about the great hollow inside her that Archie had left when he'd taken her mother away from her the night of the killing. She hadn't told him of the erotic satisfaction that had shivered through her when she'd shot him. That had been all too brief; the residue was long-term and bitter. She hadn't told him that no matter how many years passed, she feared Archie would always be with her.

The horizon to the east was pale, and the color of the river was changing. In the chilly light, she knew that even if she'd told him years ago, Eddie would still feel robbed, too.

"Lindy."

She turned around. A middle-aged man with faded, thinning blond hair was standing behind her. A wrinkled raincoat hung from his stooped shoulders. He held a valise in one hand.

"Patrick . . ."

"Please, Lindy, just a minute of your time?"

She stepped backward. His beseeching eyes seemed unnaturally bright. She'd seen that look in the nuthouse and the prison where everyone was on drugs, legal and illegal. "What do you want?"

His face changed. "You can't look at me without looking at yourself," he accused her.

She screamed. He lunged at her, grabbed her arm.

"I want forgiveness!" he cried out. "I tried to explain in my book!" he said angrily.

She broke past him.

"Lindy! Forgive me!"

"Never!" She was running uphill, past shut-up shops and restaurants. Patrick was trailing behind her, steady, angry.

Ahead, a cab was pulling into the curb. "Hey!" It started to pull away. "Wait!" She pounded on the window. It stopped. She yanked the door open and threw herself inside.

"I'm off duty, lady," the fat, mustached man growled.

"You bastard!" She slammed the door. "For god's sake, drive." She locked her door and turned to look at Patrick. He was gaining on them, his mouth open, calling out, waving his valise.

Her security man was in the hotel lobby. "Miss Oliver, I will not be responsible if you keep going off by yourself like—"

"Oh shut up," she said. The lobby was filling up with early risers—guests and her crew. "Now just stand here with me," she said, calming down, "and wait." She told him what Patrick looked like, told him what had happened. "I'm sure he knows where I'm staying. You get me moved somewhere today."

Patrick did not show up.

Later that morning, Belinda was in her room when Guy knocked at the door. "I've got to leave for Canada," he said, coming inside. He put his arms around her gently. "I'm embarrassed about last night," he said. He stroked her cheek with one hand. "This thing between you and Francine. Please smooth it out." He rubbed her chin.

"You don't smooth out something like that, Guy."

"Oh, yes," he said, supreme. "Everything can be dealt with. I've been thinking. Since we're related, it's time the families got to know each other. Next Sunday I'm hosting a party on my yacht, and I'm going to ask your people—part of our family: Sara, Vail and his wife, even Eddie. We'll cruise San Francisco Bay, have dinner, trade stories."

"That's a terrible idea."

"I thought you'd like it. We can start making some repairs. Belinda, I want to know you for a long time."

She stepped back. "Guy, the reunion isn't workable. Diana doesn't travel at all. Sara and Vail heard about you Venners for most of their lives and I don't think they have real friendly feelings. Sara said Diana was always talking about living up to the Venners."

"We *are* people you should live up to," he said, chuckling.

"Old Faith Venner never let Diana into the house, the way I hear it."

"I'll let everyone onto my boat."

"I can't. I'm shooting the film."

"Sunday's your day off. It'll be good for you and Fran to make peace."

"I'd like that, but I don't think Francine— Guy, don't do it. It gives me a bad feeling."

"Where's your spirit of adventure?"

Later that day, Belinda, Yvonne, Buttons, and Keith drove the hundred miles through the dark spare pine forests of the Cascade Mountains to the meadows and the sea.

The coast was rugged and rocky, quite unlike the polished, tamer shores of Southern California. Wide sandy beaches alternated with precipitous cliffs fringed with trees blown flat back from the sea by salty winds. It was summer, but it was windy and crisp and gray. The tide was low. People in coats and kerchiefs walked along the hard sands with bounding dogs and driftwood sticks.

Yvonne had finally put away her notebook of lists and reminders for the next day's shoot. She sat in a deck chair, leaning against the open door of the rented van. Next to her and slightly higher, Buttons sat in the front seat, looking out the windshield at the breakers. Keith and Belinda, heading toward the hard sand, were climbing over the skirt of rocks and battered driftwood piled up by the waves on the shore.

"Go walking with them," Buttons said to her.

"I'd rather stay with you," she replied. "Besides, I think they want to be alone." She put her head down against his thigh. "Me, too."

Buttons combed his fingers through her short black hair. "Me, too," he echoed.

* * *

Belinda was trying to figure out when Keith had become her best friend. She walked beside him, poking a stick at the damp sand, remembering their lunch at Musso's when he'd described the forest lake to her; he'd challenged her, dismayed, and irritated her. She thought of the time they'd met by chance in Sydney when he hadn't liked the way she'd looked at herself in the mirror. She thought of their first cantankerous script meeting for this film, and later, in Portland, when he'd burst into her office with news about the reviews of *Crossing*. That time, he'd been on his way to Los Angeles and he still hadn't left. Finally, she thought of their drive up the Columbia River Gorge . . . it couldn't have been only last night, could it? But when had he become such a complete friend? She watched the wind ruffling his hair and the way he angled his square head into the breeze as he strode along the sand.

Keith was thinking about his fear. Belinda had, almost overnight, become the most important person in his life. He walked beside her, letting the feeling fill him with its goodness and its gravity. He wanted in the most urgent way to touch her, not as a friend or co-worker, but touch her with implication in that honest, bone-deep way that spiraled emotions upward, changed lives, gave no quarter, sought no reprieve.

That morning, Keith had called the woman living in his apartment, an exciting and funny actress with whom, for the last year, he'd been informally "making plans." He'd told her the apartment was hers if she wanted it, but that he'd be getting a new place when he returned. Keith had no idea where he'd be living when he got back from Oregon; but he knew he couldn't live with anyone except Belinda. "Keith Llewellyn," his actress had said in her animated, theatrical voice, "have you gone and fallen in love on me?" He was not able to answer that even now. He hadn't felt this way before. Oh, he'd loved, he'd certainly enjoyed—but this feeling was different. He only knew that everything had altered and if he denied it, he would lose his soul and never recover.

The wind was lifting Belinda's hair, blowing it back from her head in streamers, exposing her profile and her ears.

"What are you afraid of?" he asked.

"That everything'll come unraveled. That the press will print a big article about Sky and about me, about Archie, and prisons, and that Eddie will read it."

Belinda doesn't know, he thought. Maybe it's only happened to me. "I think *Crossing* and you and Sky are old news," Keith replied, feeling intensely lonely. "The press doesn't seem real interested anymore."

"I hope so. I want to finish the film very much."

"You will." Keith watched the waves breaking against the tide pools. "Did Francine know you were pregnant?"

"No, I don't think so. Why?"

"Just wondering if she knew about Eddie."

"No, my problem is the press." She flicked a smile at him.

He was tempted to say, my problem is with you. He really wasn't thinking about the numbers woman from Venner Broadcasting. "So, what are you going to do?" he asked.

"Go back to Los Angeles as soon as I finish the shoot."

He stopped walking. "Then for the next ten days, unless something dire happens, which you can't control anyway, why don't you just relax and shoot?" He grinned at her. The wind behind him blew his dark hair straight up.

"Yes, you're right." She flung her arms out into the salty wind. "And look at all this! This is good! This is beautiful!" She thrust her face into the clean air and threw her stick into the waves.

Keith, a few steps away, watched her reach down to examine a stone. It was more than attraction, what he felt for her, but she was unapproachable right now, caught up in the film, in her fears about her son, about herself in her son's eyes. Whatever this big feeling for her was, he had to hold it inside, warm it, tend it, wait on it, and hope its wonderful, scary weight, its hugeness, didn't come shooting out of him at the wrong time.

In Los Angeles, Eddie's connection with Cynthia was by daily telephone. He thought of her constantly; his past was Cynthia, his present was Cynthia. He remembered the ecstatic detonation of touching her for the first time, and of knowing then without doubt that, having kissed her that night, he would make love with her. And, of course, he had and his memories of the night bore him now through every day. She was like a color, painting every minute, each thought and act.

"We're related." Cynthia giggled.

"Yeah, I heard." The news that had come in Venner's invitation to a party on his yacht had cemented Eddie's feeling that he and Cynthia were fated.

"But I don't believe it," Cynthia said. "It's one of Dad's games."

"My mom says we're distantly related to your dad."

"I'm glad it's distant," she whispered on the telephone.

"Yeah." A long silence ensued which proved the weight of everything they felt like saying, but weren't saying. Finally, Eddie said, "Your dad called my grandmother Diana, but she refuses to go to the reunion."

"The party started out being for the media so don't get the idea it's just a family reunion. You're coming up for it, aren't you?"

"If you had a six point eight quake scheduled for that weekend, I'd be there."

"You're like a six point eight quake to me," she said.

"God, I wish I could be with you right now."

"We've got a place in Carmel," she said, "and maybe after the reunion, you and I could go down there. Dad's going to be out of town."

The heaven of this proposition made Eddie shudder with happiness.

"The reunion!" Vail exploded. "It's a damned stupid idea. I thought we'd decided against this. I don't want to hear about it again!" The less said about the Venners, the better: they were, to Vail, incendiary. There was too much damned history. His fury about the party was actually his anger at himself: each day he told himself that now he'd talk to Eddie about Lindy, and each day he delayed.

"Dad," Edward said, "it's for the family. We've got to go."

"Son, the only Venner I ever met was that dippy old broad with a toy poodle in her lap. I don't want to meet any more of them."

"Mom," Edward appealed.

"I can't change his mind. And your grandmother is definitely not going. Neither is Sara."

"How about you, Mom?"

"No. Not without your dad." She didn't trust Venner's motivation and she wasn't satisfied by his explanation of discovering their families' connections from Sara at the film festival. She'd called Sara, who'd denied telling Venner any such thing and had suggested that Belinda might have told him, though for what reason she could not imagine.

"I'm going," Edward said.

"No, you're not," Vail declared.

"I wish you wouldn't, honey," Patsy said.

But Eddie was adamant. "I want you to meet Cynthia," he said. "She'll be there."

"She's still special?" Patsy asked.

"Yes, Mom."

"*Cynthia?* Your Cynthia's a Venner?" Vail shouted. "A son of mine involved with a Venner? God, where's it going to *end*?"

"I want you to meet her," Edward said with the calmness he'd learned to ride out Vail's explosions. "I'm going away to college soon. Please, can't you do this one thing?"

Venner's yacht was named *The Cynthia*, a hundred-foot-long schooner with two masts and five sails. Wood hulled, it was a well-known antique which Venner used mainly for parties or meetings. The wood gleamed, the brass shone.

As Edward, Patsy, and Vail stepped aboard, Guy, the genial host, dressed in white ducks and an open-necked white shirt with faux epaulets, welcomed them grandly.

"A great pleasure," he said to Patsy and Vail. "Edward, we met at the film festival, didn't we?" They shook hands. "I couldn't get Belinda out of Oregon, can you beat that?" Guy was extremely irritated at her refusal. But none of this showed as he ushered them onto the foredeck among his other guests. He glanced at Edward Wyman with new interest; Belinda's son and Archie's, the result of passion, appeared normal, even benign, a blond, well-built young man with a ready smile. Guy wondered if the boy knew he'd been adopted.

The bright waters of the bay reflected the hard afternoon sun. The breeze was soft. A waiter served drinks and hors d'oeuvres, balancing against the slight roll of the yacht in its slip.

Patsy was surprised to find Guy Venner an attractive and knowledgeable man, someone she'd enjoy knowing better, and she could see why Belinda might be drawn to him. He wore his power confidently, while he listened to his guests with an attentive charm.

A gurgle sounded to Vail's right, and he started: a waiter was pouring ice water into a glass. Parties were nightmares for Vail—he heard things happening beside him but couldn't see what they were unless he turned his head. He hovered near Patsy, remotely polite to Venner at first. But after a while he warmed up, finally telling an amusing rendition of the meeting with "old Faith Venner in that pile of stones, looked like a mausoleum, square hulking mansion—"

"Yes," Venner said, "we gave it to the National Preservation Trust. It's kind of a museum now."

"It was a museum then!" Vail said.

As Vail and Guy traded San Francisco stories, Patsy's gaze settled on Cynthia and Eddie. They were standing near the bowsprit, talking intensely. Edward was tilted toward her attentively; she saw Cynthia's fingers trail lightly over Edward's handless wrist. My God, she realized, they're lovers.

"Does your daughter go to school here?" Patsy asked Guy.

"She wants to," Guy replied, his back to Cynthia and Eddie, "but she'll go back to France for another year. It's best for her to complete what she's started there." Patsy glanced back at Eddie and Cynthia. She didn't think Cynthia would leave easily and if she did, Eddie might follow her.

"Victor!" Guy called out.

Patsy hadn't seen Victor for several years. Dressed in a black and white checked jacket, white slacks, and a Tuscan red ascot, Victor was moving toward them with an easy grace that didn't match his fixed smile or his wrinkled, aging face. He put out his hand. "Patsy," he said, "how often I've thought of you." Patsy felt both his hard slender hands fold over hers; she had completely forgotten the seductive poise of the man.

"Vic," Vail said, "what a surprise."

Guy was welcoming him like an old friend, introducing him to people nearby, most of whom either knew his books or had seen *Crossing*.

"Vic!" Eddie said, bringing Cynthia over to the circle of people now surrounding him. "Cynthia, this is my grandfather."

Victor's hand closed on Eddie's shoulder, a gesture of total acceptance, then he smiled at Cynthia, a dozen new creases appearing around his mouth. "A beautiful name," he said, letting his eyes linger a moment on her face and then on Eddie's. Then he turned to Vail, shook his hand warmly, putting an arm around his shoulder at the same time, and saying in a low voice, "Can't tell you what this means to me, seeing you and Patsy here, and Eddie." Vail's sight wasn't good enough to see the tears in Victor's eyes, but he heard the hoarseness in his voice.

"Victor came all the way from Ireland," Guy was saying, introducing a reviewer for the *Chronicle*, who started a jubilant conversation about *Crossing*.

"What a terrific man," Cynthia said, watching the knot of talky people around Victor move with him toward the railing on the other side of the yacht.

Victor's effect on women hadn't been lost on Eddie: something in his grandfather made them light up inside. "He looks kinda weather-beaten, but he's got something," he said, pleased by Cynthia's reaction. "You still want to go down to Carmel with me tonight?" he asked. "Sure you don't want to take Vic?"

"You silly," Cynthia said, secretly squeezing his hand, letting one finger press into his thigh. Eddie couldn't keep the adoration out of his eyes. "You have to stop looking at me that way," she whispered.

"Cynthia."

Cynthia turned. "Francine! I saw you come aboard but then you disappeared."

"I was below deck, dear. A couple of calls."

"Eddie, may I introduce Francine Cheney—Mrs. Charles Cheney—a really good friend of Daddy's and mine." Edward shook hands and called her Mrs. Cheney. "Francine, this is Edward Wyman."

Francine said, "And which Wyman are you?"

Cynthia pointed at Vail and Patsy. "His parents are over there."

Francine nodded politely. The yacht was filling with guests rapidly, the talk and laughter rising.

"And that's his grandfather," Cynthia said proudly, gesturing toward the crowd of people around Victor.

Francine looked in that direction casually, her beautiful hair catching the sun. When she saw Victor, she reached out for the railing. "I just felt the boat roll," Francine said, breathlessly. "I never got along with boats." Her eyes traveled back to Eddie. "Victor Oliver's your grandfather?" she asked. She saw her father's hairline, and the shape of her father's eyes. She looked again at Victor, whose leather face was stitched with pleasure as he spoke with Patsy. Cynthia was saying something to Eddie, but Francine's ears were ringing. She wrinkled her forehead and smoothed one hand down her throat. She glanced at Eddie, who was replying to Cynthia in a low voice. He was tall and broad-shouldered, like Archie, but he looked more like Victor Oliver than Archie. Eddie was leaning against the railing insolently, one hand in his pocket, his head bent toward her. Belinda's child, Francine thought, feeling her heart thump. But did he know it?

"When I came up from below," Francine said, feeling high, not knowing what she was going to say next, "I saw you two in such a close conversation. Are you dating, by any chance?"

Edward looked surprised. Cynthia laughed, leaned toward Francine, and said, "Does it show, Fran?"

"Not to everyone. Are you going to take me into your confidence?" she asked with a difficult conspiratorial smile.

Edward tugged on Cynthia's hand behind her back. Cynthia's pale eyebrows lifted. "I do like him a little." She leaned close to Francine. "And you're the first to know."

Francine, feeling stronger, surer of her direction, looked at Eddie as if to size him up for matrimonial material. "Are we talking about a serious attachment?" Cynthia nodded. Edward looked as if he might fall overboard with joy. "I thought you were going back to France soon," Francine said.

"I'm not going back, Fran."

"Guy doesn't know that, does he?"

"No," Cynthia said reluctantly, "I haven't really told him yet."

"What are you thinking of doing instead?"

"I want to go to journalism school at Stanford. Their department's really fresh."

Francine shot both of them a glance full of false admiration. "Well, if I might offer a little advice, I think you should take Guy into your confidence as soon as possible. It looks so bad if he hears something before you've spoken to him; you know how that is. And Guy is so protective of you, Cynthia. Edward should probably have a long talk with him soon. He'll want to know Edward. But you two do what you think is best." She tossed them another warm, conspiratorial glance. "And my lips are sealed."

Francine turned away and accepted a glass of champagne from the waiter. She felt wonderful. Guy would hit the ceiling when he heard that Cynthia was in love with, maybe even sleeping with Edward Wyman. Would he know that Edward wasn't Vail's real son? She would have to tell him. She pictured the scene with Guy. The crowd around Victor opened and for an instant, she saw him fully. He was looking at her. She raised her glass toward him and smiled as if she'd met him. He cocked his head. She felt the delicate sting of the champagne on her tongue. There would come a time, she knew, when she would tell Edward Wyman just whose son he really was and what his mother had done to their father.

The strong hand, with its conical fingers, clutched the pen firmly. After the first downstroke, the sloping writing spread over the page like a fire, filling it. The letters seemed conversational now, a steady flow from the mind.

So you see, Sara, why none of you are safe. It's my turn now. Remember when you fell off the horse and broke your front teeth? Were you twelve or fifteen? You'd been the leader, the favored one until then. . . . You didn't know anyone knew that, did you? I know all. Remember later, in the little theater, Sky stole the show from you. Remember the envy you felt, living in her shadow? I felt that way too. Lindy will die soon. But before she dies, she'll know shame. Everything and everyone she loves will suffer. And I will do it. It makes me so happy. I am finally happy. I hope you are frightened. You should be . . .

*   *   *

"Eddie's in love with Cynthia," Patsy said as she and Vail arrived at the L.A. airport the following afternoon.

"Crush," was all Vail said. He felt Patsy touch his elbow. He focused in on their driver who was standing to one side at the gate. "You see love everywhere," he snapped. His decreasing sight made him constantly irritable and angry. "You're like a teenager yourself, you have sex on the brain."

"It's serious," she said, preceding both men into the elevator that would take them down to the car.

"No one's serious at eighteen. He'll be in college in a month." The car was at the curb. Vail and Patsy climbed in.

"I quite enjoyed Victor," she said, remembering the special confidence with which he'd greeted her. Victor was one of those men who really liked women. "He was so touched to be there." Vail said nothing. The car moved out. "Eddie likes him," Patsy went on.

"Yes," Vail said, "I know." Patsy hugged his arm. "It'd be ironic, if Belinda married Guy Venner. You really think she's having an affair with him?"

She nodded. "Yes."

"All that Venner money."

"No, Vail." She laughed. "Something bigger."

Their driver maneuvered the car into the choking freeway traffic. Patsy was going to her office, but he had nowhere to go except home. What the hell am I going to do for the rest of my life? he wondered.

"Fletcher was in the other day," Patsy said. "He wants to cast Lindy in the lead for his new picture to be shot in Berlin."

"Great idea. For a woman who didn't have any choices a few years ago, she's got a lot now."

Patsy squeezed his arm. "Vail, if you don't tell Eddie when he gets back from San Francisco, I'm going to tell him."

"How about Lindy?"

"I've already talked to her. She knows the time has come and how lucky she's been that nothing's broken in the press. But it's just sitting in front of us like a monster. I can't go on this way anymore. Lindy said she'd be down this week to see Eddie. But if she's not here, I'm not going to wait for her or for you. I know how hard this is, but, honey, it's got to be now."

The car rushed along with the traffic. Vail felt suspended, waiting for the rest of his life to unravel: his work was gone; his son would soon know the truth and leave him. "I'm going to miss Eddie so much," he said softly.

"Oh, darling, don't dramatize. Just agree."

Irrationally, he had the sudden urge to see Diana, talk to her the way they used to.

"Answer me!"

"All right, yes, as soon as he's back."

They sank into a silence. "I think I'll see how Mother is," he said.

"Good. She's alone too much."

"It's her choice."

"Some people don't reach out very well."

Their driver dropped Patsy at her office in Century City and then took Vail home.

He realized as he walked into the front hall of his home that he was cross and sad all the time. He couldn't move around easily, though he could still see things directly in front of him if the light was good. But doing the most ordinary things took mental and physical adjustments that wore him out.

He stood in the hall and was again aware that, irrationally, he wanted comfort from Diana. That would be an unlikely honor. It sprang from the nature of his failed and hesitant heart, from being Diana's only son. He brightened; he could tell her about that pretty Cynthia that Eddie seemed smitten with. Cynthia Venner—just the kind of news his mother would secretly want to hear.

He went into the kitchen. Maria was putting on her jacket. "Are you going somewhere?"

"On an errand for your mother."

"Oh, I was hoping you'd send up some tea things for us."

"I just sent a whole luncheon tea up there," Maria replied. "She has guests."

"Who?"

"She didn't introduce me. Mrs. Lytton and someone else."

"Oh," he said. He felt disappointed. His head moved as he surveyed his kitchen. In a year, maybe less, he wouldn't be able to see the copper pots hanging above the cooking island or the herb garden in the window box or the cutlery and shiny casseroles. He wouldn't be able to cook anymore; you can't chop herbs if you're blind. It depressed him immensely. He went back into the hallway. He had nothing to do. He looked up the stairs. Maybe Sara was with Diana. That would be nice, sort of like old times. No, if Sara was there, Maria would have mentioned her. There was a stranger with her. He didn't feel up to making polite conversation. But his curiosity took over. He went up the stairs and knocked at his mother's door.

"Yes?" his mother said from inside. "Who is it?"

"Vail."

"Vail? What are you doing back?" He heard a rush of murmured conversation through the door.

"Mother, are you all right?" He put his hand on the doorknob. "Mother!" He shoved the door open.

Diana was sitting in her favorite wing chair, a luncheon tea spread on the table before her. He moved his head to see who else was in the room. Leonora Lytton was sitting at the midpoint of the tea table, a chic straw hat on her head. His mother's hand, holding a teacup, came into his line of vision. He turned his head and focused on the foot of the table.

His mother was offering Patrick O'Mara a cup of tea.

CHAPTER 22

"Get out of here!" Vail demanded. Patrick flinched. Despite the disadvantage of his failing vision, Vail's body tensed and he advanced on Patrick angrily. Leonora grabbed Vail's arm. He looked down at her. "What are you all doing? Are you crazy?"

"Vail!" Diana demanded. "Shut the door and sit down."

"Perhaps Vail could come back later," Leonora tried.

"Come *back*?" he repeated, shocked. "Get him out of here." In the past, when very upset and angry, Vail had been known to punch people out.

"Vail!" Diana cut in. "Mr. O'Mara asked to see me and I gave my permission."

"What?!"

"Now sit down or leave!"

Patrick looked smug in an elderly and pathetic way. He was seated in a high-backed antique peacock chair. "I came here hoping that Mrs. Wyman would forgive me, Vail," Patrick said. "It's the most important thing in my life." He looked at Diana with obsequious humility.

But Vail saw that his mother, far from receiving these words cordially, was instead so angry she could barely hide it. But her voice was smooth. She grasped the heavy silver teapot, poured out a cup of tea, grimly placed it on the table in front of the spot where Vail was standing. "Tea, Vail?"

"Tea?"

His mother slowly lifted her dark eyes and gave him such a look that Vail sat down and took his cup.

"Leonora," Diana said, "perhaps you'd pass those sandwiches."

Vail felt that he'd walked into the fourth dimension. Bewildered, he cocked his head and examined the elaborate luncheon. A variety of little sandwiches and canapés crowded the serving plates—hot biscuits with a chicken and celery filling, shrimp puffs, a wedge of Pont l'Évêque cheese, a wedge of Roquefort, a green salad with blossoms in it, and on the serving table behind his mother, a burnt-sugar cake with white icing rested beside a shallow bowl of cookies. It was disgusting that his mother would allow Patrick inside the house, let alone share in this spread. "My god, mother, what *is* all this?"

"I felt that if Mr. O'Mara and I could talk directly, he might leave Belinda alone."

"Belinda?" Vail asked. "What's *she*—"

"You have been pestering her, haven't you?" Diana said to Patrick, ignoring her son.

"Yes, I have called her," Patrick admitted softly. He balanced his teacup awkwardly. He was pleased but mystified by Mrs. Wyman's wonderful courtesy, the gracious luncheon, and being introduced to her oldest friend.

"Sugar?" Diana said.

"Yes, please."

"You've done more than call her, Mr. O'Mara." Diana's voice was hard.

"I had to tell Lindy—" Patrick stopped in midsentence, not sure that the time was right to tell them what Sky had said to him on the day he'd read the review of Lindy in the film. He was sweating under his jacket. "I had a message for Belinda," he said.

"A message?" Vail said stridently. "Mother!"

"Vail, button up," Leonora snapped. With a grotesque smile on her ruined but still beautiful face, she offered a plate to Patrick. "Have some of these mushroom butter sandwiches."

"Maria makes the mushroom spread with just a speck of sherry—quite wonderful," Diana said. Patrick took a sandwich.

Vail, dazed, reached for a mushroom butter sandwich.

"Too rich for you, Vail, dear," Diana said, taking the sandwich plate from Leonora and putting it at the far end of the table.

"But I like those—"

"Very good," Patrick said, finishing the tiny sandwich.

"Please, have another," Diana said. "Maria gets quite put out when there are leftovers."

But Patrick shook his head. The first one had a slightly bitter aftertaste.

Vail peered at a plate of square-cut, marinated tenderloin cubes. "Ginger seasoning?" he asked, carefully aiming a toothpick at one, and putting the sirloin in his mouth before his mother could stop him.

"Yes, dear, help yourself." Her voice was so warm that Vail looked up. His mother was making a gesture to Leonora who seemed worried.

Patrick nervously speared two tenderloin cubes from the plate, and wolfed one down.

"You'll like these little fritters more," Leonora said.

"A Peruvian appetizer," Diana said, "a specialty of our cook, quite highly seasoned." Patrick put another tenderloin cube in his mouth and took one of the Peruvian fritters.

Vail eyed the fried cylinders, knowing that Maria made nothing like them. He reached out for one. Leonora, sitting next to him, seized his thigh under the table. Her long-nailed fingers felt like talons; her bright blue eyes were staring at him. She said, "Have another tenderloin cube."

A horrible smothered sound came out of Patrick. He gripped the arms of his peacock chair, a look of amazement on his face, his mouth half open, his nostrils dilated. He started to cough. Leonora said quickly, "Pass me that cucumber sandwich, Vail," in the tone of voice she'd use if someone had made a rude sound. Vail passed the plate. Patrick kept on coughing, gripping the arms of his chair, trying to speak.

"Jesus," Vail said, rising. Leonora's claw clasped his wrist. Vail turned his head so he could see her. She was looking at Patrick with a puzzled alertness. Vail shook her off. "Is it caught in your throat—the meat?" Patrick nodded with difficulty, wheezing, trying to cough it out. "He's choking!"

Patrick was trying to rise, gagging, staring at Vail, begging, trying to regurgitate. Both women were frozen with surprise. Vail rose hurriedly, clumsily, knocking against the table to reach Patrick and to pound him on the back. He put both arms around the man's middle, but Patrick was tall and broad and overweight; Vail's arms barely joined at his belt buckle.

"Leave him!" Diana's voice was full of retribution. Patrick stared at her with horror. She darted out of her chair and slapped Vail, who drew back, shocked. An ugly urgent sound full of suppressed panic came out of Patrick. His face was turning red, his eyes bulging, the sounds of his gagging tormented.

"We can't—" Vail said.

"We can," Diana replied.

"He's choking to death!" Vail cried. Patrick fell across one corner of the table scattering dishes and food as he collapsed on the floor. Frantically, Vail knelt beside him, pulling at him. Patrick heaved desperately for air. "Sit up!" Vail commanded. "Sit up, damn you!" Vail gripped Patrick from behind again, trying to get his arms locked around his middle, trying to squeeze the deadly obstacle out of his throat. But convulsions gripped Patrick.

Diana was standing behind Vail. Leonora was at the end of the table, leaning tightly upon it, watching.

"This is true justice," Diana shouted at Patrick, her whole body trembling. "This is for Sky! She never harmed you; she helped you! She gave you money and jobs, and how did you repay her?"

Vail felt his spine shiver. Patrick's bulging eyes were terrorized; his face was mottled. His chest heaved like a bellows, and still the strangled, extreme sounds boiled out of him. Vail hung onto the flailing man, trying to press his diaphragm, but he knew Patrick was losing consciousness. His face was splotched; his tongue was protruding from his mouth, a vein bulging in his neck like a cord. The odor of his bowels climbed into the air.

It went on and on until Patrick's body shuddered horribly and went limp. Vail let him go. Leonora, who'd had a brief stint as a nurse in World War I, recovered first and took his pulse. Vail had to use the table as a support to get to his feet. He was drenched in sweat. He felt his chin trembling. He was going to cry. Diana was handing Leonora a mirror. Leonora held it to Patrick's contorted mouth. Diana hung onto the back of a chair as she wobbled away from Leonora and Patrick. She sat down heavily, a small, extremely old woman. The room reeked.

Vail stumbled into his mother's bathroom, found the taps, and pushed his face under a jet of cold water. When he returned, Diana and Leonora were sitting in their places at the ravaged table. Vail, dizzy, collapsed on the love seat.

No one spoke. Outside, a motorized lawn mower moved across a wide lawn. A loud blue jay complained. Leonora glanced at the fritters on the carpet and the overturned sandwich plates.

"You see, Diana," Leonora said in a husky voice, "we didn't have to go to all that trouble after all."

"What trouble?" Vail asked.

Leonora looked at Diana, who was staring out the window. Diana tried to speak and could not. "Our research for our little book," Leonora said, smiling narrowly.

"My god, you were going to poison him!"

Diana turned away from the window and looked at her son. "God decided differently," she said with a sigh.

"God?" Vail moaned. "We just let him die. I can't believe it."

"It's my burden," Diana said, "but I can carry it. That man murdered your sister."

"What if someone decided to do 'justice' to Lindy?" he demanded.

"It's not the same. Archie used Lindy—he destroyed her life, just took it away. But Sky helped Patrick."

"It doesn't give anyone the right to kill!" he bellowed at her.

She turned away. Her fingers crept up the front of her dress to her pearl necklace. "I don't care what you say. I don't even care what happens to me."

"Oh god," Vail moaned again. "And you've involved your friend."

"Vail," Leonora said, eyeing him carefully, "I was never convinced that the rat poison or the mushrooms would kill him. I thought they might make him very ill, and I confess I said hurrah to that." She folded her napkin. "Diana has some justice on her side. We all know how much Sky did for Patrick. He betrayed her so callously."

"Oh, Jesus," was all Vail could say. His own extreme emotions were overwhelming him.

"In the end," Leonora went on, "we didn't do anything. The Almighty did it." She rose stiffly and went over to her friend. "Diana, dear, perhaps we ought to take some of these sandwiches downstairs?"

"We ought to call an ambulance," Vail said. His head throbbed.

"We will, in a minute," Diana replied. "Stop ordering us around. We know what we're doing." Leonora was scooping fritters and sandwiches onto a serving plate, efficiently dividing the incriminating from the ordinary. Diana put the magnificent cake on a tray, took the plate from Leonora, and put that on the tray, too. Vail watched. Women are cold, he thought.

"I'll take it down," Leonora said. She tottered out of the room.

"Mother—"

"Just hush up."

"Now, listen here! We have to call them right now or they'll know you let him suffocate!"

"Well, I guess you're right, dear." Suddenly, Diana began to weep.

Vail picked up the telephone and dialed 911.

By early evening, the paramedics had come and gone. One of the police officers remained, making last notes. Diana sat on the living room sofa, weeping and recovering, then weeping again in a rhythm which, for a while, Vail thought was manufactured. But when Leonora called him over at one point, and he was close enough to see his mother's face, he realized that the domineering, remote, and noble Diana Wyman was nearly hysterical.

"Leonora, pour her a whiskey, for heaven's sake," he said, sitting down in the chair next to her.

The police officer hovered near the doorway. "I only have a couple of questions, Mr. Wyman," he said. "How did O'Mara get in?"

"Mr. O'Mara came here uninvited, begging for forgiveness," Leonora said, handing Diana the whiskey. "Diana and I were having luncheon but he wouldn't go away, maybe he was on drugs or whatever, perfectly disgusting."

"Mrs. Wyman?" the officer said to Diana.

She was sipping her whiskey. "He just insisted upon seeing me," Diana said. "I was afraid of him . . ."

"This was before we knew Vail was coming home early," Leonora continued. "We were alone here, so we thought the best thing to do was invite him in to luncheon, pretend that everything was ordinary, you know, not escalate the situation. Isn't that what we thought, Diana?"

Diana nodded. Vail peered at his mother; she was crying again. It shocked him. "My son," Diana murmured tearfully, "arrived from San Francisco and we were about to usher Mr. O'Mara out when he started to choke." Vail heard the seamless lie embedded in the truth and marveled at it. "My son was magnificent. We didn't know what to do. He hit him on the back—"

"I tried to do a Heimlich, but I couldn't get him off the floor," Vail said. "I called the paramedics, but he . . ."

The officer nodded gravely. "It's a clear accidental death. We'll let you know," he said, going to the door.

After he left, Leonora helped herself to a glass of sherry. Diana folded her handkerchief into a small neat square. Vail asked for a whiskey, which Leonora gave him.

"I must be off," Leonora said, gathering up her purse and hat. She patted Diana on the shoulder. "A very exciting afternoon, Diana. I'll telephone tomorrow." And she was gone.

"Mother," Vail said.

"I can't talk now, Vail dear," she murmured, rising. "I'm too distraught."

"We'll talk right now." Diana looked at him. "Sit down." Meekly, Diana sat down. "Patsy will be here in a minute—"

"You'll have to deal with her and with Eddie and everyone. I can't." Her shoulders were bent forward. She looked very old.

"Before Patsy gets here," he continued, "I want to know exactly what you thought you were doing."

"I can't imagine what you mean."

"Mother, I've been sitting here for the last two hours listening to you and Zip lie." He reached across and grabbed her wrist. Diana sat up straight and yanked her wrist back. "Did Patrick just appear at our door?"

"No, he did not. I asked him."

"You asked Patrick O'Mara."

"That's right," she snapped. "And I don't intend to be cross-examined by you."

"You don't have any choice," he said, feeling disturbed yet free at the same time. "I'm participating in, at best, a shaving of the truth to the police. I was in that room and I watched that pathetic man die on your carpet—"

"All right, Vail! I asked him here, and I doctored a few little cookies. He kept phoning and phoning; he was actually in Portland and chased Belinda down the street. I was afraid! I was sickened by him!" The sobs broke up her words. "He killed my child; he killed her for no reason at all. I didn't think he'd actually show up here, but when he did, I—I just went ahead with it. Oh!" she said, trembling, "this is so unnerving." She sank back suddenly, deflated. "But, you know, in the middle of our luncheon, I felt myself drawing back from my resolve. I found myself glad that he ate the ginger steak because that wouldn't hurt him."

Vail finished the last of his whiskey and put down his glass. He felt calm and strangely liberated. "Mother, this is your last interference," he said, wishing to nail down the lesson. "You must not deviate by one iota from the story you told the police today. Do you understand?"

"I don't care what happens to me."

"I'm not thinking of you! The world doesn't revolve around you! I'm thinking of Eddie and Patsy and the rest of us."

"Yes, Vail."

"You will not answer the telephone; you won't talk to reporters; you will clear everything through me from this moment on. When Patsy and Eddie want to discuss it, you will make sure I am there, or you will delay until I am there. Do you understand this?"

"Yes, Vail."

"Now, perhaps you should get some rest."

He helped her to rise. "I can do it," she said. He watched her walk slowly to the umbrella stand at the doorway, take his father's old ivory walking stick, and mount the stairs.

Vail sat down again and reached for his glass. But he couldn't find it. His hand crawled over the table surface. It had been right there a moment ago. "Damnit," he muttered.

Patsy came home a few minutes later. "My god, Vail honey, this is dreadful," she said, embracing him. "Where's Diana?"

"She's in the guest room. Her room's a mess. I can't find my glass. I want a drink." Patsy went to the cupboard and took out a fresh one. Vail gave her "the official story."

"But, it's so suspicious, you know, it being Patrick, of all people."

"I was there, Zip was there. That's what happened and when they open up his throat they'll find steak." He hoped they wouldn't do a full autopsy and find whatever else Diana and Leonora had served him. "Now you and I have to talk. Come upstairs."

Patsy was taking off her shoes. There was a new note in Vail's voice. He was in charge. "Sure," she said, holding her shoes.

Into their bedroom, a bright two-room suite at the back of the house, Vail walked over to the love seat and waved at it. "Sit down." She did that. He sat beside her so he could see her face.

"Vail, what's happened to you?"

"It's been quite an afternoon. I don't want to talk about it right now. I want to ask you a question."

"Yes, dear."

"Are you having an affair?"

"No. Vail, how can you possibly believe something like that?"

He watched her. He listened to her intonation. "I have felt this for some time. I didn't want to believe it, didn't want to face it, but today—everything's changed. Today, I want to know, I want you to be honest."

"I am being honest."

Vail listened and looked into her face. "I haven't been much of a man sometimes, particularly recently. I've felt like a failure. I've hesitated and delayed when I shouldn't have." Patsy reached out for his hand. "I've felt sorry for myself, and I've let my mother run rings around me all my life." Patsy squeezed his hand. "And now I'm virtually blind. I'm a weight on you."

"Never," she whispered.

"I want you to know you don't have to stay with me. In fact, I don't want you here if it's pity or—"

She threw her arms around him. "Oh, Vail, I don't want to live without you. I loved you the moment I saw you. If it hadn't been for you I wouldn't be doing what I love. You encouraged me. You always supported me; you taught me to set my sights high and go after what I wanted. You're stuck with me. I'm not leaving, no matter how much you beg me."

He held onto her tightly, no hesitation now. "I was so afraid of losing you. I know I'm foolish and erratic—"

"And emotional and opinionated—"

"Yes."

They collided again but this time it was in bed. They knew every curve and indent, every fault and fissure of their bodies but never had they made love so openly and humanly. And later, they sat together in the wide, disarranged bed, sipping champagne in their bathrobes, their hair messed up, clothes scattered all over the room, never out of touching distance from each other.

"I feel like I'm home again," she said, nesting her head on his shoulder. "I know you do, too." She lifted her head, stared into his sharp face. "What's different about you tonight," she asked, smoothing down his hair, "besides happiness, that is?" There was a forceful, solid quality in him again.

"Dunno," he replied. But he felt changed. "We have to talk to Eddie," he said.

"He's in San Francisco with Cynthia."

"Oh, I forgot. That damned yacht party seems like a year ago. As soon as he gets back then. Everything out on the table."

"Yes, Vail."

He threw back his head. "I'm afraid of losing him."

She put her arms around her husband. "Eddie's going to be hurt but he'll blame me more than you," Patsy said.

"No, he won't."

"Yes, he will, and he'll be right because I blame myself," Patsy said. Then she moaned, "God, I don't want him hurt. I love him so."

Vail held her fiercely.

Guy Venner and Cynthia were eating dinner together in the family dining room, a comfortable, pea green, chintzy area off the family sitting room.

"Let's take our time," Guy said, "this doesn't happen often, having dinner at home with you."

"Yes. I have a lot to say," Cynthia stated.

"You do?" Venner's eyebrows went up. "Well, shall we wait till we're served?"

She put her hands in her lap. One of the servants handed

a platter of fish around, followed by bowls of vegetables and wild rice. When everyone had cleared out and they were alone, Venner said, "Shoot. What's up?"

"I want to stay in the States, Dad. I want to study journalism at Stanford."

Venner had just sunk a fork into his orange roughly. "Don't quit in the middle of what you're already doing, Cynthia. I'll make a deal with you—finish up your last year in France, then Stanford."

She shook her head. She was going to be difficult. "I want to do it now."

"What difference does one year make?" he said, his irritation showing.

What she was about to say to her father, she had never said before. It made her uneasy. "Daddy, I just can't live so far away from home again."

"Why, you've traveled all your—"

"I'm in love with Eddie Wyman," she said with the speed of a fast car going by.

"Honey, you don't know what love is!" The instant it was out, he was sorry. It was the wrong approach. She was already rising to dispute it. "I didn't mean that," he said quickly. "I don't want you to rush into anything. You don't know him. He's going away to college, too—"

"He's going to college up here, Dad." Her mouth was set.

Guy knew he would win no battles with her this night, but that he might win over time by strategy and affection. "Just let me absorb all this news," he said. "I've got to go up to Seattle and then back here," he said, deciding at that instant to change his plans. "We'll talk about it fully when I get back, how's that?"

"I won't change, Daddy."

"Okay, but right now, let's just have dinner and chat." He brushed her with his best smile and took a big taste of his wine. Eddie would not do.

The letter lying faceup on the table was so distressing that Sara had had difficulty breathing when she read it for the first time. She'd called the investigating service immediately. "Ms. Wyman," her contact there said, reporting in the next day. "I've spoken at length to the messenger service who delivered that latest letter to you. They were instructed to deliver it on a certain day, cash was enclosed with the instructions. They know nothing of the sender. Our people are analyzing the paper again—"

"Why can't you do anything?" Sara wailed.

It was another dead end. Sara felt worn out.

How did the writer know of her childhood with Sky? Only someone in the family, or very close to it, could have known anything of that time. Sara felt again her fierce, sad, helpless envy of Sky that had eaten up years of her life. How could the author of these letters know of it? Sara paced her kitchen, sat down, paced again. She was overlooking something vital, something she'd known and had forgotten.

The teakettle was whistling. She went into the kitchen. Who, but Lindy, would know these things? She turned the screeching kettle off. Archie would have known because Sky had told him everything. Victor? No. Maybe someone connected to Lindy—but who? Only Belinda. Extremely upset, Sara made the tea. She found herself thinking about Lindy's hearing in San Francisco. It had been held around this time of year, the summer. Whenever she'd stepped out of the lawyers' offices or the courtroom or the jail, an airy, salty, summer breeze from the bay had reminded her that, even though she'd felt her own life ending, life in its fullness had been all around her.

Something nagged at her and she couldn't bring it back. Something she'd heard or read around that time. Something about Lindy. Sara turned, went to the basement door off the kitchen, and went downstairs. A line of packing boxes at the end of the basement faced her. One of them contained all the papers from Belinda's hearing.

The first sockeye salmon of the season—some of them bright red, some already battered—were leaping out of the churning water into the falls, flailing up against gravity and current on their last obstacle course. Those who made it over ran a gamut of fishers and nets, birds and bears. Of those that lived, all would find the stream they'd been spawned in years before.

"Look at those suckers go!" Fletcher Avery proclaimed to Belinda. He and the documentary crew had arrived that morning, and they now stood around the edge of Belinda's shoot.

Belinda smiled at him as the documentary video operator circled them. Fletcher was wearing a visor cap and a windbreaker that said he was A DGA MEMBER FROM HELL. His dark eyes snapped; he put a big arm around her and declared, "God, back on location again with Belinda! Is this heaven or what?"

"Would you step back, pal," Belinda said, "I got a show to run here." Fletcher roared with laughter and kissed her wetly. The video camera hummed and recorded it forever.

She was filming the demonstration scene. Thirty extras carrying placards about animal rights were standing in front of a medical research center in a parkland outside the center of town. Three cameras had been set up to cover the action.

"Tell me you're going to come to Berlin," Fletcher said. "Tell me you've read the script and you love it and you want to change your life."

"No, no, and no. Extras!" she yelled. "Over there!" Her AD sprang into action, herding them like sheep.

Fletcher groaned. "Don't say no. Say yes."

Belinda stopped moving. "Fletch, would you please move your video group back?" She turned to the crowd. "We need lots of noise from you demonstrators," she shouted.

"You got a big hole in your crowd over there," Fletcher mumbled. "And there's gonna be a big shadow—"

"Fletcher, just let me work here, okay?" She'd kicked her addiction to him, and in its wake had come a kind of irritated fellowship. They had spent the day joking around, and she'd enjoyed him.

"I'm gonna cling to you like a leech until you say yes," he said. "How much of this crap you got left to shoot?"

"Five days."

Belinda's AD came panting up to them. "Guy Venner's here! He wants to see you."

"Can't now. After the shot. Just tell him."

"Lordy," Fletcher said, mocking a moan, "what's the main man doing up here?"

"He's ticked off that I wouldn't go to a party on his yacht."

"Nah, he wouldn't come up here for that. He'd wait in his lair until you walked past and then spring on you."

Belinda was peering at the video monitor. "Outta my way, Fletch."

"Ooooo, yes, ma'am," he said.

"Okay, everyone, this is a take!"

The demonstrators, led by "Phyllis," surged forward to their mark on a grassy slope. The AD yelled: "Sheriff's deputies!" Cars, loaded with deputies, careened around the corner and pulled into a U-shaped parking lot. They leaped out. The demonstrators turned, and "Phyllis" shouted: "Hold your ground, animal lovers!" One deputy started yelling over his bullhorn, adding to the confusion. The other deputies mowed into the demonstrators. "Phyllis" went down. Demonstrators and deputies swirled around her. Belinda yelled, "Cut! That was good!" Belinda and her cameraman looked at the video monitor, checking the coverage, debating the footage. Out of the corner of her eye she saw Keith arriving.

The AD said to her, "Venner's got that cold look in his eye."

"Okay, where is he?" The AD jerked his thumb toward a limousine sitting well back of the action beneath a huge spruce tree.

Fletcher took her arm. "Don't leave the battlefield," he said kindly.

She disengaged. "Thanks for the advice, Fletch, but I know what I'm doing. Keith!" She waved at him. "Keep Fletcher out of trouble."

She walked toward the limousine under the trees. They were all here—Fletcher and Guy and Keith. A month ago, she wouldn't have counted Fletcher as a friend, but he was. That felt good. She remembered eating satay with him in Malaysia. She remembered the burning addiction to him and her terrible surprise that she could feel again. The limo ahead of her looked like a big silver fish. Was the man inside a friend, too?

"I didn't expect you today," Belinda said as Guy opened the rear door of the limousine for her. She climbed inside. "We're losing our light, only got a minute."

"I didn't expect to be here either," he said warmly, "but something came up." He pressed a button that rolled up the glass separation between the backseat and the driver. "Would you like some coffee? Or perhaps some wine? I have a very nice Sauvignon Blanc here."

"I haven't got time, Guy, the light's going." She looked out the window: her AD was talking to "Chicky," her camera crew was checking the gear, the extras were milling about.

"This won't take long," Guy said. His deep rich voice was confident, confiding. He had no doubt that she'd do what he wanted. He'd arranged to produce the film, he'd made her a director, and she was sleeping with him. "Cynthia and I had a talk yesterday. She wants to stay in the States."

"That's not news," Belinda said, still looking out the window at her crew.

"No, but the reason she wants to stay now is Eddie."

"Eddie?"

"She says that she loves him and that he loves her." He sighed. "They're so young," he said in a contented, condescending tone. "I feel deeply responsible for my daughter, and I can't just sit by, like some parents, I know you understand." He checked his watch. "I've got to fly back to San Francisco today but I wanted to discuss this with you in person. Please look at me when I'm talking." She turned to him. "Eddie's a nice boy, of course, but this isn't the right thing for Cynthia right now. I'm sending her back to France, as planned, and I want you to speak to Eddie, get him to call this off, whatever it is. You'll do that, won't you." It wasn't a question.

"You want me to tell Eddie to forget about Cynthia?" Guy nodded, smiling. "I can't do that, Guy. It isn't any of my business, and why would he listen to anyone if—if they're in love? Is that what she said—in love?"

"It doesn't matter what she said," he replied, irritated. He felt for his watch under his cuff. "The important thing is that you get it across to Eddie that he's in a no-win situation."

Belinda was still thinking of her shots. It was with a jolt that she realized she was in a crucial confrontation. "Guy, I can't talk to Eddie, I'm not a figure of authority with him, and even if I were, I wouldn't interfere. I didn't know they were in love." She was still adjusting to that news.

"Oh, they're not in love. It's a crush, temporary, a mistake." Guy Venner's bright sharp eyes had lost their sense of fun.

"How do you know they're not in love? Your daughter says they are."

"She isn't ready for love, she's a child." Guy was flushing, his back was very straight, his mouth tight.

"She has feelings, Guy. Eddie's a responsive, warm person. Why don't we all relax? Let her stay a year here, let the

relationship run its course. Maybe it's serious, maybe not."
She glanced out the window at a gaffer laying cable. She had
completely misjudged the depth of Guy's resentment.

"*Look* at me," he said.

She faced him. His cheeks were red, his eyebrows drawn
together. His mouth had flattened; the two handsome lines
around it that moved whenever he spoke, stilled.

"He isn't good enough to be serious about Cynthia."

Belinda opened her eyes wide. "What did you say?"

"You know what I mean," he said, but he seemed to have
difficulty speaking. The words came out haltingly. "He'll listen
to you. He just has to duck out of it gracefully. I don't want her
hurt. They'll forget all about it when she's in France."

"I won't do that," she said. She was shocked. "Did you think
I would do that?"

Guy uncrossed his legs, leaned forward, and took her hand.
"You and I," he said, breathily, "we have certain understand-
ings. You do this and I won't be ungrateful. But I think you
owe this to me."

"I don't owe you. Guy, don't ask this. If you want to send
her back to France, fine, but don't ask me to meddle in Eddie's
affairs."

He was thunderstruck. "I'm—dis-a-ppointed," he said, bro-
kenly. He had seen her in his life, a full partner. But now,
she was being childish, an amateur; she wasn't behaving like
a partner. "I expected much better from you," he said. "You're
not behaving like the woman I thought you were." He stopped,
his mouth curved, lips parted. "Belinda, just do it!" The hon-
eyed tone of his voice vanished. It was an order.

"It's out of the question!"

He stared at her, an accusation. "I was wrong about you,"
he said.

Belinda tried to shore up the disrepair. "Guy, this isn't a
life and death situation. What if they spend their college
years together, then get married, and raise beautiful children?
Forcing them apart usually doesn't work. I'm sure you've seen
those situations."

Urgently, soothingly, she spoke on but images were forming
in Guy Venner's imagination, images he'd tried and failed to
erase, images of Eddie's stump around his daughter's waist,
in her hair, against her cheek, and they revolted him. He'd

always seen himself as open-minded, liberal, generous, tolerant of deep differences, departures from the norm which, he'd believed, made life complex and rich. But this thing with Eddie, it was his flaw, he couldn't get past it, it made him less.

He was holding his breath. He didn't want to say anything, he knew he shouldn't. He couldn't stop himself.

"I won't have my daughter connected to a cripple!"

"A *cripple*? How dare you call him that?" she cried, astounded to hear such a thing from him. She looked into his face. It was as if a chrysalis had split apart, and another Guy Venner had emerged.

He grabbed her arms. "Now you help me, you owe me, you stop this stupid affair, or I'll stop it. I'll tell Cynthia and Eddie just what kind of a past he has." Guy's face was very close to hers and his hands gripping her arms hurt. "I'll tell Eddie who his father was and what happened to him."

She wrenched away from him and pressed back against the door. "I can't believe this," she whispered, appalled. "I thought you didn't care about anyone's past."

"This is different! This is Cynthia!" He felt out of control. It was releasing and terrifying. He fought against it but the waves of emotion and his own repulsion for what he was feeling, what he was doing, swept him.

"Eddie's not good enough because of his hand and because of what I did? This makes me sick!" She tried to open the door but it was locked. "Let me out." Her AD was standing only thirty feet from the car, reading the call sheet for tomorrow. "Let me out of here!"

Guy physically yanked her back from the door. "You help me on this," he said in a menacing voice, "or I'll shut down the film."

"What? Oh, Guy, you can't mean it."

"Test me." In the fury of a man who always got his own way, who'd always believed he'd earned the right to have his own way, he said again, his voice dead, "Test me."

"Then, goddamnit, shut it down!" she yelled, alarmed. "I can't stop you! If that's how you feel, I quit!"

Guy sucked in his breath and rocked back against the seat. "Don't be stupid, be smart, change your mind." His eyes raked her, but he felt drunk on the passionate certainty that she wouldn't change her mind, and in that instant he hated her, hated himself for allowing this to happen, hated Eddie. But he couldn't stop. He rode the crest of his power and his self-loathing.

"I am smart and I intend to be able to live with myself," she shouted, pressing buttons on the door of the car, but the control was on his side. Suddenly, she stopped. "I can't believe you'd shut down this production. What's wrong with you?" She was panting. "Can't we just call a truce and talk this over later?"

"You talk to Eddie. You get this affair stopped."

"Okay, I will."

He leaned back tensely. He was sweating. "Nice try."

"What?"

"You'll hold me off for four days, finish your shoot. You won't talk to him. You're lying."

"Test me."

He couldn't retreat from the high of pulling all the supports out from under her, of punishing her, punishing Eddie for what he'd seen in himself. Another, more intimate image of Eddie with Cynthia rose up in his mind. Air expelled from his mouth. "Keith was wrong about you."

"What?"

"He wouldn't give me the script unless you directed," he spat.

He pressed a button. Her door opened. "Shoot's over," he said, coldly. "Shut down." His heart was pounding. She hesitated, opened her mouth to say something, closed it. She stepped out of the car into the cool air. He rapped his fist on the divider in the limousine; the driver immediately started the big engine. Guy slammed the door; the car rolled away. He did not look back.

"Belinda," her AD called out, waving the call sheets. "We've found a real fuckup here."

"Later," she said, walking in the opposite direction.

"We're ready to shoot," he called out.

"You do it."

"*Me?*"

"Yes." She was walking through damp grass. She couldn't believe she'd just quit. She'd also been shut down. He'd shut her down *and* she'd quit. It was devastating. Would he tell Eddie? Yes, she knew he would, but not right away; he'd

calm down and wait to see if she changed her mind, to see if
he believed her changing her mind. God, what was wrong with
him? She hadn't loved Venner, but she'd liked him, respected
him. I have to get to Eddie, she thought. And what was all
this about Keith and the script? She strode along the grassy
path, away from the dozens of people waiting for the last shot
of the day. Sara had been right about giving the Venners a
wide berth.

She stopped walking. She didn't feel crushed and dried out.
She could survive this. It was Eddie that mattered. She'd just
chucked the film for him. Crippled—what a crock. She realized that she'd do almost anything for Eddie and it shocked
her. Would she give up her career for him? She didn't know. If
it would save his life? Yes, unquestionably. For the first time,
she wanted Eddie to know who she was. He was old enough
to know. She was big enough to tell him. And she had to tell
him, not Patsy and Vail. That, too, shocked her.

"Belinda!" Yvonne was running toward her. "Where are you
going? Do you want Fletcher directing this movie?"

Belinda put her arm around her friend's shoulder and started
walking back to the setup. "No, I don't want Fletcher directing it," she said, feeling light-headed. "C'mon, let's do the
last shot."

"What the hell's happening?"

"Get everyone together, I'm about to make a speech."

Belinda looked at her cast and crew assembled on the grassy
strip beside the trailers and equipment trucks.

"So many of you are my good friends," she said. Keith was
leaning against a trailer, his T-shirt announcing in big letters
that he was for the dolphins and against tuna salads. Yvonne
and Buttons were sitting on a bench. Fletcher was lying on
the grass. "And so many new friends," she said, glancing at
"Chicky" and "Phyllis" and "Nell."

"You're all terrific to work with, and you sure made things
easy for me, the first time out of the box." She hesitated.
Everyone looked worried. "We've been shut down." A groan.
"We're not behind schedule. We're not over budget either. It's
against all contractual agreements. But Mr. Venner has refused
to cover the expenses after today . . ."

"When the money people say they won't pay any more,

that's curtains," a gaffer summed up.

"I'm going back to L.A. and see if we can't work something out. So I want you all to take the days that are left and stay here. Maybe," she said, looking at Keith, "we can put it back together. I know you've got commitments. I'm just asking that you don't leave before you'd planned to."

She went to Keith. "You and I—talk."

"What's going on?" he asked.

They marched away from the crowd of extras and crew. "Venner just told me something interesting," she said, "before he shut me down. Actually, I quit. He said you'd refused to give him the script unless I directed."

Keith propped his hands on his waist. "Yeah? So?"

She felt like telling him off. But he was grinning.

"So, thanks," she said.

"You're welcome." He leaned toward her conspiratorially. "Venner's real pissed, right?"

"Right."

"Can you save it?"

"Price is too high, I think. I'll get Patsy on it. I have to get back to Los Angeles real fast. Can you come, too? I don't want to go down there alone."

CHAPTER 23

Cynthia hit the accelerator.

"I love it when you drive fast," Eddie said as they roared through a freeway interchange on the approach to San Francisco. "But don't get us killed. We have to make a plane."

Orange and purple streaked the sunset sky. They'd broken every speed limit from Carmel north on the 101 freeway. They were young; nothing bad would ever happen.

"Why don't you want me to come with you?" he asked.

"I only want to pick up an overnight bag, Eddie."

"Yeah, try another."

She laughed, and squeezed his thigh. "Dad'll be back tonight. I want to tell him I'll be with you in L.A. for a couple of days. It's better if I do that alone."

"I should be there."

"If you're there, we'll have to get into all of it—you, me, the future, all of it. I don't want to have that talk tonight. I'll meet you at the airport."

"You're putting it off."

"Yes."

"Why?"

She pursed her lips and tossed her head. "Dad's—difficult sometimes. The whole business about me staying here instead of going back to France—I have to really talk it out with him."

"That's not it. It's me. I'm what's difficult."

"No," she said, turning toward him. "You're easy." She squeezed his leg again and accelerated.

Vail broke the cup in half as the doorbell rang. "Goddamnit!" he cried, trying to see where the pieces had landed on the kitchen floor. Sara scooped up the two halves; Patsy went to answer the door.

"Belinda!" she said, startled. "What are you doing here? Did you finish shooting?"

"I've been shut down." Her dark hair was in streamers, some of it pulled back, some loose against her cheek. There were dark circles under her eyes; she looked impatient, exhausted, and ready for combat.

Patsy led the way into the kitchen, firing questions at Belinda, making statements—energetic, advisory, astonished.

Vail was still sitting at the marble table, trying to glue the two parts of the cup back together. Sara sat nearby, smoking a cigarette and drinking a sherry.

"Guy's shut down the production?" Sara asked. "Why?"

"Because of Eddie. Because of me. Vail, we have to talk to Eddie now."

"Hey, wait a minute," Vail said. "You don't just walk in here and make demands like that!"

"Eddie's in San Francisco," Patsy said, more conciliatory. "He just called. He and Cynthia will be here later tonight. Now, what is all this about?"

Belinda sat down. "Guy knows everything."

"What?" Patsy said, shocked. "I can't believe you'd tell him—"

"I didn't. It was someone else," Belinda said, impatiently. She felt hot and loosened her jacket. "There was a girl . . ." She saw Francine backlit against the windows in Guy's hotel room, standing there, erect and on display, a forewarning. Since then, the days were a jumble. "First it was the press," Belinda said, "then it was Francine . . . and now Guy. It's just all coming apart."

Vail was scrutinizing her, his eyes narrowed, his head tilted at an angle.

Sara said, "Francine?"

Belinda sighed. "I knew her once, a long time ago. I didn't tell Guy; Francine did."

"Who the hell is she?" Vail demanded.

"She's Archie's daughter. . . ."

Sara put out her cigarette. Her shrewd face was quite still. "Ah," she said. "She knew you as Lindy Wyman."

"Yes. She knew me with Archie."

"But how?" Vail asked, baffled.

"Vail," Patsy said, "she works for Guy. We met her at the yacht party."

"She found out who I was and she told Guy—in front of me. *That*'s how Guy knows everything. Actually, at the time, Guy didn't care very much about it, until he learned from Cynthia how important Eddie was to her. Today he demanded that I—cut off their affair, if they're having one. I refused." She thought about Guy in the limousine. "He lost his sense of decency. He went out of control. He said if I didn't do as he asked, he'd tell Eddie everything. He knows Eddie's my son."

"Those damned Venners!" Vail shouted.

"Vail, Guy won't do anything rash," Belinda said. "I know Guy. At least, I think I do. So we have some time if Cynthia and Eddie are on their way down here. But we'll have to tell him."

Patsy leaned back in her chair, a look of interest and care on her face which usually signaled analysis.

Sara glanced at Vail's clumsy efforts with the cup. She was thinking of Lindy's confession and of the hearing's transcripts that she'd pulled out of the cellar storage boxes and had read late into the night. "Was this Francine there—that night? The night Archie died?"

But Belinda was distracted. "I don't remember," she said, absently. "I don't know."

"Sara!" Vail said, swinging his head from one side to the other. "We have to talk about Eddie."

Sara sat back. "All right, Vail," she said.

Patsy, who'd been thinking about Eddie, looked up, alerted by Sara's surrender. It wasn't like Sara.

Vail turned to face Belinda so he could see her. "Lindy, a lot's happened here since you went on location. Some things changed."

"We were going to tell Eddie ourselves in the next few days," Patsy said, carefully, "when he got back."

"What happened?"

"I came to my senses," Vail said. "It took an escapade of your grandmother's to do it."

"The Patrick business?" Lindy asked, looking at Patsy.

"I told her," Patsy said to Vail.

"That was just part of it," he said, exasperated, wrestling with the antique cup and the glue. "I've been helping you avoid this moment for years, Lindy. But no more."

"Were you going to tell *me* about all these changes?" Belinda demanded.

"Of course," Patsy said.

"And was I going to be in on this scene or was Eddie just going to show up at my shoot after you told him?"

"We hadn't worked it out," Patsy said. "We never expected you to be here, Lindy."

"But you suddenly arrive," Vail cried, "full of yourself, ready to make big announcements—I don't want all of us jumping on Eddie!"

Diana, in a pale blue dressing gown, came into the kitchen. "Oh, Belinda, dear, you're home safe and sound." She gave her granddaughter a pat on the shoulder as she went to the refrigerator. "I thought you were all going to dinner at Schurl's," she said to Vail.

"We are," Vail mumbled. "What do you want, Mom?"

"A glass of milk, dear."

"We could bring it to you," Patsy said.

"I'm not in the final stages of a crippling illness," Diana said, sharply.

"Grandma, I heard—about Patrick," Belinda said. "What was he doing here?"

"He wanted to see me just as he wanted to see you. All he talked about was forgiveness," she added tartly, glancing at Vail. "Of course I forgave him. You can't live your whole life condemning someone."

"People do," Belinda said.

"I don't want to talk about that terrible day anymore," Diana said hastily. "I'm not sorry he's dead, and I was afraid for you, dear." Diana gave Belinda a tiny dry kiss on the cheek and glided slowly out of the room.

Vail put the broken cup down dramatically. "I can't do this."

Sara took it from him. He'd smeared glue haphazardly around the broken edges.

"She seems subdued," Belinda said, watching Sara clamp

the two pieces of the cup together and hold them tightly.

"Mother's had a lot of excitement," Vail said, rising.

Belinda watched her uncle move toward the sink. He seemed taller and there was something in his manner that had altered.

"I'd like to stay here until Eddie gets home," Belinda said.

"No, you're not," Vail snapped. "You'll go to your own apartment and come back tomorrow. I won't have you lying in wait for him like a hunter in a blind!"

"I'm not doing that!"

"Both of you, calm down," Patsy said, physically putting herself into the space between them.

Vail could see only Belinda's face and shoulders, but in his mind, he saw all of her hurtling off the roof of a building. He didn't believe it anymore; it was a child of his anxiety. He stared into the circle of Belinda's face. He wished he'd known her better because, paradoxically, he had the feeling he'd have liked her more.

"Sorry, Lindy," Vail said. "I'm on edge."

Belinda nodded. "Me, too."

"But I won't give an inch on this. I won't have Eddie ambushed."

"I never meant to do that."

"Of course you didn't," Patsy said. She sat down next to Belinda. "This is in our hands. We're Eddie's parents and we will do this the way we think is best."

Belinda sighed. She felt Sara's eyes on her, too. "Yes."

Vail was carefully smoothing his jacket. "Too bad about your film," he said to Belinda.

"She might finish it yet," Patsy interjected. "We won't give up without a fight. Why don't you come with us to Schurl's, Lindy?"

"No, I think I'll just go back to my apartment, air it out. I'll see you tomorrow." Keith had said he was going home; she wondered if she could find him there. She felt suspended—in a space where nothing, and everything, mattered.

Sara put the cup down. It held. She was still thinking about all that she'd read, about the new presence of Francine, about the letters which had stopped coming.

"C'mon," Vail said to Patsy and Sara, "let's go. I don't want to be late and throw his timing off. Schurl makes a very mean *timballo di maccheroncelli alla ricca.*"

"That's pasta pie to the rest of us," Patsy said.

When Cynthia arrived home after dropping Eddie at the airport, she'd found Francine dropping a fat manila envelope in the mail slot. "It's for Guy," she explained. "He'll need it for Tokyo tomorrow."

"Come on in," Cynthia said, taking in Francine's usual immaculate and expensive outfit. The dress had a huge snowy-white yolk collar and cuffs. "So, Dad is getting in tonight?"

"Yes. You look wonderful, Cynthia," Francine said as they entered the huge foyer.

"It's because of Eddie," Cynthia said simply. "Fix yourself a drink, Fran. I have to throw a few things in a bag." She ran upstairs.

A half hour later, Cynthia was standing in front of the hall mirror, putting on her coat. Francine was behind her, holding a martini which Cynthia judged, from experience, was full of straight vodka. Guy, who'd just arrived from Oregon, was standing in the front doorway.

"Dad," Cynthia was saying firmly, "I'm just going to L.A. for a couple of days. You'll be in Tokyo. No big deal. Francine, tell him it's okay to let me out of the cell block for an hour," Cynthia said, winking at her in the mirror.

Guy saw Francine open her mouth to answer, and he slammed the front door. Both women started.

"You're not going to Los Angeles," he said in a low, deep voice. The wave of violent, uncontrollable emotion had crested on his way back from Portland. Now, he was in the ebb tide. He felt stubborn and alone and committed. "You're on your way back to France. It's all arranged."

Cynthia, astounded, stared at her father's reflection in the mirror. Behind him, even Francine looked surprised.

"Don't be silly, Dad."

Guy walked up to her, put a hand on her shoulder, and turned her around. "This isn't a joke. I am a responsible parent. I'm not going to let you get carried away."

"Dad, cut it out. I'm just going to the airport. He's waiting for me."

"You know what I mean, Cynthia. Don't argue." He searched

his daughter's sharp, keen face, her bright, auburn hair. She didn't remind him of his wife, and for that he was grateful. "I only want what's best for you, dear. I know this is hard." I haven't faced her marriage, he suddenly thought, haven't seen life without my responsibilities for her. I've built something around her and it's collapsing.

But he was still flailing, trying to stave off collapse. "You've got your whole life ahead of you. You're not really in love," he said.

"I am!" she shot back. "I'm sleeping with him. We're lovers. I'm not casual about that!"

Guy struck his daughter so fast, and for the first time, that she reeled backwards more from shock than from pain. Her hip hit the table in front of the mirror; she staggered, caught herself.

"Guy—!" Francine cried.

"Go upstairs and pack for France," he said. Guy heard the words coming out of him but he didn't feel his mind form them.

"I won't," Cynthia said, holding a hand against her cheek. "You can't make me."

Guy seized her arm and started her up the stairs. Francine, upset, stood at the bottom, watching.

"You'll do what I say," Guy said, hustling her up the stairs.

Cynthia, never one to hold back, began yelling. "I won't! I'm not one of your employees! You won't break me down! Let go of me!"

Francine ran up the stairs after them.

Guy was shouting, overriding Cynthia's cries. "There's insanity in Eddie's family. You don't know what you're involved in!"

"What are you talking about," she yelled. "He's adopted! Daddy, you're crazy!"

But he shoved his daughter into her room.

"Guy . . ." Francine said from the doorway.

He ignored her. He seized his daughter's telephone and ripped the plug out of the wall. "Pack!" The wave was humming in his ears. Carrying the telephone, he slammed the door and pounded down the stairs. Francine followed him.

The house was quiet. Guy tossed the telephone on the sofa in the sitting room and made himself a drink at the bar. "You want one?" he asked Francine. She was sitting on a chair like a Victorian lady, stiffly, legs together, hands folded.

"No," she said, eyeing him. Only once before had she seen Guy behave crudely and emotionally. It had not won him anything then, either.

He ran his fingers through his hair and straightened his cuffs. "Oh, hell," he said, sitting down heavily, forgetting his drink.

"You can't control everyone," Francine said, loftily.

He looked at her angrily. He disliked the supercilious side of her. "I'll apologize," he said. "But I'm doing her a favor. Goddamnit, why can't she see sense? She's too young to make these big decisions. I don't want to hurt her. I don't even want to hurt that Eddie."

"You just want him away from her."

"That's right."

"What did you mean there was insanity in Eddie's family, Guy?"

He glanced at her sharply. "He's Belinda Oliver's kid," Guy said, roughly. "Sorry, Fran, that's the way it is. He's Archie's son."

A long moment went by. "Archie was never insane."

"No, but maybe Belinda was, for a minute." He sighed, feeling his acute disappointment in Belinda, in himself, in the man he'd never faced. But at least, he thought, he had the capacity to feel. It seemed cold. He felt divided from life as he'd known it. He'd regressed, seismically, to a creature that couldn't stand upright. But even feeling small and retrograde, crab-like, he knew he wouldn't back down.

"Go up and say you're sorry," Francine intoned.

"Not now."

"Then I'll see what she needs," she said, prissy and smooth.

Guy Venner lifted his jaw. "Just once," he said, "I'd like to see you sit in a chair like a slut."

Eddie was looking all over the crowded departure area for Cynthia. His life would end if he missed her. Hadn't they agreed to meet at the gate? He combed back through their conversation, examining each sentence he could remember. He was sure they'd said the gate. Then they were going to the coffee shop and spend the hour there before his flight.

"Eddie."

He whirled around. But it wasn't Cynthia. "Oh, hi," he said. He couldn't remember the woman's name.

"Francine. Sorry to startle you. We met on the yacht."

She looked like a picture, that was the first thing that struck him. Not a hair was out of place—it was all drawn back in some kind of knot behind her head—the wide white collar and cuffs of her suit were snowy, her skirt didn't look wrinkled, and her eye makeup was perfect. How much he would have preferred Cynthia with her expensively sloppy clothes.

"Cynthia can't make it. She sent me especially to tell you. There's been a misunderstanding at home." One of the attendants was announcing a flight. "Is that yours?"

"No, I don't leave for an hour."

They walked down the corridor to the coffee shop. Francine ordered tea. "It's better for you than coffee." Eddie had a Pepsi. They sat down at a table the size of a napkin.

"Is she all right?"

"Oh, yes," Francine said carefully. She sipped her hot tea looking at him over the rim of her cup. She could see traces of her father's blond curly hair and broad pleasant face in the boy sitting across from her. "I'd like to be your friend," she said.

Something about that made Eddie uncomfortable. "Sure," he said, looking away.

"No, I mean it. Cynthia asked me to come and tell you she wouldn't be here."

"What's happening?" he said. "Why couldn't she be here?"

"Her father's sending her back to France. Guy doesn't approve of you."

"Nothing special about me," he mumbled. "Guess *that's* what's wrong with me, isn't it?"

"Oh, there's a lot special about you," Francine said.

"It's my hand, isn't it?" Eddie suddenly demanded, not liking the woman, disappointed about Cynthia, and angry at the man he had not yet faced.

"Your hand?" she asked, startled.

"Yes, this! *This!*" He brought his handless wrist up from beneath the table. "I'm clever about hiding it. You have to be with me a while before I let you notice it."

Francine was dumbfounded. He was deformed. And to her, in that moment, he was the physical representation of what the pairing of Lindy and Archie had really meant—a distorted, disfigured union.

She was holding her cup. A wave of tea slopped over the rim. She put the cup down hurriedly and started rubbing her hand, rubbing out the tea. A spot had landed on her wide white cuff. She scoured it. It would never come out. He's missing a hand, she kept thinking. He's not whole. Guy's right. It's an ugly relationship. Guy must get Cynthia away.

"It's your family," she said abruptly. "I didn't know you were, ah, like that"—she gestured distastefully—"but it proves where you came from. That's why you're deformed."

The words hit him like a punch. "Who asked you?" he demanded. "And my family's great." He grabbed his bag and got to his feet.

"You look like your father."

That stopped him. Eddie sat down.

She hadn't planned to do it but once started she couldn't stop. "You don't know who your father is, do you?" He stared at her. "His name was Arch Moberly. He used to live in this very city." Eddie was riveted and he could feel himself breathing fast. Francine Cheney was pressed against the table rim, leaning toward him. "He was my father, too. Know what that makes you? My half brother. Want to know who your mother was?" The shock on his face was intensely gratifying. "Belinda Oliver! She wasn't called that then," she said, thrilled by his openmouthed dismay. "She was called Lindy Wyman. She's Sara's daughter. Want to know where you were born? In a county jail. Know why? Because your mother, Lindy, murdered your father—and mine. She shot him and they sent her to prison." She sat back, out of breath. "It's quite a story, isn't it? You can see why Guy won't let Cynthia see you again."

Eddie finally found his voice. "You're crazy. None of that's true."

Francine smirked, took up one of her kid gloves and started pressing her fingers into it. "It's true. You just trot back to your family and ask them." She picked up her other glove and her purse and rose. "By the way, give Cynthia up. Once she hears this, she won't want you either."

CHAPTER 24

Eddie sat on the plane, feeling cold and dry. When it landed in Los Angeles, he was barely aware of getting off or of meeting his father's driver who'd come to pick him up.

"Edward," the driver said as Eddie tripped getting out of the car in the driveway, "if you've had a little too much get some coffee before your folks get home."

"I'm not drunk, if that's what you think."

Edward marched inside. The house was darkened except for low lights in the hallway. He felt defeated. He went upstairs, dropped his bag, and threw himself down on his bed. It was then that he heard his grandmother's cane on the floor above.

He knocked on her door.

"Edward," she said, opening it, "what a lovely surprise." Diana was in a silky old-fashioned dressing gown, her hair loosely swept up on the crown of her head. "And how is Cynthia?"

Eddie felt numb. "She didn't come with me," he said, coming inside.

Diana left the door open. "You two had a little spat," she said comfortably, sitting down in her chair.

"I met someone at the airport, Granny, who told me Cynthia wouldn't be seeing me again." He felt her sharp, hooded eyes settle on him. He was deeply upset. He wanted to get it all straight right now but he knew he shouldn't talk to his grandmother about it. "When are Dad and Mom getting home?"

"Well, I'm sure I don't know, dear. They went to Schurl's for dinner. Edward, do sit down. You're making me nervous, all that walking about. Would you like a chocolate?"

Vail had recently instilled in him the idea that his grandmother wasn't capable of dealing with reality and he shouldn't lay anything complicated on her. It all had to do with the

Patrick thing. He could see how someone choking to death on her carpet would upset her, but his grandmother seemed compos mentis to him. His distress caused him to push everything Vail had said out the window.

"Grandma, who are my real parents? Who's my mom? Did she really die?"

Diana looked as if he'd slapped her. "Edward! Who have you been speaking to?" she managed to get out.

"There was this woman at the airport," he said, miserably. Barely able to withhold tears, he staggered through the entire story.

"What a pack of lies!" Diana said in a tight shrill voice. "Nothing like that could happen in our family. Just put that out of your mind." She drew herself up in her chair. Her hands clasped the arms, the skin stretched tight over her knuckles.

But Eddie was an eighties kid and he heard the terror in her voice. He knew that the sweetest thing on earth, making love, could make you die. He knew that people could kill for no reason and for any reason. Stealing, lying, bribing, cheating were ordinary—U.S. presidents did it. Everyone did it. The music he heard, the television and movies he saw—everything pointed out hypocrisy and mocked the lie in front of the truth.

Now, Diana made him truly afraid. He felt sick. "Grandma, you know!"

She was shaking her head vigorously. "I know nothing! It's all lies! Whatever she said was a lie!"

Below, the front door closed smartly. Diana jerked her head toward it, snapped her eyes back at Edward. But he was on his feet and racing for the hall. "Edward," she cried, a shrill moan of a word.

Edward thundered down the stairs. He came to a stop in the foyer before his startled parents. His father blinked and peered at him. "Eddie, what in god's name is the matter with you?"

"Just whose kid am I?" Eddie shouted, enraged and heartbroken. Patsy started to put her arms around him but he threw them off. "Or weren't you ever going to tell me?"

"Will you calm down?" Vail shouted at him.

"Why? You never do."

Vail took Edward's arm in a strong grip and even though Edward was now taller than he was, Vail started to steer him into the living room. But he couldn't see his way clearly enough and cracked his head into the archway. He staggered, lost his footing and fell.

"Vail!" Patsy cried. "Eddie, help him!"

Together, they got him to his feet. Vail, groggy, sagged against their arms. "Sit here," Patsy said when they reached the sofa. A welt and a tear in the skin on his forehead was oozing blood. "Eddie, get some cotton and rubbing alcohol or iodine or something."

When he had left, Patsy went to the telephone and called Belinda. "Get over here," she said when Belinda picked up. "He knows. Someone told him."

"Jesus, that hurts," Vail groaned, his head back, as Patsy administered the iodine. Edward sat on the floor. He wondered what his grandmother was doing upstairs and had a mental picture of her sitting in her chair, grimacing, telling lies.

"Get your father a brandy," Patsy said.

"He's not my father."

"Get him a brandy anyway!" she shouted.

"And you're not my mother," he said rising, casting a scathing and disappointed look at her. He went to the little bar table and poured out the drink.

"I'm as much a mother to you as you could ever have and I won't tolerate such talk. You've known for years I'm not your birth mother." She took the glass from him and offered it to Vail. "Now sit down and we'll tell you what you want to know."

Chastened, furious, Edward sat down.

Vail sipped the brandy. When he looked up he thought he saw Diana standing in the archway. "Mother, if that's you, you can come in," he said, "but if you say anything, you'll have to leave. That clear?" Diana made no sign that she had heard. She simply sat down.

In an excited voice, close to tears, full of rage and pain, Edward told them what Francine had said at the airport.

"Those fucking Venners," Vail muttered with malice. He reached out to put a hand on Edward's shoulder but his son shook him off. "Edward, this is all my fault. I didn't trust you or myself enough to tell you the truth right away. The truth here was—is—ugly and I didn't want you growing up with it. You had enough to deal with."

"Cut to the chase, Dad. Is Belinda my mother?"

"Yes."

"Well, *damnit*," he cried, outraged. "*Damn you*." Patsy's hand flew to her throat, and her chin trembled. "And my father was that guy in San Francisco?" he yelled at Patsy.

She nodded, wretched.

"And she shot him?"

She nodded again. "Yes. She did."

Vail could hear but couldn't see Diana making motions, moving in some way, from the other chair. "Grandma wants to remember it her way," he said to Edward, but with a warning note in his voice he added, "Grandma was part of the problem a long time ago."

But Edward was remembering his dream of "the suits" taking him away from the bare room, and the woman screaming behind him. He repeated it to Vail, yelling, accusing. "That's not a dream, is it?" he demanded.

"Part of it is! We used to take you to see Lindy when you were small, a toddler, but—there came a time when she couldn't deal with it, she sort of cracked up. I didn't take you back there."

"Was I born in a jail?"

Patsy gasped. "You were not! You were born in a proper hospital like everyone else. You were only a few days old when Vail and I took you home."

"Well, why'd you do that?" he demanded truculently.

"Because we loved you!" she wept. "Because we couldn't have children. Because Lindy's life was ruined and I didn't see why yours should be, too!" She flattened her palms against the seat of her chair and rocked back, trying to control herself. "You can't tell a little child these things, and I am not excusing what we did, or failed to do, but Eddie, you had a real hard time as an adolescent, you were always in fights, those cruel children, you had so much to deal with—it just didn't seem fair to load this tragedy on you on top of everything else—"

"You should've told me," he shouted. He stood up and looked at them. His grandmother sat straight as a stick in her chair, the ivory cane upright by her knees, one hand grasping it like a talon. Vail looked very pale; the bulge in his forehead was red and blue. Patsy's makeup was running; there were dark circles under her eyes. She looked older.

"I'm glad I'm leaving for college," he said, feeling a disappointment in them so intense that it was close to hatred. "I don't want to be around any of you." He left them and went upstairs to his room.

Belinda arrived a few minutes later. "He's upstairs but I wouldn't go up there," Vail said from the sofa, holding a cloth to his head.

"You're all so stupid," Diana said suddenly. "You could have avoided all of this."

Vail jerked up, livid. "We could have avoided all of this if we hadn't given in to you in the first place! I won't have you behaving like this anymore in my house. This *is* my house and I make the rules and there's a whole new set, Mother. Take it or leave it."

Diana pressed her lips together and rose haughtily from her chair. She looked as though she wanted to say a great deal to Belinda, but she didn't.

"Who told him?" Belinda said when Diana had gone upstairs.

"That Francine woman," Patsy replied.

"Oh, my God," Belinda groaned.

Belinda went upstairs and knocked on Eddie's door. "Eddie, it's me, Belinda. Please, may I talk to you?"

"Go away."

"There's a lot you don't know. Please, let me in."

"No."

She didn't know what to do. "I'll be down in the garden, if you want to talk, just you and me. Private."

He didn't answer.

It was a warm summer night. She sat on the bench under the jacaranda tree. On the other side of the garden, the crepe myrtle was blooming, its bright pink blossoms pale under the moonlight. Belinda felt she had reached a terminus and she couldn't see beyond it. Everything had stopped in this garden.

As soon as Francine had said that Belinda was his real mother, Eddie had felt as if something he'd always known had locked into place. He couldn't figure out why he'd felt that way.

He stayed in his room until he knew his parents had gone to bed. He crept downstairs to the kitchen, conscious that

Belinda was still in the garden. Let her wait till doomsday, he thought. He opened the refrigerator, pulled out a Pepsi, jerked it open. The cold bubbles bit into his tongue. He glanced outside but he didn't see her. He opened the back door and went out.

The air was soft and fragrant, and he paused, breathing in. He felt deeply deceived and injured. It was unjust. What had he done to deserve this?

He saw her. She was sitting slumped over under the tree on the bench. He shivered. He'd always liked her, and from the first he'd felt connected to her. Now, she was the last person he wanted to be related to. Not just related, he thought: she's my real mother. He didn't want her—he didn't want any of them. But, drawn against his will, he walked across the yard. She looked like she was asleep. He stared at her. He couldn't think of any words bad enough to throw at her.

Belinda raised her head slowly. She hadn't been asleep.

"So what is it that *you're* going to tell me." He folded his arms.

"I wanted you to know how much I loved your father."

He barked, "Yeah, sure, that's why you killed him, right?"

"Yes, it was one of the reasons. Love isn't always love; it can turn into hate. Or fear, because people are very vulnerable when they're in love. If it had been anyone except Archie that night, I wouldn't have reacted that way. I would have said, 'Up yours,' and left, but I reacted hugely because there'd never been any check on us. We made love and it was secret but as long as we were alone we could do anything. I wanted to marry him and have my baby . . . you. I was very young, younger than you are. I expected everything. I didn't think anything could ever go wrong in life. I was desperately in love with Archie and for a while, it felt wonderful. That's what I wanted you to know."

Edward slowly sat down on the grass. He began pulling a few blades out by the roots and tossing them away. He didn't know what to say at her outpouring.

"That woman, Francine," Belinda said, "she did this to hurt me, not you, Edward." You were the messenger, she thought, to me.

Eddie pulled out more grass. He hated to even think of what the woman had said. Belinda waited. The edge of her sweater had begun to unravel. She plucked at it, trying to loop one thread under another, tie it down.

"She said—she said that it's why my hand didn't show up on my body."

"What? *What?*"

He got to his feet. "You and him—that's why I'm deformed! Get it? Some kind of fucking unholy alliance," he screamed.

She leaped up, reached out for him, shook him. "No! You don't believe that!"

"No, I don't but you think I liked hearing it?"

"Now you listen to me. She wasn't there, I was there."

He twisted away from her. "Leggo. I don't want to talk to you either."

"You wait, Eddie, you listen. You have to deal with me. I was the only person there. I'm the only person who knows."

He stumbled away from her, then turned. "You know what I used to do as a kid? I used to try to think why I didn't have a hand, that there had to be a reason and one of my fears as a kid was that you or my dad had done something wrong—"

"Oh, Eddie, I'm so sorry—"

"It was just kid stuff, I didn't believe it, really. I know all the scientific reasons why hands or feet don't get formed." He began crying and snapped his head back, a wild gesture of denial and rage. "But when she said that, it was shocking—"

Belinda reached out for him, but he pulled away. "Please, please sit down." He made no move. She rushed on. "Your father and I had a tremendous love affair and it was very good for a while. You were already formed, you were already inside me before everything went crazy. And that's what it was, everyone went nuts. I paid for it, I won't pay any more, and I don't want you to pay for it with stupid shit about your hand."

"Well, I've always had to deal with it!" He broke away from her and waved his handless arm.

She seized it and wouldn't let go. "The first minute I saw you, I saw that you didn't have a hand and I loved you. I held you and I nursed you and I loved you." She let go of his wrist. "God," she said, despairing, "your hand had nothing to do with any of this."

"I know that!"

"Good! I made terrible mistakes, I've committed . . . I've failed horribly—"

He backed away from her, away from the tree, into the moonlight. "Please," he said scathingly, "no confessions. You've done enough to wreck my life."

"I haven't wrecked your life. I've made it more difficult. I would've made it easier if I could have, but I couldn't."

"Jesus . . . all these years," he said in a rush of pain, "I'm believing my mom's dead, and Vail and Patsy—"

"They're like your parents. They're the best of parents—"

"I *believed* them, I believed what they said. Anything big that came up, we always talked about it. And now . . ." He sank to the ground.

"Eddie, it was me." She went over to him and knelt down near him, not touching him. "I told Patsy to tell you I'd died. I was in prison. I never thought I'd come back here. I was ashamed. I didn't want you to know. I was afraid. Don't blame them. Patsy argued with me a lot; she never wanted to lie— I forced her to."

"Why did you come back?"

She sat back on her heels. "I don't completely know. But when something really terrible happens to you, when you do something really bad . . . I had to come back and face the ghosts. I just had to. Because, otherwise, I was just running away from the rest of my life. I did that for years, Eddie. I stayed away. But I was avoiding everything. It was a fake life. It was a life without love or connection or depth or anything. So I came back. You remember that foggy morning? You were in front of the house? I was petrified. But the moment I saw you, I knew somewhere deep inside me that I'd done the right thing—to come back. But then I started living another kind of lie because I wouldn't let Patsy tell you about me. I wouldn't let her tell anyone about me and I believed that was okay— because how could I tell a twelve year old that I was his mother and I'd gone to prison for shooting his father?"

"When were you going to tell me?"

"As soon as I'd finished my shoot."

"Great. That sure lets me know where I stand."

"I was wrong but I thought I had that long."

"What do you mean?"

"Haven't you read any of the press about me in that movie?" He looked at her blankly. "Aside from everything else that happened—Francine, everything—it was only a matter of time before somebody started delving into Lindy Wyman. I almost came down here two weeks ago. I never dreamed that Francine would do this."

"*You* did this. You had no right." He walked away.

Early the next morning Guy Venner put his daughter on a flight to Paris. "You'll see, Cynthia," he said, holding her shoulders, "you'll forget all about this when you're back in school, back with all your friends. Trust me. I want what's best for you. I always have."

The waiting room was noisy and crowded. Passengers were lining up to enter the plane. Cynthia stepped back from her father. "You believe me, don't you?" he asked.

"No, I don't."

Disconcerted, he said, "Well, you will. I have to rush but I'll wait till you get on the plane and it takes off." Cynthia read this as distrust: he feared she'd get off the plane.

"Why didn't you send an escort, someone who'd keep me chained to my seat."

This irritated Guy greatly. "I trust you to do what's wise and best, Cynthia. Now, I'll be in Tokyo for a few days, and then I'll fly to Paris and we can take a little time to ourselves, sort things out."

"You're making a big mistake," she said. She turned away from him, entered the line and walked down the ramp into the plane.

It wasn't until the flight was approaching New York that Cynthia realized they were going to land there for an hour before continuing on to Paris.

On the morning Guy put Cynthia on the plane, Vail opened his front door to find Schurl standing on the steps.

"Here's a tape of Neil's next two shows," Schurl said. "I thought it might give you a laugh. I forgot to give it to you the other night. Sara around?"

"Schurl, she was at your place for dinner, now you go to her house. She's got a house. Invite yourself over. Make a statement. Get off the pot. Thanks for the tape." He shut the door.

Vail stood in the hallway, staring up at the balustrade on the second floor, wondering what to do about Eddie. He hadn't come out of his room for a day. To every request, he'd said, "Leave me alone," through the door.

"You've got a lot going for you," Keith said to Belinda with a crooked smile. "Some people aren't lucky enough to have lost everything once. But you have, so you know what the bottom's like."

"Yes," she replied sarcastically, "I'm very proud of knowing the bottom."

"There's nowhere to run anymore. There's comfort knowing that. Makes you face what's real." He felt that now. In the hours since he'd arrived in Los Angeles, he'd awakened the actress in his apartment, spoken with her honestly. He'd packed a few clothes, his modem, laptop and a box of disks, a box of dog food, and he and Bob had moved into a Best Western motel.

"You look like hell, Belinda," Keith said. Bob's leash was tied to the parking meter about ten feet away from their table. He was looking at a pigeon with interest.

"Thanks. Can't sleep."

They were sitting at an outdoor café on Sunset Boulevard, across from Le Dôme, a distinguished restaurant now framed with small chichi cafés serving Italian and Chinese delicacies. The people at the tables around them spoke Arabic and French, Hebrew and Italian and a little English. A huge tree, locked against one wall of their café, sprayed its leaves over the outdoor tables.

"Did you tell him everything?" he asked.

"I didn't tell him what it was like in the nuthouse. What's with you today?"

He reached across and patted her hand. "Sorry. I feel for both of you. I know it's a hard time."

"I told him almost all. Even so, he'll never get over it," Belinda said.

She was in mourning, unreachable. "You don't know that," he said. "He'll get over it. You're worth knowing."

Keith felt altered: physically he couldn't live in the same old apartment, and he didn't want to see anyone he knew. Last night, he'd sat for hours in his motel room, thinking of all the reasons he should go back to his apartment, take up his life again, start writing. He couldn't put one word down on paper. Belinda's face and shape, her grainy little laugh, her excitement, her boldness, and her errors held him. He wanted to talk to her frankly about what had happened to him, about the possession of his still solitary passion, a kind of suffering that fed him so completely he had no appetite for food. He wanted to know if she felt that way, too. He imagined kissing her as he waited to kiss her.

But Belinda, in a space of her own, was sipping her wine and looking around. The trattoria was washed in the warm yellow light of Los Angeles. "Such tender California afternoons," she said. Tender. Death, lies, cowardice, betrayal could never take a seat at this table. But she knew different. "Oh, god, Keith, what to do?" she said, thinking of Eddie. "He'll hate me."

"Then you'll live with that." He put his hand on hers again, then lightly removed it. He felt taut, stretched out. He yearned to lie down beside her and feel the length of her against him, the lightness of her face against his shoulder, the lightness of her arm across his chest.

He didn't want to show her what he'd brought with him but it was better coming from him than from a stranger. "The recent press," he said, unfolding a copy of *Eye* magazine. It was a two-page spread with a huge picture of Sky, a smaller one of Belinda as a teenager. An old headline had been reprinted: *SKY'S ADOPTED TEEN DAUGHTER KILLS IN LOVE NEST*.

Belinda took it, looked at it. "They're too late!" she said, and she tore it down the middle. "You know what? I don't even care."

Bob let out a bark at a Puli going by.

Keith put Bob in the backseat of his car and drove Belinda back to her apartment. The afternoon was hot. Children played on the street; the Armenian men played backgammon on their porches. Dr. Suico's sign had recently been relettered. Belinda's apartment building needed a coat of paint. Six-foot-high graffiti grew along the walls like errant urban shrubs.

Inside, it was warm and dusty. Keith looked around without comment, unleashed Bob, and fell comfortably into a chair near the couch. Belinda opened a bottle of Evian, dropped some ice in a bowl, put them with the glasses on a table near him and sat down on the couch.

"Where are you living?" she asked. "I tried to reach you last night."

"I moved."

"Last night?"

"Yes."

"Where?"

"Motel that allows dogs."

"Why?"

"I couldn't live in the old place anymore."

"Why?"

He thought about that. The light from the window dusted her sharp face. He sighed. "Because everything changed for me in Portland." He leaned forward and touched her knee. "I can't tell you when it changed. I can't tell you if I like it or not. I can't even talk about it with you right now."

"Why not?"

He shrugged and patted her knee.

She felt her apartment closing in and opening up at the same time. His eyes were hazel in the light from the window, his mustache more brown than black. Underneath it, a faint smile tugged at his mouth. He was looking at her with a tenderness and attention that were unmistakable.

"You're beginning to scare the hell out of me, Keith."

"Yes," he said, flatly, "it's very scary."

The telephone rang and her answering machine clicked on. Belinda did not move. "Oh," a familiar voice said, "I was hoping to get you." There was a pause; the tape ground on.

Belinda said, "That's Francine." She reached across the back of the sofa to the table and grabbed the telephone. "Yes?" she said, guardedly.

"Belinda? It's Francine. Please don't hang up. I'm so incredibly sorry. What I did was terrible."

Belinda's body stiffened.

"What can I do?" Francine moaned, her voice amplified by the answering machine that was still recording.

"If you're talking about Eddie, there's nothing you can do. Don't call me again."

"Please, don't hang up. I don't want to be an enemy. I don't know what came over me. He looks like—Archie."

"He does not."

"Belinda, I'll be in Los Angeles tomorrow to help set up Guy's new offices with—with the decorators. We've bought an old landmark building in Hollywood. Guy's out of the country—and, well, would you come by, let me apologize in person? Maybe I can help you get your film back into production."

"What you said was unforgivable."

"It was, it was! I'm so sorry. Let me try to help you. Please, please come and see me. I need to talk with you." She paused. Belinda could hear her amplified breathing. "I think you need to talk to me, too. I know you do."

"I'll let you know," Belinda said coldly, and hung up. "Amazing," she said quietly.

Keith leaned back in his chair. "People are."

"I might see her."

"Oh, Christ, why? She can't bring your movie back."

"Not about the picture." Belinda hesitated. "I don't know why. I just feel—it has to be done."

Keith rose. "Okay." He groaned, "I'll take you over there— wherever the building is." He picked up the leash and Bob, hearing the sound, trotted over to him.

Belinda rose. "Hollywood somewhere." They walked to the door. "But I'll be at Vail's tomorrow."

"Well, that's okay."

They weren't thinking about what they were saying; it was cover to reach the door.

"You could pick me up there, we can have lunch, then you can drop me at the building." She opened the door. "I don't know what building she's talking about, do you?"

"No. We'll find it." There was something about her manner, the way she stood, the way she brushed a lock of hair back from her face that was private and remote. She'd be that kind of woman, he thought—unapproachable—but when she gave in it would be completely.

He stepped outside the doorway. The leash was twisted around his leg. "Okay," he said, "I'll call you tomorrow morning. We'll get our signals straight." He stepped out of the leash. Bob was restless. He wanted to get moving.

Belinda pressed one small hand flat against the doorjamb. "You can stay a while if you want—"

"I have to see my agent over on the west side."

"Oh, right, I forgot. Okay, tomorrow we'll check in . . ."

"Sure." He grinned, feeling the ecstasy of his failure to touch her, a painful absence, a physical hollow, a physical surfeit. He turned away, then instantly whirled back, dropping Bob's leash, one arm thrown wide, catching her around the waist, his other arm around her back and with a sound between a wail and a moan, he pressed his body fully against hers. Her arms shot up, clamping around his back, drawing her body even more urgently into his. His cheek was sealed to hers. "Come into my life," he whispered. He felt himself expanding against her. He was going to blow up as the tension fired into a hundred sensations. Once started, there was no stopping. His lips trembled against her mouth, pressing, receding, tasting. He heard children coming down the stairs. Still holding her, afraid to let go, he turned and stepped back inside her rooms, his arm locked around her waist. "Bob," he whispered. Bob looked confused but finally ambled back inside. Keith kicked the door shut and immediately turned, facing her, and she seemed to jump back into his arms, holding him, not letting go. Her hands slipped up to his face and felt blindly for his cheek and mouth and throat and she turned her face up and kissed him hungrily, each movement of her lips on his a new surfeit that blended instantly with a new longing. "Drown me," she whispered. He turned her, one arm around her, and began walking to the sofa, brought her down beside him, stretched out, held her length against him. She was a perfect fit.

After a moment, she said, "This is too scary, I don't want to make love to you now."

He stroked her hair, pressed her head into his shoulder. "No, not yet." It was too solemn. His former life had died and he knew that was true of hers, too. He knew that anything he felt she felt, and what wasn't didn't matter. It was an entirely new feeling. He didn't need any telling. He'd found his match.

After a while, she said, "Get up." They rose. She put her arm around his waist, her head slightly bent against his chest, and led him into the bedroom. "Lie down just for a minute." He fell on the bed and she dropped beside him. They rolled into each other's arms and lay quietly. "I didn't know I was waiting for this," she said.

"I did."

When she began kissing him, the waiting was over. He knew he wasn't going to leave that bed without feeling every inch of skin on her. He ran his hands under her shirt and felt the expanse of skin underneath. He pulled her shirt over her head and tenderly kissed her breasts. He was so excited it was like a death—too much air, too much water, too much life.

He was lifting her. She was peeling off her jeans. He was standing up and loosening his belt with emergency gestures and flinging aside his jeans. He leaped back on the bed in his socks and slammed his naked body against hers. Her hands closed against his skin. She was at once spiraling upward, into the atmosphere, and she was spiraling downward into a core. Drowning and spinning, she instantly opened her legs and he was there, pressing against her, tenderly pressing and opening, and fusing with her, inside. "Closer, closer," she said in wonder and terror, "closer."

That night, Vail went into the study and put Neil's tape in the VCR. He couldn't find the remote control. He hunted for it, growing angrier.

"Vail," he heard his mother say very close to him, from one side. He jumped. That's the way it was—people were always sneaking up. "What are you doing?" she asked. He was peering at the front of the VCR machine, searching for the button that said, Play. He heard her sit down in a chair to his left. The front doorbell rang. He knew that Maria was still in so he ignored the bell, the challenge of finding the Play button consuming and enraging him. The bell rang again.

"Maria!" he yelled.

"Oh, Vail, don't yell like that," Diana said.

Maria's voice came out of the darkness behind him, "A Miss Venner is here."

"Fucking Venners," Vail mumbled, incensed that he could not find the right button. "Don't let 'em in."

"My stars," said Diana, "is that the Venner girl?"

"I think so," Maria said. "The young lady Edward's talked about."

Vail turned fully around and saw a piece of Maria. "Okay, bring her in."

Cynthia looked tired, her clothes were wrinkled, but she was clearly pleased to be there.

Diana extended her bony hand. "I am delighted to make your acquaintance, my dear. I knew your great-grandmother. I took my triplets to have tea with her one day. Such a lovely afternoon we all had, such a vital woman. Maria, call Edward down here."

Vail cut off this matinee greeting. "Cynthia, this is not a good time for a visit. I'm going to be blunt. Edward's up in his room and he's had a rough time and he won't come out."

"Vail!" Diana said, shocked at his lack of *politesse*.

"Is he all right?" Cynthia asked.

"Yes."

"Maybe I could go up and see him?" she asked.

Vail looked at the small cameo of her that he could see. "Sure. Mother, would you show her the way?"

Diana and Cynthia went up the stairs. "This is very unusual," Diana said, stopping in front of Edward's door. "But," she sniffed, "this is an unusual time." She went on down the hall.

"Eddie. It's Cynthia," she said, knocking. "Eddie?"

The door flew open. Eddie was standing there in a pair of jeans, no shirt, his hair messed up, a look of astonishment on his face. "Cynthia . . . Cynthia!" He grabbed her. Their bodies collided. "Jesus, where'd you come from? I called and called you. I thought—I thought you didn't want to see me. . . ."

"Dad ripped my phone out."

"Huh? What's going on?"

"This morning, he put me on the plane for France. But I escaped," she whispered.

"God, this is just too good to be true!" he cried. "I can't believe you're here!"

She held onto him tightly. "So there I am on the plane going to Paris, but it stopped in New York, and I just got off. I caught a plane back and here I am."

Eddie tugged her inside and shut the door. The room was dark except for the MTV playing without sound from the corner. "He didn't send a jailor with you?"

"He expects people to do what they're told." She hugged him hard, pressing against him. "Sometimes we can't do that."

He drew her down so they were sitting on the edge of the unmade bed. Eddie put his hand on her cheek and kissed her. He looked at her hard in the gyrating light. "Did you send Francine to meet me at the airport?"

"Yes. Didn't she get there?"

"Oh, yes, she did. She said your dad wouldn't let you see me anymore, that he didn't like my family."

"That's nonsense," Cynthia said airily. "He doesn't like anyone I go out with. He'll get over it. Wasn't Fran a dear to carry my message for me?" She kissed him hard.

He drew slightly away. "What message?"

"That I couldn't meet you."

"Oh, that message. Yes, Francine was a sweetheart." He realized that Cynthia did not know anything. "Your dad'll find out you're not in France," Eddie said.

"Sure. I'm going to call him up and tell him."

Eddie groaned with pleasure. He lay back on the bed and turned on a small lamp. Then he pulled her down beside him, propped himself up on an elbow, stared at her. "I can't believe you're here." He smoothed her hair. "What's this?" he said, stroking a slight bruise on her cheek.

"Dad was really angry," she said. "He hit me. He never hit me before."

"He hit you? He *hit* you? My dad never . . . did that," he said.

"He said there was madness in your family. He was talking all kinds of nonsense."

Eddie went up on his elbow again. "There are some things you should know about, things I didn't know till I got home."

"Tell me later."

"I think you ought to hear them in case you change your mind."

"Oh, Eddie, how silly you are. I'm not changing my mind." She sat up. "I've been on two planes today just to get here. And you know—I'm famished!"

As Eddie steered her through the hallway toward the kitchen, he saw the flickering light of the television from Vail's study. He pushed the door open to the kitchen and turned on the lights. "Tough," he said, "I guess Maria's gone." He looked at her for the first time in the bright light. "You're here, you're really here . . ."

"Some kitchen, Eddie. Shall we raid the icebox?"

"Will you be all right here for a minute?" he asked. "I want to talk to Dad."

*   *   *

Vail was playing Neil's tape when Eddie came into the room.

"What's that?" Eddie asked.

"Neil's new show." Vail turned, narrowed his eyes, then widened them, trying to take in his son. "Thank god I can't see him. Bad enough to hear him."

"Yeah, well. Why don't you turn it off?"

Vail looked surprised. He'd found the remote control and he knew the buttons on it by heart. He pressed Stop. "Good idea, Son." He tilted his head, peering at a corner of his son's face, trying to see into his heart. "Where's Cynthia? Is she with you?"

"She's in the kitchen." Despite his joy at seeing Cynthia, Eddie felt the revelations piling back on top of him. His eyes filled with tears. "Oh, Dad, all this shit, it's a real bummer, isn't it?" He sank down beside Vail on the leather couch. Vail put his arms around him, held him close.

"Life's a bummer sometimes," Vail said. "But it can improve." They sat together quietly. Vail stroked his son's hair, and Eddie cried for the way it had been, in the certain knowledge that it would not be that way again.

Vail said, "I know I've done a lot wrong, but I hope you'll be able to forgive me. Can't live without you, Son. Can't do it."

Eddie smiled sadly and wiped his eyes on his sleeve. It felt good to talk to Vail again.

"Your mom's—Patsy's—upstairs. Why don't you see if you can get her to come out?"

"Nah, I don't want to. I think I'll check on Cynthia."

"Suit yourself."

Eddie examined the contents of a bookcase that he'd seen a hundred times. "Well, maybe I will." He turned around. "Cynthia's making scrambled eggs, but I don't think she knows how."

"Yipes. I don't want any experiments in my kitchen," Vail said with a phony heartiness. He leaned on Eddie as he rose to his feet.

Patsy was lying on top of the coverlet in her bathrobe. "Mom, Dad wants you," Eddie said outside the door.

"Come in," she replied.

"We have guests," he said, coming inside. He folded his arms against his chest.

"Tell them to go away. I can't see anyone." Her face had an unnatural sheen, her eyes were puffy and faintly red. "We'll be living with this for a long time."

"I thought your motto was 'shoulder on.' "

She turned her head away. She could feel his anger. "I don't have any tears left, honey. It's all so—it's all my fault. I should never have let this happen to you."

"No, you shouldn't have. But it's not all your fault—Dad's already claimed that. I think Belinda did, too." He knew he was going to start crying and yelling again, so he picked up a small silver music box from her dresser and opened the lid. The tune of the Byrds' hit, "Turn, Turn, Turn" tinkled out of it. "Dad gave you this?" She nodded. He clapped the lid back on the music box and put it down. "Mom, I thought you always told me everything straight," he said. "So I think it's really shitty, this thing about my real mom being dead," he said, struggling with the words, "and it was shitty of you to agree to it."

"Yes, it was." Patsy moaned. "I can't forgive myself, Edward."

"Well, I don't know if I can either, but I want to stop thinking about it. Can we stop thinking about it?"

He was across the room, looking angry and sad. "No," she said, surprising him, "we can't. We can only get used to thinking about it. And after a while we can put some distance between it and us, between the shock and us."

Why, he wondered, was it so hard to forgive her and so easy to forgive Vail? He had counted on her more. That was it. Vail was mercurial, always up and down. But Patsy was steady as a rock. She kept everything going. She had let him down.

"Cynthia's here," he said. He stomped out.

CHAPTER 25

Sara was wearing Katharine Hepburn slacks and a tennis hat. She marched across the garden to Belinda and gave her a hug. "Good for you," she said. "Good for you." She sat down on the bench under the tree. "How's Eddie?"

"I haven't seen him yet today."

They sat together on the bench, Sara talking about youth mending, about her repairs to Sky's house, about Vail's situation. It was hard for Belinda to believe that two nights ago, she had been in this garden with Eddie, sick with remorse, as he shouted at her out of his pain. Now the garden was full of light and warmth and color, dressed in summer. She had no sense of endings, as she'd had that night, only beginnings. And for those reasons, she found it hard to concentrate on what Sara was saying. She was waiting for Eddie; she was thinking of Keith.

"These letters," Sara was saying, and Belinda nodded. "But I know that after everything you've been through, they don't seem important. . . ."

"Maybe you'll never get another! Life is mysterious."

"But there was a line in the last letter about Sky and me and I don't understand how the writer could have known about that time." Sara peered at her daughter.

But Belinda only nodded patiently, wholly distracted by the feeling of Keith's arms.

"Belinda!" Patsy called out from the French doors. "There's a limo waiting for you outside."

"For me? It's a mistake."

"Francine Cheney sent it."

"But I'm having lunch with Keith in an hour." Belinda went to the garden gate and peered over it at the long black limo in the driveway.

"Send it away," Sara said, rising.

"Yes," Patsy said, "do that."

But Belinda said no. She looked again at the limo, beached like a black shark on the paving. She turned away. "I'm starting a new life," she said. "We all are. And part of that for me is putting all the ghosts to rest. That includes Francine now."

Sara was irritated. "Belinda, it's just possible that Archie could have mentioned something about Sky and me to Francine."

"Francine? She was a teenager, younger than I was!"

"I don't understand why you're even considering seeing that woman," Patsy said.

"Well, I don't either," Belinda said, "but I think I need to do this."

Belinda was listening to other feelings that were not about Francine or crazy letters or old retribution. With Keith had come a sense of rightness and a sense of worth. She felt that somehow, at some time, she and Eddie could be friends, that she was capable of repairing the wrongs she'd done, and if she couldn't, she was capable of living with the results.

"There was a time in the nuthouse when I knew I was all right," she said to them. "I'll never forget it. It was nighttime and I was standing in the dayroom where I wasn't supposed to be, looking out the window. The moon was huge and perfectly white. It was so beautiful. Its light on the old poplar, on the window and the screens, even on those cold walls, beautiful. It was healing." Belinda turned to look at Sara. "So I think I'll go and meet Francine, Sara," she said, walking back across the yard. "Have Keith meet me at the building—it's some old landmark in Hollywood. He'll know where it is."

"Oh," Sara said. "I still don't like the feel of this."

Downtown Hollywood was attempting a reconstruction in the midst of virulent urban decay. Reconstituted old buildings, arrayed in brick, wrought iron, marble, and tiles shot proudly up from the filthy sidewalks and towered among sordid souvenir shops and boarded-up windows of stores that waited for demolition.

Belinda, on the luxury ride in to Hollywood, found herself thinking about Fletcher, how surprised she'd been in the magnificent Malaysian highlands, the British protectorate preserved like amber in the jungle, and how addicted to him she'd become. The car slithered along Hollywood Boulevard. She thought about Guy, his commanding and charming veneer that had matched her cynicism and her ambition. The car stopped for a light at Highland where the Hollywood Hotel had once graced the corner with awnings and wide verandas and pepper trees. No trace of it remained. Her shiny piscine vehicle glided forward. Belinda luxuriated in a new sense of being home—home with its errors, demolitions, preservations, its imperfect reality. With Keith, everything felt real, solid, matched.

Guy Venner's building, twelve stories high, sat at the inter-section of Hollywood and Vine. The exterior had been sanded and painted. Ornate window frames and pristine new glass panes flashed in the sun.

Belinda stepped out of the limousine. "Nice ride," she said to the driver, "but it feels like a hearse."

He smiled. "Lotta people say that their first ride."

"What floor is Venner Broadcasting?"

"They said penthouse."

She looked up. On the top floor, under the eaves, marble and plaster sculptures were stationed along the facade. Between these sentinels huge French windows opened onto balconies that ran the length of the building.

"Lunch is delayed," Sara said to Keith and Vail as they came inside the house.

"Why?" Keith asked.

Eddie and Cynthia stomped into the living room from the kitchen, carrying a plate of tostados and chips. He looked at Patsy solemnly, truculently.

"Lindy's gone to meet Francine," Sara replied.

Eddie put down the tostados.

"In Hollywood?" Keith asked Sara.

"That's cuckoo," Eddie said.

"Where in Hollywood?" Vail demanded.

"Wherever the Venner building is," Sara sighed. "Keith, she said you would know where it was."

"It's right downtown," Cynthia said. "On Vine. It's the oldest highrise in Hollywood."

"A big gray and white building facing a corner?" Vail asked.

"Yes," Cynthia said, "it was just repainted. Have you seen it, Vail? It's terrific."

The color went out of Vail's face. He reached behind him, feeling for the chair, and sank into it. "No, I haven't been in Hollywood for years." But he had seen the corner of the building in his mind's eye. "Keith," he said, "you and Eddie, you go down there. You go get her."

Francine, turned out in a white summer suit, red blouse, and red shoes, stood in a large unfurnished room at a table heaped with fabric swatches, designs, blueprints, and the paraphernalia of decorators in motion. Beside her, a young man in a crisp jacket was examining a roll of material. As Belinda entered, two workmen in overalls, carrying buckets and brushes, were making a noisy exit.

"The idea, Mrs. Cheney," the decorator said over the banging of buckets, "is all in the upholstery and the paneling for the outer office." He swept out an arm and noticed Belinda. "Hi," he said. Francine turned.

"Come in," Francine said to Belinda.

"Mrs. Cheney," the decorator said, "I'm a tad late for lunch. Why don't we meet back here about two?"

"That'll be fine."

The decorator nodded pleasantly at Belinda as he went out.

"Quite a space," Belinda said without pleasure.

"Guy hates air-conditioned buildings," Francine said. "The tenants can have it if they want it, but you'd be surprised how many choose not to use it. Hermetically sealed buildings spread germs, but you can open any window in this building. And look at these," she insisted, going to a tall French door and opening it. A breeze stirred the wood chips and plaster dust on the floor. "We're putting plants out here, and there's room for chairs, too," Francine said, stepping out on the balcony. It was edged with a bowed, ornate wrought iron railing. Two sculptures, twenty feet high, faced north to the hills, affixed to either side of the balcony. The breeze picked up a lock of Francine's hair. She pressed her hand against her head to hold it in place. "Come look," she said.

"No, I hate heights."

"Every office along this side has a balcony." She stepped back inside. "It's a magnificent Art Deco building."

"The breeze feels good."

"I thought we might go to lunch," Francine said. She had about her, Belinda now noticed, a high energy as if she were full of hopes for all levels of her life.

"I have a lunch date. Perhaps we could just talk for a few minutes."

Francine looked surprised and disappointed. A workman suddenly appeared from the back of the suite. "I'm at lunch," he grumbled, slapping a cap on his head.

"Okay, Frank," Francine said, but when he'd gone, she added, "Good riddance. I'm firing that guy."

"You wanted to talk to me about Archie," Belinda said.

"I never said anything about Archie."

"Francine, Arch was our only connection."

"But now it's Eddie, isn't it?" She whisked a dust speck off her skirt. "I'm sorry. I meant that Edward is important, too."

"Important to me, yes. Not to you." Belinda cocked an eyebrow at Francine. She wasn't sure what she'd expected, but she felt they were already on a strange avenue. "What you did to Eddie isn't up for discussion. You did that only to get back at me."

"It had nothing to do with you," Francine said, pressing one hand over her hair, smoothing it down. "I'm sorry I said those things to him." She made a minimal, pleading gesture with both hands that looked unnatural. "It just came out. I didn't even feel like I was saying them. Has that ever happened to you? Things just come out? I'm very sorry," she said again, walking away from the windows, toward Belinda, who stood beside the table in the middle of the room. "I didn't mean it. I thought he looked a lot like Daddy—a lot like Archie."

"No, he doesn't," Belinda replied, on surer ground. She didn't want Francine to see Archie in Eddie. She stepped away from the table.

"I want to be frank with you, Belinda. I know I wanted Eddie—oh, it was terrible of me—I wanted him to feel responsible and guilty, too, for what Archie did—"

"For what Archie *did*? How could Eddie ever have any connection to that?"

"Oh, I don't mean you and Archie," Francine said, shaking her head, smoothing the lapel of her red blouse, "he's not responsible for Daddy's little faults."

"Which of his many faults do you mean?" There was something artificial, arranged, about Francine's voice and gestures that disturbed Belinda.

Francine gave a little shrug and smiled. "Oh, don't pay any attention to me. I don't know what I mean half the time," she said winningly. "I'm nervous about talking to you. Aren't you nervous?" She moved out to the balcony again and looked down. "Back at the airport, talking to Eddie, I guess I felt that you and Eddie were connected so completely—that Eddie, too, was responsible—like you—for Daddy's death." She turned. "Now, wasn't that crazy of me?" Her head was lowered, but her eyes were looking up at Belinda.

Below on the street, a middle-aged man in shiny slacks was waiting for a bus. He looked cross and worn out. He hated the grime of Hollywood and the weirdos in it. He hated that corner where the guy in bedroom slippers and the filthy suit sometimes walked up and down shouting his lungs out. Most of all, he hated the fate that had cost him his job and now sentenced him to ride buses to the unemployment office. The tall building across the four lanes of traffic, ceaselessly moving in the exhaust-filled street, was newly painted. It was considered old, but nothing in Hollywood was old. The streets in Denmark, where he'd originally come from, *they* were old. He looked up at the building and noticed a woman standing on one of the top balconies. She looked frail up there among the immense columns interspersed with the statues. The columns were Ionic. He was surprised he remembered that. He began checking the entire building, starting from the east, moving his gaze west. It took his mind off the weirdos down below with him.

Francine, on the balcony, stood at the railing, her arms crossed. She gazed at the rooftops.

"I wanted to tell you something, Lindy," she was saying. "Archie *was* the bond between us. But you don't know how much. See, I'm sure you think I hate you, but I don't." She lowered her voice. Belinda moved closer. "I don't hate you," Francine said softly, "I'm grateful to you."

"How's that?" Belinda asked, standing in the doorway.

Francine crushed her hands together in front of her, twisted them. "Oh, this is really hard but I have to tell you. I've never told anyone."

Belinda said, "Then don't tell me. Francine, why don't we just agree that a lot of bad stuff happened, and that I caused the worst of it. I truly never meant to kill Arch. If there was any way I could bring him back—"

"I don't want him back!" she shouted. "God, how could you think that?"

Belinda was completely bewildered. "He was your father."

Agitated, Francine clasped her hands tightly together again. She started to say something, then stopped, then began again. Finally she flung the words out in a tormented, aggressive voice. "He did terrible things to me. He—molested me!"

Belinda, repelled and astounded, stepped back.

"He forced me. I don't want him back." Francine stopped talking and shut her eyes, appalled that she'd said the words out loud. She pressed a hand to her breast. "That first night he came into my room and stretched out beside me. He said he was just resting.

"'So tired out,' he'd said. 'You've been through a lot, Fran, Mommy dying, coming all the way out here, you need comfort, too, adult comfort. You're not a child anymore, are you? We'll comfort each other. You can trust me. I know just what you need . . .' His voice, low and warm, had talked on without real expression.

"It was like a hum in my head," Francine said, "like something in the background. And after a while, I didn't really remember hearing." Belinda drew away, feeling both pity and antipathy for Francine. The artificiality she'd sensed earlier had come from Archie. His abuse had sucked the life out of her: there was nothing left but a pool of anger hidden under a mediocre, dull mask.

"And then he touched me," Francine said softly, rocking her body against the railing. "And I pulled away, and he said that I could do it, that I wasn't a scaredy-cat, I wasn't a baby, I was grown-up. I wanted to be grown-up." Her voice was full of hate and pride and anguish. "I wanted to please him, but I was only twelve and I didn't know how to get away from him without making him mad."

"Don't tell me anymore," Belinda said. She felt sorry for her, but she was nauseated with a new anger at Archie mixed with intense self-disgust. The sounds from the street were changing. There was less traffic. She leaned against the door frame.

"I tried hard to forget all of it," Francine said. She paced to one end of the balcony, then reversed and paced to the other end. "Sometimes it seemed like a dream or something I imagined." She stopped pacing and rocked against the railing. "And then you arrived. Do you remember when? You and Daddy were coming out of the study. I knew what you were doing in there," she said slyly. "And he knew I knew."

All the columns were Ionic, but the columns on the sister building to the west were Doric. The middle-aged man waiting for the bus had examined each one. He went back to the far east corner of the first building and started trying to determine which Greek goddesses were lined up beside the columns. That's when he saw the two women on the top floor. One was rocking against the railing like she was making a dare. The other woman stood in the big French doorway which was set under the ornate eaves. The one at the doorway reached out and suddenly tugged at the woman by the railing. There was some kind of fight, some sort of argument.

The man shouted to the crowd waiting for the bus, "Look! Someone's gonna jump. Get the cops."

"Don't touch me," Francine said, wrestling away from Belinda.

"I only put a hand on your arm. Come inside."

Francine shook her head, looking down at the people below. "I didn't imagine any of it. It was all real. Everything always came back. Something always brought it all back. But I *pushed it down*." She pressed her open palm downward against the air. She looked up. "Understand?"

Belinda stepped back and unconsciously stiffened. Francine's confession was an act of hostility.

"So that other night, when I saw you in the hallway, the night he had you pressed against the wall, I felt glad because I knew I wouldn't have to deal with him that night, because he never came into my room when he'd been with you. It was a reprieve and you did it, Lindy." She looked brightly at Belinda. "But I was jealous, too," she whispered. "He was mine."

Belinda felt sick. It wasn't the memory of that night but hearing the tone of Francine's words about Archie. "I have to go," she said.

"No, wait!" Francine caught Belinda at the edge of the door. Her grip on Belinda's arm was muscular and severe.

"Ouch. Let go."

"Sorry." Francine instantly let go. "I just want to tell you— I want to be honest about this—that I also felt cheated." She turned, walking to the railing again. She looked back at Belinda over her shoulder. "Really, Lindy, it was disgusting what you were doing down there in the hallway."

Belinda's apprehension took on new dimensions: she felt bound to Francine. "Francine, come inside. Francine, there's no reason for this. It's only chance that we know each other. It's only chance that I'm here at all—"

Francine leaned against the railing, her hands propped flat on the warm iron, her elbows out. Belinda stood stiffly by the doors, angled toward Francine, her posture at once afraid and sympathetic.

Francine turned around. "I could have killed Archie. I thought about it. But *you* did it, and I wondered if you did it because you knew what he was doing to me. Did you?" The wind was taking down her hair.

"Yes, that's why I did it. Francine, come back inside!"

"I should have made you pay for what you did," Francine screeched, "but I couldn't bring myself to do it." She was beating one hand against the railing, mired in her horrible youth.

Belinda turned away, aware again that there were different sounds coming from the street. Francine crossed the short distance between them in a second and seized her arm again.

"Oh, please, just a minute more. This is so important."

"No! Let go."

But this time Francine did not let go. A lock of her hair had come loose from the twist on the back of her head, and Francine didn't notice it.

"Let go!"

Francine was a strong woman. "You saved me by shooting him, but when you killed him, you took him away from me.

But it was also—a reprieve." Big tears rolled out of Francine's eyes and down her cheeks. She did nothing to stop them but clung to Belinda, childlike, holding her close. "It was such a terrible time. I loved my dad. He was good to me. We'd lie down together and he'd tell me things about the patients, what they said to him. . . . His patients were as real to me as my friends, realer. He told me about Sky, how awfully jealous Sara was of her . . ."

Belinda felt cold. "You've been writing letters to Sara, haven't you?" But Francine only cocked her head and smiled and turned away.

"He was a terrible man—and then you took him away," she said. "Thank god, you took him away. It was like you'd done something about him, and I respected you. Except . . ." Still holding onto Belinda with one iron hand, Francine's other hand flew to her face, covering it like a mask, fingers splayed.

The shot had echoed through the old house. She'd run downstairs, through the halls, back to the study and burst into the room. "Daddy was on the floor . . ." Belinda had fainted. Francine had fallen to her knees next to Archie. His throat had been bloody; he'd been breathing hard. He had been staring at her. "He looked so pitiful," Francine said, weeping. "He couldn't move; he couldn't tell any more stories. He was completely helpless!" Francine had dipped her finger in the blood on his throat and drawn a line down Archie's cheek. She'd painted another line across his forehead. His eyes had been full of panic as she swept her blood-soaked fingers down his nose, plugged into his ears, and over his wide mouth.

She jerked Belinda closer to her. "I could have done anything to him," she said with a huge laugh. "I detested you for bringing him so low! I should have had the guts to save myself! So I finished him off. I stopped him from breathing. Otherwise, he might have lived. You made me kill him."

Belinda struck out at her with one hand and shoved her knee with all her strength upward between Francine's legs. The woman jumped back, astonished. Belinda, panting, leaped toward the door, desperately afraid, but Francine caught her. Belinda struggled frantically against the arms laced around her. "God," Francine moaned in a high voice, bracing herself against the French door, "you saved me. I don't want to hurt you." A fist came out of nowhere, punched Belinda on the jaw, and dropped her. She fell just inside the doorway. The pain radiated through her head. Francine, sobbing, had both hands down on the railing, like a child on a fence, swinging her body back and forth in the grip of a deadly ambivalence. Belinda tried to get to her feet. The balcony swam, rising and falling.

Francine sprang on her, lifting her, dragging her. Belinda seized her hair and fought.

"I hated you! You stole him!"

"Why didn't you save yourself?" Belinda shrieked, grasping at anything that might stop the woman.

"Because he was my father and he was killing me!" she screamed.

Eddie and Keith were in the car a few blocks from the Venner building, impatiently ploughing through heavy noontime traffic.

"Chill out, Keith," Eddie said. "Dad's always seeing things. It's just part of living with Dad. I don't even want to be here on this wild-goose chase." He widened a rip in his jeans.

"Don't tell me again," Keith muttered.

"I'm not ready to see her for a while. That's the way it is. You can understand that, right?"

"Just stick with me on this one, Ed."

Eddie hung out the window, looking ahead. "Keith, the street's blocked off."

Keith hit the wheel impatiently with his hand. At a break in the traffic, he pulled off the boulevard and drove the car into the first parking lot he saw. They were two blocks from the Venner building.

"What's going on?" he asked the parking attendant. The man spoke no English. He pointed to the east and made a sign of confusion.

"Bummer," said Eddie as they set off. But Keith felt sick at heart. The blood pounded in his head; his hands tightened. Something was terribly wrong.

"There's been an accident," Keith said, hurrying through the crowds. He was sweating and felt the dampness under his arms and down his back. It was fear. He couldn't live without her.

Below the building, the crowd had grown, and police and fire engines had arrived. The street had been cleared. The middle-aged man watched the figures on the balcony with a sense of ownership. He tore his eyes from a statue when the other side of the French doors burst open. He thought for a moment the wind had slammed it. One woman broke away from the other, but the other one caught her, held her fast.

Belinda had never been so terrified in her life. The wind was whipping her hair back from her face. Francine had locked her into an embrace, strong as iron, strong as death, and she was grimly dragging her toward the railing. Belinda grabbed the knob of the French door and hung on. She gave no thought now of stopping Francine from going over; she had to save herself. But she could feel her sweaty hand slipping away from the doorknob. "I should've done this a long time ago," Francine was screaming, twisting her head around, looking at Belinda with malevolence and, a second later, affection. Belinda was losing her hold on the knob. She could see the huge space through the wrought-iron railing of the balcony, the crevasse, the tiny people below. Seconds were hours. She was going to be dragged over.

Eddie and Keith were a half block away when they heard the crowd moan, a huge sound full of hope and despair and satisfaction. Keith looked up at Venner's building. A figure hurtled off a balcony, turning in the air, skirt flying, arms up, hair streaming behind her.

She hit the pavement. Keith grabbed Eddie's arm. Eddie, bent over, was crying, "Oh god, oh god."

Keith charged forward, the sound of the woman slapping the pavement arching inside him, repeating and repeating. But he was swimming in slow motion, trying to cut through the crowd—a hive of gasping, talking people, looking up at the building and down at the pavement, moving and stretching and turning with a kind of sickened group wonder.

Keith broke through the crowd with Eddie right behind him. Down the emptied, blocked-off street, a policeman was throwing a blanket over a crumpled body. Behind him, at the curbs, other police were commanding the crowd to break it up. But the crowd kept turning around and buzzing and peering up and down, endlessly moving their hands and talking.

Keith began to shake. He stumbled over to the nearest cop. "Who is she?" he asked. His mouth felt dry.

The cop stared at him. "Look, bud, just move on, will ya?"

"I demand to know who she is," he said in a voice that didn't sound like his. "She might be this boy's mother. We were going to meet—"

"I don't know who she is. She didn't bring her purse down with her. Talk to the sarge over there."

Keith's legs were made of water. He tottered over to the sergeant and went through it again with him. "Listen, we might be able to identify that woman."

"Oh, yeah? Well, wait here a minute." He turned away and started shouting at a new crowd of people who were stepping off the curb, milling around, moving closer. The blanketed lump in the center of Hollywood and Vine was inert as stone.

Frantic, Keith didn't know what to do. He weaved against Eddie, who grabbed his arm. Keith turned back to the sergeant. "Don't you even care who she is?" he shouted, choking.

The sergeant eyed him, then reached out. "Yeah, sure," he said kindly, leading him over to the curb. "Sit down here a minute. We'll sort this out."

Numb, Eddie and Keith sat down. Eddie looked ashen. Keith was paralyzed by dread. He could see the shape in the middle of the empty street even when he wasn't looking at it. Suddenly, Keith bolted from the curb and streaked into the street toward the body. Cops looked up and pumped across the pavement at him. But Keith, grieving and frightened, was quick. He lifted the blanket.

The woman under the blanket lay on her side, half her face pressed into the asphalt. Her eye was open. It was Francine.

The cops grabbed Keith.

"It's Francine!" he shouted to Eddie. "Let go," he said to the sergeant. "I know her." Keith sank down on the curb, put his hands to his face and wept.

Eddie stood beside him, one hand on Keith's back. He watched the crowd shifting and turning and staring at them, and he thought of the woman who'd appeared out of the fog one morning on his street and said lightly, "Is there one of you at every gate?" She'd had a sort of doubtful smile on her face, as if she wanted to be there and didn't want to. For the first time, he was glad she was still there.

Keith raised his head, punched out one arm. Eddie helped him up. Without embarrassment, Keith rubbed a hand over his eyes and snorted miserably. "C'mon," he said, thickly.

Supporting each other, they walked across the empty street and into the building. The lobby was full of people waiting for the elevators. Keith jerked a thumb at the stairs and they started up. At the second floor, they punched the Up button, waited, then ran up the next flight of stairs. At every floor, they pumped out of the stairwell and tried for the elevators, then ran back to the stairs, legs weakening, muscles shaking. Keith felt the blood pumping into his neck and face and his breath shorten. On the ninth floor, the elevator door was just closing, but Keith forced his hand through the crack and slapped it open.

Belinda was sitting on the floor inside the French doors, shaking violently. She could still feel Francine's crushing embrace, feel her own hand slipping off the doorknob, feel her choking terror of the void below. She could still hear the sound of the crowd below rolling up like a sea swell, holding Francine up on the air like a sky diver, arms akimbo, feet apart, head up, death's arabesque.

That could be me, she thought, that could be me.

Keith and Eddie spilled out of the elevator. The top floor was jammed with policemen. Keith pushed past them. When they started to restrain him, he started yelling.

"Belinda! Belinda!"

She was rising awkwardly from the floor in the huge room. He flung himself into the space between them, folded her in his arms. Eddie stood back. From deep inside, Belinda unlocked a sound of relief. Keith held her.

EPILOGUE

It was Christmas vacation, a December morning five months exactly from the night Francine had accosted him at the airport. Eddie awoke in his own bed in his father's house. He hadn't been in Los Angeles since he'd started college.

He lay on his back watching the pattern of the winter sun dance on the ceiling and listening to the happy commotion in the house below. It was always like this at Christmas; Patsy was a fervent believer in seasonal rituals, and she filled the house with streams of friends, waifs, gifts, foods, greenery. But today, another level of hustle had been factored in: a wedding. Eddie dragged a hand over his face: A hundred people would be in the backyard this afternoon. Buttons Botsford was marrying Yvonne Duret.

Eddie turned over. Cynthia moved sleepily, the way she always did, content and self-possessed even in sleep. He pressed his face in her hair and kissed the back of her neck. Since September, they'd been living together in a small apartment off the Berkeley campus. Cynthia was a wretched cook; Eddie, having witnessed Vail's kitchen conjurings over the years, found that he enjoyed it while Cynthia made her applications to colleges in communications and argued with her father on the telephone. That man was a complete shit, Eddie thought. But Cynthia had a childlike conviction. "Dad always comes around," she'd say simply. Eddie hadn't seen Belinda or Keith since the grueling ordeal in Hollywood. They'd taken themselves off somewhere in Oregon, rented a house at the beach where Keith had written a new script. But they'd be here today, that he knew.

The odor of baking breads came floating in under the door. Eddie turned on his back again to watch the sun streaks. Whenever he thought of Belinda, he was with her in the garden, the night all the dark corners of his life had been revealed. And he always felt offended, trespassed against. But this morning, something was different. He was making his peace with the truth. He knew who he was and where he'd come from; whatever his childhood fears had been, they were, if not gone, going. He had a history. Good and bad, it was his to make it what he would. Or not. It was his choice.

He opened his arms wide. He was grinning when Cynthia woke up.

Later that morning, Belinda rang the bell at Sara's front door. She was picking Sara up for the wedding. There was no answer, but the door was open. She stepped inside the house in the hills that had once been Sky's. She hadn't been there since Archie's death.

"Sara?"

She headed toward the patio. But she paused in the living room, drawn by a painting of Sky. Her black hair, slightly exaggerated, filled the space around her face, one hand was raised, her head was tilted, looking off to one side. Belinda felt the undertow of her dream about Sky. I sure miss you, Mama, she thought. I always will. Sara would always be a relative, but she'd never be her mother. Maybe Sara had long ago adjusted to that.

Belinda ran her hand across the old baby grand with its crowd of photos. This was the house of her youth and much had happened in this room. But on this sunny quiet morning, no one would know it. The space seemed innocent of, even indifferent to, the acts of love and achievement and deceit that Belinda could recall.

Sara had once said that a person couldn't have a new life until she stopped living the old one. Belinda felt the weight of her passage lighten. The end of a long, long journey was merging with another trail to take another bearing.

Sara's bawdy laughter rode out on the warm winter air. Belinda stepped onto the patio.

Sara was stretched in a chaise, a ragged straw sun hat clapped on her head. Victor was sitting across from her, the faint breeze lifting his white hair.

"I didn't expect you," Belinda said to him.

He jumped up. "Lindy!" He clasped her by the shoulders, held her at arm's length. "Sara and I—we were talking over old times."

Belinda hadn't moved. "I don't think I've ever been with both of you at the same time."

Victor's narrow, blue eyes, nesting in lines, peered at her gravely. "Always a first time," he said.

"Here I am, coming to talk with Sara and I find you!"

"That's life. Sit, sit. Eddie and I got together about a month ago, up at his college. He's fine, so you can rest easy there," Victor went on, his tone elated but forced. "And when are you coming to Ireland with me? I've started a new book that's *not* about spies and treachery, and is *that* ever refreshing. You could rest up, get things in perspective. Bring Keith."

Belinda laughed. "Vic, get real. I don't want to be airlifted to Ireland. I'm not a kid anymore."

"I don't think of you as a kid," he said.

"Oh, yes you do," she tossed at him, keeping her voice light. "I know you do."

"Hey, I came for a wedding and a pleasant afternoon with the family, if that's possible," he said. God, he thought, women are wonderful but so difficult. They were endlessly engaged in an archaeology of life, brushing at old broken pots, delving into things, taking them apart, putting them together.

They were both looking at him. "I don't think of you as a kid, Lindy."

" 'Fess up, Vic."

Victor grimaced. "I never know what you expect of me."

"Victor," Sara said, "she wants a piece of you, a real piece."

"Is that what you want?" he asked.

"I want my father back with all his warts. I want you to take responsibility for the influence you've had on me. I don't want you to appear to be better than you are—or worse. I want you to be the idiot with me that you really are."

"Well, I can certainly do that without half trying," he muttered, pleased and wary at the same time.

She surprised him again. "I owe you an apology."

"You do?"

She nodded. "You tried hard to help me, and I wouldn't let you. I was wrong." She thought of Guy in the limo hoping to sink her with the revelation that Keith had made it possible for her to direct *Indictment*. "I thought I could do it all by myself; but you were right—no one can. Keith helped me once and he didn't rob me of anything by helping."

She smiled broadly at him and got to her feet, feeling great. "I guess you don't need a lift to the wedding," Belinda said to Sara.

"No. I meant to call but we got talking . . ."

In the car, Belinda had planned to tell Sara that she forgave her. But now she sensed that it wasn't necessary. The new course had already been set and accepted. "Sara, you and I can talk later, okay?" She leaned down and kissed Victor's cheek. "See you at the wedding, Dad."

Sara walked her to the door and waited until she'd driven away. She was proud of her daughter.

Victor was sitting on the end of the chaise with his head in his hands.

"Oh, Vic, buck up. She's finally getting to know her own life."

Victor Oliver raised his head. His cheeks were damp; sadness and reprieve had drawn more lines on his face. "I'm such a blunderer," he said.

Sara sat down next to him. "No, you aren't," she said. "You're just phony sometimes, dear." Her bosom rose, she chuckled deep inside, keeping it inside. "It's part of your charm, in a perverse sort of way."

But Victor wasn't listening. "She called me 'Dad,' " he said.

"Dad," Eddie said, laughing, "some joker named Keith over there wants to take our picture."

Vail was sitting in a white chair with a cushion behind him. He peered into the forest of noisy celebrating people on his lawn, and finally picked out Keith, waving a camera. The wedding had been held; the reception was in full swing.

"I detest pictures," Vail said merrily. "Tell him we don't take pictures in our family."

"I mean it," Belinda was saying to Dr. Suico and Dr. Durbin, handing them each a glass of champagne, "if it weren't for you two, I wouldn't be here." She looked across the yard at Keith, who was fiddling with his camera, then back at the two women. "I'm awfully glad I'm here."

Dr. Durbin was wearing a bright turban and a red dress. She said, pleased, "That's our job, Belinda."

Cynthia was talking to Fletcher, who had been Buttons's best man. "But you won the Emmy for *Crossing*," she said.

"Yeah, yeah." He chuckled, surveying the field of pretty women. "It was okay."

"I don't understand why an Emmy's bad," she said.

"It wasn't bad," he replied, fixing his dark eyes on her, "it just isn't good enough. That's television for you." His rough, mashed face, strangely crude and handsome, watched her.

"You're very strange, Fletcher," Cynthia said. "But I kinda like you, too."

"That's the spirit."

Schurl was comparing camera features with Keith. "This is the most uncooperative crowd for pictures," Keith said, setting his focus.

"They've always been like that," Schurl said, snapping a clandestine picture of Sara who was standing a short distance away. She put her thumbs in her ears and waggled her hands at him. "Even Sara." He chopped the air with his hands, reminding Keith of a big, sweet teddy bear.

"How is it with you and Sara?" Keith asked softly.

"Oh, man, I dunno." Schurl rolled his eyes.

"Don't let Victor put you off. He's going back to Ireland. She's staying here."

Schurl beamed at Keith.

"Belinda!" Keith called. "Over here."

Belinda, with Victor in tow, came up to them. "Schurl, have you met my dad, Victor?"

"Just once, long time ago," Schurl said, shaking hands.

Victor didn't feel the pressure from Schurl's big hand, and he didn't hear the escalating sound of the party. All he could hear was the word, "dad."

"Belinda, we're going to take some pictures," Keith was saying.

"We're not big on pictures," Belinda said.

"Don't be a spoilsport. This is what normal families do, take pictures."

Victor said to Keith, "Lindy's going to keep on directing, she says."

"Yes, she's a natural."

"Pretty hard for a woman, isn't it?"

"Times change," Keith said. "I'm going to give her all my scripts to direct."

"Why don't you do it yourself?"

"No way. I don't like telling people what to do or even talking to them that much. Belinda loves it." At that moment, Keith caught a glimpse of Diana under the tree. "She's got a lot of her grandmother in her, don't you, honey?"

But Belinda was watching Eddie and Cynthia who were standing over Diana, under the tree. She's like I was, Lindy thought, before Archie. Eddie was holding her hand, not letting go. They both look so normal and young and beautiful, she thought, happy for Edward.

"So be it," she said.

"What?" Victor asked her.

"Nothing. Old ashes. New beginnings."

Victor's gaze followed hers to Cynthia and Eddie and Diana. He was struck by how old Diana looked, yet still upright like a queen in her chair. He hadn't spoken to her in thirty years.

With a sudden decision, borne on three glasses of champagne, he went over to the woman who'd split his life in two. "Diana," he said, not offering his hand.

She raised her head. Fissures and creases marked her face but her eyes were sharp. "Yes?"

"Victor Oliver," he said, his voice grim.

"Mr. Oliver?" she repeated, querulously. "How do you do? I'm afraid I don't know you." She smiled thinly.

Cagey old bitch, Victor thought, knowing she knew precisely who he was. But he couldn't feel angry or injured anymore: she was too old; it was all too long ago.

He took her offered hand. The bones were so light under the skin they felt like glass. "How do you do?" he said.

Yvonne and Patsy came out of the house and Yvonne, holding her bouquet, joined an exuberant Buttons under the jacaranda tree. She was dressed in a short-skirted white kid suit and a small white hat. Cool and poised, Diana, talking fitfully with Victor, was seated nearby.

"C'mon, Vail," Patsy said, taking his arm, "get up. This is Yvonne's show."

"Huh? What the hell's going on?"

"She's going to throw her bouquet. Victor, you, too—other side of the yard."

"Oh, let her throw it," Vail mumbled. "Why do I have to move?"

But Patsy insisted. As he was rising, he heard his mother say to Yvonne, "Aim it that way, dear, and throw it high. Bouquets always look so special high in the air."

"Mother, let her throw it her own way," Vail said.

Yvonne stood on the bench Vail had vacated and threw the bouquet overhand. It arched high and dropped hard.

Sara caught it. Schurl, next to her, could not contain his excitement.

After that, it was wind-down time. Fletcher left to have a little quality time with his daughter; Keith and Yvonne made a special, but unexplained toast to Dr. Suico, which she accepted with a return toast to Belinda, who in turn toasted Yvonne, "my uncommon friend."

"Mom," Eddie said, sitting down next to Patsy and stripping off his tie. "Cynth and I are thinking of getting married next summer. She thinks that old buzzard will be 'around' by then."

"Guy?"

"Yeah."

"I'm sure she's right, but talk to me in a month. Right now, I'm wedding-ed out. Did you get a picture of Dad and you?"

"Nah, he refused. So did I. Kinda hokey." Patsy laughed. "Mom, I've been wanting to say . . ." He looked off, nesting his wrist in his right hand.

"Yes?"

"Been wanting to tell you that given the choice," he pressed on with difficulty, "given the choice, I mean of moms, since I have two . . ."

"Yes?"

"I choose you. You're my mom."

Patsy's hand rose, fluttered, landed on his wrist. He put his arm around her shoulder.

"A picture, damnit!" Keith was yelling.

"What is it with that man and his pictures?" Belinda muttered, walking toward the food table with Victor.

"Yeah!" Eddie was all for it.

"You call it, Eddie," Keith said, taking the lens cap off his camera. "Schurl, let's have a little support!"

"Light's good over here," Schurl said.

Pictures were taken of Cynthia and Eddie, Buttons and Yvonne, Cynthia and Diana, Vail and Patsy and Schurl, Schurl and Sara.

Almost shyly, Victor said to Keith, "How about one with me and Eddie and Belinda and Sara?"

"Great! Hey, everyone, listen up!" Keith shouted. "Picture of Sara and Victor." Keith wound an arm around Lindy. "Why don't you join them?" Keith turned and gave Eddie a push. "You, too, buddy."

The four family members lined up self-consciously in front of Keith and his camera.

"No," Schurl said, directing the action, "move in closer." They did that.

"Well, for Chrissakes," Vail said, "snap it."

"Hush up, Vail," Patsy said.

"Don't look so grim," Schurl admonished them. "God, who died?"

Suddenly, Eddie moved between Victor and Belinda and, taller than Belinda, but the same height as Victor, he flopped his arms over their shoulders.

"That's it," Keith said and he snapped it.

Few women know Washington as intimately as Maureen Dean, and only she could spin this tale of glamour, decadence, and corrupt passion in high places.

MAUREEN DEAN

CAPITOL SECRETS

When beautiful, ambitious congresswoman Laura Christen makes a move to become the most powerful person on Capitol Hill, she stirs up a secret past that could become a bombshell for some of the most powerful men and women in the country, and sets off a firestorm of controversy...and murder.

*Coming soon in hardcover
to bookstores everywhere.*

G. P. PUTNAM'S SONS
a member of The Putnam Berkley Group, Inc.